DEADLY RIDDLES

DEADLY RIDDLES

THE GREAT DIVINER SERIES
· BOOK 2 ·

AARALYNN KARMAN

Deadly Riddles

Copyright © 2025 Aaralynn Karman

For information contact:
Sunflower Petals Press, LLC
sunflowerpetalspress.com

Hardcover: 978-1-7347736-7-5
Paperback: 978-1-7347736-8-2
Ebook: 978-1-7347736-9-9

First edition March 2025

Edited by Cheyenne Nielsen
Cover Design by Damonza

For all those who thought they weren't worthy enough.

This one's for us.

Pronunciation Guide

CHARACTERS
Alaric: a-lar-ic
Malus: mah-lus
Malamone: mal-uh-MONE
Celaena: suh-LAY-nuh
Avi: AEY-VYE
Ciaus: KAI-us
Viola: VYE-OLE-uh
Celestia: sell-ess-TEEuh
Yalecia: yale-SEE-uh
Aero: arrow

PLACES
Vezchia: vez-CHEE-uh
Tungsinn: tongue-sin
Viden: VYE-den
Hora: hor-uh
Ludia: LOO-DEE-uh
Temnota: tem-NO-tuh
Soaipkia: SO-APE-KEY-uh

A Mysterious Disappearance

FIRE BLAZED IN massive plumes all around Malus. The heat thickened the air with smoke and chaos flickered in his malicious green eyes.

It was as if Malus' world was burning down around him, but he'd build it all back up just as he had shaped the Dark Forces into an army that lurks in the shadows. He glanced backward toward the Malamone Mansion, which remained untouched amongst the now crimson town of Tungsinn. The sun was setting, putting everything into an overdone reddish glow. The colorful autumn leaves rained down as fire engulfed the trunks of trees and enhanced the golden tones of everything. The wind blew the smoke through his choppy short blond hair, ash mixing in it. He pushed the hair out of his eyes, recalling the many times he couldn't stop himself from tearing it out.

Screams of men, women, and children echoed through the air, but it meant nothing to Malus. To him, this town was simply a matter that needed to be taken care of. He'd heard the rumors that had spread through the townspeople—rumors of him and what had happened to his father. Everything he loved had already died here, and a part of himself went with it. It was 1789, and decades later, the painful edge in his heart still hadn't healed. Whatever happened to the Tungsinnian people amid the destruction, he didn't care, as long as they were gone.

Malus strode past a woman carrying a small child, stumbling over the broken glass, splintered wood, and cracked bricks. She scurried away from him, through the smokey haze and stench of death. Malus watched the shadows for his Dark Forces members draped in black cloaks like him, keeping an eye out for Viola. She was deep within the fallen buildings, avoiding the ones that were on fire and likely quenching her gruesome thirst. Memories of that day back in 1718 when Viola had been changed into a vampire flooded his mind unbidden. He halted and clenched his eyes shut, trying to block out the feelings of horror and fear that had consumed him that day. Gathering magic into his palm, he opened his eyes and let his magic fly toward a caving building to splinter it apart. Hooded figures scurried everywhere, throwing fire and weapons around. People lay on the paved road, unconscious or dead. As he walked through the town, he took it all in with pleasure, casting a faint wicked grin on his lips.

Chunks of buildings, broken wood, and shattered windows were scattered around him as he entered what had been the lower end of town. The old orphanage was caving in, fire flickering from inside the windows as it consumed the curtains. A flash of black and purple appeared in the corner of his vision, and Viola suddenly stood next to him, rising to his shoulder. The wind blew her scraggly black hair against her small deathly pale face.

There was a silent pause before Malus said anything.

"I'm sorry it all had to end like this." He couldn't even look at her. They had met when they were eight on what were now the crumbling stairs of the orphanage. This was the place Viola had been raised. She hadn't seemed to care when he brought up the idea of burning Tungsinn to the ground. In fact, she'd been strangely gleeful about it. But some memories were too painful to burn away.

The door was suddenly torn open as children and nannies ran out, screaming as they tried to reach safety. Their clothes were scorched and smoke billowed out behind them like a beast reaching to pull them back into its maw.

"Malus, you know very well the orphanage was nothing to me." Viola watched them flee, blood dripping from her pale lips. The firelight flickered in her beady gold eyes. Her face was emotionless like stone yet held the sort of insanity a person only gets when they've been pulled from the depths of darkness. "It was where I was raised, but it was never home. They weren't my family. I never had a family until I met you."

Family. Viola wasn't blood, but she was the only family Malus had left. Every single day he wished all that had happened wasn't true. He wished his mother hadn't died there in Tungsinn and that his father hadn't betrayed him. But there was no going back now, only forward. Revenge was like a burning poison, driving him deeper into the darkness with every breath. He threw a ball of fire at one of the nearby buildings. The flames scorched through the wood and the building fell within a few minutes. No one would ever challenge him again. He would get what he wanted, and no one would know what he was planning until it was too late. Even the Forces of Light would believe the whole town went down with fire and chaos, and no one would ever hear of Tungsinn again.

The high-pitched scream of a child tore him from thoughts of purging and venging. His head snapped toward the crumbling edge of the orphanage, where the face of a little boy poked out. An arm wrapped around the boy and pulled him back into the smokey shadows. Hushed voices grew louder as Malus stalked closer, his black cloak billowing around his feet. Fire burned in his veins and magic crackled over his fingertips in swirls of angry colors. Viola bounced on the balls of her feet giddily as she followed.

"I smell them…" she crooned, her voice light like a ghost's.

Peering around the corner of the building, Malus caught sight of a woman and three children escaping down the road. The children screamed as they clung to their mother. Ash and blood were smeared across their skin. Malus watched them flee into the shadows, heading toward the town's edge as if they really thought they could make it out alive. He had members of the Dark Forces surrounding the entire town. The four of them would fall one way or another. Malus spun on his heel, turning his back on the woman and her children running toward a freedom they'd never get.

"Malus," Viola said, her voice spiking urgently. "That woman has a Divining Power. She's a Shape-shifter."

Malus cut a look at her as his heart rate spiked. Knowing himself, Shape-shifters were unpredictable. If he didn't stop her himself, she could change into something able to slip past his Forces. Malus' teeth ground together and his whole body tensed. Turning back toward the woman and her children, he jumped forward. His back arched with a loud crack and his teeth elongated into fangs. Dark tan fur spread across his body except for around his paws, where copper scales formed. A mane of lion hair sprouted around his head like a crown. Surging forward down the path, the beast he'd become pounded the ground with his feet. The woman glanced back at him, eyes widening at the croccotta barreling toward her. Malus let out a growl full of fury and heartache.

Behind him, Viola grinned maliciously. A soft cackle bubbled from her throat and drifted through the wind like a music box playing in a lonely mansion. Stars began to blink into existence above.

The woman pushed her children into an alleyway and let out a pained cry. Wings ripped from her back where her shoulder blades had been, covered in shiny black scales. Talons grew from her feet and more scales slithered over her growing body like a snake. The woman's eyes glowed like lava and steam blossomed from her nostrils. Malus' feet paused, claws digging into the dirt road. Where a woman had been standing now stood an obsidian dragon with fiery red eyes. Malus' heart hit painfully against his ribs. He tried to keep himself steady, but his bones felt like they were shaking. In all his life, he'd never seen a dragon, let alone a Shape-shifter who could turn into one. The feeling rushing through him made his heart sink and he shook all thoughts and emotions from his body. He'd come to destroy, and that was what he would do.

I am the son of Alaric Malamone. I am more powerful than any enchanter or enchantress the world has known for decades. With those new thoughts, he bolted forward, a growl tearing from his throat.

The dragon-woman's children ran toward her and clung to her wings, hoisting themselves onto her gleaming back. Fire burned all around them like the world was coming down. Malus' paws dug into the dirt with every quick step, forcing himself closer to the beast before him even as blood rushed in his ears.

Heat engulfed him before he could react. The dragon-woman opened her mouth to let out a blast of fire that surrounded Malus. Malus hissed and rolled across the ground as the fire tried to bite through his coat. The dragon-woman glared as screams of agony escaped from him.

It was as if the look in her eyes was saying, *now* you *know what it feels like to burn.*

Oh, if only you knew how much I really do, Malus thought even through the pain. *I burn every day; it just usually happens to be on the inside.*

Then the dragon-woman and her children took to the air, vanishing into the darkness above. No one would ever hear of Tungsinn again—or so he thought.

August 3rd, present year

All the oil lamps in the mansion were out, leaving Kora, Chad, Seth, Ebony, and a few others in nearly full darkness as night descended. The wind rattled the windows and made eerie creaks throughout the mansion. Kora paced back and forth in Malus' office, her nostrils flaring like a temperamental beast. Malus' last words kept replaying in her head, making her heart pound frantically.

"Let the girl and her friends leave. She's the Diviner—the one thing that can destroy the Dark Forces," Malus had hissed to her in those final moments as he stood as Twilight on the old fountain crumbling away in the courtyard. *"She'll come back, and when she does, she'll bring me the Death Stone. She still has to get her parents, doesn't she?"*

That was what Malus had believed—and it had cost him. Now he was nowhere to be found, and neither was Viola. *The wretched girl could be leading the Forces of Light to the mansion at this very moment!* Tungsinn had been destroyed for reasons like these—so, *no one* would know where the Malamone Mansion was and what Malus was planning.

How does he think that she'll be able to find the Death Stone when he's been looking for it for centuries? Kora thought as she continued to strut back and forth across the office.

Chad rolled his eyes and interrupted her thoughts from across the room. "Pacing isn't going to help the situation."

His annoyed, bored tone made every nerve in Kora's body go over the edge. She spun to look at him through slitted gray eyes, wavy, tangled black hair whipping around her head. Chad sat in Malus' chair behind the desk covered in papers, fiddling with a feather quill.

"Then what do *you* suppose we do, Chad? Because Viola and Malus are missing with no way to contact them!" she screeched. "And that bratty Chesler girl is gone. We had one job! ONE JOB!"

"Will you just calm down!" he shouted, jumping to his feet. His long black cloak—the one that all the Dark Forces wore—swung around his ankles. "Malus wanted the girl to get away and that is exactly what she did. Whatever he's doing doesn't matter. Neither does Viola."

"Chad, she's the Diviner! She could have wounded the two of them! Who knows how powerful she is! Yes, she's weak. But remember how yesterday she managed to knock all of us off our feet with a simple Knockback Enchant? We weren't there to see what happened after she ran back inside the mansion! So no, Chad, I WILL NOT CALM DOWN!"

His eyes suddenly went wide and his jaw slack. "She's the *what*?" Running a hand through his spiky blond hair, he began to pace the length of the room as well. "Well, that changes things."

Kora scrunched up her nose and shook her head. "Moron."

Rain pounded against the ancient windows and lightning struck through the sky, filling the room with an electric blue glow. Thunder roared outside like a monster hovering over the mansion. Ebony, her dark brown hair falling over her shoulders in messy waves, watched out the window with awe as if she'd never seen a storm before.

"Wait!" She pulled her black cloak around her tighter to block the draft that seeped through the windows, then looked at everyone in the room with alert chocolate-colored eyes. "There's someone coming up the lane!"

Kora hurried to push the curtains back and stare out the window, which looked down on the driveway lined with wagons—even the wagon left there from when they were transporting the Chesler girl and her friends. A man in a long black cloak was riding up the brick road on a russet horse.

"Well then, let's welcome him in, shall we?" A sly smile crept across Kora's face before she strode into the hall, her black boots clacking on the marble floor and echoing throughout the silent, eerie mansion.

Dents, cracks, and peeling wallpaper littered the mansion. Dust covered the old paintings that had sat there for centuries, and purple light made the place glow as lightning struck through the sky. She descended one of the curved marble staircases leading down into the massive entrance hall that opened to other shadowed rooms.

When she pulled the dark wooden front doors open, the man was standing just outside. He gave her a sinister smirk as he pulled his soaked wool hat off to reveal his completely bald, shiny head. Rain had created puddles everywhere outside, even filling the broken, crumbling fountain in the center of the courtyard. Kora smiled at the man and stepped aside to let him in.

"Thank you," he said and gave a cough as water dripped onto the marble flooring of the mansion.

Kora swung the door shut behind him, leaving the horse

tied to a broken wagon out in the night. Malus' single stable hand would deal with it. The man pulled off his wet coat and threw it on the floor with his hat.

"I apologize for the darkness, Ciaus. Ebony thought we shouldn't have any light on in case Enchanting Control or the Forces of Light came looking for the mansion. They'd hopefully assume this place was uninhabited if they could even find it." Kora's jaw tightened. "The girl escaped, if you haven't heard."

"Oh, yes, I know she escaped." He turned to look at Kora with his lavender eyes.

"Well, would you like to come into his office? Many of us are in there, trying to figure out where Master Malus is."

"Yes."

Kora led Ciaus up the set of curved staircases and down the hall to the left, darkness looming on all sides of them. Malus' office was still and silent until Kora and Ciaus pushed the door open and strode in.

"Oh, now you decide to turn up, Ciaus?" Seth straightened up from leaning against the wall, his arms crossed with narrowed green eyes. The dark atmosphere made his dirty blond taper-faded hair look darker, and the twisted face he made only seemed to add to the shadows.

"Shut up, Seth," Kora said, returning the look.

Seth paid no attention to her. "Ciaus, how about you go do your job? Break the curse on the parents of that girl."

"Actually, I have some news," Ciaus said, looking at each person in the room with his creepy eyes as a sly smirk spread across his face. "It concerns Malus."

Everyone in the room suddenly straightened up, looking at Ciaus with their full attention.

"Well?" Ebony raised a brow, resting her hands on her hips.

"There was a trial for Malus at Enchanting Control in

which I attended," Ciaus said eerily, showing no sign of worry. "He was sentenced to go to Top Rock Security Prison."

"WHAT?" Kora screeched. "A volcano? You couldn't mention that when I opened the door for you? We must assemble a team and save him before he dies!"

"My father won't die—not with that Stone of his," Seth piped in, eyes looking past Kora rather than *at* her.

"His Life Stone will save him from old age, not lava, poisonous gases, and heat, you idiot." Ebony rolled her eyes.

"Either way, the Stone will not be able to save him… because he doesn't have it," Ciaus said. "But honestly, I'm not concerned."

"WHAT?" Kora shrieked, banging her fist against the wall and causing all of Malus' daggers to rattle. Her wavy black hair fell in front of her hot and flustered face. She stepped toward Ciaus, her hand rising with the urge to wrap it around his neck. "HOW CAN YOU NOT BE CONCERNED?"

Ciaus' calm face remained set in stone, his sly smirk widening. "I have my reasons for not being concerned and I'll get to them in a moment. But first—" He took out a tiny sack of something from his pocket. "—I know exactly how to break Miranda and Oliver Chesler's curse. I will begin breaking, but first, I have something else to tell you."

CHAPTER ONE

IT ALL FELT wrong—to be there, sitting on her bed in her dorm at school, to even be about to attend school the next day, to be safe, and above all, to not be with her parents.

Aria stared across the room, hot tears welling up in her forget-me-not blue eyes. It looked exactly as she'd left it three months ago. There was the bed, which was made and still had blankets with a checkerboard pattern of Incanting Academy's colors—sky blue and black. Her wooden desk was still across the room and her black dresser still stood next to her bed.

She let out a pained sigh, wiping tears from her pale, lightly freckled cheeks. It felt like she should run away, find a way back to that mansion, and hack down the doors to get to her parents. The memory of how unkempt, starving, and hurt they were had been drilled into her brain by nightmares. A shudder passed through her as she recalled the last nightmare she'd had—one of a black cat stalking toward her, its green eyes glowing in the darkness, and a brutal laugh meeting her ears. She shook the recollection of it from her mind, not wanting to remember how blind she'd been, unable to see Malus had been right under her nose for months.

It hurt when she remembered and she never wanted to feel it again.

Since returning from the Malamone Mansion, she kept asking Mrs. Mckinney, the principal, when the Forces of Light or Enchanting Control were going to save her parents.

"I've been in talks with them every day, Aria," Mrs. Mckinney had told her one day. "But Enchanting Control claims they have other priorities and that they won't easily be able to locate the mansion." She'd sighed, rubbing her temples as something seemed to press her deeper into her chair. "They haven't permitted the Forces of Light to go out on our own to get your parents, claiming it's because we no longer have leaders, and we have no choice but to listen to our authorities. I'm sorry, but things are getting...*chaotic* out there."

Out there, as in the world of magic, Aria had pieced together.

It felt reminiscent of when her parents had gone missing several months ago. Mrs. Mckinney was doing everything she could, and yet Aria felt nothing was being done at all.

She threw her school bag and duffle bag down on the floor, refusing to unpack. School was supposed to start tomorrow, and she'd already been at Incanting Academy for days, so she should...But she couldn't bring herself to unpack anything—not the bag and definitely not the baggage she felt weighing inside her. Last month she had escaped the claws of Malus and his Dark Forces, but the weight of the world was resting on her shoulders now. She had failed to rescue her parents and now she had to deal with the fact that she was the Diviner—a myth come to life, a being with immense power living in her veins, the one said to have once been a peacekeeper among enchanters and enchantresses. How could someone live with that?

She started pacing the room, one hand tangled in her wavy cappuccino brown hair and one clutching the sunflower necklace that her parents had given her. Her breathing quickened, so much air filling her lungs that she felt she wasn't getting any air at all. The bed began to shake as she fell to her knees and finally let the tears come. Her hands pulsed as her magic took control, latching onto every object in the room and shaking it wildly.

She could faintly hear someone knocking on her door, but her heart hammered in her ears as everything replayed in her head for the millionth time in the last month—Malus turning out to be Twilight, Willow's cat; the way Viola stalked in the darkness, waiting to pounce; the moment her mother said she was the Diviner; when her mother and father told her she had to find the Death Stone and destroy it; when Malus was sentenced to go to Top Rock Security Prison. She knew he was locked away, unable to harm her, but the rest of the Dark Forces weren't. They would stop at nothing until they had her and the Life Stone back in their malicious claws.

Aria looked up from the ground, feeling as if all the oxygen was suffocating her as tears poured down her face. Each breath was like a saw, dragging and scraping through her lungs. Luke, Avi, and Willow called her name from the other side of the locked door, but she couldn't bring herself to get up, so she laid down on the floor and cried, hating how weak each whimper sounded.

Principal Mckinney had brought Aria back to the school with her, but before that, Aria had stayed at camp. She'd lingered around the camp office, finding something reassuring in Mrs. Mckinney's presence. Even after everything that had happened last year, after all the pent-up anger Aria had felt, she was grateful that Mrs. Mckinney would look after her for as long as she had to. Every rub on her back, check-in, and kind word from Mrs. Mckinney made Aria's chest squeeze.

She'd realized something—Mrs. Mckinney was one person and couldn't control everything like Aria had been unable to see last school year. Aria and her friends were *four people*, and they certainly couldn't have controlled Aria's parents still being in the Dark Forces' clutches.

It had been about four weeks since she had seen Luke and Willow since their parents had picked them up from the camp not too long after Malus' trial. Avi had been at the school with his aunt, but of course, Aria wasn't supposed to know that he was related to her.

"I'm just…taking classes early to…catch up on grades." He'd claimed as he twiddled his thumbs. "Like summer school but it's not summer school. You know?"

"Um…not really," Aria had said, trying to wrap her head around what he had even been saying.

Even with Avi being at the school for the past few days, Aria had barely seen him. She'd been tucked inside her room with a blanket thrown over her, unwilling to do anything but dwell on the thoughts in her mind—as she was doing now.

After hours of being shut away in her room, Aria slipped into the massive cafeteria filled with dozens of long, dark wooden tables, and matching benches. Loud chatter rose toward the ceiling where yellowed lights hung above, casting everything in a dreamy hue. The windows along the brick wall to the right looked out at a dirt parking lot and the thick forest crowding around it. Aria found herself watching out those windows, at the place she'd once stood with a note from her mother in her hand. Her tearstained eyes were puffy and red. She rubbed at them as if she could wipe away the fact that she'd cried.

Now, all four of them were sitting together like they used to—Aria, Luke, Avi, and Willow, but something felt off. Different. They looked at Aria, her face damp and bags lingering under her eyes. She couldn't look at them, especially Luke. After the trial, after finally realizing she had feelings for him, everything felt strange. Just looking at him made her stomach want to curl in on itself and made her feet want to run away. She had no idea how she was supposed to act anymore, especially when he was around. He was so sweet and kind, always looking out for everyone, and then she was just…Well, she didn't know what she was anymore.

The Diviner, duh, the snarky voice in the back of her mind said, making her look down, and her hand found its way to her sunflower necklace. That word rampaged through her head and her hands grew into tight fists.

Slowly coming back to her senses, the words of her friends met her ears.

"…a track team. I'm joining, and I was wondering if any of you would want to also?" Luke was saying, but Aria barely processed it. When she didn't look up at him, he said, "Aria, what's wrong?"

"Huh?" Her eyes met his blue ones. "What?"

"What's wrong?" Luke looked at her with concern etched on his tanned, freckled face, dark coffee-brown hair falling over his forehead.

A lump rose in her throat, but she choked it down and plastered on a smile that strained her cheeks. "Oh, just school."

"Yeah, sucks that we have to go back, doesn't it?" Avi brushed his hand through his auburn hair and his hazel eyes dulled with disappointment.

Willow shot him a look before saying, "School is actually a *good* thing, Avi." She shook her head, her bushy light blond hair swinging behind her in a ponytail.

Aria sighed. "Not when Celaena Malamone will no doubt be there." That was only one of her reasons for not wanting to go to school the next day, though. Slowly, her eyes trained on the wooden table, and she lifted pasta into her mouth.

"That is true, but we got through last year with her," Willow said and a sly grin slid onto her face. "And who knows, maybe she'll be so scared we imprisoned her grandfather that she won't return this year."

Avi smirked, nodding his head plottingly. "Yeah, maybe she'll take over the Dark Forces in his place and build some evil school for evil kids like her."

"That is really not something to hope for, Avi," Willow scolded.

Aria snorted but didn't respond. Her brain was slowly turning off her senses, leaving her in the quiet space of her mind. She knew her friends were speaking, but it all seemed muted even as she tried to hold onto the present.

As soon as dinner was over, she started walking back to her room to go to bed early. There were two sides of the school: the magical side and the nonmagical side. What separated them was a veil—a magical rip in the universe. The magical side was hidden in the Space Realm, where nothing existed except what enchanters and enchantresses had built within it. On the other side of the veil, the halls were silent, dim, and empty. Most people were probably still at dinner or outside in the cool, end-of-summer air. Aria walked along with her own mind wrapped up in thoughts, barely aware of the footsteps coming up behind her. A large hand suddenly wrapped around her wrist and swung her up against the wall with a thud. Her heart leapt into her throat, adrenaline pumping its way through her veins. Her hands pulsed and called for her to use the magic threatening to escape her.

Right in front of her was a tall boy, about a foot taller than her. with dark brown hair, a tightly set jawline with the beginning of facial hair, narrowed blue eyes, and thin cheeks. He had to be at least seventeen, and his arms were corded in muscle. His blue eyes bore into hers, the same open-ocean shade of Luke's. She'd never met this boy, but staring at those eyes, something seemed to click into place in her mind.

"Christopher," she said, the breath rushing from her lungs. "You're Luke's brother." She roughly pulled her wrist from his hand, pressing herself closer up against the wall as he took a step forward.

"That's right." He cocked his head to the side, his deep voice filling the space around them.

Looking at him closer, the only things that resembled he was related to Luke were his dark, ashy hair, deep ocean eyes, and tanned skin. And he certainly didn't act like Luke. An instinct in Aria told her she needed to get away. It had every hair standing on end as she recalled Luke saying Christopher wasn't the nicest to be around. Her stomach twisted as if she was stuck at the top of a rollercoaster.

Feigning a smile, she said, "Well, it was nice to meet you, but I really must be going now." She went to make a step to the left.

"You're not going anywhere right now." Christopher brought both his hands down on the wall, one on each side of Aria, blocking her from leaving. "This is a warning to stay away from my brother."

"What?" Aria couldn't quite understand. Her breathing hitched, sawing in and out of her again. She could barely hold herself back from pushing him away. He was dangerously too close to her. She could even smell the stink of sweat on him.

"Stay away from Luke. He doesn't need to get hurt because of you." Christopher glared down at her like she was vermin. "Everyone knows about the Malus trial and how you got Luke kidnapped. Stay away from him. Do you understand?"

That was it—she pushed Christopher away from her, magic clinging to his shirt and knocking him back further. Her jaw dropped, but it was quickly replaced by annoyance. "Don't you think I've tried to get him to stay away from me? I've tried to get him to stay out of all of this, but he doesn't listen!" Aria shouted, a temper building within her. "He *chose* to follow me!"

"Yeah, I know he follows you freely. Like a drooling dog if you ask me, but you're a danger to him. If you don't stay away from him…" Christopher made a fist, looking as if he might lash out as he stared at Aria. His face was beet red, aggression warring over it.

"Aria? Christopher?" Luke's voice came down the hall just as uncontrollable anger flickered in Christopher's eyes and he shot his fist toward Aria's face.

Aria jumped out of the way and Luke began running toward them, jumping at his brother to knock him to the ground. Luke pinned his older brother's shoulders back as Christopher lashed out to hit him.

"What is wrong with you?" Luke shouted at him.

"I'm trying to protect you," Christopher spat. "Mother and Father told me to look after you, but you can't stop running after that stupid girl—running into danger!"

Aria stood there, wide-eyed, as Luke wrestled with his much stronger brother. Her bones felt frozen in place, shoulders slumped and lips parted slightly.

"Protect me? You *abandoned* me when Mom and Dad got those jobs! You were supposed to be there for me, but you weren't!" Luke shouted, hurt seeping into his voice. "Why do I suddenly matter to you?"

Aria was unable to look away. Everything was getting very personal in ways she thought she shouldn't be listening to, yet she couldn't get her feet to move.

"You little brat—" Christopher grabbed Luke's wrist and yanked him off. "I may have pushed you away, but that doesn't mean you can just do whatever you want now that no one is paying attention to you."

"Luke, Christopher, what is going on over here?" Mrs. Mckinney's voice echoed from down the hall.

Christopher shoved Luke away, forcing Luke to stumble into the wall, then he glared at Aria. "Stay away from everyone, you hear? Especially my brother. Our family doesn't need to be broken up more than it already is." Then he stalked away, his breath heaving like a freight train.

Mrs. Mckinney stopped next to Luke, laying her hand on his arm as she watched Christopher disappear. "What in all three realms did I just witness?" Her body was rigid with tension, making her intimidating in her navy pantsuit. She had a kind look to her wrinkly face, though, with eyes crinkling at the corners and gray hair falling over her shoulders.

"I think my brother was trying to threaten Aria," Luke said, looking to Aria for confirmation.

She nodded, her heart pounding in her ears and shock still shooting through her. She'd been confronted by people before, even by Celaena, the granddaughter of Malus Malamone, and yet she still couldn't beat the feeling of panic. Because Christopher had been right. She was a danger to others now. Christopher just didn't know to what extent because he didn't know she was the Diviner, the one who people would kill to have under their control.

"Oh goodness gracious!" Mrs. Mckinney turned to Aria, her hand moving to her shoulder. "Aria, are you okay, dear?"

"Yeah, I'm fine," she replied, voice shaky.

"Okay, good. I must see to it that Christopher is punished, but if you need anything or you have trouble with anyone else, let me know and I'll take care of it." With that, Mrs. Mckinney gave her a reassuring squeeze on the shoulder and strode down the hall to catch up with Christopher. She rounded the corner after him, the sound of her heels clacking on the stone floor.

Aria kept her eyes on Luke as he slowly walked up to her, his own eyes on the end of the hall where his brother had disappeared. An awkward silence that made Aria's stomach turn passed.

"Are you sure you're okay and not just saying that you are?" Luke asked, looking her up and down with concern etched on his face. He was flushed—whether from fighting his brother or from something else. He placed a hand on her elbow. "He didn't hurt you, did he?"

"No, I'm fine," Aria said and tucked her arms closer to herself, feeling small.

"Good. Are you going to your room?"

She nodded as a nervous butterfly feeling set in.

"I'll walk you there," he said, falling in place beside her.

She couldn't stop herself from grinning. "Why? You think another big scary enemy might try to attack me?" She joked, but it felt good to have him at her side—reassuring.

"No." A faint smile formed on his lips. "You're more than capable of taking care of yourself, but it would make me feel better."

"Well, thank you—for helping me out." There was a twisting feeling in her stomach. It gnawed at her, telling her that Christopher had been right—Luke did follow her around, and Aria knew how dangerous that was. She tried to push it away and enjoy that Luke was with her. *Bottle the feelings up. They're not important right now.*

"Of course…But I heard what he said to you, and he's

wrong." Luke shook his head, releasing a frustrated puff of air. "He's stupid. He doesn't get to make decisions for me—"

"Luke, he was *right*." Aria stopped in the middle of the empty hallway. "I *am* a danger—to you, to everyone. I don't want to see the people I care about get hurt anymore."

"No, you're the Diviner. The Diviner saves people—"

Aria looked away, hoping he wouldn't see her jaw clench at the sound of that word. Her hands tightened into pulsing fists. Luckily, no one was around to hear his words. "But the Diviner is the one the Dark Forces want, the legend nobody believes in, the one *Malus* wants. Anyone involved with me is in danger of being captured…or worse." She started down the hall again, tears welling in her eyes. She didn't want him to see her cry. She didn't want to cry *at all.*

Luke stayed at her side, matching her strides. "I don't care."

Her fingers found her sunflower necklace, tracing the intricate golden petals. "What?"

"I don't care about any of that. You're still the same Aria I met back in March. I helped you then, knowing the dangers. Why wouldn't I help you again?" He shook his head. "I don't care what my brother says."

Aria's mouth refused to form words as they stepped up a staircase. She was speechless and the emotions were too overwhelming. They were coming closer to the door of her room. Thinking back to everything Luke and Christopher had said, a question begged to be answered. She could not help but ask. "What did you mean your brother abandoned you?"

The two of them stopped in front of the door to Aria's room. The air stood still for a moment. Luke scratched the back of his neck, his eyes focused on the space next to Aria's head rather than *her.*

"My parents—my parents got jobs in the Vezchia Realm

when I was really little. They travel around a lot, and Christopher and I used to be able to go with them, but then they put a stop to it. They study creatures all around the Vezchia Realm. They started studying more dangerous creatures when I was ten and then they started sending me to Camp Enchanted." Luke sighed, running a hand over his freckled face. "Christopher was supposed to keep an eye on me, make sure I followed rules, spend time with me...But he didn't. Christopher met some not-so-good people at camp, and he started trading with bad people to get rare and dangerous magical items. My parents don't even know, and I only see them at the end of summer and over the breaks, so I don't tell them. I don't want to ruin what few moments we have together..." His face grew red and his teary eyes avoided her face, like a part of him was breaking in front of her. She'd never seen him cry before. His voice lowered solemnly. "Good thing is, though, their job pays well..." He looked down at his fidgeting hands, eyes pained.

Without hesitation, Aria flung her arms around him, pulling him closer. She felt him tense in surprise before his hands slid across her back.

She let her face fall onto his shoulder. "I'm sorry to hear that, Luke."

Her face grew heated, but she didn't let her emotions get the best of her. The hug didn't feel like it was enough. She felt the need to fix something or show even more that she cared, but all she could do was this.

When they pulled apart, Luke's lips parted and he tucked a strand of hair behind Aria's ear. Her heart fluttered in her chest like a butterfly taking off.

"I should get to bed," Aria said, her hand finding the doorknob behind her. She opened her bedroom door and stepped inside the dark room slowly. Her heart ached having to leave him, especially after everything that had just been spoken between them…and everything that hadn't. "Good night."

"Sweet dreams, Aria," he said as the door gently closed in front of him.

Chapter Two

AT BREAKFAST THE next day, loud conversations reverberated in everyone's ears. Luke, Avi, Willow, and Aria sat at the same table they'd sat at a hundred times before throughout the last school year. It bore the same nicks and dents in the wood, the same view of the parking lot and gardens under the window. The four of them held schedules in their hands, reading over how their days were planned for them, and slowly scooping food into their mouths.

"What? I have algebra first!" Avi exclaimed, his brows raised high above his hazel eyes. "My brain couldn't even decide if I wanted pancakes or eggs. How am I supposed to figure out *math* this early in the morning?"

Aria shrugged, a smile creeping onto her face. She had two of her favorite classes first: Basic Enchanting and Potion Brewing. Excitement bubbled up inside her at the fact that she would get to surround herself with the kind of magic that made her feel alive again.

"Don't you have any magical classes first?" Luke asked, taking Avi's schedule. His lips tugged up and he pushed it back across the table. "Yes, you do. You have History and Legends right after breakfast."

Avi frowned, his voice growing gloomier. "That's not really much better. Mr. Monroy will make me wish I'd stayed in bed."

"Well, I say this day calls for a celebration!" Willow set her schedule down and smiled at them. "We're in ninth grade! We're high schoolers now!"

"Of course, *you* would say that, smarty-pants." Avi crossed his arms and smoldered mischievously. "But I suppose that's pretty cool."

Aria's first day of middle school replayed in her head. It had been such a happy day, one of the better days of going to school. But now the memory was tainted with gloom. The smile slid off her face as she imagined it—her mother and father stepping out of the car with her, looking up at the big building, stepping into a school meant for *'big kids.'* Watching her parents leave but knowing she'd see them again when the day was over.

Now it was her first day of high school and her parents were locked away. And who knew when they would finally be rescued. Her heart ached to forget her worries and wear a careless genuine grin like Willow, Avi, and Luke were at that moment.

Her eyes stung and she blinked the sensation away, a lump blocking her throat. Turning her face away from everyone else, she looked toward the cafeteria doors. She made a mistake in doing so, though, when Celaena Malamone walked in. A sly smile quirked up on her lips when she saw Aria, malicious green eyes twinkling with a smugness that seemed stained to her face. She didn't stop; instead, she swung her silky straight-as-a-ruler black hair behind her and continued walking to her group of friends.

Anger rose inside Aria at the sight of Malus Malamone's granddaughter. That family had brought misery upon Aria's.

Her hands curled into fists, but she had to force herself to stay in her seat and look back at her three friends. Even as Celaena watched her like an angry cat, Aria ignored her.

Willow's eyes trailed over to where Aria had been looking and frowned. "Hey, Aria, did you speak with Mrs. Mckinney recently?"

Aria sighed and met Willow's expectant, hopeful gaze. "Yeah, yesterday morning. But it's still the same as usual. Things are chaotic. Enchanting Control won't let the Forces of Light go out and get them because they don't have leaders…anymore." Her voice broke and she choked down the lump in her throat. *My parents are the leaders—or were the leaders.* "Mrs. Mckinney didn't say it, but I think the Forces of Light are scared to have new leaders step in. Malus has hunted the leaders for years, and every single one met their end with him. She said Enchanting Control is stepping into the situation now. But she also kind of implied that there's something…dark going on out there."

"The Dark Forces," Luke interjected. "They're keeping quiet, probably lurking, but they're active."

Willow gnawed on her lip, looking uneasy. "Well, I'll see if I can get a message to my dad. He works at Enchanting Control in the Ally Communications department, which manages connections with the Forces of Light. Maybe he can talk to someone a little higher up and get the Forces of Light clearance to go get your parents." Her eyes crinkled at the edges with a smile. "My dad is the most understanding person in the world. I'm sure he can help us."

"Thanks, Willow," Aria said, hope warming in her heart.

"Of course." Willow patted her hand and stood to leave as the bell rang, grabbing her stuff. "Oh, and his name is Acre Mudry by the way."

The Basic Enchanting classroom was just as it had been last school year, though now there was a thin layer of dust covering everything. The oil lamps hanging from the ceiling filled the room with light and an open concrete floor stretched out in front of Aria. First day of school nostalgia hung in the air like rays of sunshine. Students younger than Aria sat on cushions on the floor, in front of a green chalkboard. Aria joined them awkwardly, thinking, *how odd that I'm a year behind on learning magic, and that only just last spring I learned of it existing.*

Mrs. Helma wore a brown cardigan, sipping on coffee in the back of the room. The faint smell of pumpkin spice wafted through the air despite it being only the beginning of September. She set the coffee down on her desk before standing up and striding to close the door as the last of the students filed in. Her hands clapped together, a smile forming on her face.

"Welcome, students, to another year at Incanting Academy!" Mrs. Helma strode to the chalkboard and grabbed the white chalk. "As you all should remember from last year, I am Mrs. Helma. I will be teaching you all sorts of basic enchants and helping you to grow in your magical abilities. Today, we will start with a review on illegal forms of magic."

Mrs. Helma turned to the chalkboard and wrote *Illegal Magic* on it.

"Illegal—or immoral—forms of magic are any enchants, curses, or charms that are used to harm. Defensive spells such as the Knockback Enchant could be considered an enchant that harms, but that is not the purpose of it. The purpose is to defend, not harm. A harmful enchant is one used *specifically* to harm, and really has no other purpose. Can anyone recall what some of the illegal enchants, curses, and charms are?"

A few students raised their hands as Aria leaned back on her palms. Having only known about magic for several months, there was no point trying to answer something she knew little about.

"Gerold!"

A skinny boy with sandy blond hair lowered his hand. "All curses."

Mrs. Helma shook her head. "Not all curses are bad. Curses are a type of magic that is permanent, unless it has a counter-curse. Because of that, many curses are punishable under certain circumstances, and there are several that are illegal altogether, but not all are. Can you name off an illegal curse?"

Gerold's nervous eyes wondered across the room, contemplating. "The…the pain curse?"

Mrs. Helma turned to the chalkboard to write his answer, speaking as she did. "Well, it's actually an enchant because it isn't permanent, but yes. The pain enchant is one of the biggest ones. It is also called the Bolest Enchant, if you get into technical terms. It causes the victim unbearable pain. It has been known to drive people insane." Mrs. Helma glanced across the room. "Can anyone else tell me an illegal form of magic?"

Aria watched more hands go up, unable to understand how Mrs. Helma could talk about something so horrible so casually. Avi would be mortified of his aunt, probably joking about it if he were there next to Aria.

"The death enchant?" A girl in the front answered hesitantly.

"No, that is not a thing. There is no enchant that has the sole purpose of killing. There are enchants that could be used to kill but are not supposed be," Mrs. Helma said. "Anyone else?"

"Mind control," someone in front of Aria said.

"Yes, another big one!" Mrs. Helma wrote it on the board. "Mind control comes in many forms. Mind-readers can control the minds of others if they are strong enough, or potions can help people weaken and control a mind. A mind is one of the greatest weapons, so we should do our best to protect it."

"Does that mean Mind-reading is illegal?" The sandy-haired boy spoke out. "My little brother is a Mind-reader."

"No, it's not illegal unless it is causing harm to someone or something. When it becomes a problem or if someone is being controlled by Mind-tampering, then it is illegal." Mrs. Helma continued to write more illegal forms of magic on the board as she called on students. Soon the board had a neat little list written on it. "I do not teach you about these forms of magic to scare you, students. I teach you about them to help you. The world of magic is a scary place, and if you are not well informed on these, you could end up getting hurt." Mrs. Helma looked at Aria as if she were trying to drill the lesson into her specifically. Aria knew from experience that the words rang true.

"Always report incidences of these forms of magic being used to the Forces of Light so they can put a stop to it...Or report it to Enchanting Control." The way she almost left that last part out sent a strange feeling down Aria's spine, like somehow the Forces of Light were more competent than the actual law enforcers. And with everything going on with Enchanting Control, resent toward them began to rise up in Aria.

"The charges against someone using these forms of magic are extreme. Remember what you've learned." Mrs. Mckinney strode to the door and opened it. "Now, have a wonderful day! Class is dismissed."

Aria grabbed her bag off the floor and followed the rest of the students out of the classroom. She hurried along, weaving through the crowds coming out of the classrooms in the hall.

Voices and the scratching of chairs on the floor greeted her in Complicated Magic. Mr. and Mrs. Migotchi, an older plump couple with wisps of gray hair and kind crinkles in their eyes, stood near a rolling chalkboard in front of the class. All the students sat at desks, which must have been a new addition since they weren't there last year. Empty stone walls loomed on all sides, making the room feel oddly blank. Aria sat down at the nearest desk as Mrs. Migotchi put a paper and pencil down on it.

Mr. Migotchi adjusted his round glasses on his face and started scrawling across the chalkboard. "This school year, you will be learning more complicated enchants and even some defense, as the Dark Forces seem to have woken and are resorting back to their ways during the Dark Days," Mr. Migotchi said before taking a deep breath, voice growing heavy. "And with the recent discovery of Malus Malamone being a Shapeshifter, I think there is much more that the Forces of Light do not know yet. The best we can do is prepare you all."

Aria's heart jolted in her chest at Mr. Migotchi's words. The memories of Twilight came at her in a rush, shooting adrenaline through her veins. Whispers spread throughout the room and many eyes landed on her.

"That's her, isn't it?" someone whispered behind her and Aria sucked in a breath. No one knew her secret, but everyone knew about how she'd been kidnapped over the summer by the Dark Forces. It was hard to keep the gossip from spreading.

"Yeah, that's her," another person answered. "Her parents were taken by the Dark Forces last school year. They *were* the leaders of the Forces of Light. Now the Forces of Light don't have leaders. Without them, it won't be long before the Forces of Light fall. From what my pa said, they're already in a horrible state."

"Did Malus...you know..." The first person's voice lowered. "Did he kill them?"

Aria kept her head down and grabbed her sunflower necklace, tracing the petals. *It's just gossip. Don't let it get to your head.* Her bones felt like they were made of lead. She took a deep breath to steady her heaving chest and directed her attention to Mr. Migotchi.

"Before we begin learning all of that, though, we will be taking a pop-quiz as usual to refresh on what was learned last year. On the quiz, you will find questions on all different forms of magic—natural, basic, immoral, charms, curses, and enchants. You may begin."

Aria glanced down at the paper and her teeth clenched together in concern. She began writing down what she knew, but her mind reeled at all the things she'd yet to learn. Being a year behind and somehow being the Diviner at the same time made heat creep into her cheeks. She should know this stuff, but her mind ached at the words on the paper.

Some of the questions were easy like *'What was your favorite charm to have learned last year?'* But others were hard, and Aria could barely wrap her head around them. At the end of the pop-quiz time, she was the only one still trying to figure it out. Circling and jotting down the best she could think of, she handed it in.

As students began to pack up their things, Mrs. Migotchi spoke across the room. "Later this month we will be learning conjuring. Conjuring is a lot like teleporting, but it is used on items rather than yourself, so be thinking of what you want to bring to class to learn to conjure with. It will need to be small, but not so small that it can be lost, as we will be going outside with a few other classes."

Aria sighed, knowing very well that she didn't have anything to bring but clothes or a hairbrush.

After dinner, Aria walked through the veil to head to her room alone. The dim stone halls were empty and eerily silent. She continued down the halls with her nerves on edge, feeling as if something was watching her—like she wasn't alone. She clung to the books she had taken from the library with such an intensity they felt like they were going to cut into her arms. Footsteps sounded ahead. Three people rounded the corner, cutting off the hallway in front of her. They were dressed in leather, black, and bright neon colors like an arcade from the 1980s. The second Aria heard footsteps behind her, she turned rapidly, holding on to her courage even tighter than her books. Another three people stood in front of her, blocking off all possible escapes. The person in the middle was Celaena, a wicked smile spread across her face.

"Well, well, well," Celaena said.

Her voice made Aria shiver—she sounded like Celaena's mother, Kora. The way she spoke reminded Aria of the day she and her friends were captured in Bola. It was one of the many petrifying dreams that woke her in the middle of the night, like her brain didn't want her to forget a single moment of it.

"So, girls, this is who I've been telling you about," Celaena continued. "The Diviner."

Instant fear made its way through every vein in Aria's body and the hallway suddenly felt cold. Her body tensed up. She took an automatic step away from Celaena, not sure what Celaena would do—she'd tried strangling Aria before.

The magic in Aria's veins pulsed with a need to get out. Every time she heard that title it made every one of her nerves go off like a bomb. She hated it. She didn't want it. It shouldn't belong to her. It was a dangerous word.

Of course, Celaena would know about Aria being the Diviner. Her mother would have told her. The thought of anyone else knowing made Aria's head spin and she felt the dire need for more air.

"Malus is sure to have tested you by now, so he will know you are the Diviner. You are in mortal danger. He will want to use you," her mother had told her. *"He will know that you are the only one powerful enough to destroy the Dark Forces."*

All that power. All that responsibility. And it wasn't just her that would be in danger because of it all. Everyone she cared about would be. What if others wanted to use her for her power once they found out? Celaena couldn't possibly mean well with anything she said.

"Don't worry, Aria. We won't tell," Celaena said, grinning at the reaction she got. She lifted her finger to her lips. "It'll be our little secret."

"What do you want then?" Aria stood her ground, not breaking eye contact, even though every nerve in her body told her to run away. Celaena had drained all the color away from her skin.

"My friends wanted to meet the Diviner for themselves. Right, girls?"

"Yeah," the rest of them said with cunning grins. Malicious intent hung in the air like a suffocating fog.

"Oh, really?" Aria's disbelief made its way into her voice as she shook. "You're not going to try to trick me or tie my hands together or teleport me to—"

"I'm not going to do anything to you," Celaena patronized Aria, flipping her hair over her shoulder. "And we can't teleport in the school—"

"Then you might drag me out of the school and teleport me to Malus' mansion," Aria quickly interrupted, before part of her began to wonder why she was giving Celaena all these ideas.

"My grandfather is not even home, thanks to you, Diviner." Celaena wrinkled her nose.

"But I bet your mother will be looking for me, along with the rest of the Dark Forces."

Inside the school, Aria had no idea what the Dark Forces were planning or where they were. Were they looking for her? Did they know Malus was imprisoned? She knew they would want revenge and it was only a matter of time before they came to get it. And Celaena, the granddaughter of Malus, loved to brag, so if Aria could just get her to leak something…

"Yes, I suppose she is…but the Dark Forces don't need to look for you." A sly smile crept across Celaena's face. "Not if they *know* where you are."

Aria hadn't thought about that.

"Still, they couldn't catch me and keep me locked away then," Aria bluffed, faking a smirk. "What makes you think they'll succeed now?"

Inside, she felt like curling in on herself and wished everything that had happened in the last several months was simply a dream. What Celaena had said made Aria's hands tremble as she clenched them around her books. The Dark Forces could be coming for her at any moment.

Celaena turned furiously scarlet, then blank as if she were unsure of what to say, then amused, which took Aria aback. It was never good when Celaena was amused.

"You're right. Maybe my grandfather's best of the best is not very good at capturing you. He himself would do better at getting the Diviner."

"He's locked away, stuck as a cat," Aria said, taking an

impulsive step back. Her blood boiled, wanting more than anything for Celaena to stop saying that word. It repeated itself in her mind, stirring angry magic in her veins.

Celaena ignored her. "The Diviner will finally be captured one day. One day very soon."

"STOP CALLING ME THAT!" Aria couldn't help herself.

The word was like poison, giving her a headache and driving her mad. The sound of it put her on edge and brought every bit of magic to the surface. Energy pulled itself from her body, shooting out through her fingertips, and leaving her feeling weak. Her books fell to the ground. She let out a long shaky breath and unclenched her eyes; her body had been petrified and she hadn't even been aware of it. The wall in front of her was cracked all the way through to the other side in the Space Realm. The black void of nothingness loomed like the jaws of a beast. The coldness leaking into the already drafty hallway gripped Aria's skin. The floor had cracks running down it, leaving crumbs of it falling through into the endless void. The crack let a musky smell leak through, a slight pull threatening to drag her into it.

"So that is the power of the Diviner..." Celaena's mouth hung open as she stared into the void, eyes wide. A faint smirk spread on her face as if she expected it, as if this was her very intention. "Mrs. Mckinney won't be too happy about that."

"Oh my..." Aria stared, remembering when she had broken Mrs. Mckinney's clock. She felt overwhelmed like thorny vines were constricting her. She needed to get out of there and hide. She had caused too much damage. She had to leave before she caused more. The power surged through her blood, tugging as if it wanted out again. She quickly picked up all her books and pushed her way past Celaena's friends, tears streaming down her cheeks.

"Don't worry, we'll keep your secret!" Celaena called. "And we'll get someone to repair what you've broken."

Those last few words sounded dark and malicious, and they repeated themselves in Aria's mind even as she fled… *What you've broken.*

She ran all the way back to her room, pushed open the door, and collapsed in the darkness. The time blurred together as she sat there, her eyes red and puffy. Soon enough, she fell sideways and let exhaustion consume her like the nightmares she had every night.

"Have you ever fought in the dark, Aria?" Viola's voice trailed through the eerie darkness. "I do it all the time."

Aria's screams filled the air as she was pulled across the marble flooring of the Malamone Mansion. Then something pounced on her, claws digging through her clothes, and the pulling stopped. Bright green cat eyes gazed down on her and the Life Stone dangled in the midst of the pitch blackness. Twilight. Malus. Was there even a difference?

"Diviner." The cat spat the word out of its mouth like a curse. "Give me back what is mine."

How was the cat talking?

"Get away from me!" Aria screamed, shoving it away. A sudden burst of golden magic lit her fingertips, and she fell through the space realm, the world crumbling away beneath her. Even as black dots edged into her vision, she felt it was all her fault. Then there was nothing.

CHAPTER THREE

ARIA CREPT DOWN the hall the next morning. Her bag was slung over her shoulder, and she held onto the straps like they were a lifeline to stifle the trembling of her hands. When she reached the spot where she and Celaena had been the previous night, she breathed a sigh of relief. The massive hole in the wall was gone. Had it just been another one of her nightmares? She spotted a thin line like a scar tracing where it had been broken the night before. So, not a nightmare. That meant Celaena had kept to her word; she'd gotten someone to fix it. But what had she told them? Did she tell them Aria had been the one to break it? No single teenager should be strong enough to break through into a realm…and yet Aria had.

In the cafeteria, Willow, Luke, and Avi were sitting at their usual spot. The table was oddly quiet. Willow sat with a book propped open so she could read while she slowly lifted food into her mouth. Luke and Avi quietly chatted in front of her, but their conversation paused when Aria slid onto the bench beside Willow. Luke turned to Aria, who sat in front of him, and studied her.

"Good morning," he said. "How are you?"

"Um, good." Her voice sounded off so she forced her lips to tug up in a half smile.

Maybe it was because she had bags under her eyes from the nightmares that kept her restless, or the twinkle missing from them, but Luke sighed. It was like he could see right through her, but he didn't press.

Willow glanced up from her book, a hopeful light sparking in her eyes. "I got a letter out to my father this morning, so it's on its way."

"Thank you," Aria said, the tightness in her chest loosening a little. "That's good to hear."

Willow gave a little smile and turned back to the thick hardcover sitting in front of her.

A light blush bloomed on Avi's cheeks. "What are you reading about, smarty-pants?"

Willow's eyes trailed up from her book to meet Avi's eyes. "It's about trolls."

"Does it say in there what a troll who likes to dance is called?" Avi asked, grinning mischievously.

"No, what—"

"A trollerina!" Avi laughed.

Willow rolled her eyes and evidently tried to fight the smile spreading across her face. Aria snorted, shaking her head at Avi's ridiculousness when the clacking of heels came up behind her. Her mind instantly shot to Mrs. Mckinney. Maybe Mrs. Mckinney had something new to tell her. Maybe Willow's letter had somehow already managed to reach Acre, her father, and he had managed to convince Enchanting Control to give them clearance. Maybe she had news about her parents. But when Aria turned, it was Celaena behind her.

"You're welcome." Celaena's tone had an edge like a blade. She raised her eyebrows, clearly expecting a response.

"For what?" Aria glanced at her friends to see they were listening.

"I got someone to fix the gouge you put in the veiled side of school." Celaena's emotions looked closed off, so Aria couldn't determine whether she was irritated, angry, or bored. Or maybe all of them. "You know, the one that you created last night—the one that someone could have fallen through and *died* because of you."

Aria clenched her teeth, shame washing over her. "It was an accident."

"We all have mistakes to fix, Chesler." Celaena rolled her eyes. "At least I was there to fix yours."

Aria shook her head and blew out a puff of air. "What do you want? A payment of some kind?" She raised an eyebrow. "Because it's not like you to do something out of the kindness of your heart. You clearly want something, or you're just trying to play with my head." Aria huffed out a frustrated breath. "Did you tell someone that I was the one who did it and you want to bask in the feeling of being superior, or what?"

Celaena looked at her blankly. "No…I don't expect anything from you. And no, I kept your secret. I told you I would. I simply told Mrs. Mckinney that me and my girlies found it that way. I'm doing this for free."

"Why?" Aria lowered her brows, pinning Celaena with a fierce gaze.

"It's the least I could do, since—Well, it's probably best that I don't ruin the *surprise*…" With that, her mouth twisted into an evil smirk and she walked away.

A pit opened up in Aria's stomach and her hand pushed her food away. She turned back to her friends to see they were staring at her with wide eyes. A rush of questions about the broken wall enveloped her.

"Um, you did *what?*" Avi's eyes were wide and concerned. "Man, I wish I would have been there to see that. I've never seen the Space Realm. I bet it was cool."

Willow shook her head, looking mortified. "I bet it was scary."

"It would have been scary-cool then!" Avi smiled, completely ignoring the fact that Aria had destroyed a part of the school and added a potential danger to it.

Luke leaned closer with concern etched on his face. "Are you okay? You must have been very shaken."

"I was, but I'm fine," Aria said, sighing. "I'm just glad no one got hurt."

Luke's studying eyes traveled across her face. Aria shrunk in on herself, tucking her arms close to her and fidgeting underneath the table.

"And I'm glad that *you* didn't get hurt. I'm sure we all are." Luke pulled back as well, shooting a look at Avi, who smiled sheepishly. "Just stay far away from Celaena. Nothing good ever comes from her."

Aria nodded, her mind on whatever surprise Celaena might have in store for her.

The next two weeks passed strangely. Every day, she got up, ate breakfast, spent most of the day learning, and talked with her friends. It almost felt normal, if it weren't for her parents missing, talk of the Dark Forces and the Forces of Light coming up in nearly every conversation, and spending her days in a magical school. Everyone had something to comment on about what had happened over the summer, spreading rumors that got farther and farther from the truth every time. Aria, Willow, Luke, and Avi were nearly inseparable when classes were out, except for when Willow went to visit her mom and little brother in the close town of Forest's Edge. Her father was away at work. Celaena kept to herself most of the time now that Aria didn't have any classes with her, but there was a callous look in her eyes every time Aria saw her.

It was Friday, the day of learning to conjure, and the whole school was acting rowdy with the thought of the weekend. Early that morning, Aria searched her room for something she could bring to Complicated Magic so she could learn conjuring. After pulling out all of her things, she decided to go to the library. Bringing a book would be much better than bringing her hairbrush. She got way more books than she'd planned, so after dropping them back off at her room, she scurried to Complicated Magic. In class, everyone was talking with anticipation of conjuring the items they'd brought. They'd all lined up at the door and then were led from the classroom to the other side of the veil, and then outside.

The sun had risen a bit, but the morning dew still covered everything and goosebumps tickled Aria's skin as the fresh air washed over her. Mr. and Mrs. Migotchi led the class to the back of the school, where a few other classes already were. The forest surrounding the school crowded around the clearing behind it, students milling about through the grass.

"As we said before, this class will be taken with a few other classes today," Mr. Migotchi said. "Like teleporting was last year, this will also be a complicated enchant to learn. It will take many classes to master."

Some other teachers and staff that Aria didn't know mingled among the students filling the clearing. They helped space students out, taking their objects and putting them ten feet from them. Excited voices blew through the clearing. Students talked amongst each other in anticipation, unable to stay still for even a second. Aria stared ahead at the little book she'd gotten from the library, now ten feet away in the grass. It was a worn green hardcover with golden detailing and a fraying placeholder sticking out from the bottom. Magic stirred in her veins, calling her like an old friend.

"To conjure is to make an item disappear from one place and reappear where you are. As said before, it is a lot like teleporting except that it is used on an object." Mrs. Migotchi strode through the crowd of students, her voice booming over all the others. "There is also the enchant of deconjuring, which is the enchant of making an item disappear from where you are and reappear somewhere else. We will start with conjuring."

Aria had teleported before, but that had been with help. She chewed on her lip, hoping she'd be able to figure this out without knowing how to teleport on her own beforehand.

"Just like with teleporting, you must be able to picture where the item is. You must picture it in your head. You must be familiar with it. In order to get it to you, you must picture it as though you already have it. Reach out through the atoms in the world and magically connect with it. Then teleport it into your hand. This is why we're starting with something small."

Aria looked at her book in the grass, trying to reach out and grasp it. It shifted in its spot, but it didn't disappear and reappear in her hands. She closed her eyes, holding out her hand for it, and willed it to conjure itself. She felt nothing, as if her magic lay dormant in her veins, disobeying her. She shook her head to herself, thinking that was a ridiculous notion. Her magic belonged to her; it didn't have a mind of its own. She tried again and still the book didn't reappear in her hands.

Other student's items were vanishing and reappearing in

their hands. Aria blew out a puff of air and tried again, but a light touch at her shoulder startled her from her concentration.

"Calm down," Willow's light, airy voice came from beside her. The wind rattled the fabric of her sky-blue jumper around her legs. "It takes practice."

"Oh, hey. You're in one of the classes here?" Aria looked around, hoping to see that maybe Luke and Avi were too. Instead, she saw Celaena across the clearing with her eyes and a callous grin pinned to her.

"Yes, and so are Luke and Avi." Willow pointed to where Avi was joking with Luke, making it so the two of them were barely paying attention to the lesson. Avi spotted the two of them and waved, flinging his arm wildly back and forth. Willow waved back before turning to nod at Aria's book in the grass. "I see you're having trouble."

"Yeah…" Aria sighed.

"Don't worry. Avi hasn't gotten it either and his aunt started to teach him conjuring last school year."

"But he knows how to teleport?" It didn't add up in Aria's mind.

"That's because he paid attention in *that* class." Willow glanced at Avi with a pinkish tint painting her cheeks.

Aria's lips tugged up and she glanced between the two of them.

"Focus and don't force it," Willow continued. "Don't let anything hold you back. You can do it. I believe in you. Know that you're not alone." She gave Aria a delicate pat on the shoulder. "Welp, I should get back to my object."

Then Willow gave her a smile and strode away, leaving Aria confused.

"What was that supposed to mean?" Aria whispered to

herself. Willow was a Mind-reader, and she gave Aria the distinct feeling that she knew something even Aria didn't know.

Aria turned back to the book and closed her eyes, picturing it was in her hands. She willed it to move from one place to the next, attaching her magic to its very atoms. A connection like an invisible thread spread through the air to the book. The connection gave a fierce tug at Aria's command. And then, she felt it in her hand. She opened her eyes with a faint grin to see her fingers wrapped around its aged spine.

She looked up from the book and over toward where Willow, Luke, and Avi were. Luke waved and she lifted her hand to wave too. Warmth settled in her heart and a weight felt lifted off her shoulders. Then Celaena caught her eye. She was watching Aria with intensely narrowed eyes, reminding Aria of that surprise she'd mentioned…

While the rest of the school chatted in the cafeteria, Aria sat in her room during lunch, trying to figure out how the Divining Powers worked. She believed she should know anything she possibly could about previous Diviners and the powers that ran within her own blood, but what she wanted was to throw the books at the wall. Everything she read was something she'd already learned before. She hardly knew what she was even looking for, but she felt she needed an answer to *something*. It felt like there was some puzzle inside her that was missing a piece, and if she didn't find it, she felt she wouldn't be complete.

She gave a sigh and slammed the one she was reading shut. Dust flew up into the air from its old, weathered pages. Lunch would probably be over soon enough, and she had learned hardly anything. Hurried and flustered, she opened another of the books, hoping there was some satisfactory answer within the pages.

The Diviner has long been a story that children love hearing, elders love sharing, and writers have loved debating about. Few people believe the being to be real, and therefore it has been claimed a myth. The only way to find out the truth would be to read the legendary Ancient Scrolls.

It has been said that nearly two thousand years ago, the Ancient Scrolls were made to hold all the knowledge in the universe. They were crafted by the most knowledgeable creatures known. The Ancient Scrolls told stories and legends, but also every truth. The Diviner would be among those mentioned in the Scrolls, the information on all previous Diviners jotted down on the thin parchment. Not much is known about these Scrolls, but they are a big part of history despite many believing them to be a legend. Over time, what has been known about both them and the Diviner has become blurry, and no one knows what is really truth. The Scrolls are said to remain in the one place they can be safe: Viden's Library of Knowledge. There they are well protected, and a supposed curse was put on the library, making it so that no one dares enter. Sadly, because of that, the information we wish to write for you is inaccessible. So, here is what has been gathered about the Diviner not from the Ancient Scrolls but from the legends and myths.

The Diviner lives the average lifespan of any other human, but because of their healing abilities and immense powers they tend to live longer by a few decades. The power the Diviner wielded is said to have been unmatched. It is the type of power that could tear civilizations and worlds apart. With the five Divining Powers—Shape-shifting, Nature-manipulation, Healing, Mind-reading, and Omni-communication, the Diviner is the true bridge and peacekeeper between all. A Diviner is not reborn or reincarnated, but rather, their powers are transferred to the next infant with a worthy destiny. It could take several years before a new, worthy infant is born—

Aria shut the book, teeth grinding together and mind aching. She could barely even process the information. Her, worthy? The true power of the Diviner and all five of the Divining Powers had been stripped from the Diviner before she was even born. And now she was one? She had always felt like a grain of sand on the earth, and this book wanted to tell her that she was worthy of the Diviner's powers? Nonsense.

Why me? Aria shook her head and rubbed her face. *Why do I have to have a power I can't even use? Why do I have to be the one the Dark Forces want? Why can't I just be normal?*

She grabbed the book abruptly, flipping back through the pages to reread one line: *Now, the Scrolls remain in the one place they can be safe: Viden's Library of Knowledge.*

If the Scrolls told the truth, she wanted them. Every book she read couldn't give her the exact information she wanted. Only the Scrolls could. Everything would tell her she was a myth cooked up to make children go to sleep at night. But the Scrolls held the answer to who she was, *what* she was. They would tell her exactly why it had taken so long for a Diviner to be found, right? They would tell her why she was chosen and not someone else. They would tell her why everything was happening to *her*.

Aria didn't know when or if she would ever be able to read them, but the desire bloomed in her heart.

She grabbed her sunflower necklace that hung around her neck and traced the petals, trying to calm her racing mind. The bell abruptly rang and she got up from the bed, stuffing all the books back in her bag as she hurried out of her room. The last one wouldn't fit, so she carried it. It was a heavy, old, dusty book that told old stories on different creatures like dragons, mermaids, and sphinx. She had hoped the previous Diviners would be among the stories, but they weren't. The Diviner seemed so inhuman to her, like a creature always clawing at her heart and mind.

Hurrying to the veil, she entered the mundane side of the school, where students were moving about the halls in hurried paces. She held the book close to her to hide the title, knowing well enough that many other children at the school didn't know about magic, and might not ever find out about it.

Noise filled her ears as she pushed through the crowds of rowdy people. Everyone was eager for school to be over for the week; she could tell. An elbow jabbed into her ribs as she pushed past a black-haired girl, Aria not paying attention to who it was. Her arm was knocked out of the way and the book slipped from her hands. As the book fell, she caught sight of Celaena's cunning grin as she walked around the corner. The papers inside the book fell out and pages ripped, flying about the floor. One of the librarians had told Aria to be careful with the weathered book and for good reason. Now it was a giant heap of leather, pages, and random students' papers that they'd left behind inside it. The hall was clearing out, leaving Aria alone. She got down on her hands and knees to collect everything into a pile, her hands shaking. She had messed up enough last year with yelling at Mrs. Mckinney and breaking her clock. Now the librarians would be angry with her for ruining a book. All she had wanted was information about herself. Everything in her trembled, pushed over the edge, and ready to crack.

"Here, let me help, Aria."

A soft hand found hers as she reached out for the pages.

She looked up and she saw Luke's face, so close to her own. Right then, she could see all the shadows and highlights of the light reflecting off his blue eyes. She felt butterflies fill her stomach and her breath shuddered. Heat crept into her cheeks.

"Thanks," she said, still scrambling for the papers.

Luke handed her a couple, then picked up the leather cover. She heaved the stack of papers into her arms, standing slowly and carefully. Luke lightly set the cover on top of it all.

"Do you need help carrying it to…" He trailed off, looking at her with a question written on his face.

"The library. I need to take it to the library." Aria finished, her cheeks on fire. "I would love some help."

"Then I'd be happy to assist."

They stood there for a moment, wavering in the empty, silent hall. It was as if something was keeping her there, gluing her to the spot.

He reached for the book, growing closer to her. "I can carry it for you, if you would like." His eyes darted from the book to her eyes, then fell to her lips.

She moved her hand slightly, forcing her body to hand the book over like he was offering. His eyes moved to her own again and he somehow grew closer. Aria took a step back, her back brushing the wall. She licked her lips, not sure what was happening. There was a want waking within her that she'd never felt before, and she wasn't sure if she *should* want it. Luke was supposed to be just a friend, nothing more. And yet, his face was growing closer to hers.

"Aria?" He looked at her with his full attention, another silent question lingering in the air.

Her mouth wouldn't form an answer to whatever the question was. Her brain wasn't even working properly anymore. She wasn't sure which one of them was moving, or if they both were. But one second, they were inches apart, and the next, the pages were falling onto the floor again and her lips were about to brush against his—

The sudden sound of an explosion made her pull away, every nerve inside her going off and her heart thumping against her ribs furiously—whether it was because she had *almost* just kissed Luke or because of the sound, she didn't know. Another loud sound racked the building, sending shakes throughout the floor and walls. Dust fell from the ceiling.

Something was wrong—very, very wrong.

She looked to Luke with terror etched into her face as the cacophony of crumbling met her ears. The floor shook beneath their feet.

"Let's go!" He grabbed her wrist and pulled her along with him down the hall.

They ran toward the noise as screams erupted from the classrooms in the front of the school. The halls passed in a blur, their feet carrying them to stairs that led down to the very front of the school. Stopping dead at the top of the stairs, Aria's eyes went wide. Gaping holes were left in the front wall. Staff fled from their offices, where walls were crumbling away to reveal the outside. Dust was everywhere and shouts rang out from every classroom now. Aria hurried down the stairs with Luke right behind her so she could get a better look outside. Horror overtook her entire body and she had to force herself to breathe. Her heart seemed to stop beating and her blood chilled when she saw five cloaked figures standing out in the parking lot. The golden daggers embroidered on their shoulders gleamed in the sunlight.

CHAPTER FOUR

ARIA'S LUNGS FILLED with sharp breaths, but she felt like she was suffocating.

"EVERYONE GET OUT OF THE SCHOOL USING THE BACK EXIT. HIDE IN THE WOODS!" Mrs. Mckinney's voice belted over the loudspeakers. "THIS IS NOT A DRILL! THERE ARE INTRUDERS IN THE PARKING LOT!"

Doors were thrown open and panicked cries flooded through the school like a tsunami. Everyone rushed out into the hallways, pushing and shoving people. Order was lost in the chaos as they tried to get out. The cloaked figures started toward the school. The faint smell of smoke wafted through the air.

Luke held tight onto Aria's wrist and started for the back of the school.

"What are you doing?" Aria pulled her hand out of his grasp.

"Getting out of here," he said, nodding toward the enemies in the parking lot. "You heard what Mrs. Mckinney said—We have to get to the back of the school."

"No, we have to find Willow and Avi," Aria argued. "The Dark Forces are here for me, but they'll recognize you guys. I have to make sure they get out of here safe too." Aria took off up the stairs, trying to remember where Willow's advanced biology class was at.

"Aria, wait up!" Luke was right behind her in an instant. "You're so stubborn."

He continued to speak and reason with her, but all his words were lost. Images of losing her friends at camp when it had been attacked flashed through Aria's mind. She rushed down the hall, pushing her way through the fear-stricken crowd. Elbows knocked into her ribs and shoulders bumped each other, noise echoing all around her.

She stood on her tippy toes to look over heads. "WILLOW! AVI!"

"Aria?" Avi's voice called from somewhere to the right of the hall.

Luke and Aria shoved forward until they found him following his class to the back of the school.

"What's going on? Who's the intruder?" Avi asked, eyes alert as they darted between each of them. "And where's Willow?"

"The Dark Forces—they're here!" Aria said, nearly hyperventilating with her heart hammering in her chest like a mallet. Her bones rattled underneath her skin. "They're here for me."

"Do you remember what class Willow is taking?" Luke asked no one in particular.

"Advanced biology," Avi said immediately.

Luke lips tugged up and a knowing look twinkled in his eyes.

"What? It's not like I have her schedule memorized or something…It's just down the hall—" Avi's voice was cut off as the wall next to them exploded in a shower of dust, chunks of wall, wood, and stone.

"We need to hurry," Luke shouted over the noise, stumbling backward. "They're going to bring the whole building down on us."

Aria shot her hand out, magic gathering in her palms, to direct a massive chunk of wall away from falling on them. Her backpack slipped to the floor. Clouds of dust stung her eyes and pushed into her airways, forcing her to heave and cough. Screams filled the air, and when the smoke cleared, she saw the hallway was emptying. A shadow appeared in the broken, crumbling doorway of the classroom next to them. Blinking away the dust in her eyes, her vision cleared and she raised her hands to defend herself. Magic lit on her fingertips. Worried voices grew farther away as the hallway cleared out, leaving behind lost backpacks, papers, and crimson stains.

The air around them twisted as if the Dark Forces' malice was laced with it, and the hairs on Aria's arms stood up. Black fog began filling the hallway, shifting and thickening by the command of the hooded figure in the doorway. The Black Smoke enchantment leached the hallway of light until all that could be seen was the vague silhouette of the figure.

"Run!" was all Aria could scream at her friends before the fog started wrapping around her limbs.

"Malus wants you back, little Diviner," a voice came from under the hood. It was feminine and sounded so much like Celaena's cruel, taunting voice, which could only mean one thing. It was Kora, Celaena's mother.

Light pierced the darkness, and Aria could see Luke and Avi's figures just a few feet away. Dust danced in the light before drifting to the ground, where debris sat among shattered glass and bricks. In the doorway, the figure took off its hood to reveal a wavy, black-haired woman with pale skin and gray eyes.

"We underestimated you once and we will not be doing that again," Kora said, her voice darkening like a violent storm. "We will carry you out kicking and bleeding if we must."

Luke bolted toward Kora and rammed into her side,

sending her to the ground. Magic lit in his palm, glowing blue and reaching for Kora. The magic reached a mere inch from her face before she pushed Luke off of her. He hit the wall with a sickening thud. A powerful blast blew past Aria in the direction of Kora. Plumes of dust went up around her, burning her eyes. A green light lit up the hallway and then someone was groaning. Sounds of fighting surrounded her—shuffling feet, crumbling walls, magic flying through the air with a whistle, and hisses of pain. Someone hit the wall beside Aria, crashing to the ground near Aria's feet.

"Hey, Aria," Avi said through clenched teeth. "Wanna use some awesome Diviner magic and blow Kora up like you did with that wall on the other side of the school?"

Aria gathered her strength and pulled away from the fog that was wrapping around her. It stung at her skin, linking around her leg like a chain. She stumbled forward and slammed into the ground on her stomach. A groan escaped her lips. "That doesn't sound too bad right now."

"Stupid children," Kora tutted and Black Smoke descended on them completely again, shutting out Aria's sight.

"Run!" she shouted again, but she didn't hear her friends retreating. She turned over just as Kora grabbed her wrist. "Avi, you and Luke just run! I'll catch up!"

"Let's go," Kora said, her wicked smile faintly visible through the dark. "Malus is waiting."

"Malus is locked away!" Aria shouted and slipped her clammy wrist out of Kora's grip.

Another hand wrapped around her wrist and she twisted it, shooting her fist toward a face, but stopped when she saw it was Avi. He ducked out of her fist's path and helped to her feet as she whispered an apology. Together, they hurried away, tripping over bricks and chunks of building in the darkness. Her skin felt radioactive, and her heart raced to keep up with the panic spreading through her. The school was silent as she listened for Luke ahead of her. Then she slammed into his chest and nearly knocked him over. He grabbed Aria's hand, intertwining his fingers with hers like an anchor to keep her at his side. Kora let out a ferocious shout as they turned the corner. Her voice echoed against the cracked walls, following Aria as she ran.

"You can run but you can't hide. We will tear this school apart *brick by brick!*"

A shiver ran down her spine. More stone crumbled from the walls and ceiling.

The fog around them shifted, slowly fading into a toxic green color. Aria gasped, fear gripping her. Black Smoke was often summoned by the Dark Forces and every aspect of it could be manipulated, even the toxicity of it. Her lungs began to burn and she coughed, starting to feel dizzy.

"We have to get out of the fog!" Aria yelled and pulled Luke down another hall where the fog dissipated away. "Where's Avi? Willow!"

Willow's voice came then, laced with fright, "Don't worry, we're right behind you." Her hand lightly touched Aria's shoulder.

"Willow!" Relief filled Aria's voice. "Kora is right behind us."

They continued down the halls, running as fast as they could. The school was like a maze of too many halls and doors, just like the Malamone Mansion had been. They needed to get to the staircases and then to the back of the school where all the students would be gathered to escape. But Aria's heart was hammering in her ears, and she was short of breath, little specks moving into the edges of her vision. She tried to breathe in deeply, but her heart was beating too fast, and all the air felt as if it was being sucked from her lungs. Memories she didn't want to remember forced their way into her mind. Her sweaty hand slipped from Luke's. Her head felt like it was spinning, unable to focus or understand anything but the dire need to collapse. Every muscle in her body felt weak. She forced herself to keep going, trying to push the feeling and the memories away. Her knees shook and tears streamed down her face. It was too much. Breaths coming in rapidly, she thought it was the end. She fell to the ground on her side before she could stop herself. Her hand slipped from Luke's and she wrapped her hands around her sunflower necklace like a lifeline. She gasped for breath and begged for it all to stop. Everything around her was a blur and all the noise seemed to grow soft and distant.

"Aria!" Luke dropped to his knees at her side. She could barely even tell that it was him with how blurry her vision had become. Every word he said echoed as he repeated it. "You've got to get up!"

"What's happening to her?" Avi grabbed her arm and tried to pull her up with Luke.

"She's having a panic attack." Willow was at her side in a second, wrapping her arms underneath of Aria to sit her up. "Aria, it's okay. We've got you. You're going to get out of here. This will pass and you'll be okay."

Luke tucked her hair away from her face. "Hey, hey we've got you. Everything's going to be okay. We just have to get out of here." He turned to Willow and Avi. "I could try to carry her? We have to keep moving."

Still gasping, Aria felt like she was going to die. She could hardly move and sweat was pouring down her back. The Dark Forces would come and they would have her for sure, just like last time. She needed to get out of the school, she knew that. If she didn't, they would get the most powerful weapon in the universe. But she felt consumed by this hopelessness and cowardice. She was trapped in the cage of her mind, unable to break free.

"Just breathe," Willow's calming voice came again, her hand rubbing Aria's back. "Come on, let's get you up."

The emotions slowly began to recede. Breathing as slowly as she could, Aria fought against the onslaught of hopelessness. Willow and Luke had her almost to her feet as she came back to her senses.

"My chest hurts." Aria laid a hand against her heart, feeling it squeeze and twist like a knife was stuck in it.

Willow and Luke helped to steady her on her feet, Luke's voice next to her ear, "It'll be—"

The walls started falling down around them.

"I do not think you know how to play hide n' seek, children," Kora teased, her voice seeming to come from everywhere.

Aria's eyes darted around, unable to locate her in all the dust that was rising up around them.

Luke wrapped an arm around Aria's back to get her to move forward. "Come on."

"Uh-uh-uh, you four aren't going anywhere," another wicked feminine voice echoed around them.

Aria stumbled forward, a scream tearing from her throat as Luke was ripped from her. She spun around to see him dragged across the floor, a ball of magic already forming in his hand and bouncing lights off the walls to find a target. Something ensnared Aria's leg, yanked her, and her back slammed into the scattered plaster. The breath left Aria's lungs at the impact and she struggled to reel it back in. Two shouts beside her told her Willow and Avi had been pulled to the ground as well. Her hands grappled for the rope-like thing wrapped around her ankle and felt leaves. A vine.

"Not these vines again," Avi grumbled, slashing at them

with a slicing enchant. The vines broke apart, falling to the ground…until new ones just replaced the old ones.

The vine slithered away from Aria's ankle, leaving her there like an unloved rag doll.

"Aria!" Luke screamed. Aria could barely see him as the magic flickered out of his palm like a dying fire, the vines too tight around his wrists.

Aria sat upright so fast it made her head spin. Luke was being dragged back down the hall by vines, screaming her name over and over again.

"Luke!" she called, but she couldn't see him through the dust anymore.

She looked around her with her hands raised to protect herself and saw that she was now alone. The sound of her name had been silenced, along with all other sounds. It was just her and wreckage now.

A figure started coming down the hall, then another, and another, each hovering a few inches off the ground. As the three people got closer, she saw the dark green, leafy vines tightly restraining them. The closer they got, the easier it was to see through the ever-growing darkness of the hallway and all the dust. The three figures fought against the vines, slicing at them and kicking, but the vines only constricted them tighter. They fought to breath, eyes bloodshot and faces turning scarlet.

"Luke! Willow! Avi!" Aria screamed, realizing the figures were her friends. Her feet slapped against the floor as she rushed toward them. She reached out to slice her hand through one, magic already forming in her palm.

"Aria, watch out!" Willow shouted at her, but not before icy chains of Black Smoke wrapped around Aria's wrists, harshly pulling her backwards. Then the fog began to twist around her ankles, holding her in place.

"Well, well, well," Kora said as she walked up from behind Luke, Avi, and Willow.

Beside Kora, Ebony strode forward with vines draped across her shoulders like an accessory—the same vines that held her friends hostage. Aria glared at them, searching for some plan in her mind as the icy bite of the fog dug beneath her skin.

Kora strode up to just in front of Aria, cocking her head to the side with a cunning grin. "If I am not mistaken, I heard you say that Malus is locked away. It's kind of funny that you would think such a thing. Malus is powerful and feared for a reason."

"What are you talking about? Malus *is* locked away." Aria's hands were stuck in the air and her feet were planted firmly on the ground. "I watched him at the trial." She grunted as she tried to pull away from the fog laced around her, but it only seemed to tighten its grip. Her blood felt like ice in her veins even as she glared daggers.

"Oh, did you now?" Kora sneered and walked around her like an amused lioness stalking her prey.

"Malus *is* locked away! He's a cat!"

Ebony and Kora broke out in laughs.

"If only Viola were here to hear you," Ebony laughed.

"But she's not," a deep, annoyed voice came up from behind Aria. "Now, can we just get this job over with?" As the man stepped around Aria, she saw that it was Chad, a blond, spiky-haired man who seemed to be a thorn in everyone's side.

"Oh, but Aria needs to see the truth," Kora said, her voice rising an octave. "That Malus never went to prison. In fact, he never even went to the trial."

Aria's heart beat painfully in her chest, a panic barely able to stay at bay. "No, NO! I WAS THERE!" She felt like she might faint. "I SAW HIM!" The cold, vileness of the Black Smoke rubbed at her skin as she yanked at it, leaving red flesh behind.

Kora shook her head and made a mock-caring face. "No, you saw a cat."

"He *is* a cat!" Aria's voice shook. "Enchanting Control took him to Top Rock Security—"

"No, they didn't. Malus was not at the trial. He was not even in that little cage that you trapped him in." Kora's face was alight with wicked amusement. "You see, little Diviner, you took a little, harmless cat to the trial. I wonder what has become of that cat now…Probably still floating over lava in a volcano, watched and fed by guards who don't know the truth…"

"No, no, no…" Aria's head was spinning in a whirlpool of confusion. Half to herself, she said, "I don't understand."

"Well, it's quite simple, actually. You took one of Malus' many cats—he's quite fond of them, so he has a great many. The judge at Enchanting Control knew it was not Malus, but still sent the cat to prison. Poor cat…" Kora explained, her smile widening when she saw the horror on Aria's face. "And you want to know what's even funnier? You truly thought you were getting away. Children, we *let* you walk away. Back on that fountain—" She looked over at Willow with a savage face. "—When you realized your little kitty was actually Malus, he told me something. He told me to let you go because you'd lead him to the Death Stone." Kora looked back at Aria, her grin falling away. "But Malus' plan didn't work out. Instead, you followed him and stole the Life Stone. Now he won't stop until he has both you and it back in his possession."

The looks on the faces of Aria's friends were drenched in pure terror from where they hung with vines wrapped around them.

"Malus spoke to you while he was a cat?" Avi's eyes widened with realization. "Then you're an—"

"Omni-communicator?" Kora smirked. "Yes, yes, I am."

"The judge at the trial…" Luke asked as he struggled

against Ebony's vines. "How did he know the cat wasn't Malus then, if what you're saying is even true? Why didn't he say it wasn't Malus?"

Ebony joined in, hands on her hips. "Because the judge is a very dear friend of ours. His name is Ciaus."

Aria recognized that name from the day they were taken from Bola. He was a potion master for Malus. But that didn't mean it was true. How could a potion master also be a spy and a judge?

"No! You're lying." Aria tugged on the Black Smoke harder even as it constricted around her more. "All of it is a lie!"

"No, it's not," Kora said, hostility lacing her voice. "And now, Malus is waiting for you, little Diviner." A silver dagger appeared out of nowhere in her hand and she pointed at her throat. Aria froze at the blade so close to her body. "You and the Life Stone you took from around his neck."

Aria had to resist looking at Luke, the person she had given the Life Stone that way it would be hidden. The mention of her being the Diviner made her blood boil. Her palms pulsed at the reminder and her fingertips lit with sparks of magic. Fury fueled the magic and sent it spiraling through her veins.

Kora turned her back on Aria, sauntering over to her friends with the dagger clutched tightly in her hand. She lazily pointed it at them like this was just another errand that she could end as easily as she wanted to. "If you try to fight your way out of this," Kora met Aria's eyes, "I will make them hurt…Now *sleep*."

Exhaustion hit Aria like a wave, drowning her in its force. Her limps began to sink lower, her eyelids felt like they carried an immense weight, and she could barely bear standing. The magic she'd had rising to the surface began to flicker away. She pushed her eyes open wide and took a deep breath, trying to fight the enchantment sinking into her like poison.

Kora's eyes bore into her as she forced her legs to keep standing. "The Diviner will—"

"DON'T CALL ME THAT!"

The power surged through Aria again, up to her fingertips, and then out, filling the hallway with an eye-burning light. Her skin glowed, spreading out light like the sun, but she couldn't see it. She had to clench her eyes shut. The blast was so powerful that it made her fall to her knees, magic swirling through the air around her. It was like the air was soaked in it.

The roar of the walls coming down filled her ears, and Kora, Ebony and Chad violently swore. Shouts resounded, and stones hit the ground beside Aria, grazing her skin. The fog dissipated at her command and let in the gloomy, dusty light. The rough floor dug into her knees as she gasped and trembled at the power that had just exploded out of her. It was as if the very essence of her power had been pulled on and gone out of control. But she had to keep fighting.

Ebony was a heap of black fabric on the ground, clutching her arm close to her. Blood trailed down Chad's forehead, but he stood, looking much more annoyed than before. The vines around Luke, Avi, and Willow shriveled up and turned a dying green color, falling to the ground. They each breathed in a sigh of relief and scrambled toward Aria with worried glances at the heaps of black cloaks.

Luke grabbed her arm and pulled her back to standing. "Are you alright?"

"Yeah." Aria balanced on her wobbly feet and summoned magic into her palms. Her eyes pinned a piercing stare on the Dark Forces members. "I'm not going anywhere, and neither are they."

Blood dripped down Kora's chin from the fall, having hit the stone that was littering the floor of the hallway. The way she smiled with blood slick on her teeth made Aria's skin crawl.

"Get behind me," Aria whispered, gesturing for her friends to move behind her.

Luke shook his head. "As if we'll listen."

"You don't have to fight this battle alone," Willow said, standing beside Aria, along with Luke and Avi.

"*Not* fighting this battle is also a choice," Avi whispered, voice shaky. "We could just, you know, *run.*"

"You fool yourself, little Diviner." Kora strode closer, pointing her dagger at them. "You are *nothing* compared to us—compared to Malus."

The words cut like glass, piercing Aria's heart and breaking her down. They felt so true despite the immense power that she knew ran in her blood. All her life she'd felt insignificant. But despite the hurt the words caused, she didn't let her feet give out from under her. She didn't let the tears escape. Instead, she kept her hands raised and her power surging through her veins, ready to unleash itself as if it begged to. Her breathing was becoming steadier now, a piercing glare aimed at Kora, Ebony, and Chad. All of them were standing up now, waiting with their hands raised, smiling with hostility—except for Chad, who only ever seemed annoyed.

The power within her rose into her palms, the magic growing stronger. A black, shifting ball of smoke faded into existence above her hands. She remembered that lesson with Mrs. Helma last school year when she had been reviewing the summoning of Black Smoke. No one else in the class had learned how to summon it, but Mrs. Mckinney had said she should learn it. Mrs. Helma had told her to make it change color, but Aria didn't know how.

"At that moment, your power did what it wanted to, but you have to control that. See, you may not have known how to shatter that clock, but your gift did, which means you are capable. Believe in yourself."

Believe in yourself.

Black Smoke suddenly started filling the hallway up again, wiping the smiles off Kora and Ebony and leaving Chad wide-eyed; not many people knew how to summon Black Smoke. It was the Dark Forces who'd begun using it decades ago. The fog reached the ceiling, weaving through the cracks in the walls, digging beneath the rubble, and turning the hallway into darkness.

"Get to the stairs," she whispered and grabbed hold of Luke's clammy hand. Pushing Willow and Avi in front of them, they started blindly through the dark.

"Blasted brat!" Kora cursed before everything became eerily silent.

Light pierced through the darkness up ahead, the stairs to go down into the entryway approaching. Avi was already scurrying down them with Willow heading down after him. The sunlight from outside poured into the entryway, where the walls were now nothing but rubble. The roof was caved in in places, leaving the doorway barely intact, the office crushed, and broken slabs of stone were strewn across ground beneath. Luke and Aria started down the cracked stairs after Willow and Avi, taking two steps at a time.

Then a powerful force pushed up against Aria's back and she flew over the railing, barreling toward the stone, plaster, and wood littering the concrete ground. It was as if everything happened in slow motion—Luke reached his hand to catch her as she fell, and a look of utter horror crossed his face. Then Luke tumbled down the stairs as she hit the floor. Agony racked her body and the wind was knocked from her lungs, making it hard to breathe. She could hear Luke groaning several feet away at the base of the stairs, cries escaping her own mouth. There was pain everywhere, the worst of it in her head and back. Everything was blurred, but she spotted three black, hooded figures walking down the stairs very slowly. One of them stopped at the base of the stairs and kicked Luke in the side. A groan tore from his throat.

"Leave him alone!" Aria screamed, her voice sounding hoarse like sandpaper against metal. She tried to stand but her knees buckled and she coughed. She tasted something metal and felt hot blood running down her face. Tears streamed down her cheeks, making everything look red and smeared together. "Don't hurt him!"

The three approaching figures were getting close, but Aria still couldn't stand. Every bone in her body felt like it might snap. Her head spun. She felt she might vomit right on their shoes. One of the figures squatted down to her level and grabbed her by the chin, their short nails digging into her skin. Flashbacks of Viola played through her head, making her cringe away like a hurt animal.

A blurred smile spread across Kora's face. "Oh, *we* won't hurt *you* anymore if you come easily…but I have no doubt Malus will."

"Luke…I need to help him…" Aria pushed Kora's hands away from her and tried to crawl towards him, barely aware of the hands that were grabbing her arms and trying to pin them behind her. Cold metal pressed into her wrists and she pulled away, fingers feeling the links of a chain.

"*Sleep,*" came close to her ear, magic drilling into her mind.

Every sound became muffled as she swayed on her knees, her breathing slowing. She dug her fingers into the ground as if she could dig herself deeper into reality and farther away from the exhaustion digging into *her*.

"Leave our friends alone, you people with bad taste in

clothing!" Avi's voice shouted from somewhere. His blurred figure stood in the middle of the demolished school's entrance.

"What—" Ebony's voice was cut off as two hands were ripped from Aria's arms.

There was a bang behind Aria and she slipped to the floor, unable to sit up anymore. There were suddenly warm hands on her, picking her up and dragging her away with gentle grace. All she could see was white and black specks.

"Mrs. Mckinney, she's bleeding," Willow's voice came from behind Aria. Her arms were around her, holding her close.

Avi's blurred figure had lights dancing across his hands as he fought back and forth. A second figure fought beside him, a woman with long gray hair. Mrs. Mckinney. She glanced at Aria with a smudged facial expression, then back at the cloaked figures.

"Luke…" Aria tried to say. "Help him…"

"GET OUT OF MY SCHOOL!" Mrs. Mckinney shouted, magic blasting from her hands toward the stairs. "YOU ARE NOT WELCOME HERE!"

Stone fell from the crumbling staircase, landing beside Aria in a heap. Willow's arms tightened around her and dragged her farther away from the wreckage.

"Not until we get what we've come for," Kora snarled.

"Well, unfortunately for you, that won't be happening," Mrs. Mckinney ground out, her voice sounding fierce and aged—a side of her Aria had never seen before. "I will fight for my students until my very last breath."

There was a smile in Kora's voice. "That can be arranged."

There was a loud crash and Aria's eyes fell closed against her will, plunging her into darkness.

CHAPTER FIVE

WHEN ARIA OPENED her eyes, she had to blink several times. All around was an eye-burning white, from the sheets on the bed she was laying on, to the walls of the room. The strong smell of disinfectants in the air stung her nose. She sat bolt upright and glanced around the room, which was filled with rows upon rows of infirmary beds. Immediately, she recognized it to be the infirmary from when she had been attacked by Stranger's Vine. The infirmary at camp. The office had been destroyed by the Dark Forces over the summer, so how it had already been rebuilt was a mystery.

Aria's brows furrowed at being in the infirmary. *Strange, I was not injured.* Then a wave of pain shot through her body from her head to her toes. She felt like she had been stabbed with millions of shards of glass down to the bones. She didn't know why she was at Camp Enchanted, but the answer would have to wait.

Throwing her legs over the side of the bed, she saw that Luke was in a bed next to hers. She quickly stood up and tried to walk over to him, but a sharp, stabbing pain in her right arm made her stop. She looked at her arm to see a needle stuck in it with a tube leading up to an IV. She tore it out, biting her tongue and tasting blood to stop herself from crying out. Then she tossed it aside and hurried over to the side of Luke's bed. He had an IV in his arm as well, but he looked fine, dark lashes splayed across his freckled cheeks as he slept peacefully. Not a bruise or scar was left on him.

The door opened and a wrinkled, blond-haired woman walked in. A pin on her white smock read: *Cassandra Ruff, Healer,* the same woman who helped heal Aria after she'd been attacked by Stranger's Vine.

Aria took a step back from Luke's bed and asked in a rush, "Why are we at camp? What happened? Where are the rest of my friends?"

Cassandra put up a hand to stop her. "The school was no longer safe. It had been destroyed. The Dark Forces made sure to leave nearly nothing left of it." She paused, eyes softening. "Molly Mckinney sent them away and made sure that you and your friends were brought here on a bus, along with everyone else at the school. There is no need to worry."

"Mrs. Mckinney?" Relief flooded Aria, recalling the last moments before she went out. "She's okay?"

"Yes, she is," Cassandra gestured to the bed. "Now, if you would please sit back down—"

"I need to see my friends." Aria started for the door, but Cassandra caught her wrist.

"You are hurt."

"No, I'm fine," Aria said, despite the soreness that was lingering over her body and the painful throbbing in her head.

Cassandra took her by the shoulders, led her back over to the bed, and forced her to sink back down into the plush of the mattress. "Your head was split open."

For a moment, Aria just stared, and then realization sank

in. Her hands went to her head, where gauze was wrapped around her forehead. "How? Can't you just heal it?"

"You hit the concrete ground, Aria." Cassandra readjusted the pillows behind Aria and motioned for her to relax against them. "And no, a part of your skull was fractured. I cannot just heal it. If I did it right away, it would not heal properly. It's not a simple fix when it comes to certain parts of the body and certain injuries. Bones, especially skulls, are one of those certain things. I have done what I could, but you will have to stay here—in the infirmary—until you are completely healed. Once I am done, there won't even be a scar left."

Aria laid back against the pillows of the bed, her hands shaking. "Fine...but will you please make sure Willow and Avi come to see me?" She grabbed her golden sunflower necklace and traced the petals to give her hands something to do.

"I will," Cassandra said before walking over to Luke to check on his vitals.

"What happened to him?" Luke looked so peaceful in his sleep, but Aria felt a pang for him. She felt it was *her* fault anything had even happened to him. His brother had warned her to stay away.

"Minor injuries," the Healer said. "He's all healed now, but we still needed to keep an eye on him after everything he went through."

Aria pulled the white covers over her to block out the drafty air and closed her eyes, images of Kora, Ebony, and Chad flashing through her mind as if trying to remind her of everything she'd been through.

When she opened her eyes back up hours later, the lights were off, and Luke was no longer in the bed next to her. The curtains were open now, so she could see the starry night sky. What time was it? The feel of the air and the look of the vaguely lit sky said it was early morning. Her head felt a lot better, but it still throbbed slightly like a bruise. She sat up and looked around to find that at the foot of the bed was a tray of food. There were waffles, a cup of syrup, bacon, eggs, and a cup of orange juice. The sight made her stomach growl. She took the tray in her hands and began to eat, flavor bursting over her tongue. When all the food was gone, she finally saw the little note stuck under the edge of the plate. She picked it up and read it.

I hope you are doing better. Miss Ruff tells me you will be able to leave the infirmary tomorrow morning. Come see me when you're ready if you'd like. —Mrs. Mckinney

Aria smiled before setting the note back down on the tray and leaning against the pillows again. She closed her eyes, letting sleep take over.

⸺✳︎⟨✳︎⸺

"Wakie wakie, chicken bakie," Avi's voice came at her side.

Her eyes fluttered open, the late morning sunlight nearly blinding.

"Dude, she needs rest." Luke shook his head in disapproval.

He, Avi, and Willow were at her bedside, staring at her. Waiting for her to wake with wide expectant eyes and bodies practically leaning over her bed, they looked like stalkers. Aria's eyes flew wide open and they took a step back.

"Oh, hey, guys," she said, pushing herself into a sitting position.

Willow gave her a soft smile. "How are you feeling?"

"I'm fine." Aria resisted the urge to touch her aching head where the gauze was wrapped around it.

"Don't lie," Luke said as if he knew that deep down there was a pit opening up in her stomach.

She sighed, crossing her arms. "Fine, I feel horrible." Hesitating, she gnawed on her bottom lip. "Not just because of my head, though—because of what Kora said."

"Yeah, I've been thinking about that all day," Avi said. "I bet she's lying, though. We were there. We chased Malus all around that mansion. It was the same black cat the whole time."

Willow sucked in a breath at the mention of that cat. "No, Kora wasn't lying." She sighed and looked down at her hands. "She believes Malus is free, whether because he broke out of prison, or because he was never sent to it like she said."

Avi shot her a quizzical look. "How do you know? You never even touched her."

"I could sense her emotions and the emotions that were radiating from her meant she wasn't lying. When a person lies, they feel nervous and unsteady. They don't feel so prideful and believable, but Kora did. She was fully confident."

"She could be wrong," Luke piped in. "Just because she believes she's right doesn't mean she is."

"And let's not forget that she and Celaena are nearly one and the same." Aria's gut twisted at the thought of Kora being right. Her mind couldn't fathom it. "If Celaena is good at lying and hiding things, Kora is too."

"Yeah, but how do we know what is true without walking up to the Malamone Mansion and knocking on the door." Avi mocked, his voice rising several octaves and cracking, "Hello, Mr. Malus, we know you're a mass murderer and whatnot, but we just wanted to check in and see if you're in the jail we put you in. You aren't? Okay, we'll come back *never*!"

"This is really bad." Aria's eyes wandered across the room as her heartbeat picked up and her breathing quickened. Her head spun and she felt as if she was about to retch. Malus might be free and there was no way to know for sure where he was or what he was doing. "He won't stop until he has me. And if he has me and the Death Stone, he'll be able to destroy everything."

She wanted to throw something and let tears pour down her face where no one could see. Everything in her hurt too much and it needed a way out. Her nails found themselves digging into one of her hands.

"We'll figure this out together," Luke said, grabbing Aria's hand. The touch sent sparks of embarrassment up into her face, remembering how they'd almost kissed. "You're not alone."

Aria wondered if he remembered that moment in the halls as detailed as she did.

Of course, he does, a snarky voice said in her mind.

Avi looked at Willow and blushed before opening his mouth to speak. "For the last two days, me and Willow have been helping the staff—"

"Two days?" Aria's eyes went wide. She couldn't have been in the infirmary for two days.

"Well, if you count the day of the attack after we got here, yesterday, and so far today, that sort of makes two days," Avi said. "Anyway, we've been helping the staff. The students are in a panic, the Forces of Light are weak, and the staff is trying to figure things out. The attack really shook them. No one expected it."

"Celaena warned me she had a surprise." Aria looked down at her hands, shame settling in her stomach. "She'd said the Dark Forces knew where I was. I should have said something about that to Mrs. Mckinney...Speaking of Mrs. Mckinney, how is she? The Healer said she was okay after the attack but—"

"Yeah, she's fine," Avi said. "She really knows how to kick some Dark Forces' butt!"

Willow nodded in agreement. "She was even better than

Kora. Considering she's much older than her, I bet she's been studying the art of magic even longer. There was so much practice and wisdom in the way she fought. She's *really* good."

"Like a magical powerhouse," Luke added with a faint smile.

A million more questions bubbled up in Aria's mind. "And what will happen now that the school is gone? What are the Dark Forces doing?" She paused, searching each of their faces like they held the answers. "How are we safe here? What's going on out in the world? Have we heard from Willow's dad? Is there—"

"Hold on," Luke gave her hand a reassuring squeeze. "We'll answer all your questions the best we can…But we don't know everything. The Forces of Light refuse to tell anyone what is going on outside of camp." He sighed, shaking his head. "We don't know what the Dark Forces are doing out there. All we know is that something is stirring and that we haven't received any news from Willow's dad."

"Hopefully we will any day now," Willow said, strained hope on her face.

The door opened then, and Cassandra walked in carrying a clipboard.

"Oh, hello, children. Excuse me," she said and gently pushed through to get to Aria. "Time for Aria's last healing." She carefully unwrapped Aria's gauze and pressed her hand to the red, painfully split skin on her forehead.

Aria bit down on her tongue as the skin stitched itself back together. All the pain in her body seemed to evaporate, leaving nothing behind, not even a scar. She breathed a sigh of relief, fingers tracing over the smooth skin near her hairline.

"Thank you." Aria threw her legs over the side of the bed.

"You're welcome, dear." Cassandra smiled. "Now, you're free to leave."

Aria stood up, still a little unsteady on her feet, and beckoned her friends to follow. They started walking toward the door and out into the lobby. The benches that had once lined the log walls were gone. They were probably trashed after the Dark Forces attacked over the summer. In fact, a lot of things looked different in the newly built office. The flooring was tile now, and logs only went halfway up the walls before it changed to yellow floral wallpaper. The layout of the building was still the same, though. She paused and glanced around as a thought came to her.

"If Kora was right and Malus isn't actually imprisoned, Mrs. Mckinney should know," Aria said. "And Celaena shouldn't be here. After she tried strangling me over the summer, I wanted to tell Mrs. Mckinney, but I couldn't because I needed to use Celaena to find my parents. I don't need her anymore." Her jaw tightened. "And after the attack on the school…All she'll do is cause harm like her parents and grandfather."

"Then we should go talk to Mrs. Mckinney." Willow strode across the lobby to the door on the other side of it, beckoning for them to follow.

The four of them stepped inside the room full of rows of wooden desks and busy staff. Intense noise hit their ears from phones going off and the voices of people answering them. The air was thick with body heat and the smells of ink, paper, and a vanilla candle. Fresh air circled in from an open window that looked out on the massive camp parking lot. A plump woman with a curly white bob-cut sat at the desk in the front row. A corded phone was pressed to her ear as she watched them enter.

"Yes, you can come pick up your son. We will retrieve him from the cabin he was assigned shortly and have him waiting in the parking lot," Miss Stax answered someone on the phone, then set it down and began scribbling down notes in a rush. A second later, the phone screamed to be answered again.

"We really weren't kidding when we said things are crazy," Avi said.

Aria looked past her to the back of the room where Mrs. Mckinney sat taking phone calls and doing paperwork. Gesturing for her friends, Aria led them across the room. They stopped in front of Mrs. Mckinney's desk, and she looked up with a half grin. She looked thinner than usual, her gray hair framing her wrinkly face, and draped over the collar of her tan pantsuit. Bags hung under her eyes. Aria wondered how much she had slept since the attack—or if she'd stopped working for even a second.

"Aria, dear, it is great to see you are better. And you as well, Luke," Mrs. Mckinney said kindly, eyes crinkling at the edges. "What can I do for you?"

Aria took a deep breath, trying to calm her racing heart. Her fingers found her sunflower necklace. "Malus might be free."

Mrs. Mckinney's eyes went wide and she dropped the pencil she'd been holding. "What?" She paused, glancing around. "Keep your voice down. What makes you think that?"

"Kora, Celaena's mother, helped attack the school. I know you saw her," Aria said. "She claimed Malus was never even at the trial…that we caught an actual cat, not Malus…"

Willow looked down shyly, surely remembering what she thought had been her pet cat, Twilight. What she thought was her pet had really been a monster.

"But the judge—" Mrs. Mckinney started.

"He works for Malus," Aria answered. "At least, that's what Ebony said. He's a spy."

Mrs. Mckinney gave her a quizzical look. "Ebony?"

"She works for Malus too."

"And you believe them?" Mrs. Mckinney furrowed her eyebrows.

"I don't know," Aria answered honestly. "There's not much proof other than—" She glanced at Willow and shut her mouth. She was about to reveal Willow's Mind-reading abilities. Willow shook her head, her eyes alert with worry. "There's not much proof other than their word," Aria finished.

"Then I want you to forget what they said," Mrs. Mckinney said with a sigh. "You are all safe here. We'll contact each of your parents and see if they can get you if they wish to. Everything is going to be okay. Don't worry yourselves with what the Dark Forces told you. The Dark Forces say things to invoke fear and uncertainty. Fear is a great weapon in the hands of evil, but do not fall prey to it."

"And what about *my* parents? Have they been rescued yet?" Aria's voice lowered hopelessly. "Or is that not happening because the judge who said that might actually be a spy for Malus?"

Mrs. Mckinney ran a hand over her face, looking pushed over the edge. "Everything is going to be okay, Aria. I want more than anything to get your parents back for you." She took a deep breath. "But right now, I have well over four hundred children that need protecting and parents that need to be contacted. I will work everything out." Something else seemed to occur as her eyes studied Aria's face. "Just promise me you'll stay here and be careful. Clearly, the Dark Forces are hunting you because your parents are the leaders of the Forces of Light. I wouldn't wish the Dark Forces to put a target on anyone's back, so I'm sorry to see they have one on yours."

"Um, thanks," Aria said awkwardly. *There's actually much more to why they're hunting me.* "What about Celaena?"

At that, Mrs. Mckinney rubbed her chin. "What about her?"

"Her mother and father are part of the Dark Forces, and

her grandfather is Malus. Her mother attacked the school," Aria said, unable to understand why Mrs. Mckinney wasn't seeing what she saw in Celaena. "Celaena shouldn't be here at camp. She's a threat to everyone."

"Aria, dear, we are not our parents or grandparents. Some people can become just like their parents, but others are nothing like them," Mrs. Mckinney stated. "If you had Celaena's future in mind, which would you prefer Celaena become? Just like her family, or like you and your friends here?" She folded her hands together. "My job is to protect the children I am entrusted with. By keeping Celaena away from her family, I believe I am protecting her. You may not understand now, but I hope one day you will." Mrs. Mckinney sighed. "Have a great day, dears."

Aria turned around, stunned, and started walking away. Her friends trailed beside her. She glanced at them and lowered her voice. "But Celaena is already exactly like her mother in every way. There's no changing that."

The four of them stepped outside, the brisk air blowing over their skin. It smelled of autumn leaves and pumpkin spice already. The office building was completely rebuilt, but there were still several buildings within eyesight that were piles of shattered glass, charred wood, and smashed plaster. The rubble was still slowly being cleaned up from the Dark Forces' attack that happened over the summer.

A glimmering in the sky caught Aria's attention and she looked up. Over the whole of the camp was a shimmering bubble-like shield giving off a rainbow hue from the sunlight shining through it. Aria couldn't help but imagine the camp stuck inside a little snow globe.

"It's a Protection Barrier to keep the Dark Forces out in case they come back." Willow looked upwards at the sky as well.

"Why didn't they have that over the summer? Especially after the camp was attacked?" Aria asked, remembering running between the cabins to escape the Dark Forces.

"Protection Barriers take a lot of energy to keep up, and eventually they start to weaken," Willow said. "When we arrived in the buses from the school, all the teachers and staff helped put it up. But it weighs on them. It takes their energy and turns it into a shield." Willow sighed and Aria recalled Mrs. Mckinney's tired, drained expression. "They said they'd find something else to use as a protection, but other than this, all they have up is an Anti-teleportation Charm."

"Can't they just take it down for a few hours while they regain their energy?"

"The Dark Forces would use that moment of vulnerability and attack again. As you said, they're not going to stop coming." Willow looked at her with soft, saddened blue eyes. "Not until they have what they want."

"Then I know what to do," Aria said, changing her gaze to each of her friends. She sighed, determination flickering in her blue eyes.

"What's that?" Avi had his hands in his mustard jacket.

"I have a lot of practicing and learning I have to do first, but I'm going to do exactly what my parents told me to do." Aria thought back to those moments in the Malamone Mansion. *"He will want to use you."* She didn't want to be a puppet on a string. "I'm going to find the Death Stone and destroy it."

CHAPTER SIX

THE SMELL OF pine trees and grass filled the air around the tall oak tree. Its leaves were turning golden and orange like fire. So many memories lived in the space surrounding the oak tree—memories of making a Tracking Potion, laughs between friends, deadly plants, and warning alarms going off. Aria, Luke, Avi, and Willow had been gathered around the tree for hours, away from the anxiety that festered throughout the rest of the camp.

All the students that had been brought to the camp were acting like bothered ants, running and ranting about the camp. Even the students who didn't know of magic and weren't supposed to know had been brought to keep them safe from the Dark Forces' claws. Even after two days—as Avi had said—they still were in a panic. Their voices could be heard even from the edge of the forest, shouting and pointing at everything like it was some sort of magical essence. Aria recalled the day she'd been told magic was real and how she hadn't been able to believe a word. It had felt like a pit had been gouged out in her stomach…And these other kids had found out by having their school *torn to the ground*.

Aria, Luke, Willow, and Avi couldn't handle the chaos that was now taking place in the mess hall, where everyone had gathered to ask questions. Mrs. Mckinney had to shout over all the noise. Guilt stabbed at Aria's heart, knowing she hadn't treated her politely last school year. She couldn't fathom the amount of stress Mrs. Mckinney was now under.

Aria and her friends had gone to listen to Mrs. Mckinney speak, but there wasn't much to know. It was laid out simply—the school was destroyed, kids were welcome to go home, and anyone who stayed was to be taught by the teachers from the school while things were figured out—if they ever were figured out.

A cool breeze blew through the treetops and all the animals of the forest seemed to be awake, gathering food for the winter. In the distance of the forest, the end of the shimmering Protection Barrier could be seen. Aria had been surprised to find that the Protection Barrier went so far while the Anti-teleportation Charm didn't. Avi's voice floated through the air as he talked about something he found on the internet back at school. Willow flipped through a book, and Aria peered down at the information on the page. Out of the four of them, Willow had been the only one to get out of the school with her backpack.

The pages of Willow's book were filled with different enchantments, charms, and curses. If they were going to find the Death Stone and likely come across the Dark Forces again, they'd need more than luck and a few simple enchantments to get them out alive. As Kora had said, they wouldn't underestimate them again, and Aria's heart squeezed at the thought of facing them again.

"So, what does that enchantment do?" Aria asked, pointing to a page in the book. "Should we add it to our list of things to practice?"

"It just makes someone vomit, which is not of any use." Willow turned to the next page, trailing over words as she read. "Not unless you want them hacking as they chase after you."

Luke and Avi were supposed to be learning along with them, but they couldn't seem to focus. Luke started pacing, mumbling words to himself that no one else could hear, and Avi was still going on about something.

"—But isn't that crazy? I mean, why would anyone eat an animal that's poisonous?"

Willow turned toward him and raised her eyebrows. "Avi, what in the name of Viden are you talking about?"

"Um, people eating spiders and snakes."

"That's disgusting." Aria's lips tugged up and she had to resist a laugh. "Luke, you want to look at these enchantments with us?"

"Oh, sure." Luke came to sit down next to her, a slight smile on his face as they peered down at the pages of the book.

He was so close to Aria that butterflies fluttered around in the pit of her stomach. His smell of mint and fresh pine engulfed her. She squeezed her eyes shut for a moment, trying to block out the images her mind replayed of that memory when they'd almost kissed in the hallway. Luke was practically marked as *off-limits*—they were supposed to be just friends.

Or are you? The voice in the back of her mind slid into her thoughts.

Oh, shut up! Aria couldn't help glancing at Luke, her eyes landing on his lips. *Stop it!*

Willow suddenly stood up, pulling Aria from the thoughts that were distracting her. "I think that's enough for today." She grabbed the book off the ground and wrapped her arms around it. "But y'all should definitely practice what we've just spent the last several hours studying." She threw a look at Luke that

Aria didn't understand. "We should go to the mess hall and get some food."

Avi stood up so fast that he almost fell right back over. "I agree. I'm starving!"

"And once we eat," Willow continued, "I'm heading to Mr. Monroy's class. He's teaching about Viden's Library of Knowledge if anyone wants to come with me."

"I think I'll pass," Avi said, giving a grin. "Knowledge isn't my sort of thing, smarty-pants."

At that, Aria snorted and Luke looked at her, a faint smile on his lips. She tried to push that nervous feeling fluttering around in the pit of her stomach, but it wouldn't go away.

She quickly looked away from him and at Willow instead. "I'll go with you."

If Mr. Monroy was teaching about the Library of Knowledge, maybe she could learn more about the Ancient Scrolls she'd read about before the school was attacked. Maybe she could learn more about what she was, why she was, and about her true power being stripped from the Diviner before she was even born.

They left the forest and walked down the paths that wound throughout camp, a cool wind blowing through Aria's hair. As they walked, Aria played with fire in her hand. It was warm and had a pulse to it, like that of a heart. It felt so alive and natural. Nearing the mess hall, the smell of delicious spices and smoked meats wafted up out of the chimney. Aria, Luke, Avi, and Willow marched up the steps and inside, taking in big whiffs of the mouth-watering smell. All the students that had come from the school were piling into the mess hall too. As soon as Aria and her friends sat down, they started stuffing their faces, especially Avi. He took a bite of his sub, the toppings dripping onto his plate.

"Dis is 'o 'ood," he mumbled with his face drenched in dressing.

Aria stared, her eyebrows raised.

"What? It *is* really good," he said after swallowing. "At least, it's better than cafeteria food."

Aria shook her head, a smile quirking up at the edges of her lips. Underneath the table, her hand guided objects on the table to move around as practice, just like Willow had said to do in the forest. A sudden electric pulse like a shock lit in Aria's fingertips. The bottle of ketchup tipped over and started squirting across the walkway, but it never made it to the floor. There was a nerve-shattering pause. Aria bit her lip as she swallowed her food down. That was definitely not what she had meant to do, but the look on Celaena's face was hilarious. Celaena stood there in the walkway, holding her tray of food, ketchup running down her side. Her face was scarlet like a hot iron, and her nose wrinkled with disgust. She turned her face towards Aria so quickly that Aria thought she might lash out and try to strangle her in front of everyone. And people were definitely staring.

"You'll pay for that. Just you watch," Celaena ground out. "I'm surprised you're even still here. I thought my mother would have gotten you for sure. Especially after she threw you over the railing like a rag doll." She swept her hair over her shoulder and strutted away.

A monster tried to claw its way out from inside Aria, but she kept it at bay, preventing *herself* from lashing out. Her palms pulsed the way they had in the hallway of the school as the Black Smoke had restrained her. She looked down at her hands, now glowing like pure sunlight, and pushed the magic away. This was not the time for it to get out of control. Not again.

"Hello, everyone!" Mrs. Mckinney's voice called from the

middle of the mess hall. "I hope you are all doing well! Remember, all of you are allowed to call your parents. Some of you have been or will be notified of your parents coming to pick you up." She took a deep breath, looking shaky and worn too thin. "I—I just want you to know that you are safe and that everything is being worked out by the Forces of Light…But…by the looks of it, school will be taking place on the campgrounds for the rest of the year. We already have some classes running for this evening and tomorrow," she said, her hand tapping anxiously against her leg as if she were trying to count each reassuring beat of her heart. "And remember, return to the cabins you were assigned before curfew."

A sudden burst of questions exploded across the mess hall.

"What about the Dark Forces?"

"Why did they attack our school?"

"I want to go home!"

"Can I learn to use magic?"

Several minutes later, Aria was back outside, the cool air brushing against her skin. She wished she had a jacket, but she didn't have any spare clothes. She had no idea what was going to happen, and that fact scared her. As she walked down the paths, Willow was already way ahead of her with a pile of books in her arms. Aria summoned different enchantments into the palm of her hand but didn't release them. The sparks of magic quaked in her palm and poofed out of existence. It had wanted to get out of control in the mess hall, and now it didn't want to appear for long. Maybe it was the nerves. She felt like she was on the edge of a cliff, knowing she had to jump. There was so much she needed to know, so much she didn't know, and she needed to practice what she already knew if she was going to save her parents *and* now also get the Death Stone. This weight was becoming too much on top of the fact that she was the Diviner, as if all of it were crushing her and she couldn't breathe.

She heard the crunch of gravel and dirt grinding together behind her and, thinking it was Celaena, she quickened her pace. Celaena said she would pay, and Aria was not in the mood to deal with her hostility. She rounded onto a path on the left, forcing her feet not to slow down.

"Aria!" Luke's voice called behind her. "Aria, can we talk?"

Aria stopped and spun around. Luke was a few yards away, hurrying to keep up with her. When he reached her side, he blew out an exasperated breath. Aria started forward again, not wanting to be late, and he matched her pace. His eyes locked on the trees surrounding the camp off in the distance.

"So…" he said, scratching the back of his neck.

"So…" She glanced at him through her peripheral vision.

"Um…I—I was wondering—It's just I thought…uh… Maybe I've got this all wrong…" He looked away suddenly, his cheeks flushed. He scratched the back of his neck so hard and fast that it turned red. "What I'm trying to say is that… uh…I just thought that there had been something…um…"

Luke stuttered and mumbled, and Aria couldn't understand one word of it. He ran his hand through his hair. Doubt and uncertainty began to sink its claws into Aria's mind with every second. Was he asking if he could give the Life Stone back to her? Did he want out of the horrible mess that Aria had gotten him into? Was he tired of being her friend? Was that moment in the hallway not what she'd thought it had been? Her heart ached with sadness and she kept her eyes ahead, not looking at him. The cabin where Mr. Monroy was teaching was just a few feet away.

"Luke, what are you saying?" She stopped in front of the door.

"Um…" For several moments, he kept his head down and mumbled.

Aria raised her eyebrows, waiting for what it was he was trying to say. She'd never seen him struggle so much with words. An angry knot twisted in her chest, hearing Christopher's words in her head. *You're a danger to him.* Maybe those exact words had gotten into Luke's head too.

"Luke, I'm sorry, but I really can't do *this* right now." Her eyes burned and she looked away from him, blinking away the feeling.

"What?" He suddenly looked up, his hand dropping from the back of his neck to his side. "Why?"

"I have a class. The same one Willow's taking."

"Really? I didn't think you liked Mr. Monroy."

"He may not be the nicest, but it's about the Library of Knowledge," Aria said. "In the Library of Knowledge are the Ancient Scrolls, and in those, information about the Diviner… about *me*." She frowned and couldn't stop her face from falling.

"Right…You're the Diviner…" He sighed and turned around with his head hanging. Looking like something had just been broken inside him, he slowly walked away with his face flushed all the way up to his ears.

Aria stepped into the cabin, which seemed so cold compared to the sunny outside. A tugging feeling to go back outside and apologize to Luke rose inside of her, but she pushed it to the edges of her mind. Only a few people were in the room, which seemed to have Mr. Monroy in a great mood. He towered above everyone else in a gray suit that clung to his bony figure, with a little beret neatly placed on his gelled black hair. His face was devoid of emotion, but at least he wasn't annoyed or angry. Aria laughed on the inside because she knew how much Mr. Monroy disliked students. Willow was in the back, eagerly writing down as many notes as she could fit in her little notebook.

Mr. Monroy's thick accented voice—which sounded like something hard and foreign—filled the room. "The Library of Knowledge, also known as Librinino es Viden in the secondary Viden language, is located in Viden, the capital of the Vezchia Realm—"

Aria made her way to stand next to Willow, listening to every word like it contained the greatest of information. "What does he mean capital?" she asked Willow. "Is it like how we have capitals in this realm?"

"Yes," Willow said, excitement lacing her voice as she spoke. "Viden is the biggest city in the whole Vezchia Realm, and the richest too. It was the very first town to be built in the Vezchia Realm, and over the last two thousand years it's grown into the metropolis it is today. That's why it's the capital." Her blue eyes seemed to glitter. "Everywhere else is just towns and villages. Viden is where everyone wants to live, and I can see why… with knowledge at the center of the city!"

"No talkin', ladies," Mr. Monroy said, which took Aria by surprise—she would have expected him to yell.

He paused as many people around the room scribbled down notes. Aria found herself wishing she had a notebook, but all her things had been left behind in Incanting Academy. Perhaps she could see about getting one from a staff member.

Mr. Monroy continued, "The library was the first thing requested to be built by the first king and queen of the Vezchia Realm. The first king and queen are said to have been Omni-communicators and they befriended one griffin and one sphinx. That is just a myth surroundin' the ancient library, of course. These two creatures are said to have helped in creatin' the Ancient Scrolls, which contain all knowledge in the universe, even the things humans don't know. The griffin and sphinx are said to keep these Scrolls updated on each new change in the universe. The biggest things they are rumored to focus on are historical events, wars, and the Diviners. Don't get too excited, though. No one's known to have been in the library for centuries, except for one team on a mission." Mr. Monroy glanced at Aria, something she didn't understand hidden within that look. "Information on what's really inside it is confidential and only known by certain highly-ranked Forces of Light and Enchanting Control officials. They say the doors to the library are unlocked," Mr. Monroy's voice darkened, "but no one's dared enter it because of a supposed curse."

The urge reignited itself again. Aria had to see the Scrolls and read them. *What if they aren't just legends?* After all, she'd been one herself.

⸺⸱⸺☾⸺⸱⸺

"What was I thinking?" Luke shouted at himself, plopping down on the edge of Avi's bunk and sinking into it. He slightly hoped it might swallow him whole and save him from the embarrassment of everything.

Every fabric in the cabin was blue, including the dusty carpet, which was a deep indigo like that of the night. He and Avi were alone, leaving an awkward silence between them as the jittery feeling inside Luke continued to grow.

Luke tapped his feet against the floor with all the frustration he felt. "I couldn't even get the words out and she just stared at me...I'm so *stupid!*"

"Luke, you're not stupid," Avi said. "Her not listening was stupid. How could she not listen to what you have to say?"

"No, Avi, that's the thing. I barely said anything! We almost kissed, I think, and—and I couldn't even have the guts to tell her how I feel..." Luke gave a sigh, his head spinning. "I know the situation we're in is difficult, but so is this feeling. I can't keep being around her every day and then not function properly. I can't get her out of my head. Just staring at her makes me think of that moment we shared in the hallway—" His head fell forward into his hands. "I just—All I did was mumble and stutter. And Aria is *not* stupid."

"That's not even what I said." Avi gave him an awkward pat on the back. "I'm just trying to make you feel better."

"It's just, she's so brave and beautiful and she never gives up, even with everything that's going on around us…But I don't know what I was thinking." Luke shook his head, thinking back to that day in the hall before the attack, then that moment when she'd lit the hallway with eye-blinding magic as if she were light itself. "I thought she liked me, but maybe I was wrong. I mean, after all, she's the Diviner…She wouldn't want a guy like me."

Avi sat down next to him, chewing a piece of candy he'd found in his cubbyhole at the back of the room. "I'm sorry, man. But if you ask me, women are strange. They don't make sense to me."

The door opened and Christopher, Luke's older brother, and his friend, Charlie, walked in. They both towered over Luke and Avi, looking down on them like they were somehow less. A black mustache was starting to grow on Charlie's bronze skin, a perfect match to his gelled black hair and dark eyes. He leaned against the bedpost, his gray shirt hanging loose on his body.

Christopher raised an eyebrow and spoke as if interrogating them. "What are you two talking about?"

"Nothing," Luke stated with an edge like a blade to his voice.

"Someone's in a bad mood. What? Did little *Miss Dangerous* dump you?" Christopher chuckled as he strode to his cubby at the back of the room. Luke thought it was empty, but maybe he'd kicked over a younger teen and stolen something from them earlier.

"We were never together," Luke said through clenched teeth as he stood.

"Really?" Charlie joined in. "Because I really thought you and that brown-haired girl who got you kidnapped were a thing? No?"

Hurt crept into Luke's voice. "We're just friends."

"Well, don't be," Christopher said as he turned back to the group. "Ditch her."

A muscle ticked in Luke's jaw and his body tensed with the urge to lunge at his older brother. For years, his brother had ditched *him*. No one deserved something like that, and Aria only had her friends now.

He shot a glare at his older brother, one that screamed rage and hurt at even the idea of that. "Not in a million years."

Aria and Willow walked up to their log cabin—cabin number thirteen—talking about the lesson. There hadn't been much more about the Ancient Scrolls, after all. Or at least not as much as Aria had hoped for. They opened the door and stepped inside, blocking out the cool, evening air. The sun painted orange and pink hues across the sky as it set, and now a crisp breeze was wrestling with the trees. It knocked a few browning leaves from their branches. Inside, the cabin smelled like dried roses and lemon. The cabin was warm like a blanket smothering them in comfort, and a silence hung in the air. A breath of relief escaped Aria at the sight of the cabin being empty.

Perhaps there's a bonfire tonight, Aria thought.

Willow plopped down on her burgundy bed sheets, dragging her hand against the spot where Twilight—Malus—her cat would always lay. She frowned and drew away from the spot as if there was a phantom of that monster still there. Aria's eyes softened as she climbed up the ladder into her own bed above, letting her gaze wander. Three bunk beds lined the walls of the cabin, and two cubbyhole shelves sat on either side of the one at the back. Everything was covered in maroon and deep reds, making it look like a warm fire inside the log cabin. Outside the windows, the glow of buildings lit the camp under stars beginning to blink into existence.

Something drifted to the edges of her mind and pecked at her like an angry bird. She felt like she had broken something and now she so badly wanted to fix it, but she couldn't erase what had happened. Aria sighed and grabbed her pillow, wrapping her arms tightly around it as if that would hold her together.

"Aria?" The way Willow's tone sounded was as if she was about to give a young child a lecture about what they did wrong.

"What?" Aria tapped her feet against the bed's ladder; it was all she could do to stop herself from pacing the room. She wanted to ignore this wretched, twisting feeling inside herself, but it coursed through her like poison.

"Are you alright? I can feel your anxiety."

"What? I'm fine." It was such an obvious lie, she knew. Especially when Willow already knew the truth, being a Mindreader; she could feel Aria's emotions radiating through the air.

A smile quirked up at the edges of Willow's lips as she said, "Okay…but if it has something to do with Luke…"

"Luke?" Aria jumped down from the bed, flinging the pillow back up onto her sheets. "Why would it have anything to do with Luke?"

"Does it?"

"Um…" Aria hesitated, grabbing her sunflower necklace to trace the petals. She felt like such a jerk for leaving him, not bothering to let him find the words to whatever it was he was trying to say, even if it was that he wanted to end their friendship. "He wanted to talk to me, but I blew him off and went into class. He was stuttering, but it sounded like being my friend was *wrong* for him."

Willow's eyes went wide. "Wrong for him? He said that?"

"I—I think so…"

"I doubt it." Willow stood up and gave a mischievous, knowledgeable look.

Aria's eyes squinted as she searched Willow's face for some kind of answer. "You know something, don't you?"

Willow had known some of their deepest secrets for months, so she was bound to know *something*. Ever since they'd met, she'd secretly been reading their emotions and thoughts.

"Oh, just that for the last several months you two have been radiating feelings for each other, but as of recently, those feelings have been going haywire." A giddy giggle bubbled out of Willow. "It's like your emotions drank several gallons of caffeine each."

"What?" Aria stood, her mind coming to a complete halt—that was definitely not what she expected to hear. After how Luke acted, she'd thought it was the complete opposite.

"Something happened between you two, I can tell."

Aria's stomach clenched and she glanced away. A nervous feeling began to creep through her limbs like a snake. "Um… maybe there was something…We…uh…we *almost* kissed."

"What? Your first kiss!" And that was definitely not what Willow expected to hear. "How? When? Where? Why?" She smiled with anticipation as she stepped closer to Aria, looking like she might start jumping up and down. Or maybe she'd just levitate as if she were on a cloud.

"Right before the attack at the school, my books fell and he helped…" A smile was now playing across Aria's lips as she remembered it. The way his soft hands had brushed against hers, and then, the way their faces had grown closer. Then the sound of the walls exploding.

"Well, I thought it was bound to happen one time or another."

"But we didn't actually kiss. I don't even know for sure if I'm ready for that." Aria's brows narrowed and her eyes shot to Willow, realization dawning on her. "Wait. What *exactly* do you mean by *that*?"

"Well, haven't you ever wondered why Luke called you over to his table that first day we all met?" Willow gave her a dimpled grin, crinkling the edges of her eyes. "Aria, Luke likes you, and he has since day one."

Aria felt tension leave her just by hearing those words. Her heart stopped and the world faded away. *Luke likes me. Maybe he still does like me. What if what Luke was trying to say earlier had something to do with that almost kiss?* She suddenly felt so dumb. How did she not see that he liked her? Why couldn't she just listen to him? A tingling feeling filled her stomach as she began to gnaw on her bottom lip. She traced the petals of her sunflower necklace, debating whether she would march out of the cabin and apologize to him right that second or not.

"Aria?"

Aria could feel Willow's eyes on her as her own eyes wandered. "Hmm?"

"Maybe we should just get some rest? I can tell what you're thinking—and I don't need to use my Divining Power to know that," Willow said. "I think maybe it's best if you wait until tomorrow. Sleep on it."

"Yeah…" Aria sighed and strode to Willow's cubby, pulling a book from it. "We have a lot to do tomorrow."

"Practice makes perfect, as they always say."

Aria paused, watching Willow sit back down on her bed with grace. She thought about how Willow had known all their secrets for months and how she'd known Luke liked her. There were probably a lot of other things she knew.

A sneaky smile swept Aria's face. "Willow, you know Avi likes you, right?"

Willow looked up as a light peach colored her pale cheeks. "Um…yes. I've known for two years."

"Really?" Aria raised an eyebrow. *And she never said anything?* "Well…do you like him?" Aria waited for an answer as Willow's blush deepened. "I don't mean to pry. If you don't want to answer, you don't have to. I was just curious."

"Yes, I like him. I think he's funny and sweet. And so caring too!" Willow's face turned dreamy. "He was the one that asked if I wanted to help the staff. His aunt and the rest of the teachers were under so much pressure when we got here, so he asked if I'd help him assist them."

"His aunt—" Aria was about to question how Willow knew that Avi was looked after by his aunt, then thought better of it. Of course, Willow would know. She sat down next to her on the bottom bunk. "Why don't you tell him you like him if you know he likes you?"

Willow opened her mouth to speak, then sighed. "I'm not sure if either of us are ready for that. Not yet. I like being friends. Eventually, maybe I will tell him."

Aria patted Willow's shoulder before standing up. "I respect that. Want to do some studying?" She held out the book.

Willow nodded and they spent the rest of the time before bed on their stomachs, flipping through books on the burgundy carpet. But Aria's mind kept growing distant no matter how much she tried to focus.

When they both grew tired, they put the books away and Aria climbed into bed with a yawn. The other members of the cabin hadn't entered yet—if there were any others. Elaine and Natalie from last summer could have been from Incanting Academy, but she didn't have any classes with them, so she didn't know. And Celaena was likely off stalking through the night like a predator.

"Talk to Luke tomorrow," Willow teased as she flicked off the light.

Aria could imagine Willow's grin as she pulled her bed sheets over her. As much as there was relief coursing through Aria, there was also unease. *Luke likes me! And I just blew him off.* Her scratchy jeans, constant thoughts, and nausea-inducing headache made the night restless. There was too much weighing on her, and she feared that if she couldn't figure it out, she'd break before the Dark Forces even had a chance to get to her.

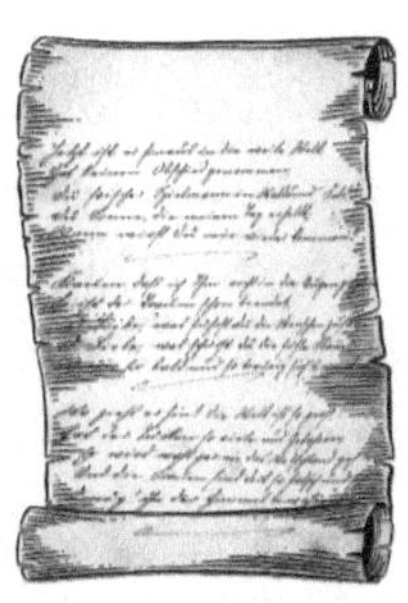

CHAPTER SEVEN

DUST DANCED IN the sunlight beaming through the chilled cabin's windows as Aria sat up out of bed, pushing her heavy comforter off her. The smell and feeling of fall were thick in the air, even in the small number thirteen cabin. Aria climbed out of bed, careful not to make too much noise, and strode across the room to the thermostat by the bathroom door. She turned the heat up, a chill racking her body.

Glancing around, she saw that Celaena, Elaine, and Natalie were in the cabin, likely having come in late at night. Celaena was still asleep, or at least she looked like she was.

Knowing her, Aria thought, *she could be faking, waiting for the perfect moment to strike like a stalking panther.*

Elaine's dark curls framed her espresso-toned skin as she slowly lifted her head and blinked away sleep. Above her, Natalie let out soft snores and hugged her pillow, her long blond hair splayed around her in a mess.

Aria crept past them and into the bathroom to quickly take a shower—only to put the clothes she had back on. She wished she had at least one change of clothes, but it was all still packed in her room at Incanting Academy, lost within the Space Realm. The veil was likely still there, with no way to access it now that the school had been destroyed. The cabin had extra supplies for campers, though—toothbrushes and such—so Aria dug through the drawers to find a hairbrush. Then she pulled the brush through her wet tangled hair.

Outside, a soft breeze blew through the trees, carrying the smell of the forest. Aria smiled at the sight of autumn leaves as she walked down the trails that wound throughout the camp. Fall had always been her favorite season; it gave everything more color, the weather was just right, and she loved when she got to have apple cider and donuts with her parents. She bit down on her lip and her shaky hand found the sunflower necklace her parents had given her, tracing the golden petals again.

A memory flashed before her glassy, tear-filled eyes. It had been about five years ago, yet it seemed like it had been a lifetime ago when she and her parents had visited a local orchard. She'd been ten then, oblivious to the secrets her parents had been hiding and the magic that ran in her veins. There had been a whole pumpkin patch bigger than a football field, an orchard with the loveliest apple trees, and donuts dusted in cinnamon and sugar. She and her parents had sat at a little shaded picnic table, the wind blowing through the trees—Aria imagined she could still feel its soft breeze brushing her skin as she walked down the path. Her father, of course, had told her some of the cringiest jokes known to mankind. The sound of her past laughs filled her ears, a bittersweet smile tugging at her lips. She fought to hide the twisted feeling inside her. It was like a caged animal, growling and tearing at the bars to escape. A tear dripped down her cheek, leaving a trail in its wake. She could still hear her parents' voices through the fading memory as if they were right there next to her. But it wasn't real. Aria looked up, pulling herself from her memories and pushing everything back down as she wiped away the tears.

I don't need to cry, she scolded herself. *I need to be strong.*

Being strong was hard, though, even if there was no other choice.

Down the path, Luke was coming toward her, which made her suddenly hyperaware of everything—her feelings, her most-likely puffy eyes, her stringy wet hair, and every thought going through her head. She felt like running and hiding after the conversation she had with Willow last night. Now, she wished Willow was with her, not still back in cabin number thirteen… But, instead, she would be…alone…with Luke.

It's just Luke, she reminded herself. She breathed in deeply and put on a fake smile, shoving those raging, depressing emotions farther away. *It's just caring, handsome, kind Luke. My friend.*

RUN! A voice in her head screamed protests at her. *You are going to mess this up so badly!*

As Luke neared her, she decided then that she would *not* bring anything up about yesterday, about whatever Luke was trying to say. *I could* mess up. *And then Luke might think I am weird…or that I don't like him.*

Well, you are *weird,* said the sarcastic voice in her head. Her smile nearly fell off her face.

"Hello," Luke greeted, a slight smile on his face. It looked forced, or maybe that was just because of the bags hanging under his eyes.

"Hi." Aria's hands grew clammier by the second and she couldn't keep her eyes locked on his.

"So…um…h-have you seen Avi?" he asked, scratching the back of his neck anxiously. He looked away with nervousness in his eyes. "I woke up and he wasn't in the cabin."

"No, I haven't…" There was an awkward silence between them for several moments that seemed to last years. Aria's eyes kept darting to his lips, which she wanted to smack herself for. In a sudden rush, she said, "Maybe he's in the mess hall?"

"Yeah, maybe. Would you like to walk there together?"

Together. It was just a word, one Aria had to have heard millions of times, and yet, it still lit sparks within her. He wanted to walk with her, alone. *Together.*

Oh, pull yourself together! You've walked and talked with him plenty of times! Her snarky conscience could have been rolling eyes at herself. *You sat alone in a room with him once! This is no different!*

Aria clenched her hand tight, trying to block out the voice. "Yes, I'd like that."

The next several minutes were spent in silence as they walked, which made Aria's fingers begin tracing the golden petals of her necklace. Luke scratched the back of his neck continuously again, just like yesterday, with his eyes trained ahead of them. Aria desperately tried to think up some way to start a conversation that wouldn't be awkward when Avi came running up to them from the mess hall.

"Oh, hey, Luke!" Avi exclaimed, his tone laced with something that sounded like fake surprise. He waggled his brows knowingly. Aria raised one of her own eyebrows in confusion before he turned to her. "And hello, *Aria*!"

"Hi…" She looked between the two of them, wondering if maybe Willow shouldn't have told her everything about Luke liking her. Avi was only making the situation more awkward.

He smirked. "They're handing out clothes and a backpack to everyone inside the mess hall."

"Seriously?" She couldn't wait to get out of the dirty clothes clinging to her body.

"Seriously, what?" Willow's voice came from behind Aria, curiosity and something akin to amusement in her voice.

Aria turned—and her stomach seemed to do the same—to see Willow standing there. Her hair was wet and stringy, no longer bushy, indicating that she had showered, but she still wore the same clothes she'd been wearing since the attack. She wore a knowing look on her face, but not one that suggested she knew anything of what was happening in the mess hall. Her eyes darted between Luke and Aria like arrows telling her what to do. Jitters ran beneath Aria's skin and heat spread across her freckled cheeks.

This is so awkward… The voice came back again. Aria could imagine someone sitting in the back of her mind, reclining, and watching as the scene played out before her with amusement.

"They're giving everyone in the camp clothes and a backpack," Avi answered, meeting Willow's eyes.

"That's spectacular!" Willow exclaimed and her eyes lit up, a blush creeping across her cheeks. "Let's go inside then!"

Noticing the color flooding Willow's face, Aria smirked and shook her head. *At least I'm not the only one.*

Noise hit their ears like the loud beats of a drum inside— nearly the whole camp was talking and trying to get the new clothes that had been brought. Mrs. Mckinney was in the center of the massive, high-ceilinged room with multiple bundles of clothes piled on one of the tables next to her. She passed out bundle after bundle to the long line of campers stretched out between tables. Aria and her friends joined the back of the line. She tried hard to look anywhere but right in front of her where Luke's back was, but no matter how hard she tried, she still felt like the most awkward person in all the realms.

"Good to see you, dears," Mrs. Mckinney said to them as she handed each of them clothes and a backpack. "These are compliments of the Forces of Light." Then she changed her attention to Luke and Willow, "Luke, we have been trying very hard to reach your parents and tell them of the attack, but we have been unable to. We will make sure they get the message, though. We want to make sure that they know you are safe and that they can pick you up if they wish to." She paused, her face sincere. "And Willow, we have contacted your parents. Your mother will be coming to pick you up in a few days."

The world seemed to stop.

Willow froze, staring at Mrs. Mckinney like she had a million words she wanted to say. Avi grabbed her lightly by the arm and pulled her away with his lips pressed together. Aria blew out a sigh, her head suddenly swarmed as it processed everything.

She and Luke followed close behind, and Aria could have sworn Luke muttered, "Good luck trying to reach them."

Her face fell, recalling everything he'd said about his parents and the jobs that kept them from their children.

"No, no, no," Willow repeated over and over, shaking her head as they plopped their clothes down at a completely empty table. Her breaths were loud and desperate. "If my mom picks me up, how am I supposed to help you?"

Aria, Luke, and Avi looked over their clothes as they listened to Willow. The clothes were plain white, black, and tan, but they looked warm and cozy. There was a black jacket, several pairs of white socks, a few pairs of jeans and comfy pants, and several shirts and other essentials. She shoved it all in the backpack as Willow went on beside her.

"I want to be here to help you. If I leave, I won't be able to do that. How will I help you find the Death Stone? How will I help you fight off the Dark Forces? How will I—"

"Maybe it's for the best, Willow," Aria said, feeling a pang as sharp as needles when she saw Willow's offended face.

Willow narrowed her eyes and put her hands on her hips. "What's that supposed to mean?"

Aria had seen Willow's parents and her little brother when they'd arrived at camp to pick her up after Malus' trial, but she'd never actually met them. Thinking about Willow going home to be safe with them, her head became lost in the chaos. She wasn't sure how to feel about Willow leaving. If Willow was gone, she'd be out of harm's reach and the Dark Forces likely wouldn't find her. But another part of Aria *wanted* Willow to stay. She wanted them *all* to stay at her side. It was selfish, she knew, but she didn't want to face the Dark Forces alone. What lay ahead was dangerous and scary. They would all be safer if she went by herself and they stayed behind, like what she had wanted them to do a few months ago. Of course, they hadn't listened then and she was sure they wouldn't listen now. It was too late now to change how things had played out, anyway. Malus and the rest of the Dark Forces knew who they were, which meant there was a target on each of their backs.

"Just…just that it would be safer if you were out of harm's way," Aria said in a rush and quickly turned to get some breakfast.

Willow started after her with Luke and Avi at her heels. "Aria, that is not your decision to make," her voice was firm and held no room for argument. "You know I would come with you if I could, just like last time. And I *will* come. I'll figure out a way to when my mom shows up. I have a few days, so that should give me some time. I'll just read more, and I'm sure I'll find something," Willow paused, letting out a breath. "And hopefully we'll be hearing from my dad any time now. I don't understand why it's taking so long…Anyway, some books I could read—" Aria stopped listening as Willow started listing off several titles of books. She picked up a tray of pancakes and eggs before backtracking to the table they had chosen. As she sat down, she sighed. Her friends were so determined, perhaps too much for their own good.

Luke sat down next to her, their arms brushing and sending a wave of sparks across Aria's skin. Her heart skipped a beat and she had to force herself to keep looking down at her plate of food as she ate. Heat crept up her cheeks under his gaze, but she still refused to turn, refused to sink into the beautiful shades of blue that were his eyes.

"We'll just have to hope that the Forces of Light aren't able to reach my parents," Luke said. "They probably won't, though, since my parents are in some remote place in the Vezchia Realm, studying creatures."

"What about Christopher?" Aria couldn't help herself—she just had to ask. And with that, she locked eyes with him. "Won't he try to stop you from following me? Won't he try to keep you here until your parents are able to come?"

Luke looked at her thoughtfully, pondering something. He licked his lips and there was silence for a moment before he spoke. "I don't care what Christopher thinks or does. He can't stop me—nothing can."

Aria's breath caught in her throat and she felt her heart begin to flutter. That urge that she had felt in the hallway right before the attack came back, but she tried to shove it down. She looked away again and continued eating, not furthering the conversation.

Luke and Avi had gone off to who knows where—they didn't say—a few hours ago. So, Aria and Willow walked down the trails that wound throughout the camp alone. They'd changed into warm long-sleeved clothes to block out the autumn chill blowing through the air, and the temperature continued to decline. There'd been an unnerving silence between the two of them for a while, which could have been because Willow was flipping through a book. But she'd been doing that for only the last ten minutes. For the last few hours, she'd been distant.

"Oh, maybe I could clone myself?" Willow murmured to herself. "But I would have to be a skilled illusionist to do that."

"Illusionist?" Aria asked, glancing over at the book that Willow had her eyes pinned to. It looked like it had something to do with the mind.

"It's someone who can use magic to manipulate what another person sees. Usually, Mind-readers are best at it because we can manipulate the mind directly. But it generally requires a potion to weaken the person's mind," Willow replied. "Technically, any enchanter or enchantress can do it, but it's harder. You're accessing all their senses and controlling them yourself… It says people often become ill because of it. I don't want my mom to have to go through that." Then she fell silent again.

"Wouldn't that be illegal, Willow?" Aria's brows furrowed, thinking about how the illusionist thing sounded sickening. "Mrs. Helma said mind control is illegal."

"There are many loopholes in the law," Willow said quietly. "Honestly, they really need to have the laws reviewed."

Aria glanced at Willow as she flipped the page. Willow's back was board-straight and her jaw was tight. If there was one emotion Willow hardly ever showed, it was anger and annoyance. Now was one of those times that she seemed to be letting it show. Aria crossed her arms to block out some of the chill— also because guilt prodded at her, and she needed a way to hold herself together.

"Willow, if you're mad at me—"

"Mad at you?" Willow looked up at Aria with bunched brows. "Why in the name of Viden would I be mad at you?"

"I don't know. It's just—in the mess hall—"

"Aria, I understand what you were trying to say. You were right in a way, but that doesn't mean I'm going to give up hope in trying to help you," Willow said. "In fact, that's what I'm doing right now. I'm looking up ways to somehow trick my mother so I can stay here, or clone myself, or…*something*." She sighed. "I'm not mad at you. I'm just stressed out. I'm not going to stand by and return home for my own safety while you go off risking your life. I'm not going to abandon you."

For a few moments, there was silence as they neared cabin number eighteen. A smile suddenly spread across Willow's face, one that said she knew something, one that sent Aria's stomach sinking.

"So…" she began. "What were you and Luke talking about?"

"What? When?" Heat crept up into Aria's face as if she were hovering over a volcano. She hoped that Willow wouldn't be able to see her face turning red, but then again, Willow would just be able to sense the feelings rampaging through her.

"This morning," Willow looked at her cheekily. "As soon as you left, I woke up to see you leaving. I followed you at a distance before catching up at the mess hall. What were you two talking about?"

"Oh, nothing," Aria said, which was the sad truth. She probably should have said something about the previous day or her feelings. Guilt branded her heart because she knew she should have apologized to him. Her head filled with thoughts of what the conversation *would have been* if she'd said what she was feeling.

Luke, I like you. Do you like me too?

Do you realize how incredibly creepy that sounds? The voice in the back of her mind seemed to be laughing at her. She blew out a puff of air.

What about: Luke…about yesterday…I'm sorry I left you so quickly. What was it you wanted to tell me?

Aria, I like you and I always have.

Now you're just fantasizing, her anxiety snarked.

"Aria?" Willow's voice snapped Aria out of her thoughts and fantasies.

"Huh?" Aria turned to her, trying to wipe away the smile that had appeared on her face.

"I asked you something."

"Oh, sorry."

Willow looked at her with a slackened jaw and repeated herself, "What do you mean *nothing*? You mean, you didn't ask him about yesterday?"

"I—I—I couldn't…" Aria's shoulders slumped as they turned around cabin number eighteen and headed up into the forest where the oak tree sat.

"Well, you'll have to say something at some point," Willow told her.

Up at the oak tree, Aria started pacing the forest floor, trying out different enchantments that she had learned either at school or from Willow's collection of books. Meanwhile, Willow sat on the ground, scanning pages so she could figure out how to escape her mother.

"Oh! What if I went home with my mother and then tele-ported back here?" Willow looked up from the pages, her eyes bright with possibility.

She waited for a response. Aria summoned Black Smoke into her palm and let it swirl down to the ground, pulling more from the air around her.

"But wouldn't your mom figure out where you went? Or

prevent you from leaving?" Aria had a look of skepticism on her face as she made the fog curl itself up a tall pine tree like a vine. "Not to mention the Anti-teleportation Charm surrounding camp. You'd have to teleport to outside of it, like right here. And then Mrs. Mckinney would just question why you're back."

"It's still worth a try. I'm going to try it," Willow said, but she kept flipping through the book with determination.

"Hey!" Avi's voice called from behind them.

Leaves crunched and sticks snapped as Aria spun to see Luke and Avi making their way up into the forest. Avi had a pencil tucked behind each of his ears and Aria could only wonder why. They'd both changed their clothes at some point and were now bundled in warm sweaters.

"We were looking everywhere for you guys, but then Luke said you may have come here," Avi said, grinning. "So, here we are."

"I'm just practicing and Willow's…looking for ways to escape her mom," Aria said, blood creeping up her neck as Luke walked towards her.

"May I join you then?" The ghost of a smile tugged at his lips. "Perhaps I can learn from the master?"

"Oh, sure," she laughed. "But I wouldn't call myself the master."

Aria continued twirling the Black Smoke around a tree and Luke watched her as she did it. Nerves rattled around inside of her, feeling his eyes on her. A spark lit in her fingertips and the smoke turned red. Aria's eyes went wide and she tried to change it back, hoping whatever she'd done wasn't harmful. The bark on the tree turned dark with moisture, then the wood splintered, and began to decay. Her heart sped up as she tried to regain control over the magic pouring from her fingertips. The fog started to falter as she felt her hold on it slipping, and then it dissipated into nothing. She reached for the tree, touching the ruined bark. She'd never changed Black Smoke into something that could damage. Mrs. Helma had never even taught her how to. She stared down at her hands as if something was wrong with them—like they were a broken toy that couldn't be used anymore. She'd lost control. Again.

"S-sorry, I'm not in your way or distracting you, am I?" Luke asked. He scratched the back of his neck as the wind blew through the trees, shaking leaves out of the branches.

"No, no." Her eyes landed on his freckled face and deep open-ocean eyes. *Yep, a distraction.*

She turned her head upwards at the trees. Leaves rained down on them in golden, umber, rusty, and orange colors. One landed right on Aria's head and Luke reached his hand out to lift it from her hair. He smiled a bright, kind smile that made Aria's heart strike faster against her ribs.

She grinned back at him and gestured toward the trees. "It's beautiful, isn't it?"

"Yeah," he replied, but he wasn't looking at the trees.

A tapping noise came from over by the large oak where Willow and Avi were sitting. Avi had taken the two pencils from behind his ears and was now banging them on two rocks like they were drums. Aria shook her head, laughing on the inside, as he began humming a silly tune. Willow stared at him with amusement, her book still propped open.

Aria summoned fire in the palm of her hand to practice, feeling its warmth and pulse like that of a heart. It felt alive and was so beautiful to watch dance back and forth. She silently hoped that her magic would stay under control. Carefully, she tossed the fire between her hands, imagining all the ways it could be used against the Dark Forces. Luke stood a few feet away raising rocks into the air, his gaze hard as he pelted them against a tree. The bark gave way to dents with each slam of the stones. He glanced at Aria as she tossed the ball of fire into the air. It flickered and grew.

Avi began adding strange lyrics to his random song as the ball of fire soared toward the massive oak tree he was leaning against. *"If you spell Avi with just 'a's you can call it—"* He suddenly let out a high-pitched scream that sounded like, "AHHHHH!"

The ball of fire landed right next to Avi and lit the grass with flames. Aria's eyes went wide and Avi hurried to back away. Her blood ran cold as her heart leapt into her throat. Horror flashed across her face and her veins lit with power. She reached out her hands, feeling an intense instinct, a calling. She'd felt it before in the Malamone Mansion, that strange feeling of knowing exactly what to do even though she had no idea what was about to happen. She reached for water and it came, pulling the moisture from the air and grass. The grass immediately turned brown as she pulled the life of water out of it. It collected in the palm of her hand and she quickly tossed it down on the fire. The flames went out instantly but the grass beneath was scorched black. Luke, Avi, and Willow turned to her with wide eyes and dropped jaws like they'd had the shock of a lifetime.

"How in the name of Viden did you do that? I've never— *ever*—seen anyone do that before." Willow put down her book and closed it. She stood up and walked over to Aria as Aria herself tried to register what had just happened. "Did Mrs. Helma teach you that? Like how she taught you to use Black Smoke?"

"No, no. I—I have *no idea* how that—" Aria stared down at her hands as energetic light crackled across her fingertips. "I just thought I could do it...and did."

Something Mrs. Helma had told her floated into her mind

as she sucked in slow breaths to help steady herself. *"At that moment, your power did what it wanted to, but you have to control that. See, you may not have known how to shatter that clock, but your gift did, which means you are capable."*

"That's not the first time you've said something like that," Luke told her with a look of intrigue on his face.

"Aria, you should be more careful!" Avi grumpily crossed his arms, his two pencils lying on the ground. "You nearly burnt my clothes *and me!*"

"Sorry, sorry. I didn't mean to." She looked down at the ground shamefully. If she didn't figure out why her magic was going haywire soon, someone else would get hurt.

"It's okay. Accidents happen," Willow reassured everyone. "But we now know that Aria can do…well, whatever it is that she did."

"Yeah, but—but." Avi huffed but seemed to give up, standing to stretch his legs.

Aria bit down on her lip as everyone began gathering up their things, and together, they headed out of the forest and back into the camp. Willow was wrong, though. Walking down the paths, Aria tried to remember how she'd summoned the water, but she couldn't. She was the Diviner. She was powerful. But in that moment she didn't feel powerful. She felt *uncontrollable.*

CHAPTER EIGHT

THE WEEKS PASSED somehow both slowly and quickly at the same time—the sun sank sooner every day and as soon as it was back up, so was Aria. Every day, her magic crackled under her skin like a fire waiting to spark, and no matter how draining it was, she continued to practice. She refused to let another accident like the one with Avi happen again, so she'd wear herself down to the bone if it meant she could have everything under control. Halloween would be tomorrow, so she decided that would be her one break, but only because Willow insisted.

Leaves coated the ground like crunchy snow as Aria walked down the trails, a large book in her hands called *The Mystery of Vampires*. The sky was cast in sunset orange, and in half an hour, it would be pitch black with stars starting to dot its surface. Already, short garden lamps along the camp's paths were beginning to brighten, and in the cabin windows, lights were being flicked on.

Willow trudged alongside Aria, her face angled toward her feet as her hands coiled her hair around a finger. Her teeth were sunk into her bottom lip, gnawing on it. Aria's chest knotted up seeing her in such a state, almost always panicked.

Willow's mother, Iris Mudry, had never come to get her. Acre Mudry, her father, had never replied to her letter.

"He'd never even gotten it," Willow had said through tears weeks ago. "Mrs. Mckinney didn't want to tell me because she doesn't want me to worry. She's holding back a lot, but I read her mind and got *some* information." She'd shaken her head, as if unable to believe it. "The message was intercepted and never even arrived at Enchanting Control…And then the—" She'd broken off, choking on a sob.

And then the uprising happened. Aria could picture it—a battle within Enchanting Control, papers being thrown about the place, magic hitting against its marble walls. The law enforcement fighting against itself. And who had started this uprising? Willow's father.

Or at least that's what was to be believed. Thinking of everything Willow had said, Aria couldn't fathom it.

"My dad is the most understanding person in the world," Willow had said back at the school. Then after finding out about the uprising, she'd said, "I don't understand it. My father would *never*. He chose his job to help people, to be a bridge between Enchanting Control and its allies, like the Forces of Light. He's a *good* person and a good dad."

Recalling that, Aria's chest felt tight. She had thought things like that when her parents had been taken away from *her*.

Now Willow's father was on trial like some kind of criminal, despite everything Willow had said, despite everything about it that didn't make sense. But something dark was stirring out there in the world of magic, and Aria had read about the Dark Days the Dark Forces had caused centuries ago—those days when terror had its claws sunk in every person, when the

Dark Forces reigned, and fear of losing the realms to them was strong. It seemed those days were beginning again, even if no one wanted to admit it.

"I haven't received a phone call from my mom yet this week," Willow said now beside Aria, eyes darting up from the ground.

Her mother had decided it would be best if she stayed at camp, where it would be safe—further proving something wasn't right out there. She'd made many phone calls to Willow in the office, explaining how she wished she and Willow's five-year-old brother, Elm, could be there with Willow in this time of stress. Or she'd say she wished Elm could be with Willow at camp, so that he was away from the trial situation too, but because he was autistic and hyperactive, he couldn't. He was a "runner," as Mrs. Mudry put it in one of her calls. So, she was left dealing with her husband on trial and her son all on her own.

"I'm worried something happened with Dad, or with little Elm. None of them deserve this." Tears glistened in the corners of Willow's eyes. "At the end of the last school year, Elm was having some issues. Everything he sees and hears is too much for him and it sets him off. I wish my mom didn't have to deal with all of this at once. My dad should be able to be there for her. *I* should be able to be there for her. Everything is just so unfair." Panic was spread across her face again, just like so many other times that month.

Aria recalled Willow trying to find ways to not have to go home, so she could stay and help her. Then her father was accused and her mother thought she'd be safer at camp. Now Willow wanted more than anything to be able to help her family get through this dark time.

Willow's voice cracked beside Aria as she continued. "I

know we've talked about this numerous times already, but it makes me worry even more. Dad works in Ally Communications at Enchanting Control, and one of their allies is the Forces of Light. The Dark Forces have every reason to go after him and the rest of those who work in Ally Communications." Her voice was shaky and full of hurt. "They could have information that the Dark Forces want, and that's why they could have started the uprising as a distraction. What if they have him now? What if he's not simply being held by Enchanting Control anymore? What if the Dark Forces took him like how they took *your* parents?" Her voice broke on the words, a lump clearly stuck in her throat. "I just want to see him again, to know he's okay. I want to hear his voice and his laugh and see his smile. I can't imagine what he must be going through right now." Tears streamed down her face and sobs racked her body, lips trembling.

Aria reached out her hand and laid it on Willow's shoulder. "I know. I know the feeling, Willow." Tears pricked her eyes, but she forced them away. "I'm sure we'll hear if something happens. Mrs. Mckinney wouldn't keep that from you. There has to be a brighter side at the end of this."

"I'm sure you're right." Willow wiped tears from her eyes, hands shaky.

Everything in Aria squeezed as one thing Willow had said spun through her head. *What if the Dark Forces took him like they took* your *parents?*

She shook it from her mind, not wanting to dwell on the hurt that filled the air between them. Her eyes began scanning the book again, trying to fill her head with as much information as possible. She felt like Willow, having read all the books she had in the last few weeks. Willow recommended the book to her a few days ago when Aria had asked a question about vampires. She couldn't even remember what the question had been, but those nightmares of Viola stalking through the dark, waiting to pounce and torture her kept replaying in her head.

Vampires are granted the ability to live forever unless killed by unnatural sources such as a stake through the still heart or burned alive. If there is one thing a vampire fears most, it is fire.

Aria remembered Viola saying something about how her heart didn't beat and she didn't need to breathe. Trudging down the path, she skimmed the next few pages.

Once a person is bitten, the vampire venom starts to change the body completely, but it is a slow process. The venom creates cracks along the skin as it trails through a person's veins, though those will heal when the change is complete. A person may experience sudden waves of hunger and extreme violence. Once the venom reaches the heart, the heart stops, all senses become supernatural, and the body changes to become easy to prey. A few misconceptions that have to do with vampires are that they fear garlic, can't go in the sun, and sleep in coffins. None of those are true. Vampires are one of the most dangerous creatures in all the realms.

Aria was torn from the book as two teenagers, probably thirteen years old, ran past them with sheets thrown over their heads. The sheets had holes cut for their arms and eyes, and they had drawn ghost faces on them.

Another crunch of footsteps on the gravel path sounded behind them.

"Hey, Willow," a sneering voice called from behind. "How's the criminal's daughter doing?"

Aria's jaw tightened and her hand caught Willow's wrist. "Just keep walking."

The last thing Willow needed at the moment was someone poking fun at her again. The gossip that had sprung up in the camp over the last few weeks like weeds had everything to do with her, and it all traced back to the voice following them now.

"Oh, you're going to outrun me now?" Celaena teased, growing closer from behind. "That's a pointless effort. We're going to the same place." She laughed and strode around them to block their path.

Aria glared, teeth grinding together. "Get out of our way, Celaena."

"Wow, you sound really unpleasant to be around." Celaena's voice sounded so sickeningly innocent. She turned toward Willow, cocking her head to the side. "Anyway, I just wanted to know what it's like being the daughter of a criminal."

Aria's gaze turned sharper. "I could ask you the same thing."

Celaena scoffed, shaking her head. She slowly backed away with her nose bunching up in rage. "I have a bonfire to be at."

She spun on her heel and strutted down the path, turning in the same direction as the young teens who'd run by a few minutes ago. They'd likely been heading for the huge bonfire that sat in the middle of camp. Everyone had been talking non-stop about it because of the ghost stories and special treats that the camp would be having. Willow had been eager to go to it, so of course, that's exactly where she and Aria were heading. Luke and Avi had run back to their cabin to grab jackets and an extra pair of socks to layer over the ones they already had on. Aria and Willow had already done that when they woke up at the crack of dawn that morning with the weather feeling as if winter was just a block away.

"Eeek!" Willow's face lit with a grin. "I wonder what type of treats they'll have! Oh, maybe cupcakes? It's been a while since I had one of those!"

It amazed Aria how fast Willow could change her emotions. One second, she could be in the depths of despair and the next she could be jumping with joy, quite literally. She jumped up and down a little as they turned the corner. The smell of smoke and roasting marshmallows over a fire wafted through the air. The bonfire was massive, reaching its fingers for the pinkening sky as campers crowded around it on wooden benches that circled around the whole thing in rows. Halloween-themed rice crispy treats, cookies, cupcakes, and finger foods were being carried around everywhere. The smell of the sweets permeated the air and made Aria's mouth water.

Willow and Aria hurried past the bright, dancing fire. The relief Aria felt as the fire swept away the chills of the evening air made her sigh. The blazes cast a red-orange glow on every camper's face in the vicinity, two of them being Luke and Avi. They were both several feet away, pushing food into their mouths from a nearby table. The wind ruffled Luke's hair and he pulled the hood of his black jacket up over his head. Beside him, Avi looked like he was trying to keep warm from a winter blizzard with his hood on, pulled tight around his head, and the multiple layers that acted as blubber. As Aria and Willow approached them in the dimming light, Aria raised one of her eyebrows at Avi.

"Hey, don't judge. I need to stay warm." Avi said around a mouthful of food. "The ghost stories are enough to make me shiver."

Aria bit back a laugh and Willow reached for an orange-frosting cupcake. More campers were gathering around for the Halloween celebrations. As Aria glanced around, it was hard to imagine that so many campers were still at the camp. Surely, more parents would have wanted their children to come back home after such a devastating attack at the school. Or maybe, like how Willow's mother had said, it was safer at camp than outside of it. Her eyes landed on Celaena, and then Elaine and Natalie who were crowded around her. The three gossip-spreaders, who'd turned Willow's situation into something to talk about. Aria's face twisted into a glare and Celaena saw it, returning her with the same look but sharper like a blade. She turned away, back to her friends with a frustrated breath clouding in front of her face.

"Aria, would you like to take a seat?" Luke asked, scratching the back of his neck. Aria noticed how he was always doing that. He'd scratched so much that the skin looked red and irritated.

"Sure," she said, giving him a smile. "You should really stop scratching."

"W-what?" He quickly took his hand away from the back of his neck and shoved it into his pockets. A pink tinge spread across his face. "Oh."

Aria, Luke, Avi, and Willow sat down in the front row beside the bonfire with lots of sweets loaded into their hands. The heat of the flames enveloped them and lit their faces in an orange glow. Aria was already taking a bite of a sugar cookie when Celaena stood up, a twisted smile playing at her lip.

Now what? Aria thought to herself, giving an exasperated sigh.

Celaena always had something up her sleeve when that cunning grin was on her face. And it was never good.

"Happy Halloween, everyone!" Celaena's voice was raised an octave higher than normal and sounded way too sweet to even be possible. Her fake personality made Aria want to puke. "I know it is not Halloween just yet, but it will be tomorrow. I was the one who convinced the camp's board to host this little event and even helped make some of those goodies you are enjoying. There will be even more goodies, crafts, and events taking place tomorrow, which anyone is welcome to join in on."

Aria instantly spat out the cookie that she had been chewing onto the dirt ground. Luke looked at her with a questioning face as she wiped her mouth with the back of her hand.

"Knowing Celaena, it's probably poisoned," Aria said and he let out a soft chuckle.

Avi suddenly tossed his chewed-up cupcake on the ground too, coughing as if he'd had something go down the wrong pipe. Willow gave him a pat on the back, her eyes widening. He kept gagging, his breathing hitched. She grabbed him by the arm and smacked his back again, her face searching his in concern.

"Avi—Avi, are you alright?" Willow leaned over in her seat as he bent over in a coughing fit.

Everyone else was busy listening to Celaena tell a spooky story that they hadn't noticed Avi coughing and spitting on the ground.

"F-fine," he managed and stopped coughing altogether. "Just making sure I got the last of those poisoned treats out of my mouth."

"Seriously, Avi!" Willow kept her voice low enough that no one seemed to look in their direction, but she was on the edge of raising it. "You had me really worried there for a moment!" She rolled her eyes, but there was the faintest smirk on her lips. "Celaena's every word may be poison but that doesn't mean she'd poison the food."

Avi looked sheepishly at her with a blush across his face before straightening back up in his seat. Meanwhile, Luke and Willow ate the sweets one after the other.

"Are you sure you don't want one?" Luke offered Aria one of his chocolate cupcakes with orange frosting.

Aria shook her head. "No, but thank you."

"Okay, then." He ate the cupcake instead with a kind grin.

Aria turned her attention to Celaena, whose face was cast in the reddish glow of the fire. The sky was darkening, and stars were beginning to show themselves. Shadows appeared in Celaena's attentive audience, and as the fire danced and she moved about, the shadows moved eerily too.

"Starlette tip-toed around the corner, but everything was in total darkness. She was so terrified that she couldn't help screaming." Celaena was telling a dark, supposedly scary story. Everyone was practically sitting on the edges of their seats with glee glinting in their eyes. "The vampire was hiding in the darkness. She heard it laugh and felt it creep closer to her. Starlette took off down the hallway, nearly stumbling over in her heels. If she could just leave the palace…If she could just hop in her carriage…But then Starlette was stuck to the walls, cold hands holding her there. All she could see was the faint flash of white teeth."

Images flashed across Aria's eyes, pulling her away from the story and the bonfire. Instead, *she* was pinned against one of the walls inside the Malamone Mansion. Viola's rotting breath lingered right in front of her face…and then she felt the pain, the horrible agony of nails digging into her skin. She tried to push away the traumatizing memories and all the fear that came with them. Then she was back in front of the bonfire again, her breath coming in quick, her heart beating strikingly fast against her ribs, and her blood running cold through her veins. She pulled up the hood of her sweatshirt, hoping it would hide the fear reflecting on her face, and listened to Celaena's story again.

"Starlette ran and ran, pure agony covering her arms where the vampire's hard grip had held her. She may have escaped the vampire's grip, but she still needed to escape the palace." Celaena strode around the fire, winking as she passed Aria. "Everywhere was dark, and she could hear the witches, werewolves, and vampires calling her name. Their voices echoed throughout the castle's halls. And then Starlette was thrown against the wall!"

The crowd of campers' eyes went wide with what may have been intrigue. They waited to know more, to hear the rest of the *exciting* story. Aria's breath shuddered as the memories began to spin through her mind again. She squeezed her eyes shut to make them leave her head, but that only made it worse. The darkness, the pain, the threats—it was all there in her head. *"You are the Diviner,"* her mother's voice echoed through her.

"The voices of past victims called out to Starlette, wishing to be freed. Starlette had lost her parents to the werewolves, witches, and vampires. Now she could hear their voices. They wanted her to escape, and she was so close to the castle doors… Until a witch stepped in front of her and summoned magic into her palms," Celaena continued, a daggered smirk showing on her face. "Starlette would have to try her best to escape now… but maybe it was not her destiny to."

The nightmares made another reappearance and Aria found that one hand was gripping her sunflower necklace and the other had Luke's fingers interlaced with hers, holding on tight to the present.

"Aria?" Luke's voice came softly in her ear. "Aria, what's wrong?"

"Go away, go away, go away," she repeated softly to herself. Her eyes were clenched shut and nausea was kicking in. Her head spun out of control.

"Haven't you ever fought in the dark, Aria? I do it all *the time…"* Viola's wicked voice echoed, along with her vicious, twisted laugh. *"There are only two options in life: rule or be ruled. I am the ruler now,"* Malus had told her right before he had her locked away in a wine cellar. "Get out—get out of my head."

"Oh, Aria, are you okay?" Celaena's voice came loud and clear for everyone to hear.

Aria's eyes shot open and she raised her head slightly, vision sharpening with a glare. Her hands were clammy and sweat slicked her forehead despite the cool air. She tried nodding, but it looked more like a shake of her head with how much she was trembling.

"This story isn't too scary for you, is it?" Celaena's voice still sounded sweet and innocent, like she was talking to a five-year-old. "It just has vampires, witches, and werewolves." She knew exactly what she was doing. Afterall, one of her talents was creating humiliation.

Everyone chuckled around her, staring at Aria with smirks. They thought it was funny that she was scared because of some story. That monster inside her begged to be released. Sparks crackled across her fingertips. All the feelings knotted up inside her was like a lump weighing down in the pit of her stomach. She felt a tear slip down her cheek as more people laughed. These people were telling stories of terror and trauma, of innocent people getting hurt, and *laughing* about it. They enjoyed the misery of whoever this made-up Starlette girl was. But, of course, this was Halloween. And for Aria, it was all real.

"Aria, are you okay?" Luke asked her again. He gave a squeeze of her hand, looking her right in the eyes.

Avi and Willow's eyes bore into her as well with concern written plainly on their faces.

"I'm fine," Aria bit out, her eyes trained on Celaena.

"So, it's not too *scary* for you?" Somehow, Celaena's voice had managed to get higher and laughs resounded around the bonfire.

Aria was about to retort when she heard a distant, hostile, wicked laugh in the distance. She looked around, but realized it was just her head messing with her again. She recognized that laugh—it haunted her every single night and would for the rest of her life. But her heart fell to the deepest part of her stomach when she saw that everyone else was looking around for who had made such a malicious laugh too. If they had heard it… then that could only mean one thing. Aria's nightmares were about to happen all over again.

CHAPTER NINE

ARIA BOLTED TO her feet, making her head spin, and looked at her friends as the color drained from her face. Her lungs strained, but she forced herself to suck in a breath.

No, this can't be happening. Her mind felt like a whirlpool trying to drown everything else out. The smell of smoke lingered in the air as hope burned away.

Luke, Willow, and Avi stood beside her, bodies tense and huddled together. Their treats fell into the dirt. Silence cut through the night air like a blade. All around, campers looked through the darkness, listening for the malicious cackle. The air shifted as tension soaked it. Hushed voices began to fill the space around the bonfire. Celaena's face remained emotionless and unbothered as her eyes met Aria's from across the campfire. She gave a wink, then motioned for her friends to follow her. The group of them melted into the crowd like shadows. Aria snapped to attention and felt the power in her veins spark as she started after Celaena.

"Aria, no!" Luke called after her, the sound of his feet carrying him toward her soft in the dirt.

Aria gently pushed several campers out of her way as she hurried after Celaena and her friends. Her blood ran like icy water in her veins. The chill of the air bit down to her bones and rocked her with shivers. That wicked laugh replayed in her head, making magic hum defensively in her veins. Celaena and her friends disappeared around the corner of a building, the night traitorously cloaking them.

"Aria, what are you doing?" Willow was right behind Luke with Avi at her feet, all in a rush to stop Aria. "If that laugh came from who I think it came from—"

"Celaena planned it all out again. Last time the camp was attacked—" Now that Aria thought about it, it really had been Malus who had led the Dark Forces to the camp, so she stopped herself. "She hinted at the school being attacked, though. She—she is involved somehow."

"What? You aren't even making sense!" Avi shouted, hurrying to keep up. "We have to get an adult! Or hide! The Forces of Light need to know the Dark Forces are here."

"All this time," Aria continued, Avi's words not registering. "All the gossip, the jeering, the hints at something going on out in the world of magic, and now *this*. It ends now."

Celaena's group picked up pace, forcing Aria to run to keep up with them as the shadows tried to swallow them. She turned down another path, passing several cabins and the mess hall. A loud vibration, like a building collapsing, made Aria's feet halt. The Protection Barrier rattled violently like a powerful blast had been hit against it.

"WHAT WAS THAT?" Avi stopped in his tracks and looked upward.

Off in the distance, fire was being shot against the Protection Barrier. The fire made the orb-like shield glitter and orange glows lit up the camp like fireworks. Shouts and laughs resounded off in the front of the camp. Sirens blared.

The sounds of panic were everywhere now as Aria and her friends started forward again, nearing the entrance of the camp. Her heart pounded her ribs like a mallet somehow faster than it had before. Sweat beaded up on her forehead despite the autumn chill in the air, and her body wouldn't stop trembling. Crimson tendrils flew overhead and reflected in her eyes as she searched for Celaena. But Celaena had disappeared along with her group of friends. Aria, Luke, Avi, and Willow passed the office and stopped in the nearly empty parking lot. A cloud of fog gathered in front of Aria's face as she growled in frustration, spinning around to see where Celaena had gone. The moon was high in the obsidian, star-covered sky, allowing light to fall on the campground. Still, it was too hard to tell where Celaena had gone. Shadows clung to everything like cloaks.

Aria turned around to head back down the campground's paths. *Maybe she turned behind one of the cabins—*

"Oh, little Diviner!" a voice called from nearby and Aria's blood ran cold. Kora.

Aria slowly pivoted on her heel as if the night air were trying to freeze her in place. In the dark, it was hard to see them in their pitch-black cloaks, but a closer look revealed their silhouettes. The Dark Forces stood just outside of the parking lot where the Protection Barrier ended. There were so many of them, and in the darkness, it was too hard to count them all. The mention of her being the Diviner made something inside her recoil and a fire bloomed in her chest. She really hoped that no one else was around to hear Kora say such a thing. It sounded dangerous like a volcano about to erupt.

"Malus is tired of waiting for you. After centuries, I'm sure you can imagine how impatient he is," Kora continued. "Oh, and your friends are welcome to come too!"

She made it sound like a delightful thing, but Aria knew what truly awaited anyone who was captured by the Dark Forces: pain and misery.

"Bring this barrier down, foolish girl," Viola's voice called. "I know you can do it."

Aria's breath came quickly as she surveyed the barrier. Their group began another round of tossing flaming explosions at it, but the protection didn't relent despite its shaking. Would it continue to hold, though? Or would it eventually wear out? It had been standing for over a month. What if it was already too weak? What if it fell like the school?

"Come quietly and maybe things won't turn out so bad for you." Viola's twisted smile gleamed in the firelight being lit in others' palms, her fangs exposed.

"We'll get to you one way or another," Kora said, "and we'll tear everything down to do it. So, stop hiding like a *coward.*"

Aria shook, her sweaty hands clenched at her side. She couldn't stand seeing them, letting them taunt her. She started back the other way, fear making her heart strike against her ribs like the bang of a drum. *Coward,* her mind screamed back at her. Luke, Willow, and Avi stayed by her side, their eyes darting back to the Dark Forces lurking just outside the barrier.

"GET BACK HERE YOU LITTLE GIRL!" Viola screeched and her voice sounded like nails scraping across a chalkboard. "YOU CANNOT JUST WALK AWAY FROM US!"

"Aria, what are we doing?" Luke asked as he followed.

Avi matched his pace with theirs. "Or how about, what are we going to do about *them*?"

"I—I don't know..." Aria muttered, unable to think straight. "I mean, they can't get in...right?"

"In all the books I've read, a Protection Barrier cannot be broken unless…" Willow trailed off. "Um, unless a strong enough force can break it. It also weakens the longer it's up because it requires a lot of energy. Sometimes a person can't handle the amount of energy and it breaks on its own."

"*Great*," Aria said sarcastically. She pointed back in the direction of the camp's entrance. "Are they a strong enough force to break it?"

"Possibly, but there is only one way to know for sure…and that's if they *do* manage to break it." Willow bit her lip.

Aria's heart sank lower and a pit seemed to open in her stomach at the thought. She would never have a moment of peace for as long as she lived. A headache built up inside her head like clouds for a storm. All the sirens blaring around camp didn't help either. Her friends continued to follow after her as she turned the corner leading to Luke and Avi's cabin—cabin number thirty.

"Aria, where exactly are we going?" Avi asked with an urgency in his voice, his eyebrows raised.

"Somewhere we can talk without being heard," Aria said, keeping her voice low.

She had no idea where Celaena and her friends had gone, nor did she know how many Dark Forces members were there. If Celaena was sure to have gone anywhere, though, it would have been to cabin number thirteen. And the Dark Forces were surrounding the whole camp, fire slamming against the Protection Barrier from all sides.

"Well, *that* was specific," Avi said, sarcasm lacing his tone.

In a matter of minutes, Aria was charging up the pathway that led straight to cabin number thirty. The lights were off inside as she grabbed hold of the door handle and yanked it open.

"Aria, why in the world—" Avi was saying before Luke pushed him forward inside the darkened cabin.

Willow and Luke filed in and Aria closed the door. In a rush, Aria drew the blue curtains closed before turning on the light. The blaring sirens and resounding panic were muffled by the walls slightly, but the red glow of fire still managed to flash through the curtains' fabric.

On October 14th, they'd celebrated Luke's fifteenth birthday in the cabin. Aria's presence had kept Christopher away while they'd eaten and played games, but something had still felt off. Even now, it was as if an intense feeling of loss and loneliness took over the room. The room was messier than she remembered too, with dirty laundry and card games lying everywhere.

She looked back at her friends. Luke sat comfortably on a bottom bunk, Willow stood awkwardly in the middle of the room next to Aria, and Avi desperately tried to clean up the clothes he hadn't put away. As he grappled for all the laundry, his face turned hot and splotchy. He threw the clothes in his backpack and sat down next to Luke, glancing at Willow with a pink tinge to his cheeks. Then they were all looking at Aria with expectation as if *she* should tell them what to do.

"Um…" Aria started. "I think we should…uh…gather our things. Be prepared to leave if something goes wrong…" She wanted to slap herself—she didn't sound confident in the least. Not to mention that her plan wasn't very stable. Taking a deep breath, she continued. "If they break through, the camp will be surrounded. Everyone here is in danger. The Dark Forces will do anything to make sure they leave with me." Aria shook her head. "And we're not enough to fight them off. We'll have to leave to make sure they leave too. Hope that they follow us…and take this battle somewhere else." She gnawed on her bottom lip, taking in their reactions to the plan. "Unless anyone else has any ideas?"

"I agree with Aria," Luke said.

Willow nodded. "Yeah, me too."

"Um…well, I'm already done." Avi raised his backpack into the air before plopping it back down at his feet.

"Okay." Aria's eyes wandered over the room. "But don't forget blankets and other essentials. And *food*. Don't forget that again."

A loud blare sounded from the speakers outside, causing the windows to rattle. Mrs. Mckinney's voice repeated across camp several times. "ALL CAMPERS AND STAFF, PLEASE MEET IN THE MESS HALL *IMMEDIATELY*!"

"Alright, you two get your things together quickly. Willow and I will have to later," Aria said as she and Willow made their way to the door. "Put a Shrinking Charm on your bag so that everything you need fits."

The mess hall was filled to the brim and the panicked talk of everyone reverberated off the walls. Aria and Willow had to push past everyone while trying to make it to the front, where Mrs. Mckinney was standing up on a table shouting over the noise. The body heat of so many people cluttered together radiated through the hall. An elbow knocked into Aria's ribs and she stumbled to the side, shoulders hitting someone else. Brash murmurs met her ears. She ignored them and pushed forward again, grabbing Willow's wrist to pull her through the crowd too. After all, the Dark Forces were there for *Aria*. If anyone should hear what Mrs. Mckinney had to say, it was her and her friends.

"Good—Aria, Willow—you're here." Mrs. Mckinney took a deep breath and yelled over the campers again. "Quiet, please! Many of you may not yet know, but the Dark Forces are once again at our doorstep. The Protection Barrier surrounding the camp should keep them away, but I know they will not relent. Eventually, the barrier *will* wear out and they *will* break through." She looked out over the crowd solemnly, watching as that fact sank into every person in the room. "There is something here that they want, and we will make sure we find out whatever that is. If the Dark Forces want it, it won't lead to good."

Aria's heart seemed to stop beating when she heard those words. Her body stilled as the color bled from her face. They wanted *her*. But no one could know that. The Diviner was a legend, a myth, and a tale to tell children to give them hope. If anyone found out the Diviner had come back, and that Aria was exactly that...

"We have backup on the way to drive the Dark Forces out," Mrs. Mckinney continued. "It is estimated that they will arrive tomorrow night. I'm still trying to gather news, but it seems a Forces of Light base has been attacked—"

"Attacked?" Voices rose above Mrs. Mckinney's, creating a resounding mess of chatter. "Who attacked them? The Dark Forces?"

"Yes, yes." Mrs. Mckinney held up a hand to silence the crowd. "Now, we have staff members all around the camp keeping an eye on the Dark Forces. We will not let harm come to you. " Mrs. Mckinney sighed, emotions waning over her face so quickly that Aria couldn't determine them. The bags under her eyes were severely pronounced, though. "For now, all of you are allowed to sleep in your own cabins. We will have the sirens turned off so you can sleep. If you hear the sirens go off again for any reason, come here. We will protect you and for-tify this building."

Mrs. Mckinney climbed off the table and started making her way through the crowd. She laid a hand on the campers' shoulders, whispering apologies to them as if this was her fault. "I'm sorry you have to go through this. Everything's going to be okay."

Oh, Mrs. Mckinney if only you could know if that were true…

Aria and Willow pushed back through the tons of campers to the door. Everyone was making a beeline out of the place, urgent whispers hitting Aria's ears. As soon as they burst out into the cool night air, they started running down the path while Willow mumbled something inaudible.

Aria could only guess she was muttering about the Forces of Light base that was attacked. Aria was thinking about it too. If a base was attacked at the same moment the Dark Forces showed up to get the Diviner, it could only mean that the base attack was a distraction. It would stop aid from being able to come to the camp. It would give the Dark Forces time, and that's all they needed.

Cabin number thirteen neared, its lights on and silhou-ettes moving in the windows. They hurried up the path, pulled open the door, and slammed it shut behind them, causing the windows to rattle.

Aria's eye landed on three faces and her own face contorted to a look of rage. "YOU!"

Celaena, Elaine, and Natalie stood in the room, looking innocent as they neatly folded up their clothes and tucked them into their cubbies. Warm cozy pajamas now hung off their figures. A wicked grin swept across Celaena's face as she turned around to see Aria.

"Yes, Aria?" she asked, pursing her lips and using a sweet,

innocent voice. "Are you going to get mad at me that I didn't attend whatever it was in the mess hall? Because I sincerely doubt it was of any importance."

"You knew they were coming, didn't you?" Aria shouted and her throat felt like it was on fire. Her hands shook violently at her sides, starting to pulse and crackle with magic. The magic started to take control and her hands began to glow. She quickly shoved them in her back pockets and took a deep breath.

"Who?" Celaena swept her hair over her shoulder and cocked her head to the side.

"The Dark Forces!" Aria had been down this same road once, and Celaena's fake innocence was getting on her last nerve. It took every amount of control she had not to lunge at her.

"Oh, them. I didn't know about that. I mean, why would I?" Celaena's brows knitted together. "What's there to be worried about anyway? They're here for *something*, then they'll leave. So I say, let them have it." Her malicious smile crept wider. "Can you think of what they might want, Aria?"

Aria abruptly turned to Elaine and Natalie, who surprisingly didn't look the least concerned. "What about you guys? You don't care that the Dark Forces are here?" A sharp edge made every word sound like an insult.

"Don't speak to my friends like that," Celaena retorted.

"Celaena's right." Elaine's dark eyes avoided Aria and she grimaced. "The Dark Forces are trapped outside of the camp, so there's nothing to worry about anyway. They can't get in and we can't get out."

Aria rolled her eyes, furious with how Celaena could so easily manipulate people into siding with her. Elaine and Natalie had barely even known Celaena, and then suddenly they were *best friends?* Aria abandoned the conversation and headed to her cubbyhole instead.

"Willow, let's just do what we got to do," she said vaguely.

Celaena smirked, crossing her arms. "Who knows, maybe they're here for Willow. After all, her father *did* start an uprising in Enchanting Control." She leaned against her bedpost and watched them lazily. "And who would start an uprising in the magical law enforcement building but the Dark Forces? Perhaps he's with *them*."

"Wow, Celaena, you seem to have given this quite a lot of thought." Aria cut a glare at her.

Willow joined Aria at her side, pulling open the bins on the shelves. "Yeah, and my dad works in Ally Communications, which sides with the *Forces of Light*, so that doesn't even make sense."

Celaena shrugged, but a muscle in her jaw ticked and she stayed quiet. Aria stuffed all of her cubbyhole's contents into her backpack. Celaena watched them with her eyes narrowed. Aria held her hand over her backpack as she walked back to her bed. She felt a pulsing beat form in her hand before a blue glow radiated from her palm and coated the bag momentarily. She climbed up her ladder and stuffed one of her two pillows inside the bag as the blue glow faded away into nothing. Willow had taught her the charm earlier that month, so now anything that entered the bag would be shrunken to fit.

"What are you two doing?" Celaena snooped, observing their every move like a hawk.

"None of your business," Aria stated as she shoved her bag into the corner of her bed. She pulled off her shoes and threw them across the room where they landed by the door.

Celaena strode toward the door swiftly, a scowl on her face. Before anyone had their covers pulled over them to keep out the cold draft, her hand fell over the light switch. A sudden pitch-blackness descended in the room and Aria had to feel around to find her blanket and cover herself with it. She didn't have pajamas on, but she supposed it didn't matter.

"Goodnight, Chesler. I have a feeling you'll need the sleep," Celaena said, and Aria was sure there was an evil smile bent on her lips.

Aria closed her eyes, but that didn't block out the constant banging as the Dark Forces tried to break through the Protection Barrier, nor the fear that was poking at her like a million needles. The cold seeped through her blanket like the panicked feeling that was digging its claws into her. She tried to steady her breathing, tried to calm herself, but she couldn't. Not when the Dark Forces were just outside, wanting to lock her away for the rest of her life.

A sudden bang rattled the whole cabin. It jolted Aria from her sleep—not that she had gotten much sleep—and she sat up, breathing heavily. Eyes widened and frantic, Elaine, Natalie, Willow, and Aria glanced at each other. Celaena leaned against the wall behind her bed, sitting with her arms crossed. Everyone stared at the door as if something was about to bust it down. Aria tore off her blanket and jumped down from her bed, waves of shock bolting up her legs. In a rush, she threw open the door, ignoring her rats' nest of hair and her need to change her clothes. A biting wind blew past her and scattered leaves across the path. Her eyes went wide with terror as she saw the translucent Protection Barrier cracking to pieces above her, its shimmer fading away under the dark, clouded sky. It was like the glass of a snow globe shattering. Her heart froze in her chest and her blood ran cold, a clamminess building in her hands. She shook in the doorway, a million thoughts rushing through her mind so fast that she couldn't grasp a single one.

A vicious laugh broke through the sirens that were beginning to blare throughout the camp.

Kora's voice rose above it all. "TRICK OR TREAT, CAMP ENCHANTED!"

CHAPTER TEN

"NO, NO, NO, no," was all Aria could manage as she instinctively stepped back into the cabin, swinging the door shut. They were trapped. The whole camp. The Dark Forces had them surrounded and no one would be able to get out fast enough. Her hands began to shake and it felt like there were fists wrapped around her lungs, panic surging through her. Prickles ran up her spine and her stomach churned at what was happening.

"Aria, what is it?" Willow asked, her eyes wide now as she stood in the center of the room.

Adrenaline pumped through Aria's veins, clouding her thoughts like a raging storm. All she could feel was the fear and fury that burned through her like lightning. Energy crackled over her fingertips, begging to be set free and destroy everything in its path. She held her hands tightly at her side.

"It's broken." Aria's words were only a whisper. "The Protection Barrier is broken."

Willow gasped before scrambling to grab her backpack from off the floor next to her bed. The sirens blared through the walls, screaming with urgency.

"We need to get to the mess hall," Aria said as she started for her ladder. Her sweating, trembling hands nearly slid right off as she climbed and reached for her backpack.

"Why would you go there?" Celaena stood from her bed and swept her black hair over her shoulder.

"That's where the Forces of Light want everyone to meet." Aria glanced at Elaine and Natalie. "And I suggest you go there as well. They're going to try to fortify the building—"

"Key word there, Chesler," Celaena cut in. "*Try*. The Dark Forces are in the camp. They want something and they aren't going to stop until they have it. This camp will burn because whatever they want keeps evading them."

Aria shot a daggered glare at her. She and Willow drew their blankets and pillows off their beds so that they were completely empty and stuffed them into their bags. The door thudded shut behind Elaine and Natalie, leaving Celaena behind. Celaena stared Aria and Willow down as they grabbed their shoes and slipped them on.

"Ignore me all you want, but…you aren't going anywhere." Celaena stepped forward, positioning her hands on her hips. Her face twisted with a hateful frown.

"Oh, really?" Aria turned to her as her hand found the doorknob. "And what are you going to do to stop me?"

"I—I" For once, Celaena was at a loss for words. She gulped and glared daggers at the two of them. "The Dark Forces will take you. I only need to aid them."

Aria eyed her for a moment, but Celaena made no move toward her. She swung the door open, allowing the panicked cries and yells of fear to meet their ears. Then she and Willow stepped out into the chaos.

Celaena's voice shook the door behind them. "GET BACK HERE, CHESLER!"

As soon as the door slammed closed behind Aria, the smell of smoke stung her nostrils. The sky above was shrouded in dark clouds that flickered with electric blue light. A few seconds later, a roar of thunder ripped through the air and a single raindrop landed on Aria's face.

Willow and Aria made their way down the paths, hurried steps carrying them forward. A lump rose in Aria's throat. They walked so quickly that the buildings, trees, and paths seemed to pass in a blur. The leaves crunched beneath them and the cold air bit through the fabric of their clothing. More raindrops began to hit the path, turning the dirt to mud that sucked at their shoes. In the distance, a fiery scarlet glow bloomed, the trickling rain doing little to put it out. Smoke billowed in the wind.

The mess hall was just in sight down the trail. The doors were wide open and all of camp was pouring into the building. She tried to quicken her steps, the hairs on her arms standing on end. She felt as if she was being watched, as if something was hiding behind one of the cabins as she passed. Her gut twisted.

It's just up ahead…

Something pushed against Aria's back and her knees buckled, splashing into the mud as more rain began to pelt against her skin.

"Trick or treat…" a cold feminine voice whispered through the air as if it were the wind itself. "I think I'll choose *trick.*"

Willow landed next to Aria, mud caked in her blond, thick waves. Aria spun on her knees, pulling Willow back to her feet as she stood. Her eyes searched the muddy path around them in a circle, landing on nothing but still cabins, puddles of brown water, dark gray clouds, and pounding rain. The rain sank down to Aria's skin, making her blood run cold. There was no one around to which the voice belonged.

"An Invisibility Charm," Willow breathed, raising her hands slowly. "We can't see them, but they can see *us*."

"Oh, a smart one," the voice came again, this time to Aria's right.

Aria's hand clenched at her side, frigid blue magic flickering in her palm. With that one motion, the drops of rain around her froze to shards of ice as sharp as daggers. Aria flung them out toward her right where the voice had come from. The ice shards missed, stabbing into the ground.

A laugh floated through the air. "Nice try, Diviner…"

This time, the voice was moving slowly closer. Aria moved to take a step, raising her hands again, and found her feet wouldn't move. Eyes snapping to her feet, she didn't *see* her feet at all. What she saw was earth and rock rising around her ankles as if the ground were trying to drag her down into it. She tried to lift her foot again and still, it didn't budge. The ground had her shackled.

Willow's hand landed on Aria's shoulder as she too tried to move out of the rock that had shot up around her feet. "N-nature-manipulator." Her breathing came in rough and her face was scrunched in concentration.

Aria's narrowed eyes shot back up toward where the voice seemed to have come from last. "Ebony."

"So, she remembers me." Suddenly, a cloaked figure appeared a couple of feet in front of them as if it had blinked into existence. The figure lowered their hood, revealing a head of long, wavy brown hair and a smirking, smug face of a woman. She lifted her hand, directing the earth to creep higher up around Aria's legs.

Magic lit in Aria's palms and surging scarlet magic soared toward Ebony. She sidestepped it and swished her hand through the air. Something wrapped around Aria's wrists and tugged her toward the ground. The rock around her knees crumbled as they bent, sending her to the ground where mud splattered her skin and the earth dug into her legs. What had ensnared her wrists turned out to be vines, pulling her hands closer and closer to the ground. Aria let out a frustrated yell and tugged, glaring at Ebony. Lightning crackled across the sky and thunder rumbled like a monster overhead.

Beside Aria, Willow threw ice blade after ice blade at Ebony. They flew through the air, slicing her black cloak to shreds. The gaps in her cloak revealed black leather pants and a leather corset with spare daggers hanging from the sides. She threw up her arm, creating an invisible shield that sent Willow's ice shards hurtling back at her. Willow ducked, but not before one grazed her skin and crimson blood ran down her arm. Within the span of a blink, Ebony disappeared again.

"Willow!" Aria shouted as she wrapped her hand around the vines pinning her down. Her eyes fixed on Willow's hand clenched around her arm, on the blood staining her fingers.

"Shh, she'll be fine," Ebony's voice crooned in her ear. "But you...I don't know if I can say the same."

Instinct urged on the fury inside Aria, commanding her to use it. She felt the pull of water at the same time that she released the flames. Water and fire countered each other, but together, they were destruction unleashed. The vines began blazing, fire scorching them. The water was pulled from the very essence of the plants, disintegrating them into nothing but ash in the blink of an eye. With her hands free, she caught hold of wet invisible fabric blowing in the wind beside her. Aria tugged and with all her strength, pushed herself toward Ebony. The earth around her feet crumbled even as it tried to stay latched onto Aria. Her backpack slipped from her shoulder and rolled across the dirt path. She landed on top of Ebony, still invisible beneath her, and magic stirred in the air around them.

Ebony's fist connected with Aria's jaw and she went rolling through the mud. Willow fell to her knees, kicking away the earth that had been trapping her, before jumping back up and running toward Aria as her backpack fell away. Colorful balls of magic and sparks flew through the air as more hooded figures stepped out from around the cabins. Aria and Willow's backs pressed together, circling as hooded figures crowded around them. Magic soared over Aria's head and she ducked, retaliating with a powerful blast that sent two hooded figures to the muddy ground. Aria's mind went blank as she fought, arms moving, magic crackling around her in a crazed blur. Even with each burst of magic that lit her fingertips, even with Willow taking care of the hooded figures behind her, it wasn't enough.

"Aria, we can't fight them all. We can't—"

"We *have* to," Aria said through clenched teeth, her energy becoming strained. "To stop is to give in."

Ebony, who now stood visible, suddenly stretched her hand up toward the dark sky. The hooded figures around them paused and leapt far away from her, tension as thick as the clouds above hanging in the air. Blue light lit the sky again, the lightning zigzagging through the clouds like a beast with hundreds of outstretched claws. Before Aria and Willow could jump out of the way, the lightning struck the ground just over ten feet away. A blinding flash of light filled Aria's vision and she fell to the ground, electricity burrowing deep into her bones. Her chest hurt and she gasped for breath, clutching where her heart was as if it were about to give out. Her face twisted against the white-hot pain traveling down her limbs. A moment passed and the feeling melted away, leaving her trembling in a puddle of mud. She slowly turned over to see Willow lying a few feet away, not moving.

Aria crawled across the soggy ground, heart hammering against her ribs. She gripped Willow's arm and shook her, watching her chest for any sign of breath. "Come on, Willow. Breathe." Tears pricked her eyes. "Please. Please, breathe!"

Willow's chest rose and relief flooded Aria like a tidal wave.

"She's just unconscious," Ebony remarked. "Would you like to join her?"

Aria tugged at Willow's limp body before a leather-gloved hand suddenly wrapped around her bicep and tore her from her friend. She dug her feet into the sludge even as two hooded figures' hands pressed hard enough against her arms to leave a bruise. They dragged her through the brown puddles and forced her to her knees in front of Ebony, who grinned wickedly.

"You could have killed us!" Aria snarled. "After everything, I would have thought you wanted me alive."

"I summoned *magical* lightning," Ebony said, her hair hanging in rain-soaked strings around her head. "It wouldn't have killed you unless it actually *touched* you, which it *didn't*."

Aria looked past Ebony toward the mess hall in the distance where the last of the campers were pouring into the mess hall. Surely, someone had seen the lightning. Soon enough, the doors would close and they'd be locked outside with the Dark Forces who wanted to tear them apart. The figures behind Aria pressed their fingers harder against her arm.

"Must suck, you know—to be you," Ebony sneered, looking down at Aria like she was something foul she'd stepped in. "Anyway, *sleep*."

Exhaustion gripped Aria's mind.

No. Aria clenched her teeth and pulled as hard as she could from the figures' grasps. Her magic pooled into her palms, an electric blue glow radiating from them. Sparks flew from her palms as she directed the current of magic at the hooded figures. They were blasted backwards and landed with a splash in the mud. Turning toward Ebony, she knocked her off her feet in a colorful swirl of magic that clung to her. Shreds of Ebony's cloak stuck to the sludge. Power surged through her veins like a ravenous fire. She unleashed that power and fury on all the Dark Forces members in the vicinity, the magic swirling around them. Her grip on her control slipped and it lashed out in all the ways it thought it could. Color blinded her vision and someone screamed. Her skin turned golden like the stars, and energy drained from her with every burst of magic. Electricity crackled in the air. Aria struggled to get a hold of the magic, breathing in deeply, and drawing it to a stop.

The uncontrollable power reminded her that she was the Diviner.

And even though she hated it—hated that immense power that made her different from everyone else—the magic ran through her in powerful ways.

Ebony struggled back to her feet, glaring at Aria as she wiped mud from her shredded cloak. Aria quickly darted back to Willow and shook her shoulders, watching as her eyes slowly opened and took in the scene around her.

"Willow, let's go!" Aria said urgently, pulling Willow to her feet to get her off the rain-drenched ground.

Holding her free hand out, she conjured she and Willow's backpacks into her hand. As soon as Willow was steady on her feet, Aria handed her bag to her and dragged her along quickly, down the wet paths and toward the mess hall. Willow glanced back at the slumped Dark Forces members and Ebony behind them, at the colorful glows emanating from their bodies, the ripped cloaks, the footprints in the mud, and the scorch mark left behind from the lightning.

"A-Aria, what did you *do* to them?" Willow's eyes snapped to Aria's face as if there'd be an answer written there. "What happened?"

"Umm, Ebony tried to electrocute us…" Her mind reeled, thinking of what *she'd* just done. Thinking of the *magic* she'd just used. "We can talk about it later."

What Aria did scared even *herself.* It just felt like defense, like an instinct buried deep inside her. It was powerful and angry, like a blistering fire. Yet she didn't even know what she'd done. Her mind had gone blank and then colors were blinding her. She felt as if all her energy and magic had been completely drained.

A few campers were still pouring into the mess hall as they came up to it, the noise somehow managing to escape through the walls. Willow and Aria wiggled their way through the doors and crowd, the noise loud in their ears. The doors slammed shut behind them and a lock clicked in place. Mrs. Mckinney stood above the crowd on a table, yelling so that everyone would listen to her, but the anxious talk throughout the hall was too deafening for anyone to pay attention.

"Campers! Campers!" Mrs. Mckinney tried to yell again, an urgency lacing her voice.

A hand caught hold of Aria's wrist and she stopped, turning to look into Luke's blue eyes. Avi was right next to him, both of their faces contorted into looks of fear. Backpacks were slung over each of their shoulders.

"Aria, are you okay?" Luke asked, concerned eyes looking her up and down. "You're covered in mud and—your *arm.*"

Aria followed Luke's gaze to see that her arm was already bruising from where the hooded figures had held her. She tucked her arms in closer to herself. "Oh, I'm fine. We were attacked. Nearly struck by lightning."

"Um what?" Luke's eyes looked as if they'd pop out of his head. "What do you mean *nearly*?"

She was about to wave it off like it was no big deal, claim she'd tell them all the story later, when her eyes snagged on a small bloodied scratch along his jaw. "Luke, you're *bleeding*."

He lifted his hand up to it, running his fingers along the cut. "We got attacked too. Kora and Chad found us, and although Chad wasn't much of a threat, Kora certainly was. A few staff members found us, took over the fight, and told us to get here before she could do much."

Avi's eyes were pinned on Willow, who held her hand wrapped tightly around her arm. He strode toward her and gently removed her hand to see the shallow cut and the blood caked to her fingers. "Who did *this*?" He met her bright blue eyes.

"Ebony," she said.

He pulled his backpack off and dug out a big red handkerchief out of the front pocket and wrapped it around her arm carefully. "It's not much, but it'll do for now."

"Thanks." Willow gave him a small smile.

Worry curdled in Aria's stomach. "Has Mrs. Mckinney said anything?"

"Other than '*The Dark Forces have broken the Protection Barrier*' and '*Campers*', no," Avi answered, giving a roll of his eyes as he stared around at all the petrified campers. "No one will be quiet."

Just then, there was a banging on the mess hall door, causing every camper to turn in that direction and a silence descended on the room. Aria's skin pickled as anxiety jabbed at her like a million white-hot needles.

"Oh, come out, come out, wherever you are…" Kora's voice crooned from outside.

The blood drained from Mrs. Mckinney's face. Aria's feet shifted forward, urging her to go out and stop all of this, but Luke caught her wrist.

"Stay inside, campers." Mrs. Mckinney's voice seemed louder than ever now over the eerie silence. "The doors are locked."

But that doesn't mean they won't tear them down.

Rain beat against the yellow-curtained windows, and outside of them, hooded figures surrounded the hall with their faces unseen beneath their hoods. Viola was out there too, her straggly black hair falling around her shoulders and her vampire fangs exposed around a wicked smile. Lightning flashed in the clouds and thunder rolled over the mess hall. Aria's sweat-slicked hands shook violently and she clenched them tight. Her legs wobbled and her mind spun as nausea tried to knock her off her axis. "Oh, little Diviner, come out, come out." Kora banged on the door again as gasps and whispers went up all around the mess hall.

"Diviner?" Voices floated to Aria's ears.

"The Diviner's not real."

"What are they talking about?"

"They're the Dark Forces. They're delusional."

Aria's heart sank lower and lower into the pit of her stomach by the second. Every word froze her in place, head spinning. If people found out…She didn't want to think of it.

"Aria…Aria…" Kora's voice was like a ghost's carrying across the mess hall. "Bring us Aria Chesler and we will leave your dreadful little camp alone. No harm has to come to anyone but her and those who stand in our way."

Even at a distance from the door, Aria heard the terrible

words that stung like fire, and everyone else heard too. Gasps and stares met her. Everyone's eyes were wide—whether with fear or admiration, Aria didn't know.

"You're the Diviner?" Elaine asked, standing just a few feet away in the crowd of campers. She sounded and looked in awe, but fright was twinkling in her wide brown eyes.

Aria didn't answer. She backed up, desperate to get away. Sweat built up on her forehead and her mouth felt dry as sand. Luke put a steadying hand on her shoulder but she didn't register it. Nothing felt real—it felt like she was locked in a nightmare.

"T-the Diviner hasn't been around for centuries…" Natalie trailed off, standing right next to Elaine. Her green eyes looked at Aria like she was something to be studied. "How are you the Diviner?" When Aria didn't respond she added, "Well, are you?"

Something in Elaine's expression changed with realization. "Of course, she is, Natalie. It all makes sense. Over summer she goes missing, she claims to have captured Malus, and then he is locked away. Everyone knows Malus has a strange obsession with power. And here the Dark Forces are for *her*. Because she *is* the Diviner." Elaine's voice rose higher with a tone sharp enough to cut steel. "They're here for her again, putting us all in danger like over the summer and like when the school was destroyed!"

She wasn't far off from the truth, but each word was like a stab to the chest. The fact that it was the truth hurt most of all. Aria *was* putting them in danger, and they didn't deserve that.

"I say we hand her over to the Dark Forces. Let them have her," Elaine said, but she didn't move, just like Celaena hadn't earlier. It was a threat, but there was fear and uncertainty under it all.

"No one is being handed over to the Dark Forces,"

Mrs. Mckinney's voice boomed over the crowd of frightened campers. "Aria—whether the Diviner or not—will stay at this camp like the rest of you."

"Have it your way then," Kora's voice called from the other side of the door, like she had heard everything, and then the doors burst open.

Everything happened all at once. Mrs. Mckinney yelled for campers to get out, she and other staff members ran toward the Dark Forces with magic crackling in their palms, and screams erupted around the mess hall as the Dark Forces poured in.

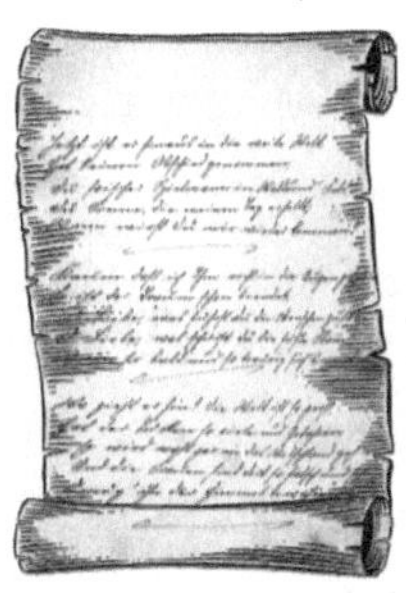

CHAPTER ELEVEN

CHAOS WAS SPREADING around them like wildfire, with panic reverberating off the walls. Mrs. Mckinney was near the door, fighting against the wave of Dark Forces members. The colorful magic exploding through the air could be seen from all the way across the massive room. Aria, Willow, Luke, and Avi pushed through the crowd toward the back of the mess hall. Everyone else seemed to be heading the same way, the back door already propped open for the campers to spill out of. A sweaty, shaking hand wrapped around Aria's wrist and jerked her backward as she was nearing the door.

"I've got her! I've got her!" Elaine's voice rang through the crowd. "Over here!" Her hand gripped Aria's wrist with such an intensity that it felt her bones might snap.

"Let go of me!" Aria shouted and grabbed hold of Elaine's fingers to pry them off her.

"No! You are a danger to us all. As soon as you're gone, they'll leave!" There was desperation in Elaine's voice. She started trying to pull her through the crowd as Luke, Avi, and Willow reached the door. The three of them spun back around as they noticed her absence.

"Aria!" Luke's voice carried across the mess hall.

Aria's magic rose up inside her, a pulsing heat gathering in her palms, and she let go of it. A Knockback Enchant blasted Elaine away from her, her back slamming onto the floor with a thud. Aria turned away, a sharp, twisting pang left in her chest at having to use her magic against Elaine. Elaine was innocent, simply someone who had been brainwashed by Celaena. She was scared and looking for safety, Aria knew that. But she knew fear often brought out the worst in people.

As more Dark Forces members pushed their way through the main doors of the mess hall, shoving campers out of the way, Aria hurried to the back door. She glanced back at the staff members and Mrs. Mckinney fighting at the front of the hall, guilt squeezing her chest. Luke, Avi, and Willow were already stepping outside into the cool, Halloween air. Turning away from the chaos, she ran for it. Her name was being shouted throughout the crowd, but she ignored it and pressed forward.

Elaine was right—as soon as she was gone, the Dark Forces would leave. She could only hope they would try to follow her and nobody else would have to get hurt.

Outside, rain pounded against the muddy puddles harder than before. The wrinkled, dried leaves made crunches and mud sucked at their feet as Aria and her friends hurried down the paths. Hooded figures were still converging on the mess hall. The sight of it made tears well up in Aria's eyes, but she blinked them away and kept running. Her legs grew wobbly as they headed toward the large oak tree that sat at the edge of the forest. The magic in her veins had taken so much from her in just a few moments of fighting. She pulled on every last bit of strength she had left to keep going.

Black dots edged into her vision just as something came at her from her side, sending her to the ground with immense force. The wind was knocked from her lungs as her side rammed into the path and her head slammed into the mud. She let out a cry as the impact shot waves of aching through her body and something sharp cut into her arm. Hands gripped her, holding her to the ground. She couldn't see anything but black fabric and smelled the distinct scent of rotting flesh and metallic blood.

"Hello, Aria," an eerie, ghost-like voice crooned in her ear. It was Viola, her voice and laugh the very thing that haunted her at night.

The fabric blew out of Aria's face and she looked up to see sharp, perfectly white vampire fangs in her face. Her heart sank to her stomach and her skin crawled, every part of her body trembling with fright. She couldn't help but cringe away. Viola enjoyed inflicting torture and suffering, that much Aria knew.

"ARIA!" Luke screamed and she could hear him splash through puddles as he ran towards her. "Get away from her!"

Viola let out a hiss like a cat, baring her fangs, as she directed her glare at Luke. He had his hands raised in defense. Magic crackled over them, blue and electric, about to be released—until one of Viola's dagger-like nails was placed against Aria's neck.

"I wouldn't do that if I were you…" Viola tutted. "The boy thinks he can save her. How pitiful." She wrapped the neckline of Aria's shirt in her grasp, scraping Aria's skin with her nails. With the strength of a bull, she pulled Aria to her feet in one swift motion, before wrapping her arm around her neck in a chokehold. She gulped as Viola ripped her backpack off with her free hand and flung it to the side.

"KORA! EBONY! I HAVE THE GIRL!" Viola screamed, causing a ringing in Aria's ears. She looked at Luke with a face of dark malice. "Now, where were we?"

Viola's fingernails were pointed right at Aria's throat. One wrong move could end it all. Aria tried to pull back, but right behind her was Viola, holding her in place. She stayed as still as she could, trying to keep her neck away from the sharp nails placed against it. Luke still had his hands raised, along with Avi and Willow, looks of horror on all of their faces. The three of them looked between Viola, Aria, and the nails placed at her neck. Gears seemed to be turning in their heads.

"She's needed alive," Luke said, his breath heaving. "You're just bluffing."

Viola's smile widened. "I know how to hurt people without killing them, but make them wish they were dead."

At that, his jaw tightened. Even Willow looked clueless as to what to do, and she usually knew everything.

"Let her go," Luke said, but he didn't look one bit confident; his hands were shaking, and Aria could see the sweat beaded up on his forehead now. "Don't hurt her."

A wicked smirk swept across Viola's sickly-colored lips. "Hmm…I don't know…It just seems so tempting…" She let her nail trail along Aria's neck, leaving a scratch behind.

Aria winced, her breath shuddering. She wanted to call her magic and defend herself but didn't want to risk moving in a way that would cause Viola to claw at her throat.

A sudden black flash appeared behind Luke, Avi, and Willow and an arm wrapped around each of their necks before they could react. A brutal smile spread across Kora's face when she appeared behind Luke, pinning his arms behind him and putting him in a headlock. Willow and Avi fought against the hold of Ebony and Chad. One other hooded figure appeared next to Aria and Viola's right, where Aria's bag lay.

"Gamaliel, check her bag for the Life Stone," Viola demanded.

The hooded figure grabbed Aria's backpack and unzipped it. He reached his hand inside the bag and felt around. It felt like a lifetime before he zipped it back up and tossed it to the side.

"Nothing but clothes and bedding," Gamaliel replied. "The Life Stone's not in there."

"Where is it, girl?" Viola asked through clenched teeth, beginning to slowly dig the tips of her nails into Aria's neck.

Aria let out a cry and tried to pull away, but that only made it worse. Tears streamed down her cheeks.

"STOP! STOP!" Luke screamed, his voice sounding hoarse. He fought against Kora's grip, pulling one hand free and reaching for Aria as if he wished to pull her away. "She lost it! She lost it!"

Viola stopped and narrowed her eyes at him, a tinge of blood on the tips of her fingernails. Aria felt a drop slide down her throat at the same time she felt a tear drop down her cheek.

"She *lost it*?"

"Yeah," Luke lied, feigning confidence in his words.

"Well, I'm sure Malus will be able to sort out the truth," Kora interrupted, carelessly pushing Luke to the side.

He tumbled to the ground before bolting back to his feet and lunging at Kora. He pushed her to the ground with an Immobile Enchantment sparking in his palm. "You're not taking her anywhere."

Kora shoved him off her and gave him a swift kick to the stomach. He gripped her foot, tripping her so she fell, and magic pooled in his palm again. Kicking him away from her, she stood up and turned away from him like he wasn't even worth her time. "Viola, I'll teleport the girl, you, and Ebony, to Tungsinn."

Aria's hand wrapped around soft, silky black fabric just as Ebony and Chad released the rest of her friends. Luke stood, chest heaving.

"Try anything again and the little Diviner will suffer for it," Kora said as she strutted toward Aria and Viola.

Luke made a step forward and Viola pressed the tip of her fingernail against Aria's throat. Heat pulsed in Aria's palm, and she felt a blaze spark on the fabric. The warmth of it heated her numb, fear-stricken skin, but it was spreading. And fast. A scream erupted from Viola and she released Aria, sending her to the ground with her trembling legs.

"FIRE!" Viola screamed, jumping up and down and swatting at the blazing fire dancing across the fabric of her cloak. "YOU INFERNAL BRAT!"

She fell to the ground, rolling back and forth in the dirt. The fire would not relent, though, and was singeing through her clothes. High-pitched, inhuman screams pierced the air.

Kora and Ebony dropped to their knees at Viola's side, their eyes scanning the spreading fire. Gamaliel followed after them to help.

"Chad, get water, you moron!" Kora commanded, glaring at him.

Chad was startled out of his inaction, but he crossed his arms over his chest and disappeared from the scene.

"Viola, hold on," Ebony said as she worked Viola's cloak off her.

Aria picked up her backpack and flung it over her shoulders as fast as she could. Luke wrapped his arm around her, steadying her on her wobbling feet. The icy bite of rain hitting her skin made her shiver. She pressed her hand against her bleeding throat as they began running down the path, leaving the Dark Forces.

"Aria, are you okay?" Avi asked.

"Of course, she isn't, Avi," Willow said, giving a shake of her head.

"We'll get that cleaned up as soon as we're safe, Aria,"

Luke told her, but Aria was barely paying attention. All she could focus on was the oak tree approaching. If they could hide behind it for even just a few minutes, they could figure something out.

They turned the corner around cabin number eighteen and headed into the forest, stepping over all the fallen branches the wind had blown out of the trees. Aria winced at the sharp, stinging pain in her neck. She pulled her hand away to find it coated with blood.

"Aria, it's okay. It's okay," Luke reassured her in her ear. "You're going to be okay. We'll make sure of it."

Once they reached the tree, Luke helped her onto the soft, wet ground. She lifted the top of her shirt to her neck to soak up the blood. Avi started pacing back and forth in front of her while Willow sat down, trying to get a look at her wound.

"Where are we going to go?" Avi asked, throwing his hands up into the air. "Because this place is no longer safe for us to stay here. If we stay, they'll stay. We can't take them all. Eventually, they'll get Aria if we do stay, and that would mean…"

"Danger for the whole world of magic," Aria whispered.

Luke nodded. "There is only one place we can go—where we won't be torn to shreds just by teleporting somewhere we don't know—and where the Dark Forces can't find us." He gazed off through the trees, looking as if he was contemplating something. "And that's Diamond Falls."

"Diamond Falls?" Avi's eyebrows raised and he shook his head. "Remember what happened last time? Last time we were captured by the Dark Forces!"

"That was because we went to Bola," Luke said. "If we steer clear of it, we should be fine."

"And what about the Timber Giants?" Aria's voice sounded soft and hoarse. "They almost killed us last time."

"Timber Giants are generally kind, Aria." Willow's eyes were soft. "We just have to be cautious. They probably felt threatened when they saw us."

"It's the only option we have," Luke said. "We need to get out of here."

Aria nodded in agreement, sending a wave of aching through her neck and her teeth clenched together.

"From one dangerous place to another." Avi let out an annoyed groan and flung his hand into the air before squatting down next to them. "Whatever. Let's just get out of here."

"I'll teleport us there, then," Luke said as he grasped Aria's hand.

Willow took hold of Aria's other hand and Aria clenched her eyes shut, trying to clear her head. Everything suddenly went silent. The rain stopped pelting Aria's skin. The thunder rolling overhead abruptly stopped. Lighting wasn't flashing on the other side of Aria's eyelids. But a rushing wind seemed to be all around them. The air started to change, stirring up energy full of static that made the hair on her head stand up. A tingling feeling tickled her skin as if her limbs were falling asleep. Then Aria felt as if she was flying ten feet into the air before she was dropped into the freezing water of Diamond Falls.

CHAPTER TWELVE

THE TEMPERATURE OF the water clawed into Aria's limbs, sinking down to her bones, and racking her body with shivers. Her head sank beneath the surface and water plunged into her nose. Luke's firm grasp around her hand pulled her back to the surface, the cool autumn air prickling her skin. She coughed and spat water from her mouth. Willow and Avi were already wading to the shore, drenched in water and shaking to their cores.

"I—I didn't e-expect to be d-d-dumped in water...again." Aria trembled as she and Luke pushed themselves through the frigid water.

Luke's arm wrapped around her back, helping keep her stable. "Yeah, sorry about that."

As they made it to the shore, Aria took in the beauty of Diamond Falls. Just a few months ago, she had been there while it was summer. It was gorgeous with the crystal-clear waters and cascading waterfalls, the bright green vegetation and red birds flying through the skies. But now, in autumn, it was somehow even more stunning. There was a crisp, calming scent of pine and the leaves were now a mix of gold, brown, orange, and red. Back at Camp Enchanted, nearly all the trees were only half-full of leaves, but at Diamond Falls, they were immensely filled. Wind was blowing through the branches, raining leaves on the four of them. The sky above was clear and calm, the sun shining down on the glistening lake. The water may have been able to chill bones, but it was still as beautiful as last time, with the teal waters that truly did remind Aria of diamonds.

Aria plopped down on the ground by a tree, one hand held firmly against her neck and the other trying to ring out her clothes. Willow was already going through her bag before she cast it aside, shaking her head in frustration.

"I wish I were a Healer instead of a Mind-reader, Aria," Willow said. "I don't have anything to help close up your wound other than clothes. I'd have to shred something, though." She gripped her arms, shaking as a rush of wind blew past. "It's freezing out here. We need to get out of these clothes and make some sort of camp…Then we can figure things out."

Luke sat next to Aria, pulling off his own bag. He held out his hands palm up and closed his eyes for many minutes, the lids of his eyes moving as his eyeballs moved beneath. His hands lit with a faint light and then a red box appeared in his hands, *First Aid* written in black marker on the top.

"I can take care of Aria's wound," he said, then closed his eyes again. A dark green packed-up eight-person tent conjured up in his lap and he grunted at the sudden weight, pushing it off him. "And there's some shelter." He looked up at Willow and Avi. "If you two could set it up, we each could take turns changing in there. There are three rooms in it and the windows can be zipped closed so you can't see into it."

They stared in amazement for a moment at what Luke had just conjured before they started into action.

"Y-yeah, I suppose we could do that," Willow said, picking up the tent. "Avi, could you help me?"

Willow and Avi started unzipping the tent and pulling it out. Luke kept the first aid kit in his hand and turned to Aria, opening it.

As he started pulling out gauze, peroxide, antibiotics, and other medical supplies, Aria said, "Where did you get all this from?"

Luke swept her hair back and took off her sunflower necklace, traces of blood stuck to the petals, then set it carefully in her hands. He squirted some peroxide on a cotton ball before applying it to Aria's neck wounds. Both a shiver and ache went through her neck as his fingers skimmed her skin. She blinked away the tears gathering in her eyes. She didn't know if it was the pain of the wound, her soaked clothes, or simply that Luke was so close, but she couldn't stop trembling. Her heart was pounding way too fast.

Luke took a deep breath before speaking. "My parents, my brother, and I used to hike a lot and we would come here often. In August, before school started up again, I had to put all of this in storage. My parents' things for their job needed somewhere to go while they were home with us, so I packed it away in the garage." He paused, a weary look of sorrow passing over his face. "Good thing I was able to remember where it was so I could conjure it."

Willow and Avi—Avi doing the least amount of work—had the tent nearly all the way up, but it kept flopping over. It was massive and had a huge room in the center, and one on each side.

"Willow, where does it say this pole goes?" Avi held up a black bendable pole.

"Oh, no wonder it keeps falling over!" She took it from him

and stuck it in the ground at the base of the tent, then fed it through slots on the side of one of the rooms, before stabbing it in the ground on the other side.

"It still looks a little floppy…Did we do it right?"

"Let me check the directions," Willow said, a frustrated edge creeping into her voice as she grabbed the instructions off the ground.

Luke pushed a strand of Aria's brown hair back behind her ear, gazing at her face. She looked back at him. Heat crept up into her cheeks and she licked her lips, remembering that moment in the hallway right before the attack.

"Hey, Luke, how do you put this thing up?" Avi called, pulling Luke's attention away. "Because I think Willow's confused." He let the side of the tent he was holding fall to the forest floor and Willow let out a sigh.

"I'll be there in a minute," Luke muttered before grabbing gauze and helping wrap it around Aria's neck.

She couldn't take her eyes off him, a tingling feeling in her stomach. Her teeth sank into her lip as the gauze rubbed against the wound, and she winced. Luke pulled away but kept his eyes on her.

"Th-thank you," she said, her voice sounding hoarse.

"You're welcome." He shoved everything back into the first aid kit. Then he left it beside Aria and got up to help Willow and Avi.

Aria's head pounded like her heart, which was still rapidly beating against her ribs. She closed her eyes and bit down on her tongue, trying to push away the pain that was coming in waves over her neck. But then visions flashed behind her eyelids of the camp; fire, screams, and black cloaks billowing in the wind. The Dark Forces had caused destruction and fear, and Aria's stomach tightened at the thought of them creating more.

What if they didn't leave the camp? Aria could only hope that they would follow after them. Try as they might to find them in the expanse of the Vezchia Realm. Aria had put the people around her in enough danger by simply being there.

"Ta-da!" Avi said, letting go of the dark green tent. It stood sturdy, wide, and as tall as Luke, with a closed zippered door and closed windows.

Willow unzipped the door and climbed inside with her clothes while Luke and Avi stood outside, shaking in the cold wind that was picking up. Aria was trembling too, her fingers and toes feeling as if they were going to turn blue. Leaves rained down on them in both bright and muted colors. How could such colors look so warm when it was so cold out? Luke glanced over at Aria and their eyes met, pity flickering in them when he saw her.

Aria was bundled up into warm clothes, three layers of socks in place of her soaked shoes that were sitting outside the tent. She had her thick hoodie that the camp had provided on, and was wrapped up in the blanket she'd stolen from her bunk bed back at camp as well. With so many blankets and pillows strewn all over the inside of the tent, it was nearly cozy. The floor was lumpy and hard like a rock, though, and the cold air pressed through every layer with determination. And it was only getting more frigid as the sun slipped farther down the horizon.

Two pieces of fabric hung from the ceiling of the tent to serve as walls, creating a room on each side of the tent. Luke and Avi were several feet away in the far-left room, meanwhile, Aria and Willow were in the far-right room. The middle room served as the main room where all the bags and food were kept.

Luke had conjured more camping supplies, including food and more blankets and pillows hours ago.

He and Avi were whispering about what to do from the other room, but Aria was so exhausted that she couldn't focus. The day had passed by, and none of them had brought up that subject yet. Aria didn't want to think about it, so she couldn't blame them for not wanting to earlier either. What was there to do? The Dark Forces were just going to keep coming after them. There was only one solution, and only that one thing spun through her mind.

The words of Aria's mother and father echoed through her head. There had always been things they had not told her—she knew that now, but there was one thing they had forgotten to mention the last time she had seen them…when she saw them bound by iron and tears.

"You are the Diviner…" her mother's words floated into her mind.

Her parents had told her of the Life Stone and the Death Stone, that she had to destroy them, but not *how* to destroy them. She didn't even know where the Death Stone was. But she had to find it. For her parents. For the realms. And for herself.

Willow sat up from where she lay next to Aria, bundled up underneath blankets. She tapped Aria's shoulder and scooched closer. A bandage was tightly secured around her arm in place of Avi's red handkerchief from earlier.

"Aria…back at camp and at the school…Your magic isn't fully under your control, is it?" Willow kept her voice down so Luke and Avi couldn't hear from the other room. Aria looked the other way, her stomach twisting with shame. When she didn't answer, Willow continued, "Something is bothering you. I mean, I know that is obvious, with everything going on. But I mean something more—something bigger is bothering you. I can feel it."

"You know, you'd be a great therapist," Aria noted, then sighed. "There's a lot of things bothering me. We literally just fled camp while it was being attacked today and I don't know if anyone will be alright. All we can do is hope they've left to follow us." She looked down at her hands as if there was something wrong with them. "But this power thing…I don't know. That started after the Malus trial. It's as if my magic thinks it can do whatever it wants—like it doesn't belong to me."

"Or maybe it's the opposite?" Willow suggested.

Aria's brows furrowed, trying to comprehend how her powers acting as if they didn't belong to her could have an opposite. But she was drawn from the thought and conversation when Luke spoke up from the other room.

"Aria, we need to decide on what we are going to do next. If we stay for somewhere too long…" He trailed off, Aria knowing what he was going to say.

If they stayed somewhere for too long, danger was sure to find them. *Nowhere is safe anymore.*

Aria took a deep breath as Willow yawned beside her. "I know. I know what we have to do. We have to find the Death Stone, and before the Dark Forces do," she said. "And we'll figure that all out, but I'm sure we're all exhausted. Let's get some rest and we can talk about it in the morning."

She turned to ask Willow what she'd meant about her powers, but Willow had fallen asleep. Feeling like she'd missed an opportunity to understand, Aria looked back down at her hands as if they held the answers buried deep inside her.

CHAPTER THIRTEEN

THE SUN HAD set hours ago, and the temperature of the air now felt like ice itself. Inside the tent, Luke, Avi, and Willow slept wrapped up in thick wool blankets. Outside was nearly pitch black except for the golden, glittering fairies dancing through the air behind trees, scared to come too close as Aria made her way through the silence. Last time Aria had been at Diamond Falls, she had never stayed up late enough to see the animals and creatures that woke with the moon. There was a beauty in the darkness—it made what little bit of light there was shine brighter. And in the still calm that autumn brought, it offered peace.

There were too many things running through Aria's head that needed to be solved. Even after telling Luke that they should all get some rest, her mind wouldn't fall asleep.

At the bank of the Diamond Fall's Lake, Aria sat down. The water was calm with the full moon reflecting on its surface and the wind was still. The air pricked at her skin even through all the layers she wore. She sighed, clouds appearing before her face. The crunch of the leaves and the snap of a stick alerted her, and she quickly stood up, the frigid water from the lake pooling into the palms of her hands with ease. Shards of ice appeared in the air beside her, ready to find a target. As she turned around, her heartbeat picked up with her anxiety.

It was just Luke. He was standing a few feet away, cautiously staying back with his hands raised above his head as if in surrender, a half-smile quirking up at his lips. Aria loved that smile—it made her heart flutter back to a normal rhythm as the water in her hands fell back into the lake. The shards of ice clattered to the ground and melted away.

"Sorry, I didn't mean to scare you," Luke said, putting his hands down and walking towards her. "Couldn't sleep?"

"No." Aria sat back down at the shore and pulled her knees in close to her chest.

Luke plopped down next to her, giving a sleepy yawn. Aria watched the moon cast glimmers on the water and her hands absentmindedly went to her throat. Usually, she'd wrap her hands around her necklace as if it could reassure her of something and keep her safe. But it was tucked safely in her backpack, so her fingers gently moved across the spot Viola had dug her nails in. Luke watched her closely from the corner of his eye, and Aria assumed he thought she couldn't sleep because of the injury. Their eyes met and he quickly looked away, a strange silence falling on them for a few moments.

"Aria, whenever you're hurting, you can tell me what's wrong. It's not fair if we laugh and talk together, yet you cry alone." Luke turned toward her, his blue eyes soft. "You don't have to bottle it all up and hide it."

A moment of silence passed as she simply stared at him, unable to form words. She wanted to shove the cork on that metaphorical bottle deeper so it couldn't come undone, but maybe Luke was right.

"I couldn't sleep because of everything that's happened,"

she said, deciding to be honest and open up. "We have to find the Death Stone and we don't even know where to start. It's as if this quest is a hundred riddles without answers. The Dark Forces attacked the camp *again* because of *me*, and I can only hope that they left." She paused, turning her head towards him. "Why couldn't *you* sleep?"

He looked down at his hands, rubbing them together. When he spoke, a cloud of fog appeared in the air. "I can't sleep knowing you're out here in the cold. What Viola did to you—I know I could only do so much to heal it. I just want to make sure you're okay."

I'm fine, is what she wanted to say. It was on the tip of her tongue, but she held it back, knowing it was a lie. Instead, she looked out over the lake again and sighed.

Silence hung between them again for many moments as glittering gold fairies danced along the edge of the water several feet from them.

"Aria, I know you worry about the camp. But you can't blame yourself because of what the Dark Forces did. It wasn't your fault. I'm sure that by us leaving, they left too. They're after us, not the campers."

"They're after *me*, Luke," she said. "You, Avi, and Willow are a part of all this, but it's me that the Dark Forces want. They want the Diviner, and they'll destroy anything in their way to get to it." Hot tears started to well in her eyes. She tried to fight them back, but one spilled down her cheek. "My parents are imprisoned b-because of m-me. Malus could have k-k-killed them al-already." Her voice cracked as shudders racked her body. Her fingers longed to wrap around her sunflower neck-lace, one of the few things she still had with her that reminded her of her parents. More tears welled up in her eyes. She'd been shoving those cries down, but now they were escaping along with the words. A knot of embarrassment balled up in her chest at saying such burdening things.

"Aria, Malus won't—he hasn't…They know too much for him to do that." Luke gripped Aria's free hand, scooting close to her and tucking the hair that was hanging in front of her face behind her ear. Tears stained her face, darkening her eyelashes.

"But soon, if we—if *I* don't stop him, he *will* kill them." Fresh tears poured down her face, her parents' own tear-stained faces flashing in her mind like a haunting memory. "He only cares about capturing me now…capturing the Diviner."

Her face fell into her hands and her body shook at an onslaught of thoughts running through her head. Luke wrapped his arm around her back, drawing her against him, and held her close.

"The way Elaine and Natalie looked at me in the mess hall—it was as if I'm a monster," Aria said, imagining it in her head. "This whole Diviner thing doesn't feel human. So much power running in my veins…I've never been special like that. It doesn't feel like it's really there—like this is just some kind of curse to torture me with." A lump lodged in her throat. "I *feel* like a monster."

"Aria, you're not—"

"Yes, I am Luke." She looked away, her wet, glassy blue eyes shimmering as the stars and moon reflected in them. "I am different than everyone else. I'm powerful and have magic that nobody else is capable of having…even if I can't use it yet…"

"So, what? Everyone is different in their own way. The choices and decisions we make are what make us good or bad." He caught her chin, forcing her to look at him. "And you, Aria, I know are good. You're a good person who bad people want to use. But your powers are not you. You're the same Aria I met when you joined Incanting Academy. And I—I—" He broke off as a creak sounded through the wind.

The leaves rustled and the breeze swept over the lake, rippling the moon's reflection. Another loud creak echoed. The two of them looked around, Aria wiping the blurring tears from her vision. There was nothing around but the forest and leaves rustling in the wind.

"I still don't know what we're going to do, though," Aria said, her voice breaking on the words. "We have no one, and my parents didn't have the chance to tell me how to find the Death Stone."

"Sometimes we can't depend on other people for things…" He sighed before a painful look crossed his face. "Sometimes you just have to take a leap of faith." His face contorted, but Aria had a hard time reading it in the dark. All she could discern was a frown, the moonlight glinting in his sorrowfully soft eyes. "I mean, just look at what happened to my family. Christopher, my parents, and I used to be so close…" His voice broke on the last word. "But I'm alone now, and I have to take that leap of faith. And that leap is towards you…towards hope."

Tears streamed down Aria's cheeks at his words. *Hope.* "Luke, don't let go of your family. You will never know how deeply someone means to you until you call their name and they don't respond. Family is everything, even if you grow in a different direction than them. We each have our own paths to forge. We each have our own leaps of faith to make, just like you said. And mine is toward hope too."

Aria gazed up at his face as a tear dripped down his cheek. A shudder of her breath shook her body and she grabbed his hand. She still hadn't admitted her feelings to him, but people do crazy things when they're tired. Fatigue was getting the best of her and she knew they should head back to the tent, even if what she truly wanted was to stay in the moonlight, right there with Luke, for hours on end. Luke seemed to know they should head back too. So, he held tight to her hand, helped her up from the shore, and they walked back to the warmth of the tent in silence.

The sun rose with the bird songs and the soft autumn breeze that flung golden leaves across the forest floor. Aria had bags under her eyes and her bones felt like they might snap. The aching in her neck was muted now and she could feel it already scabbing over. Willow was the first to get up, pulling out all the snacks Luke had conjured the day before. She threw a package to each of them before plopping down next to Aria in the tent and bundling back up under the thick blankets. Sitting in the main room, they each tore open the packs, their stomachs aching with hunger.

"So, what are we going to do?" Avi said around a mouthful of dried jerky.

"Well, since we have to find the Death Stone, we should go to Viden." Willow dumped her honey and oat bars into her hands.

"What's in Viden?" Avi asked.

"Honestly, do any of you read?" Willow blew out a frustrated puff of air. "In Viden lies the only other copy of the Death Stone Riddle, which was copied after some Forces of Light spies infiltrated Malus' rank. Now it sits in the Library of Knowledge."

Avi blinked, dumbfounded, at her. "Why didn't you tell us that *yesterday?*"

"After what happened yesterday, we all deserved a few hours of a break. I'm sorry I didn't mention it," Willow replied. "Any of you could have remembered, though. We all took the same classes at one point, and it says it in nearly every textbook that talks about that subject."

"Where is Viden, though?" Luke asked.

"That, I do not have an answer to." Willow poured the rest of the contents of the food package into her mouth and shoved it into her bag. "There are maps that show where it is, but I read books, not maps."

"We can just teleport," Avi said. "We've been in Enchanting Control before, and that's within the city."

"No, we can't. There's an Anti-teleportation Charm on the entire city." Willow shook her head. "Enchanting Control's lobby is one of the only places the Anti-teleportation Charm doesn't apply, but even if we did teleport into Enchanting Control, that would be a horrible idea. There are spies in Enchanting Control…" She trailed off, likely thinking about her father, the sketchy trial, and everything Kora had said.

"Fine, then scratch that," Avi muttered.

A sudden, loud creak resounded from outside, startling all of them. It sounded like the same creak that Aria and Luke had heard the night before. Willow urgently unzipped the front of the tent and rolled out of it, onto the leaf strewn ground. Aria, Luke, and Avi followed after her, dropping their belongings in the tent. Outside, the wind was chilled and shifting, a loud creak coming from one of the trees. A tree near the bank of the lake shifted in the wind. The tree was shorter than all the others with autumn leaves higher up in the tree than usual, giving Aria the impression of an afro. It twisted and moved, making Aria and her friends step back. The branches turned to arms and the base uprooted, showing two feet—if Aria could even call them that. Aria and her friends' eyes went wide, and their hands raised in a defensive position. The limbs of the tree had hands, feet, and fingers, but no toes. Moss clung to the tree's body like splatters of paint in random spots. Two large eyes rested in the middle of the trunk in what must have been a face. Facial features looked to have been carved from bark by a skilled craftsman, and Aria knew at once with a jolt of her stomach that she was staring at a Timber Giant.

They all gasped and took an instinctive step back, their hearts hammering against their ribs. Aria's blood ran cold and every nerve went off, telling her to run. Last time they'd seen a Timber Giant in these woods, they'd nearly been killed.

"I say we run on the count of three," Avi whispered.

"Dear Diviner," the Timber Giant said, the tone of its voice deep, yet almost in a young kind of way. A small patch of moss grew above his lips like a faint mustache. He spoke unsteadily as if he was unsure of himself. "D-did Strom speak right? Strom speak E-en-gee-lish?"

Aria gasped and her jaw dropped, frozen in place. "H-how do you know?" The words tumbled out of her mouth, and she wasn't sure whether she was asking how the giant knew she was the Diviner or how he knew English.

"Strom be by w-water. Strom be by Diviner and Diviner's love."

"What?" The blood rushed into Aria's face, her eyes darting to Luke.

"Th-that is not what we are," Luke said, his face a shade of pink as he pointed between Aria and him. "We're not in love."

A snort behind her made Aria glance backward to see Avi and Willow rolling their eyes. Her cheeks reddened. The Timber Giant seemed to tilt his head, looking perplexed. "Diviner a-and boy not in love." It sounded more like a confused statement than anything else. "Diviner need to be at Viden?"

"Y-yes," Aria managed. Her head was in a whirlpool of thoughts, mostly about the last thing the tree had said, along with the fact that the tree could speak *English*. "Do you know how to get there?"

"Strom take you to Viden. Yes, Strom will." The tree was matter-of-fact in the way he spoke, looking between the four of them with soft, gentle eyes.

"Are you Strom?" Willow asked.

"Strom is me," replied the Timber Giant. "Strom been to Viden before this time."

"You've been there? And you'll take us?"

"Yes," Strom answered, a smile seeming to cross his face. "For Diviner, Strom will take thee." With a shake of the ground, he dropped to one of his bark-covered knees and pressed one hand to where his heart may have been if he even had one. "Tis been centuries of waiting for Diviner. Now Diviner c-can bring us c-creatures out of slave-work. Dis a dark world. Now Diviner can bring peace. Strom will take Diviner and friends to Viden—to the Stone Riddle."

Chapter Fourteen

ALL OF THEIR things had been packed up and shoved into their bags a couple of hours ago, including their wet clothes that had dried out in the sun. Now Strom walked beside Aria, staring at her with admiration twinkling in his black eyes. Somehow his dark eyes could hold so much emotion in them. He looked at her as if she were something out of a daydream, which put her on edge as they trekked deeper into the forest. Willow had once said Timber Giants were kind creatures. The first Aria had met of their kind hadn't lived up to that, though. Strom was the opposite of those giants in every way, with his kind words, help, and his wise guidance. He was so unfamiliar, yet she felt guarded by him as if he were a lifelong friend. It made so many questions bubble up inside of Aria's head.

Strom led the way, saying something occasionally about how he was taking the Diviner to Viden. He walked carefully with each step like he was afraid he'd squish the dying grass too much. One of his fingers trailed along the bark of a tree as they passed it, a smile bent at his lips.

"So pretty," Strom said softly and turned back to Aria again. "Got to protect the forest. Forest is home."

Aria thought back to those barbaric Timber Giants she'd met over the summer for what had to be the millionth time since meeting Strom. It was no wonder they'd attacked—Aria and her friends had walked right into their home.

"Timber Giants be protectors of forest, protectors of forest's creatures," Strom added, gazing at the woods that stretched out before them with what seemed like no end.

Luke was on Aria's other side, silent as their feet crunched through the fallen leaves. The birds chirped and sang songs high up in the trees, and red firebirds soared above the treetops. A crisp, chilly air filled Aria's lungs and bit at her nose. The tips of her nose and ears were going numb from the cold, and she didn't want to imagine the thought of what it would be like when the snow started to fall weeks from now.

Back at home, she had loved waking up in the mornings of November to find light dustings of snow covering the grass. As soon as her father would come home, the three of them would run outside and try to catch snowflakes on their tongues as they fell from the cloudy sky…But that was a long time ago.

She pulled herself from the memories, trying to keep her focus on getting to Viden. Strom had said that it was far away, or in his own words, *"sun-sights away from them."* Willow had to help interpret that, but she could only figure that it was many days away, possibly even weeks or months.

"Strom, how do you know English?" Aria couldn't keep herself from asking, as the question had been nagging at her since they'd left hours ago. The previous Timber Giants she'd met spoke their own language.

Strom's voice turned soft and rough as if the words were painful. "Strom be a slave a time before now. Strom do slave-work for rich in Viden." He looked down at his rough hands, where his bark-skin looked sanded down from use.

Aria immediately regretted asking. Moments ago he'd looked so full of delight, but the look on his face now made her heart ache. She tried to think through his words and fix the broken English so she could understand him better, but Willow was faster.

"In other words, Strom worked for the rich people in Viden. I've read about the slavery of Timber Giants in a book once." Willow laid a hand against Strom's bark-covered arm at his side. "I'm sorry to hear that, Strom." A look of empathy crossed her face, the brightness of her blue eyes dulling.

"That's a thing? People do that?" Aria's lips twisted in disgust and her eyes narrowed as she thought of it.

Then she noticed the white stripes along Strom's back, a stark contrast to the color of his bark. Small ground-out white grooves were struck along the edges of the stripes. Aria's face fell as she realized they were scars, likely from a spike-covered whip.

"Sadly, yeah." Willow glanced at the scars too, then at Aria. They shared a silent look of mournful understanding but didn't say anything.

"Timber Giants be tough, strong, good to build things." Strom sounded resigned as if that's just the way it had to be all these centuries since there was no one willing to stop the cruelty.

Willow continued to add onto what Strom was saying. "Viden is the richest city in the Vezchia Realm, and all those who can afford it enslave Timber Giants to build homes, businesses, and do what they can't—or really, to do what they're too lazy to do…It's been going on for about three hundred years." She looked at Aria, her eyes softening. "Ever since the Diviner disappeared."

Aria's heart squeezed and her face fell. "But the Forces of Light—why don't they do anything?"

Luke broke in, his voice low and aggravated. "Because they can't. Enchanting Control is above them in power, and Enchanting Control refuses to do anything about it. Sure, they're both allies, but the Forces of Light have to abide by their rules. I don't know. There's something sketchy about it all."

Strom sighed, causing a creak in his body as he took in the carbon dioxide from the air and released oxygen. Hatred for Enchanting Control grew in Aria's chest, more than it already had since hearing that the judge at Malus' trial could have been a spy. Aria pondered how Strom was out in the wilderness if he'd been enslaved but didn't question him. The topic seemed tainted by despair.

"As soon as I can, I will end it." It took everything in her to say the words. How could she end something so much bigger than herself? But it's what Aria felt she should say, and what Strom deserved to hear. Even if it felt like a lie.

The sun shined high in the sky, casting rays of light through the golden leaves above them. Strom was on his knees—or at least, that's what they appeared to be—as he searched for something in a large bush. A breeze blew through the air, stirring up Aria's hair. She pulled her jacket tighter around her. Their backpacks lay in a pile against one of the tree trunks nearby as they searched for some food. Willow, of course, was searching for mushrooms, which had sickened Aria over the summer. Leaves rained down on them, covering up anything that may have been edible.

Strom drew his hands back from the bush and a smile lit

up his face. "W-winterberries!" Many teal berries were piled in his hand.

Aria's brows furrowed. "Aren't winterberries red?"

At one of her old homes when she was six, there had been a winterberry bush in their backyard and she would always pick them. They had been shiny and red in the winter, but these weren't.

Strom looked confused as if what she was saying was in another language—maybe because it wasn't his first language.

Willow reached for a handful of the teal berries. "The Vezchia Realm is different in many ways, being that there's magic everywhere. I'm sure that this is one of those ways." She popped the berries into her mouth, her eyes widening. "*These are delicious!*"

"Better than mushrooms, I bet." Aria smirked.

Avi chuckled beside her. "Don't even say that word or we'll be forced to eat mushrooms again."

They sat on the forest floor eating the berries for a while, with their backs up against trees. Aria watched curiously as Strom sat cross-legged and ate the berries too. Seeing the Timber Giant being so human-like made her want to know more about him, about those scars on his back, and about other Timber Giants. Still, she kept her mouth shut about *that* and decided to talk about other things.

"So, Strom, what do you like to do for fun?" Aria asked and popped a berry into her mouth.

Strom's face lit up with passion. "Strom like to play with animals." He pointed up at an animal with sunset orange fuzzy fur, pointy little ears, and huge starry eyes running across a branch. It looked like a living puff ball.

Avi's eyes grew wide. "I want it!" He reached his hands out as if he could grab it despite being several feet away from it.

Willow gently pushed his hands down. "You're not keeping a Treeburt as a pet."

Avi pursed his lips and crossed his arms, face beginning to look like a stormy cloud. "Other people keep them as pets."

"Strom also like to plant," Strom continued cheerily. He pointed to the foliage around them, the leaves turning brown with the turn of the season. "Strom plant seeds around forest. Winter coming, so Strom not plant them now."

Aria smiled and her eyes twinkled, humor rising into her mind. *A tree giant that likes to garden.*

"I'm thirsty," Avi said, pulling his backpack into his lap. He dug through it and pulled out a canteen, one of the things Luke had conjured the day before. The top popped off and Avi lifted it to his lips, only to find it was empty. "C'mon! We just left Diamond Falls this morning!"

Aria turned away from Strom. "Hold on, let me try something." She closed her eyes and tried to remember the feeling she'd felt when she pulled water from the grass and air to save Avi from the fire, and how she did the same thing to save herself from Ebony.

Her magic gathered in her palms, crackling with waiting energy. She felt the pull of the water and the pulsing of her heartbeat in her veins before the water was sucked from a patch of grass near the base of the tree. The grass immediately turned a dead brown as the water pooled into Aria's palms. She opened her eyes and lifted it into the air, hands circling around it to manipulate its movement. Everyone stopped and stared between her and the water, jaws slack.

"Willow, could you purify this?" Aria asked, reaching out to pass it over.

Willow nodded and started into action, pulling the water

through the air and into her own palms. "Everyone, pull out a canteen please."

Aria's hands grazed all the other objects floating around in the void of her bag until she found her canteen. Beside her, Luke and Avi dug theirs out as well. Willow pulled dirt, bacteria, and grass from the water hovering above her palm. The pile of stuff fell to the ground and got lost amongst the foliage. Avi set his canteen in front of her and she filled it, then repeated that with Luke's, Aria's, and her own. They sat there, drinking their fill, as a red bird slowly crept towards the pile of berries Strom was creating. The bird was about three feet tall, startling Aria as she watched it grab a teal berry with its sharp, black beak. Up above the treetops, the red birds had appeared so much smaller. Golden, scarlet, yellow, and orange feathers covered its folded wings, but they all looked ruffled, dirty, and ragged. Its back was bent forward like it held a crushing weight. Yellow, crusty, mucus-looking stuff was caked up under its shiny, tear-filled eyes.

"How fascinating," Willow said, crawling toward the creature with wide eyes. "A phoenix. They're known to be lucky. To have one come so near us...I would say we are in luck with something."

"We never get lucky," Aria muttered, her eyes locked on the peculiar bird.

"Not with that attitude, you won't."

Avi held out his handful of berries to the bird and it suddenly burst into flames. Strom fell backwards, avoiding the fire so it wouldn't touch his wooden skin. With wide eyes, everyone else fell back away from the burning bird. The fire scorched through the phoenix's feathers, but it didn't even scream. Aria's heartbeat drummed in her ears as the flames went out. The bird was nothing but a pile of ash now. Bile rose in Aria's throat. That had to be one of the most disturbing things she'd ever seen.

"*What* in the *world* was that?" Aria paled, her eyebrows raised.

The ashes shifted on the forest floor before a featherless, pink head poked out from the dust. Sleepy black eyes blinked at them and its black beak opened up to yawn.

"Phoenixes are reborn," Willow said, smiling at the remarkably cute creature that sat before them, covered in ashes. "It's amazing, isn't it? They live on forever, catching fire when it's time for them to die and be born again from their ashes, just like dragons."

"Dragons are reborn too?" Aria's eyes went wide. "So, there's no killing those things?"

"If something else kills a dragon, they die permanently. If they die on their own, they are reborn," Willow answered with her eyes trained on the little bird. "Same with a phoenix."

The phoenix stood up and shook the ashes from its peach-colored, fuzzy skin. Its eyes gleamed as if a fire were radiating inside them.

Avi grinned. "Aw, it's so cute."

"It looks naked," Aria muttered, the edges of her lips quirking up. "I mean, it is kind of cute though…"

Avi leaned forward and reached out for it with his hands.

"Avi!" Willow's eyes widened and went to pull his hands back, but it was already too late.

Avi picked up the ash-covered little bird, rubbing its tiny head. "I'm going to keep her."

"Avi, it's a wild creature! You can't!" Willow crossed her arms and glared at him. "I just told you that you couldn't have a Treeburt, so now you want a pet *phoenix?*"

Aria looked at him as if he had truly lost his mind. "Not to mention, it's a liability!"

"But it's just a baby…" Avi said, pushing out his lips to make a pouty face. "I'm going to call her…Celestia."

"How do you even know if it's a girl?" Aria asked.

"Because female phoenixes are born with lighter peach fuzz," Luke answered for her. His voice wasn't unkind, but Aria felt it should have been obvious even if she didn't know. "Males are darker in color."

The firebird hopped out of Avi's hand and wobbled over to Aria. She cringed away from it, afraid of it bursting into flames again. It hobbled into her lap and started up her arm before she could move.

"Ah, what's it doing?" Aria watched it nervously. "It's not going to attack me, is it?"

The phoenix got to her shoulder and reached its beak out to grab the gauze around Aria's neck. Aria sucked in a breath at the gauze rubbing at the wound underneath. She reached up to grab the bird just as the gauze came away and fell to the ground.

"Aria, no!" Willow said, her eyes lighting up. "She wants to heal you. Pheonix tears have healing abilities."

Aria felt the firebird press its face up against the wound and she ground her teeth against the pain. Then she felt a tear slide down her throat and the discomfort faded away. A warmth spread across her neck like pure sunshine and she lifted her hand to touch her throat. There was nothing but smooth skin there now. The firebird wobbled its way back down Aria's arm and over to Willow's injured arm, eyes gleaming. Strom leaned forward, watching the bird with his eyes twinkling.

Aria simply stared in awe, understanding just how lucky she was that Celestia had found them. Then she stood up before grabbing her bag and sliding it onto her shoulders. "Whether she's coming with us or not, we need to get moving again. Night is going to come quickly."

As they gathered their things, Celestia snuggled up in Avi's hands like they were a warm bed. The little firebird peered sleepily at the five of them, eyes landing on Strom curiously. He waved at her with a smile and her eyes fell closed.

As the sky started to lighten the next day, Aria lay bundled in the blankets next to Willow in the tent. Her legs felt like noodles from all the constant walking the day before and her mind grappled for rest that didn't want to come. Luke and Avi were in the other room—Avi already awake, talking to his new pet, Celestia. As much as Aria didn't like the idea of taking a creature from its home and having it as a liability, she had healed Aria and the very presence of the firebird seemed to warm the tent. She also brought Avi some happiness. Celestia too seemed to be clingy to Avi, always watching him as he spoke to her and responding with soft songs. The bird loved to sing—even now, she hummed a tune to Avi. Willow stirred and sat up at the noise, before trying to shake Aria from her pretend sleep. Aria rolled over and kept her eyes clenched shut, begging sleep to wash over her.

"Aria, wake up," Willow said.

Aria responded with a grunt and in her head, she thought, *But I don't want to.*

"C'mon, Aria. We need to get going." She tried to roll Aria onto her back, but Aria was stiff as a wooden plank.

She must have given up because she disappeared from the room and the sound of ruffling bags came from the main room. Then a snack pack hit Aria in the face and she rolled over, shoving it away from her.

"Get up…Please," Willow said, forcing a welcoming smile on her face.

Aria sighed and shoved her face into her pillow, mumbling a *No.*

Willow plopped down next to her, patting her on the back. "Did you not sleep last night? What's up?"

"Not *me*," Aria said, drawing the blanket over her head.

Avi laughed at Aria's reply from the other room and Celestia mimicked the sound through a strange song of hers.

Finally, after ten minutes, Aria pulled her own blanket off and they got ready to take down the tent and leave.

As they continued, hilly terrain and snow-peaked mountains grew close, making it hard to see them completely from the ground. The farther they went, the more trees had fewer leaves left to fall. The ground was coated in browns and reds that crunched under their feet. Aria's hands grew so cold she had to stuff them in the pockets of her jacket.

"You really seem to know the area, Strom," Willow said as they made their way to the edge of a creek. "Thank you for helping us. I'm not sure what we would have done without you."

"Strom know forest. Strom live here with family sunarounds before now...Before we be slaves." Strom looked down at the creek before stepping into it with a splash and walking to the other side.

"Your family?" Willow's voice was light as she followed Strom by hopping on boulders.

Aria, Luke, and Avi started across the rocks, avoiding the slippery spots. Aria crouched low, balancing her weight, and stepped on the stones.

"Stromses family be captured and taken to Viden with Strom. Slaves family be," Strom answered as they got to the other side of the creek. "Then all Timber Giants try to escape. Enchanters and enchantresses use fire to burn. Strom and others got out. Family did not." Strom's head hung low. "Sun-arounds ago. Now Strom live in forest for sun-arounds."

Avi gulped and quickly wiped his hand over his eyes. "I guess that's something we sort of have in common."

Aria tried to piece together Strom's words and correct the broken English. Strom's family had been captured and taken to Viden to be used as slaves. She guessed that 'sun-arounds ago' could mean years if 'sun-sights' meant days, weeks, or months. It was really confusing, and if she was right, she still didn't know how many years ago that had happened to Strom. How long had it been since he'd escaped and lost his family in the process? She had so many questions she wanted to ask him, but she felt asking wouldn't be kind.

However, she couldn't just ignore what he'd told them, so she spoke carefully. "Strom, are you sure you still want to take us to Viden? We don't want to force you to go back there."

"No force. Strom take you. Strom help friends." The Timber Giant looked at her with a kind twinkle in his eyes. "Viden never take Strom again. Strom is free."

Aria sighed and turned to Willow to whisper under her breath. "Do you think this is a good idea? What if they want to take him back? What if they try to make him a slave again?"

Willow's lips twisted as she thought. "I doubt they'll stop us. By coming with him, they might just think he's ours."

Aria huffed, hating the way that sounded. A pit of empathy opened in her stomach for Strom.

They continued through the forest, Willow walking beside Strom to talk with him. Her voice carried in the autumn wind. The scurrying wildlife crept away, deeper into the foliage as they passed over crunching leaves. Avi held Celestia close with her sleepy head leaning against his chest. The little phoenix still looked like a naked bird with peachy fuzz, so Avi let her nestle up in one of his socks to keep warm.

"Do you often see any other Timber Giants in the forest?" Luke asked from Aria's side, listening in on the conversation Willow had started.

Strom glanced at Luke, Aria, and Avi behind him. "Yes… Strom stay alone, though. Strom travel forest—meet new giants."

"Hmm," Luke said, nodding along. "So, you like to travel? My family likes the forest a lot too. We used to hike and camp at Diamond Falls often."

"Pretty forest." Strom grinned and his eyes twinkled. "Strom like forest. Strom like to meet new Timber Giants."

Aria looked around at the trees filled with golden leaves, the green grass peeking out from under the leaves that had fallen, and the mystical animals hiding in the undergrowth. It truly was a gorgeous place to be.

Celestia's eyes opened slowly, and she wiggled herself out of Avi's sock. He helped her out, shoving the sock in the back pocket of his jeans. The little firebird then began to chirp in Strom's direction. He turned toward her and gently trailed a finger over her wing like he was touching porcelain. Celestia hopped onto his bark-covered finger and wobbled up his arm, singing a little song as she went. When she reached his shoulder, she settled down in the shadows of his leafy afro and looked down at Avi. Strom turned his head slightly with a soft creaking sound to look at her, and his lips tugged up.

"Do you make any friends during your travels?" Aria spoke from right behind Strom, continuing to follow him through the forest.

Strom looked back at her, then at her friends. "Yes, Strom do. Strom make friends here. Aria—the Diviner—Luke…

Avi…W-Willow…Celestia all Stromses friends." He said each of their names carefully, trying to pronounce each one correctly. Never once had he said their names; he'd only ever called them his friends. His eyes grew soft as he gazed at them like they were the greatest treasures he could find.

"The best of friends," Aria assured him with a grin that touched her eyes.

They all grabbed hands and swung them into the air, cheerful laughs bubbling from their throats. Even Celestia joined in, singing a loud and cheery tune from where she perched on Strom's shoulder.

"Team riddle-breakers!" Avi announced as they lowered their hands. "You know, because we're on a quest to find an old riddle, crack it, and get the treasure it leads to?"

Aria shook her head with amusement twinkling in her eyes.

The next few days passed, and with each one, they grew closer to the mountains in the distance. After hours of walking, on the fifth day since meeting Strom, the clouds began to darken with dangerous intent. Aria hoped whatever storm was coming would wait until they could find somewhere to take shelter. They started walking uphill and Aria had to use more strength to push herself forward. The trees around were mostly pine now with pillowy moss spreading across the ground and trees. Moisture was thick in the air. The wind picked up, blowing the needles at Aria and her friends, and a few leaves fell from Strom's thick reddish afro.

Strom hurried to lead them uphill as the sun started to disappear behind the dark clouds. Aria took a deep breath and pressed on, avoiding the undergrowth and rocks. Only a few more days and they'd reach the top of the mountain where snow lay across the ground. In the distance, the sound of thunder resounded through the sky.

"I don't like the sound of that," Avi said, glancing upward at the gathering of dark gray clouds.

"Strom, we need to find shelter," Aria said. "Where can we hide from the storm?"

"Strom know cave. Cave up mountain," Strom replied, gesturing up the huge, wooded incline.

Massive rocks and steep inclines of stone covered the terrain in front of them. He pointed and pressed onward. Whatever Strom could see, Aria could not; the trees covering the mountain were blocking her sight of everything. Another boom of thunder met their ears as the darkened sky lit with the purple glow of lightning.

"Let's go," Avi said quickly before hurrying up the mountainside with Celestia in his hands. "I don't feel like being electrocuted!"

"I can confirm the feeling isn't pleasant," Aria commented.

Aria, Luke, Willow, and Strom followed after him. The trees were getting hard to maneuver around, all of them growing closer together. A massive stone cliff jutted out of the side of the mountain several yards away. A large crack in the cliff revealed a cave that Avi was already ducking inside.

A snowflake fell from the dark sky, landing on the tip of Aria's nose before crackling lightning cast everything in purple. Aria grew closer by the second to the opening of the cave, Luke, Willow, and Strom right behind her. Snow started to fall from the sky more rapidly, the icy air biting beneath her many layers. The white flakes lay in the pine trees and on the frozen ground as Aria ducked inside the cave. Luke and Willow came in next, and then Strom bent over to fit inside as well. He blocked the entrance with his body, shutting out the flurries of snow that had been managing to get into the cave. The ice-cold temperature of the stone flooring wiggled through Aria's clothes. She brought her knees in towards her chest and wrapped her arms around them, shivering.

Luke plopped down next to her, and Willow next to Avi. She looked up at his face like there was something mesmerizing about him, and a pink tint crept into his cheeks. Avi turned his attention to his little firebird as his face turned splotchy despite the chill. Willow smiled, shifting a little closer to him. Celestia hopped from Avi's lap almost mischievously, leaving him alone with Willow, and strutted toward the center of the cave.

"Hey, come back here!" Avi hissed, reaching toward his little firebird.

Celestia caught fire, the light flickering in each of their eyes. A golden glow hit the cave walls. Almost immediately, it began to warm, the heat sinking to Aria's bones. A chill racked her body and she grabbed her backpack. She dug through it and pulled out her blanket, laying it across her and shivering. The warmth enveloping her made her frigid limbs burn. Luke, Avi, and Willow, followed her lead and suddenly blankets were being laid against the rocky ground and wrapped around their frigid bodies.

The flames Celestia had made across her feathers danced beautifully in the darkness of the cave. Strom watched her with intrigue, the golden glow reflecting in his dark eyes.

"So pretty," he said, but he kept his distance. "Celestia good little phoenix for warming Stromses friends."

Fatigue took over Aria and she yawned. She didn't think she'd get much sleep in a rocky, stone-floored cave, but she leaned her head back against the wall. Lightning crackled and thunder roared outside. Aria's eyes fell closed and she yawned again. Slowly, sleep took control, and unknowingly, her head fell onto Luke's shoulder.

<h1 style="text-align:center">CHAPTER FIFTEEN</h1>

FOR NEARLY A week, they continued up and across the snowy mountains. The more they ascended, the more the snow piled up around their ankles. The temperature dug its claws into their skin and shook them to the core with each step forward. The worst was at night when they either ducked into a cave or put the tent up on the rocky ground. The air seemed to freeze like a lake of ice, sinking through the blankets and causing their teeth to chatter. Even with Celestia warming their surroundings, it was restless at night for all of them—aside from Strom, who apparently didn't need sleep and didn't feel the cold. He could sleep if he wanted to by planting himself to the ground and drawing energy from it, but he never felt tired.

"Luke, do you think you could conjure a house?" Avi complained one night as the wind blew against the tent. He'd pulled his blankets tighter around him and snuggled closer to the main room where Celestia was steaming. "I really want some heating right now, and maybe an actual bed too."

"Sorry, dude," was all Luke had said in reply.

Every day, Strom would tell them old stories he'd been told

as a young Timber Giant. Listening to his warm voice outside the tent often lulled them to sleep like a cure to the icy air.

"Sun-arounds ago Wind talked to his brothers—Winter, Summer, Fall, and Spring. Spring kind, so Wind promise Spring to send rain for the flowers. Winter started a fight, so Wind sent ice to make him sad. Fall need help, so Wind help shake away the leaves. Summer not want help, so Wind only made visits to Summer."

The stories he told didn't always make sense, but they were wonderful to hear nonetheless, and he often mentioned his mother whenever he spoke of them.

During the week, Celestia's feathers had begun to grow, so now she only looked like a half-naked chicken, her feathers short against her pink skin. Avi was trying to teach her to fly every day that they walked on level ground, but she mostly just stared at him as he flapped his arms. One day she did try to take flight, but then drifted back to the ground as she shook with fright.

"That was a nice try," Avi assured her, flapping his arms up and down in encouragement. Willow giggled behind her hand.

The morning sun was just coming up over the horizon in the distance as they were making their way down the other side of the mountain range on the sixth day. It was hard to discern, but something massive was in the distance below like a white blob of stone covering the earth as far as the eye could see—a stark contrast to the fields of farmland stretching on for miles at the bottom of the mountain range. This side of the mountain had fewer trees and more caves, and the snow melted away the more they descended.

Days later, when they finally reached the bottom of the vast mountains, they stopped at a wide lake full of crystal-clear water. A river flowed from it, heading through a mountain pass. The golden rays of sunshine reflected on its surface. They filled their canteens at the edge of the sandy beach and sat around to rest their aching legs. They eventually dipped their toes in the water, until a current latched onto them like a monster reaching for prey, threatening to drag them into its depths.

As Aria pulled away, her voice came shakily, "Let's go farther up the lake and we can bathe. The current is too strong here."

Avi's eyes widened and he opened his mouth to speak with a blush rushing into his face.

"She doesn't mean together, Avi." Willow shook her head, but there was a red hue on her own face.

As they split up and walked away, something black shifted beneath the waters like a blot of ink. A shiver ran over Aria's skin and she hurried away from it. Much farther away from the strong current, she held her hand above the water to heat it up, making it bubble and steam in the chilled air. They bathed behind the rocky nooks and camped before starting their trek through the fields in the morning.

The rising sun painted the sky pink and orange. Pressing forward over the moist dirt, they took in the expansive farm-land. Throughout the fields, there were little homes and barns, where animals could be seen. Aria spotted chipock—strange chicken-peacock hybrids—cows, horses, sheep, but also other strange animals she'd never heard of before. Farmers watched them curiously as Aria, Luke, Willow, and Avi followed Strom into the distance. The ground no longer looked lush and green; it was full of dirt and dried leftovers from plants. The farm-ers were loading what little amount of food was left of the harvest into wagons to take to the city. A few Timber Giants helped push bigger wheel barrels full of dirt or vegetables. These Timber Giants were a few heads taller than Strom, with big bushels of autumn leaves atop their heads. Strom waved at them with pity in his eyes and they broke into smiles at the sight of one of their kind, but Aria's heart sank. Their voices filled the space around them, all words she couldn't comprehend. Strom understood the other Timber Giants, though, and he replied in the same language.

"Byo! Byo! Livi ta yamea!" Strom called cheerily to another Timber Giant as they all passed.

Aria looked onward to the expansive stretch of white marble wall so many miles away and pressed forward. When the farmers disappeared from the fields, slipping into their homes for the night, Aria, Luke, Willow, and Avi set up their tent again and rested.

As the sun rose anew, the thirty-foot-tall gates and walls of the city stood before them with the sunlight glistening against their white stone carvings of vines like snow. They could only tell they were the gates because of the perfectly straight crack in the white stone. There were also two gray stone statues situated on each side of the gate—one of an angry sphinx that had the head and body of a cat rather than a woman, and one of a flying griffin.

"Great, just great," Avi said sarcastically, throwing his arms up into the air. "We've come this far, and the gate's closed. How in the world are we supposed to open *that*?" He gestured at the height of the gate, which was no doubt several feet thick as well, and raised his eyebrows.

"Ask and enter," Strom said simply.

"Huh?" Avi's eyebrows somehow managed to rise even higher on his forehead.

Aria stepped forward and let out a shaky breath, clouds forming in front of her face. As loud as she could, she yelled, "Hello! Can you open up this gate for us?"

For a moment there was silence except for the breeze that was blowing through the valley, and then the griffin and sphinx's heads turned in the direction of Aria.

From the griffin came a man's voice as if a speaker was lodged in its throat, but there wasn't technology in the Vezchia Realm, so it could only be magic. "Tell us, are you friend or foe to the crown of Viden?"

"That's not creepy or anything," Avi muttered under his breath, brows furrowed at the statues.

"Um...I'm Ar-Liliac Del..aware..." Aria said slowly and carefully. No one could know who she really was. There could be spies anywhere. "We are with the Forces of Light, if that is what you mean."

"Is there anyone else with you?" A woman's voice came from the sphinx's mouth now.

"Just my friends, a pet...and a Timber Giant." Aria looked backwards at her friends, Celestia, and Strom, hoping there wouldn't be a problem that Strom was there.

"We will meet you on the other side," the woman's voice came again before the grinding of stone filled the air and the gate began to pull outwards toward Aria.

Light from the other side poured through the seam of the gate. The hustle and bustle from inside Viden met Aria's ears as the entrance opened wider to reveal the beauty of Viden. Just like they could see from a distance on the mountain, thousands of white stone buildings were built in neat rows. Trees stood in gardens with their bare branches stretched toward the sky. Fallen leaves lined the streets and filled the flowerpots decorating the fronts of buildings. Wooden shutters were open on every house, some people staring out at the city bustle below. Blue was everywhere—from Viden's royal seal on indigo banners hanging from torch posts to the signs and other banners hanging off buildings. Aria stepped forward through the gate onto the gray brick road, which was just as perfectly paved as the homes and gardens were perfectly kept. Luke, Avi, Willow, and Strom came up from behind her and Aria heard one of them gasp at the beauty.

"Welcome to Viden," that same woman's voice came from Aria's left and she realized two people were standing on either side of the gate. The other person was a man standing to Aria's right.

"If you need any help, please visit the Enchanting Control Office Building located in Enchanting Square," the man said with a slight smile on his face before saluting.

Aria nodded in appreciation before starting forward into the crowd of people walking up and down the streets of Viden. Chatter met Aria's ears as she slowly gazed at the towering buildings and gorgeous details of the city. Around her, people were carrying baskets with children running around at their feet. One child held a fuzzy orange creature with wide eyes—a Treeburt—like what they'd seen in the forest over a week ago. There were other pets here and there too. Cats, small mystical creatures, and little lizards could be seen in windows, open doorways, or out on the streets following their owners around. Objects floated through the air in the square as people tried to sell their products and shout their wares to passersby. Aria didn't have to even see the magic surrounding the place and hundreds of people to know it was there. She felt it grazing her skin like a powerful energy.

All around them, people stopped to stare at Strom at the back of their group, and baby Celestia trying to flap her wings in Avi's hand. Willow stared up at the buildings, her mouth wide open in astonishment at the city. A jittery feeling coursed over Aria's skin as people watched Strom, but they didn't stop them in the streets. She blew out a strained sigh, watching Strom take everything in with saddened eyes.

"Alright, we need to find the Library of Knowledge," Aria

said, glancing around at the signs placed on street corners and oil lamp poles.

They walked forward and people moved out of their way to let them down the streets. The smells of cakes in a bakery, flowers carefully preserved in a shop, sweet candles in another shop, and pumpkin spice engulfed Aria's senses. She took it all in, wishing she had time to spend exploring the whole of Viden. Every nook and cranny seemed full of life and pure joy as they turned onto a particularly fancy street that branched off toward a row of houses.

Aria spotted a Timber Giant fixing a shutter onto a massive two-story house on the corner. The house was adorned in exposed wooden beams lined with gold trimming and exotic plants sat in the flowerpots below every huge window, unharmed by the fall weather. Aria figured they were magical plants. The Timber Giant fixing the golden-trimmed window shutter was much taller than Strom. The Giant spotted them walking down the street, his eyes falling on Strom. Aria glanced between the two of them, noticing their differences. Strom somehow looked younger, his bark-skin lighter and his leaves healthier. The other Giant somehow looked older and worn out with more grooves like wrinkles set into his skin. His eyes sagged solemnly, and his shoulders slumped like a horrible weight rested on them.

"Strom, how old are you?" Aria asked as they turned down onto another street.

Strom waved at the other Timber Giant with a kind smile. "Strom ninety-five sun-arounds."

"You're ninety-five years old?" Aria's eyes just about popped out of her head. "How long do Timber Giants live?"

"A thousand y-years," Strom said, looking at Aria for confirmation that he'd said 'years' right.

"Dude, you're *old*," Avi said with a silly grin.

Willow spoke up softly beside Aria. "Timber Giants *can* live to be a thousand years," Something in her tone suggested that most Timber Giants didn't make it to that age, though. "They hit maturity at one hundred, so technically, Strom isn't much older in maturity than us, though he's been alive a lot longer."

Aria's brows furrowed as a thought struck her. "How come Timber Giants didn't confirm that the Diviner is real if they can live for so long? Many had to be alive while the last Diviner was alive over three centuries ago."

Strom tilted his head slightly as if in contemplation. "Mother was four hundred ninety. Mother tell Strom about Diviner when Strom young. Timber Giants no talk with humans who hurt. Timber Giants stay in forest."

Aria still thought they could have said something to humans about the Diviner, but she didn't press about it. She could understand why Timber Giants would steer clear of humans if they thought they'd cause them harm or trap them in lives of slavery.

They continued down the cobbled street lined with white stone buildings, keeping an eye out for the library or a sign that could lead them to it. Celestia flapped her wings more in Avi's palm, starting to lift into the air.

"Yes, good job!" Avi cheered her on with a smile on his face. "You can do it!"

Then the bird suddenly took off, flying down the bustling street. The eyes of people pinned to the soaring phoenix, mouths gaping.

"Celestia!" Avi called, running after her as she led them down the crowded street of small businesses. "Celestia, come back!"

Luke, Willow, Aria, and Strom took off after them, dodging people in the bustling roads. The white-stone buildings around them got taller, each attached to the other, the farther they went down Shlyvin Street. Gray stone balconies hung off the fronts of many of the buildings with stone pillars spiraling down to support them.

"Celestia!" Avi called as Aria came to a stop at the end of the street.

There was a wooden sign on the side of the street with directions carefully written in blue paint: *The Library of Knowledge*. Below that were five translations of it into other languages. An arrow pointed in the direction of where Celestia was flapping her wings in the air, waiting for them over River Street.

"She's showing us the way," Aria murmured, her eyes wide and focused on the firebird. She sped after Celestia with Strom, Luke, and Willow following her. Avi was already far ahead of them, continuing to call Celestia's name and drawing the attention of the crowds.

"Avi, stop!" Aria told him as she caught up with him. "We're getting looks from people. Remember, no one can know we are here. The Dark Forces could be anywhere, just like Bola."

Flashes of that horrible, thief-filled town crossed through her mind and she had to shake them away.

Over the buildings, Aria spotted a massive circular tower taking up the center of the city with the sun glimmering on the golden flecks encased in its marble structure. A golden, pointed roof topped it, which had to be thousands of feet in the air. How it stood so straight made her mind spin and the breath leave her lungs. It looked like it could have had a hundred floors. Staring at it made her stomach drop; she had never in her life seen such a tall structure, and the fact that it towered over all the other buildings made her sure that *that* was the library.

"Guys, there it is," she tried to say but the words were lost; she felt breathless.

Celestia turned the corner towards the center of the city and they followed. The crowds dwindled the closer they got to the tower.

People cast concerned looks their way and Aria heard someone say to another next to them, "What are they doing? The library is cursed! To even go near it—"

Aria and the others turned onto a massive, circular, and desolate street surrounded by the backs of shops, where the only building in the middle was the library. Marble steps led up to two giant, golden doors, and on either side of them were the same statues that they had seen at the gates of the city. Blue banners with the winged horse symbol representing Enchanting Control hung beside the doors. Not a single window broke through the perfectly smooth surface of the tower.

Aria was the first to rush up to the doors of the library, staring at them like they were treasure. Next to the door hung a golden sign with something etched into it, the sun glimmering on its surface.

Knowledge is power. Knowledge is key. Seek ours if you dare but take that which does not belong to you and you'll surrender your life.

Luke, Avi, Willow, and Strom were right behind Aria now, eyes scanning the words. Celestia rested on the head of the griffin statue to her right with her head tucked beneath her pink fuzzy wing. Worry began to seep into the air around them, though the little firebird seemed unaffected.

"Um…what is that supposed to mean?" Avi nodded toward the plaque, concern lacing his voice, and he raised his eyebrows. "Because if it means we might die in there, I vote on staying out."

"Viden values knowledge above all else, so of course they

will protect it somehow," Willow said. "But we need to go in there to get the Death Stone Riddle."

"Yeah…" Aria sighed and clenched her cold hands shut, remembering what she'd heard someone say on the streets just moments ago. She knew the legends surrounding the library. But if they didn't go in there, they wouldn't be able to get the Death Stone Riddle and find the Stone before the Dark Forces. Then Aria and the realms would be even further doomed. And she also wanted to get her hands on the legendary Ancient Scrolls for her own reasons.

Aria shook her head, squeezing her eyes shut against the fear digging into her like claws into skin. "Strom, Celestia, you'll have to stay out here. I don't think you'll fit through this door, Strom, and…Celestia…it's better you don't suddenly light yourself on fire and burn everything to the ground."

The four of them dropped their backpacks to the ground with a thud and Aria clamped her hand on the golden handle of the door, the cold metal biting into her hands.

"As Diviner wishes," Strom said, giving a bow.

Aria's stomach dropped at the sound of her title so close to civilization, but at least no one was around to hear. The word echoed through her head as if it wanted to haunt her, but she pushed the door open and stepped inside. Luke, Avi, and Willow followed her into the Library of Knowledge.

CHAPTER SIXTEEN

SHE SHUT THE door behind her with a loud thud and her mind silenced itself, along with every other sound. Her breath caught in her throat. The library was breathtaking, and there was so much of it that it was hard to take it all in at once. Rows upon rows of wooden bookshelves went as far as her eye could see, same with the floors that went upward. A golden spiraling staircase started at Aria's right and wound its way upward along the edges of the tower, toward the other floors filled with shelves full of books, scrolls, and old tomes. The floor was a perfectly smooth, slippery marble with golden flecks embedded in it. Spiraling pillars of quartz went straight up through the many, many floors to support them. Those floors disappeared into the shadowy expanse above, but Aria guessed there had to be at least a hundred. The air smelled of paper, dust, ink, and rocks, but there was also a sweet freshness to it. Dust and cobwebs covered everything in thick layers, indicating the library hadn't been touched in decades, possibly centuries. The heavy silence within the library felt like a physical thing hanging in the air.

She started forward, eyes focused on the dark wooden

bookshelves. Golden plaques were mounted on each of the bookshelves with words that described what each section was for, but they were etched in a different language.

"Books." Willow seemed breathless, her eyes wide as she took in the immense collection of written works.

Luke scratched the back of his neck anxiously. "Where should we look?"

"Maybe we should split up…" Aria trailed off, her stomach swirling at the thought of it. It made sense, but the words etched on the golden sign outside echoed through her head. "Remember, we're looking for the Death Stone Riddle."

"I really don't like the whole splitting up idea. Maybe we should think this through?" Avi asked, but Luke and Willow were already nodding in agreement. "Fine, but the smarty-pants here better not get distracted."

Aria took a deep breath and then turned down a tight aisle of bookshelves that were loaded with tattered, wrinkled books and scrolls. Ancient sage, rusty red, woody tan, and indigo spines were lined up on the shelves with titles printed on them. The words were hard to discern, as most were worn out and faded, and others were written in an entirely different language. Aria's heart slowly sank lower into her stomach as her brain clouded with doubt that they would find what they were looking for in this vast sea of books. She drew one of the books off the shelf and pulled it open. Dust flew up at her face and the aged paper crinkled beneath her fingers. Luckily, the words were written in English, even if they were faded and looked to be scrawled with a shaky hand.

The creation of the Vezchia Realm, methinks, befell at the morn of our universe, just like the Space Realm. The three realms, however, hadst once been merged together as one. Yet, were torn apart and separated into three diverse realms when a powerful source entered the world, which would explain the rips in our universe known as veils. Another theory of mine is that that source was the Diviner hundreds of years ago.

Aria slapped the book shut and slid it back on the shelf. "So, I'm in the theory section of the library."

She sighed and continued down the aisles of bookshelves. Her hair stood up on her arms and a warning to be cautious tugged at the edges of her mind. A spot on her back tingled as if eyes were bearing down on her. She looked behind her, on top of the bookshelves, and down the aisle ahead of her, but all she saw were the tomes and scrolls. The stillness and silence of the library remained. The only sound was the soft fall of her feet as she continued past the shelves condemned with dust. She took a deep breath, trying to clear her head and focus.

Willow sat on the ground, leaning against a bookshelf, with a book in her hand. Dust clung to her fingers like a new skin. Everything around her was silent and she had not the faintest idea of where Aria, Avi, or Luke was. The stillness and absence of emotions pressed down on her, making her stomach give an uneasy turn. But then a flicker of curiosity and hunger edged closer.

She smiled to herself. *Probably Avi.*

The book in her hand was extremely thick and heavy, and no matter how many times she flipped to the back of it, the pages never ended. Everything was written in different languages with meanings to words. It was like a giant language dictionary. The cover and spine were dark green, and golden words were faded on the front, so she was unable to read most of them. It had attracted her attention almost as soon as she turned down the aisle, being the thickest and oldest-looking book on the shelves. If there was one thing she loved more than books, it was words. They made up the very books and language she knew. She could only guess she was in the language section of the library. She wanted to sit there and hold that book for ages, scanning the delicately written words and filling her brain with the knowledge this library provided, but her friends needed her. They were somewhere in the library, searching for the Death Stone Riddle, and she needed to as well. She stood up with the thick, green book of languages, dusting off the layers of cobwebs that had caught on her. The book crinkled as she closed it, sending more dust into the air. Glancing around, she started off down the aisle again with her arms wrapped tightly around the book of languages.

There were oil lamps in the library, each of them burning brightly, and yet it still seemed dim. Aria had searched many rows of books and still had come up with nothing. She was still on the first floor and was sure she'd barely put a dent in it, not to mention all the floors above her. The thought of that made sweat gather on her forehead. Her legs ached from how little rest she and her friends had gotten, but she pressed forward through the shadowed aisles. Exhaustion burrowed into her bones and weighed her down like lead. Taking a deep breath, she walked out into a circular clearing where many square wooden tables sat with oil lamps glowing on each of them. Yellow light illuminated the space, making it feel like Aria was walking through a hazy dream. Looking up at the darkness leading toward the ceiling far, far above her, it looked like she was in the center of the library.

Gold ten-foot-tall bookshelves circled the clearing, leaving gaps only where the clearing branched off to other aisles. Filling the gleaming bookshelves were scrolls cased in gold, and wooden ladders were attached to each of the bookshelves, reaching for the highest shelves. Golden signs hung from the sides of them, reading: *The Ancient Scrolls*, as well as those words in many other languages. Scrolls and books were neatly laid out on all the tables, and many of the Scrolls were rolled up in more golden cases.

Aria walked toward the tables, her heart beating in her ears. The Ancient Scrolls held all the information in the world…even about her. All the answers were right there in front of her. They were real, and she'd read every one until she found what she was looking for. She picked up one of the golden-encased Scrolls, which was covered with a thick layer of dust. After wiping off all the dust, she saw the words clearly etched into the casing: *The Magical Divide.* She carefully unrolled the thin parchment wrapped up inside, the ancient paper crackling as she did. The words were written with black ink in unreadable cursive. They started to glow golden and Aria's eyes went wide. She felt the urge to drop the Scroll when her hands loosened on it, the light of the paper reflecting in her blue eyes. The glowing faded away and the cursive became readable English.

At the dawn of time, there was earth and space. There were people and animals. There were those with magic and those without it. And containing all of this was one realm in which everything was at a balance. Slowly, however, mundanes began to grow jealous and division broke through the realm. One-thousand-fifty-six years after the universe was created, it was torn apart. With this tear, a powerful being was discovered, and that being was the Diviner. The very first Diviner went by the name of Cormac Delvini.

But little did the people realize that Cormac, the Diviner, had been the one to tear the universe apart, leaving it torn into three different realms: one full of magic, one with none, and one void of anything. Cormac had lost control, having no one to help him understand the amount of power in his veins. Rips in the universe known as veils are now littered throughout the world, allowing magic to bleed into the Mundane Realm—

Aria put down the Scroll with horror flickering in her eyes, her hands shaking. She didn't want to read another word, one of her own memories crashing down on her. When she'd broken through the wall and into the Space Realm at Incanting Academy, she'd lost control. The same power Cormac had then now ran in her own veins. She tucked her hands down at her side as if she could hide her powers from herself, fear curling through her like a venomous snake.

But then again, she'd wanted to come to the library so she could know more. She wanted to know the full truth, even if it made her terrified of herself.

She read on a little further in the Scroll, but it only talked of the first enchanters and enchantresses and the wars between magical and mundanes that had lasted hundreds of years. Aria walked away from the Scroll and toward the massive collection of Ancient Scrolls organized on the golden shelves. She climbed up one of the rollable wooden ladders and started going through all the different Scrolls rolled up into golden cases. She read titles like *The Dawn of Time, The Creation of the Library of Knowledge, Viden's Kings and Queens, The Disappearance of the Diviner, The Creation of the Life and Death Stones,* and more on all the events throughout history. Aria pulled out *The Creation of the Life and Death Stones* and read through it, hoping it would have some hint as to where the Death Stone was or even the Riddle itself, but it didn't.

All it said was, *The Death Stone was hidden in a place Alaric*

Malamone trusted most; a place where it would be safely guarded by loyalty. However, because we are bound by our own wisdom, we are unable to write or speak of the location. Aria set it back on the shelf and began looking for something that might have to do with her again.

She had no idea how long they'd been in the library or how long she'd been looking at the Ancient Scrolls, but she was exhausted. She was up at the top of the ladder now, reaching for the highest shelves. Her eyes scanned the words etched into the golden cases of every Scroll until they finally landed on one that read: *The Diviners' History.* In a rush, she grabbed the Scroll and scurried down the ladder with her heart beating in her ears. Her hands were clammy and shaking. She didn't know what she would read in the Scroll—if it would be good or bad. She didn't even know what it was she was looking for other than an explanation. She unrolled the Scroll and started skimming it as quickly as she could to get to the point. At first, it only spoke of the first Diviner, Cormac Delvini, and the second one named Leo Ephna, who had lived to be nearly seven hundred years old.

Diviners usually lived longer than the average human being, living to be at least one-hundred or older due to their immense power.

Aria paused, her eyes freezing on the words. Her heart sank. She wasn't sure she wanted to live that long. If she made it through this, would she be forced to watch everyone she loves pass on while she's still alive? She shook the thought from her mind, determined to ignore it until the time came.

The Scroll also spoke of wars Diviners had helped fight in and bring to an end. It said Cormac had tried to keep peace between the mundanes and magical beings as his powers grew over the centuries. Rare gifts were spreading throughout the world, and one day he'd found he had all of them. As he grew old and the pressure around him intensified, he lost control… And then the world of magic broke into an all-out war that lasted hundreds of years.

Finally, she came to a part where it spoke of the creation of the Forces of Light and the Diviner being among their ranks. She slowed her pace, soaking in every word as the paper she'd already read piled up at her feet. It spoke of Evangeline Voland, the Diviner Aria knew to have been the last. Then Alaric Malamone and his Stones came up. Her heart thrummed with the urge to read and find a reason for her being the Diviner, but she breathed in deeply and tried to calm herself.

After the death of Alaric Malamone, the Diviner went into hiding in a place we are bound by wisdom not to state. The Divining Powers were stripped from her and she slowly died at the age of forty-two. For three hundred years, there was no Diviner, and it became a myth that there ever was one. Exactly three hundred years after the Life and Death Stones were forged on August 2nd, another Diviner was finally born. It seems that this young Diviner's path is shadowed with secrets, though, as we write this. It is peculiar to Yalecia and I that this Diviner was the only one worthy enough in three hundred years, and that she was born on the exact day that the Divining Powers were taken from Evangeline. The future is an undetermined thing, though, and it looks like young A.C. will have a dark future ahead of her. After all, she is the one chosen to save us all from the evil Malus Malamone and his Dark Forces will soon release.

The words became unfocused as tears blurred her vision. Her hands trembled even more now, sweat beading up on her forehead. The words played over and over in her head like a haunting melody.

A.C. To those who didn't know her, it would look like a

random initial, but she knew it as *her* initials. *The only Diviner in three hundred years? The only one worthy enough? No, no, no!* She wanted to scream and throw something. There was a twisting feeling in her stomach, like a knife, and she hated it. She hated the fact that she was the Diviner. It put a heavy weight on her shoulders and it was pushing her beneath the tidal waves, drowning her in a power she didn't want—a power she couldn't truly have because it had been locked away hundreds of years before she was even born. She dropped the Scroll and it fell to the floor with a metal clang, echoing in the silence of the library. Something gray flashed in the shadows of her periphery and she turned, but it was already too late to react. A beast jumped out from behind one of the bookshelves, and a scream erupted from her throat.

CHAPTER SEVENTEEN

A LONG, HIGH-PITCHED SCREAM echoed off the walls of the library followed by a loud crash that resounded in the empty shadows above. The second Luke heard the sound, he knew it was Aria, and she was in trouble. He let the book he had been looking through fall to the floor, dust billowing in the air. His feet hit the marble floor as he rushed down the aisle, turning the corner to find a dead end. He turned back around, panic squeezing the breath out of his lungs.

"Aria!" he called. "Aria, where are you?"

She didn't respond, her screams fading away like sand in an hourglass. Like time running out.

Luke's heart began to race faster and sweat slicked his hands. "Aria!" His voice cracked, a lump forming in his throat.

He didn't want to think of what could be wrong, but the words from the plaque outside the library doors forced their way into his head.

Surrender your life.

There had to be a way around these bookshelves that seemed to loom around him like a trap, but he couldn't remember how he'd even gotten down the aisle. Everything looked the same. He turned and ran back the way he'd come, getting lost in tomes as blood rushed in his ears.

Avi's voice broke through his panic. "Luke!"

There was a bookshelf to his right, but through the spaces between books and cobwebs, Avi's figure was visible.

"Avi," Luke blew out a sigh of relief and started shoving books off the bottom shelf to get to the other side.

He drew book after book off the shelf, cobwebs catching on his hand. Dust filled the air the more he threw to the floor with a thud. It seemed Avi was doing the same, for there was his face looking back at him through the bookshelf.

"Move, I'm going to wiggle through," Avi said as he shoved the last of the books out of the way.

Luke took a step back as Avi started sliding through the bottom level of the shelf and over to Luke's side. "Um…are you sure you're going to fit?"

"Yep," Avi said just as he rolled across the marble floor at Luke's feet.

"Where's Aria?" Luke grabbed Avi's hand and pulled him to his feet, a worried look contorted on his face.

"I don't know. This place is like a maze."

Luke sighed, staring at the walls of bookshelves looming up around them. Beckoning for Avi to follow, he started down the aisle.

Avi brushed his hands against his pants to get the grime from the books off, frowning. "I know we really need to find Aria, but you would think this library would be cleaner if Viden truly likes their knowledge so much." He threw his hands up. "I mean, this city is rich! Why can't they hire a janitor to dust off these books? It's a good thing I didn't read the books because if I did, my hands would be as dusty as yours."

"You didn't read the books?" Luke spun his head toward him. "Are you serious?"

"I *am* being serious! Dust mites and respiratory issues are very serious things!"

They turned the corner, Luke shaking his head. "If we read a little bit of the books, then we can figure out what section of the library we're in, and then we can figure out where the Death Stone Riddle might be."

He picked up the pace, his head filling with horrible possibilities. They needed to find Aria, not to mention Willow. Time had passed by in a blur, so who knew how long it had been since they'd seen either one of them. The pressing silence weighed on him and he couldn't stop the tremble that had taken over his body. Aria's scream echoed through his head as if to taunt him.

She's fine. She's the Diviner, he reminded himself and took a deep breath.

Then he heard her voice, growing closer with every step and saying something incomprehensible, but there was also another deeper voice that had a wise ancient feel to it. His heart rate spiked as they abruptly turned into a clearing at the same time Willow did on the opposite side from them with a huge green book in her arms.

Aria was in the center of the clearing surrounded by tables and at her feet lay a wrinkled, unrolled scroll. She didn't look harmed as her wide eyes landed on him and Avi, but fear flickered in her eyes. When Luke drew his eyes away from her, he saw exactly why. Hovering above a wooden table near a golden bookshelf was a griffin. It had a head like an eagle's, a body like a lion, wide wings, and was covered in dark and light gray feathers, just like the statue outside. Its wings slowly flapped up and down in a gentle way, but there was nothing about this beast that seemed gentle. Black talons stuck out from its bird-like feet like daggers. Its black beak was sharp and pointed, with studying yellow eyes like a cat's.

"Ah, so her friends come to see me too," the griffin said and a smirk seemed to appear on its face. Its voice was deep, sophisticated, and felt like it held all the wisdom in the world, just like what Luke had heard before entering the clearing.

He, Willow, and Avi took in a sharp gasp and Willow's jaw dropped. Luke's eyebrows shot up, body freezing in place. Across the clearing, Willow's eyes were trained on the griffin, her head likely spinning with all the explanations she could think of.

"Did that griffin just t-talk?" Avi sounded breathless. "That's not supposed to be possible…unless I'm suddenly an… Omni-communicator."

"Please, call me Aero," the griffin said as he landed on the empty table below him. "And yes, I can talk. So can my dear friend, Yalecia. We both can talk, read, and write because of the curse laid on us by a past King and Queen of Viden thousands of years ago. In fact, we even wrote these Scrolls behind us." Aero paused, yellow eyes landing specifically on Avi. "And no, Avi Braxdon, you are not an Omni-communicator."

"H-how do you know m-my name?" Avi asked shakily and took a step backward.

"Yalecia and I know *everything* but the future," Aero answered. "We know each person's name—that you four are Aria Chesler, Avi Braxdon, Luke Avaenu, and Willow Mudry. We know the day the world came to be, and every event throughout history. There is not a thing from the past or present that we do not know. That is our curse. In fact, I was just talking to this little Diviner here about what she was reading from the Scrolls we wrote."

"How do you—" Avi was about to ask.

"I know *everything*," Aero interrupted. "The Diviner here says you four need to find the Death Stone and therefore need to find the Riddle. I know where it is."

Aria turned in Aero's direction and looked at him in his yellow eyes. "Forget the Death Stone Riddle. Can't you just tell us where the Stone is?"

Aero tutted and jumped to the marble floor, talons scraping it. "I cannot let that information fall into the wrong hands. I also cannot let you go alone to the Death Stone Riddle. But I can take you to it."

"What *wrong hands*? I'm the Diviner," Aria said, cringing as the words left her mouth.

Her hands slid behind her back, hiding her palms as if afraid of the power that she had. Luke watched, pity squeezing his chest. She'd never realize that she was made to be just as she was, would she? She'd never realize that her power didn't define her heart. That her power was a beautiful part of her that deserved to shine, not a thing doomed to control or destroy her.

"Believe it or not, Aria Chesler, but not every Diviner was perfect. Everyone makes mistakes and unleashes secrets meant to be kept hidden." Aero studied her for a moment. "Whether you are meant to read the Riddle or find the Death Stone won't matter. I am bound by magic to keep it protected and to protect the darkest pieces of knowledge from others."

"What do you mean?" Avi cut in. "You mentioned a curse. What—"

"Yalecia and I were *befriended* by the first King and Queen of Viden nearly two thousand years ago." Aero made it sound as if there really was no friendship between the King and Queen, and Aria found her mind wandering back to everything she'd read about the library's legends. "The Vezchia Realm was newly discovered and needed a safe haven, which became Viden. The

King and Queen didn't want the history of past wars between those with magical bloodlines and mundanes to die out. So, they found us and bound us to this place with a type of magic that has long been forgotten…magic that would be frowned on and locked away, as it should be." He looked down, eyes narrowing slightly. "Only those with the permission from the King and Queen themselves are deemed able to seek this knowledge. We were put in here to guard it and write down the truth of everything as it comes to be. Guarding it means not allowing it to get into the wrong hands, protecting it, and making sure it never leaves these walls—whether in a physical or *other* form…That is why we are cursed and why you can't go to the Riddle alone."

"I don't understand." Willow's brows furrowed and she stared at him intently, as if trying to find an answer to something in his beady eyes. "Why would you show us the Riddle at all then?"

Aero seemed to smirk again. "The Death Stone Riddle is written in another language that none of you know. Showing it to you would not harm anyone if you can't comprehend the words."

Willow's eyes flicked to the book in her hands, her eyes revealing that a strategy was forming in her head. At the same time, Luke's heart fell. Aero was right, but what other choice did they have?

And the griffin knew that. He watched them with a challenging expression, waiting for them to accept his offer. There was no other option even though those beady yellow eyes made Luke's skin prickle unnervingly.

Aria seemed to come to the same conclusion as him, their eyes meeting. "Then show us to it, Aero."

The griffin strutted past her and the tables with his head held high. "I shall."

Aria noticed that the more they climbed the seemingly end-less marble staircase, the newer the books seemed to get. The spines were not as ancient-looking, but dust was still thick on the shelves as if they had been sitting there for centuries. Along the edge of the staircase was an intricate golden railing, and to the other side was a marble wall that opened to other floors occasionally. Aero was in the lead, silent with his eyes trained ahead. Footprints appeared behind them on the dusty floors and cobwebs clung to Aria's shoes. Looking up at the pitch-blackness that stretched toward the ceiling, dread filled her stomach. The tower was so tall that she couldn't see all the floors still left to go past. She walked with her arms crossed tightly, the words from the Scrolls replaying in her head. She felt that maybe crossing her arms would help hold herself together.

"How much longer do you think we will have to climb these stairs?" Avi complained. "My legs hurt." He was half-bending as he walked beside Luke and Willow, likely hurting his back too.

Aria had been thinking the same thing. They already had been walking up the marble staircase for well over thirty min-utes. She almost wanted to grip the railing for support.

"Right now, we are in the 1500s, so not too much longer." Aero glanced back at them, amusement twinkling in his eyes.

"1500s?" Avi asked, lifting himself from bending over. He raised one eyebrow and blinked a couple of times.

"This library is nearly two thousand years old, and as more books, scrolls, and knowledge were collected, we had to add more floors upward," Aero said.

They continued up the rounding staircase. Aria gazed over

the railing to look down at all the floors below them, the first floor so far below that it was cast in shadow. It only grew farther away as they passed more floors bursting with books and knowledge. Across the circular tower, the other floors could be seen like a great balcony covered in shelves.

Aero glanced backward at them before turning to the right onto what had to be the thousandth floor. It looked the same as the first floor; it was a maze of dusty books and wooden shelves. The tomes bore less scratches and worn covers, but not by much. Shadows clung to every nook and cranny, giving it an eerier feel than the first floor. Aria's magic stirred in her veins like a warning.

"Here we are. Follow me," Aero said as he started strutting down an aisle that had a sign reading: *Mundane Mythology*.

Avi, Luke, Aria, and Willow followed after him, Willow scanning the titles of all the books in the aisles. Her fingers trailed along the spines despite the cobwebs. Aero led them down many rows of books and Aria found it hard to keep track of where they were. Had they turned left then right, or was that two aisles ago? Up ahead, a glass case could be seen in the center of a small clearing. It was tall like a podium and had gold details tracing around the edges of it in a vine pattern. Inside laid a piece of yellowed paper that rolled up at the ends. Aria's breath caught in her throat, her heart racing as they approached it.

"Here it is—the Death Stone Riddle," Aero said and walked around the glass podium once before coming to a stop next to it.

Aria stepped forward and touched the glass case gently as if she could reach through it to grab the thing they'd come for. She stared down at the ancient words carefully scrawled across the thin, yellowed parchment in another language. This language had a lot of lines and dots in the middle of words. It was completely unrecognizable. Just looking at it made Aria's head spin.

Willow flipped through the book she had been carrying around nearly the whole time they had been in the library. The paper crinkled with each flip of the pages. "If I could just find that language in here…" She glanced at the curvy swirling symbols on the ancient paper, then back to the Riddle.

"I doubt very much that you will manage to find it," Aero watched each page she flipped to carefully. "That book is filled with millions of languages, some wiped from existence and others still around today…The chances of finding it before your time is up in here are slim. There are only two people who have managed to read the Riddle."

Avi crept closer to the glass case but locked his eyes on Aero. "The people who'd read the Riddle before—were they Omni-communicators?"

"No, they were not," Aero said. "The Riddle is cursed so that no one but those who are born of the blood from that language *and* who understand that language can read it. Only those with that blood can read it or translate it. That applies to even Omni-communicators."

Aria's head turned away from the glass case and to the griffin. "But this is just a copy of the Riddle." A million different questions ran through her head, and here she was standing in front of a creature that had all the answers.

"The very words that make up the Death Stone Riddle are cursed. That information died with Alaric Malamone."

Aria had only found out magic existed several months ago, but that kind of dark magic seemed unreal. Only the same kind of magic that had made the Life and Death Stones could make strung-together words cursed. Thinking of it made her blood chill.

Forcing herself to focus, she thought back to another thing Aero had mentioned. "You said only two people have ever managed to read the Riddle. If this is a copy, were they the ones who copied it? Who are they?"

"Miranda and Oliver Chesler." Aero said, watching as shock hit Aria like a brick. "Miranda Chesler is descended from the people of the Riddle's hidden language. Only your parents have been able to read the Riddle and escape with the knowledge of the Death Stone's location. They copied it for the Forces of Light, and then it was put here to be guarded."

Aria's brows furrowed as she tried to comprehend everything being thrown at her. "But why didn't they translate it? Why didn't they share the information? Why—"

"Enough questions, Diviner." Aero's voice turned sharp and deadly. "Keep asking questions and you may no longer be welcome here. Certain information is best kept secret."

Aria shut her mouth, the glass case cold underneath her fingers. All this new information spun through her head like a tornado. A cursed riddle, her parents solving it, her parents keeping secret after secret, her mother being descended from the old language the Riddle's written in. All the secrets they'd kept from her just kept piling up, and it *stung*.

But if Aria's mother was descended from the Riddle's hidden language, then Aria was too. Which meant she could solve it if only she knew the language.

Time was ticking, and she doubted Aero would be patient much longer. As he'd said, their time would be up eventually.

Aria looked back down at the Riddle intently, trying to make sense of it all. A sudden poke on her shoulder drew her gaze away from the symbols and strange letters, and she turned to look at Avi.

Worry was evident on his face as his eyes darted around. "Aria, something seems wrong."

"Huh?" Aria asked, glancing to her sides. She felt the hairs on her arms stand on end and her heart hammered in her chest like something was watching them. Of course, Aero was standing only two feet away and staring at them, but no. This feeling was something else.

"I don't know what it is, but I think we should get out of here," Avi whispered as quietly as he could.

"Okay, just as soon as we get this out of here," Aria said so softly even she barely heard the words leave her mouth as she tried pulling on the golden lock that hung from the case.

"I am afraid we cannot let that happen," a woman's voice boomed from behind them, startling Aria, and she spun around.

Sitting on top of one of the tall bookshelves was a sphinx, her wide feathered wings folded at her sides and her furry, tan catlike tail flicking in agitation. Most of her fur was a dark cream color and two foxlike ears poked out through the fur on top of her head. Everywhere Aria had ever seen paintings of mythical sphinxes, they had the head and torso of a woman, but this sphinx had the body and head of a massive cat. She leapt down from the bookshelf with a thud and bared her many rows of razor-sharp, spiked teeth. Her black claws scraped against the floor.

"What is not yours shall not be taken. Pay the price if you try," the sphinx said, a wicked smirk spreading across her feline face. "Unless…you can answer my riddle."

Aria glanced at her friends on either side of her. Willow was still trying to find the language in her book, urgency in the way she hurried to flip its pages. Luke shook his head as if telling her not to answer it, that it was risky and irrational to even try. Avi glanced from her to the Death Stone Riddle and back again, indicating that he thought they should just steal the Death Stone Riddle and leave.

Aria turned her head back toward the sphinx and breathed in deeply before asking, "What is the riddle?"

The sphinx strutted forward a few steps as her smirk grew and Aria's skin crawled. There was a hostile challenge in the beast's eyes like she had her prey trapped and was simply toying with it. Aria's hands grew clammy and she had to fight the urge to grab her sunflower necklace.

"Some try to hide, some try to cheat, but time will show, we always will meet. Try as you might to guess my name." The sphinx sat down on the marble floor, staring Aria straight in the eyes as she thought over the riddle.

"Aria…" Luke's eyes shot to hers.

"Some try to hide," Aria repeated to herself in a whisper, but nothing was coming to mind. "Some try to cheat…"

"They will not be able to guess it, Yalecia." Aero's face had gone solemn. "They are but children, but they can't leave with the Death Stone Riddle and they've already asked so many questions. This knowledge in the hands of others is dangerous." He sighed. "You know how much I hate to do this, but we are bound by our curse. I say we end them now and get it over with. We can make it quick and painless."

"But what is the joy in that?" The sphinx smiled and it exposed her fangs. "It is so very rare that humans journey into our library and it is *so* very boring. Now is our chance to have some excitement. It's been so very long since we've had a good meal…" Yalecia stretched her paws out in front of her, hind legs readying for a pounce. "Time is running out, children… Five…Four…Three…Two…"

"Wait! Wait!" Willow suddenly burst out and put one of her hands out as Yalecia lifted her clawed paw toward Aria. Aria's eyes widened, she stepped backwards into the podium, and it tottered at its base. "The future—the answer is the future!"

Yalecia lowered her paw to the ground and cocked her head to the side as if contemplating. "That is…a very good answer…but it is also wrong. The correct answer is your fate, that being death."

The sphinx stuck out her claws and launched herself forward as Aero took to the air. Everything happened at once in a rush and all Aria could figure out was that her heart was hammering in her ears, sweat was beading up on her forehead, and she was stepping backwards into the Death Stone Riddle's stand. She bumped the case with so much force that she slipped, trying to get away from Yalecia as she reached for her with her claws, and she fell into it. The stand crashed to the marble floor and shattered, Aria landing on top. Glass bit into her skin and dark blood stained her hands and the floor. Tears streamed down her cheeks and then there was the sharp, burning feel of pain everywhere.

She heard Luke calling her name and Avi pleading with Aero as they threw enchantments at him in the background. She fought to get up, whimpering at the pain that lanced through her hands and back. Yalecia raised her paws to lash out again. Aria collected magic into the palm of one of her bloody hands and shot a Knockback Enchant at her. The sphinx was thrown backwards and landed in a heap near a bookshelf.

"Why are you doing this? Aria is the Diviner!" Avi yelled as he battled Aero a few feet away. "She's supposed to save people! She's a good person."

"We are well aware, but we are bound by our curse and wisdom not to let anyone take what belongs to the library," Aero responded and he kicked out with his back legs, knocking Luke into a bookshelf. "We can't let you leave."

Willow wrapped her arms under Aria's and pulled her to her feet, not letting go of the thick book in her hands. Glass fell to the floor with a clatter and blood dripped from Aria's hands. Pain clung to her everywhere, panic squeezing all the breath from her lungs as adrenaline pumped through her veins.

"I don't know where the blood is coming from." Aria stared down at her hands with teary eyes, biting on her lip. Her whole body shook uncontrollably.

"It's okay. It's okay," Willow assured her. "Don't touch anything. It could push the glass in deeper if it's still in your skin."

Aria did as she said and Willow bent down to grab the Death Stone Riddle lying under all the broken pieces of glass. It made a crinkling sound in Willow's grasp as she rolled it up before tucking it in her hoodie. Then she grabbed Aria's wrist and led her down an aisle of bookshelves, tucking the book she had under her other arm.

"Luke, Avi!" Willow called over her shoulder.

"We're coming!" Avi yelled back and then a crashing sound met their ears, followed by several others. "Oh, no!"

"Avi!" Luke shouted, worry thick in his voice. "*What did you do?*"

Loud thuds echoed through the library, the sound of wood splintering and books falling. Dust began to cloud the air. The bookshelves were tumbling down toward the floor like dominos, and they were heading straight for Aria and Willow.

"RUN!" Luke screamed. "We'll meet back up with you!"

Willow's grip tightened on Aria's wrist and they ran as fast as they could across the marble floor as bookshelves barreled toward them. Tomes and scrolls flew off the shelves all around them. They turned the corner, the stairs growing closer just ahead of them. A low growl broke through the crashing of bookshelves and thudding of their feet. Fear racked through Aria like lightning, burning her skin and heart as it beat horribly fast.

"We're right behind you!" Luke called from behind them as they reached the long, marble steps.

"But so is Deadly One and Deadly Two!" Avi shouted, causing Aria to glance back at Yalecia and Aero leaping over the bookshelves and into the air.

A growl resounded through the library.

Luke and Avi's feet hit the stairs at a run behind Aria and Willow. Aria's legs felt numb, but it came with waves of stabbing caused by the bounding of her feet on the stairs and the glass that may have pierced her jeans.

Yalecia and Aero dove off the floor, over the railing, and soared through the empty middle of the tower before coming back around and diving toward the stairs. The four of them ducked as claws swiped above their heads. Avi slipped on the marble steps and rolled down them, groaning with each thump. Luke, Aria, and Willow rushed after him, keeping their heads low to avoid the strikes from Yalecia and Aero. Yalecia's claws caught Willow's jacket and a tearing sound ripped through the air. Luke's hands rose at chest level, colorful magic crackling in his palms like lightning. A blue glow shot toward Yalecia and the sphinx swerved away as the enchantment skimmed past her wing, her giddy laugh echoing throughout the library.

"Little children, stop running from us! You can't win!" Yalecia yelled just as she tore through the golden railing like it was a piece of paper and Avi came to a stop. She reached out her clawed paw, grabbed him by his shirt, and threw him from the stairs. A scream erupted from Avi's throat as he fell towards the first floor, disappearing into the shadows.

CHAPTER EIGHTEEN

"AVI!" WILLOW, LUKE, and Aria screamed at once.

Shock shook Aria to the core, and before she could think, she jumped past the broken railing. She plummeted down through the air so fast, collecting her magic in the palms of her hands. The air whipped in her face, filling her lungs with so much oxygen that it felt like it was choking her. Avi was several feet below her and the ground was growing nearer by the second. She closed her eyes for a moment and called on Black Smoke, pooling it in the air around her. She then commanded it to wrap around Avi's body below her and it brought him up toward her, but the ground still rushed to meet them both.

With her free hand, Aria reached out in the air, grappling for something to hold onto, but there was nothing but empty space all around. The air blew her hair around her face. Aria closed her eyes, a pit growing in her stomach. When they reached the bottom, it would all be over. There was nothing she could do to slow their fall.

She summoned more Black Smoke above her, forcing it to wrap around her own body. The fall grew slower, the ground still growing closer. Panic seized her again and the fog dissipated into nothing as they hit the bottom floor. A loud crunch met her ears and her heart jolted as if it had been struck by lightning. A large pile of something white was just below her, and Avi was lying on top of it with wide eyes. They gasped for breath, the pile of whatever they were on shifting beneath them.

"AVI!" Luke and Willow's voices echoed off the marble walls of the library far above them. "ARIA!"

"Avi, Avi!" Aria shook Avi's shoulders violently to get him to sit up and move. "We need to get out of here."

He just stared up at the ceiling, his eyes wide and his chest rising and falling rapidly. "I thought I was going to die…"

"Yeah, well…" Aria wanted to comfort him somehow, but if they didn't escape the library quickly, they *would* die. They'd become meals for the guardians of the library, as Yalecia had said.

Above them, Yalecia and Aero dove at the steps to reach Luke and Willow as they bounded down the stairs. Their shouts and screams were faint but clear enough to still echo throughout the otherwise silent library.

"ARIA! AVI!" Luke screamed again with panic laced in his tone.

"We're okay!" Aria shouted back, continuing to shake Avi. "Avi, we need to go!"

He finally pulled himself up and took a deep breath. His eyes widened in horror and he tucked his arms in closer to himself. "Um…Aria…why are we sitting on top of a pile of bones?"

Aria looked underneath them more closely, having ignored the snapping objects they had fallen on, and her body froze up. Breaking white bones were underneath them in a pile as high as half of one of the bookshelves. They shifted beneath their weight. One of Aria's hands was planted on a human skull.

Luke and Willow ran for their lives down the staircase. Willow's heart thumped in her ears. Aria's voice echoed back at them, and relief flooded through her like a wave. She glanced at Luke and felt the evident relief and worry washing through him too. They bounded down the stairs faster in desperation, keeping their distance from the railing.

The first floor was growing closer, but it still seemed ages away and the guardians of the library were gaining on them fast. Yalecia dove toward Willow and swiped her claws toward her back, catching the fabric of her jacket. Willow was jolted backward and slammed her back into the steps. Pain shot through her back and side in waves. She groaned, trying to force herself up as tears formed in her eyes. Yalecia advanced, landing just above her with her fangs bared. She leaned down toward Willow's face, drool hanging from her open mouth and hunger flickering in her eyes. Willow tried to push her dead weight from the steps, a scream of horror tearing itself from her throat. Flames formed in Luke's palms, and he shot them at Yalecia. The fire seared the side of her face, and with a deep roar of agony, she took to the air again. Willow rolled away with her stolen book clutched tight to her side and winced at the throbbing in her back. She put a hand to it, trying to straighten herself, but the slightest touch sent agony through her back. It was either bruised or broken. She dreaded to think the worst. She blinked the tears out of her eyes and pushed through the pain anyway. Luke grabbed her hand to help her down the steps, his hands hot and sweaty.

"I really hate to ask this, but is it possible to go faster?" Luke wrapped an arm under her arms to help support her.

"I'll try." Willow walked quicker, adrenaline rushing through her veins and muting the pain. If it hurt now, it was going to hurt a lot worse later.

A loud thud behind her sent panic radiating through the air. She glanced behind her to see Aero creeping up behind them.

"Run!" she screamed, pushing Luke to move quicker despite the pangs beating into her back. She bolted down the stairs, gritting her teeth against it.

Aero leaped for them with his beak snapping at their backs. Willow's legs ached, and she could see the way Luke's wobbled. Aero was wearing them out, and soon enough, they would lose his and Yalecia's game. As Aero jumped towards Luke, his sharp talons struck out. Luke jumped forward, pulling Willow with him, and together, they rolled down the stairs. Screams broke from both of their throats as they thudded down the steps. Each tumble down the next stair was even more painful than the last. The steps hit Willow from every direction, the world spinning out of control. Nausea hit her, bringing bile up into her mouth, but when they finally reached the last step, they were alive. The book Willow had been carrying fell out of her grasp and slid to the floor. Willow gasped, gritting her teeth against the aching that just breathing caused. Her ribs now felt bruised and black dots crowded her vision.

"Oh, little children!" Yalecia yelled. "Come back here!"

Luke quickly stood and grabbed Willow's hand to pull her to her feet. "We need to find Aria and Avi." He picked the book of languages off the floor and handed it to her, watching over her shoulder for the library's guardians.

Willow glanced at the golden doors only a few feet away, wishing more than anything they could all walk out into the cold air right that moment. "Alright, let's go."

Shaking off the pain from their falling, they took off across the marble floor and turned down an aisle of ancient books. Willow reached out with her mind, searching for any emotions that felt distinctly like Aria or Avi.

"There will be no leaving this place." Yalecia's voice echoed from somewhere above. "You must meet your fate."

Aria and Avi were climbing down from the pile of bones, and with each movement they made, a loud snap came from beneath them. Aria's eyes were squeezed half-closed, trying to somehow shut out each snapping sound that resounded from beneath her hands and feet. How Yalecia and Aero had gotten so many human and animal bones when nobody had stepped into the library in decades, Aria didn't know. She didn't want to think about it either.

Her whole body ached from the glass that had pierced her skin, but she still couldn't tell where it was coming from. She shook the pain from her thoughts and focused on getting out instead. Her stomach twisted in revulsion and bile rose in her throat at the skeletons shifting beneath her. She opened her eyes when she heard many bones crash to the marble floor, along with Avi as he slid down the pile. Blood trickled from his nose and he wiped his arm across it, smearing it on his sleeve.

"I have a lot of complaints I will have to make with the city for this inconvenience in checking out books." Sarcasm laced his tone and Aria rolled her eyes.

She glanced up at the stairs, but Luke and Willow weren't there, and neither were Yalecia or Aero. She bit her lip and grabbed her sunflower necklace, blood slicking it.

"Let's just find Luke and Willow and get out of here." Aria slid down the pile of bones, her whole body tense and cringing as her skin touched them. She beckoned Avi to follow her, and they hurried down a shadowed aisle of bookshelves.

They ran to the end of the aisle and Aria peered around the corner. Her eyes grazed over the shadows and vast space above them to make sure Yalecia and Aero were nowhere in sight. Seeing it was clear, they crept down the next row of books, the sounds of their feet touching the floor feeling too loud in the now eerie silence. Aria felt on edge and the hairs on her arms were sticking up again. Avi looked back and forth behind her, but it seemed there was no one watching them even if it felt like there was. They peered around the corner, which was empty as well. They stepped down the next aisle, and Aria could only hope they were going in the direction of the door, Luke, and Willow.

"This place is like a maze," Avi whispered behind her.

He was right, of course.

"I bet there is a reason—" A beast leaped from the top of a bookshelf, causing Aria's voice to break.

Yalecia's paws gripped Aria's shoulders and knocked her to the marble floor, tearing through her sleeves. The breath left her body and dots clouded her vision. Long, razor-sharp claws scraped at the marble floor as Yalecia pinned her arms to it. Aria tried to pull out from underneath Yalecia. The beast's jaws hung open as her teeth lowered toward Aria's face, drool dripping onto her cheeks. A scream of panic tore from Aria's throat.

Avi grabbed a book off the shelf and threw it at Yalecia's face. Her eyes diverted to him and she growled.

"Leave her alone!" Avi screamed, colorful sparks forming in his palms.

The enchantment soared through the air like an arrow directed at Yalecia. Grabbing Aria by her arms, the sphinx took to the air and the magic hit a bookshelf instead. Tomes fell to the floor and the sound of splintering wood resounded. A high-pitched scream echoed off the walls and bookshelves as Aria dangled ten feet from the floor, claws digging into her skin. Aria kicked her legs in the open air beneath her, a thrill of fear opening a pit in her stomach. Darkness loomed at the edges of her vision like her sight was just waiting to give out.

Avi threw a forceful push at Yalecia and it caught her wing, knocking the sphinx off balance. Swerving to the left, her grip loosened on Aria's arm. Aria plummeted back down to the ground and hit the marble floor just as Luke and Willow rounded the corner. Pain spread through her body and she couldn't stop the groan that escaped her lips. Luke bounded toward Aria and dropped to his knees beside her as coughs racked her body. He wrapped his arm around her shoulder, shielding her. Black spots edged into her blurry vision. She blinked several times, trying to clear herself of the dizzying blur and the aches stabbing through her.

"Let's go!" Willow shouted. "Aero is not too far behind us!"

Luke offered Aria a hand and she took it, letting him help her to her feet. Then he pulled her along, back the way he and Willow had come. They ran, lungs heaving with every step, through the aisle of bookshelves and the cobwebs they were infested with. Yalecia was hot on their trail, growling from somewhere behind them. Avi continuously threw enchantments at her over his shoulder, but he hit the shelves more than the beast. Books fell to the floor and shelves tipped over with reverberating thuds. Dust billowed in the air. Yalecia soared toward them, claws outstretched and a hungry look in her eyes.

"Come on, Avi!" Willow cheered him on, but there was a plea in her voice. "You can do it!"

Finally, Avi scored. One of his enchantments hit Yalecia in the chest and a blue glow sank into her. It threw her backwards several feet and caused her to swerve in other directions, knocking tomes and scrolls from the shelves. She slowly fell to the floor as the Immobile Enchantment sank in.

Aria, Luke, Avi, and Willow turned the corner and Aero launched at them from the tops of the bookshelves. Aero pushed Luke to the ground and Aria fell with him. Aria grabbed Luke's arm, trying to pull him away from Aero. Luke kicked out at the beast's face and slammed his foot into his neck as he scooted backward. Aero opened his beak, grabbing hold of Luke's leg and biting down on his shin. His face grew red and a scream broke through the near silence.

Aria stood, searching her mind for something to do. Avi shot a ball of red magical sparks at Aero, but he swerved away with Luke's leg still clamped in his mouth. Luke screamed, flailing about, his face drenched in sweat. Aria's gut twisted and her hands wouldn't stop trembling. Vomit threatened to come up as blood ran down Luke's leg and pooled on the marble floor. She pulled on the magic in her palms, calling on every ounce of strength she had. She needed to get her friends out, she needed to put an end to this, and she had to save Luke. Her whole body shook in fear of everything that was happening at that moment.

Willow lifted the thick book in her arms high in the air and threw it at Aero, smacking him on the head. Aero dropped Luke and fixed his gaze on Willow. Luke lay motionless at his feet, his eyes fluttering closed as tears ran from them. Aero spread his wings wide, rising on his hind legs to tower above them.

"How dare you," he snarled. "You dare take what does not belong to you. I tried to appease you children, and you treat me like this." Hunger flashed in his yellow eyes.

"You treat *us* like this!" Willow screamed at him, conjuring the book back and raising it above her head again.

Aero spread his wings, using them as leverage to leap toward Willow. "You have a price to pay."

The magic in Aria rose, spilling over in streams of color that leaked from her palms. Electric green, ruby red, cobalt blue, and glittering gold lit the air like the northern lights, dancing around her.

"Get out of here!" Luke screamed, a plea of desperation in his voice.

Aria pulled on that magic and let it burst out of her ten-fold, letting it flow toward her target. Her hair lifted from her shoulders, magic making her skin glow like she was coated in stardust. Panic surged through her and all books on the shelves flew towards Aero. They knocked him into a bookshelf, his eyes wide with fear. Aria saw her reflection in the yellow of his eyes, a radiating reflection of pure power.

Magic crackled through the air, filling the aisle with light. It was like sharp electricity that prickled Aria's skin. Fear stirred in her stomach and Aero's body glowed faintly, forcing his body to go limp and his eyes to fall closed. Aria watched, trying to pull all her magic back into her palms. The blinding light and magic radiating from her skin receded and she fell to her knees. She stared at her palms in horror, remembering the words she'd read in the Ancient Scrolls. All that power and more, and she'd called on it. Whatever she'd done, she didn't know exactly. Her mind felt blank and clueless, but she never wanted to do that again. To make a creature like Aero feel fright over her made something in her seize up. She ran a hand over her sweaty forehead smearing blood across her face. This power that could make the very air burst with energy and magic was what had torn the world into three realms. She didn't want it.

Avi ran to Luke's side as Aria crawled toward him. Willow clutched her book against her chest, standing over the three of them. Her eyes met Aria's, studying her. Aria ignored the looks cast at her and tucked her arms under Luke's.

"Avi, can you get his feet?" Aria's voice sounded drained of spirit.

Avi did as she asked, careful of the deep wound Aero had made. Luke looked up at Aria through heavy lidded eyes, grime smeared on his face. His jaw was tight, excruciating agony clear on his face. She looked down on him, unable to keep the pity out of her eyes as Avi and her limped down the aisles with him. There was so much she felt she should say to him and so much explaining she felt was needed, but she didn't really want to talk after everything that had happened.

Soon enough, the golden doors were in front of them. Willow held one of them open as they stepped out into the sun. When the golden doors thudded shut behind them, Aria let out a long breath. They'd gotten the Death Stone Riddle.

CHAPTER NINETEEN

THE COLD AIR sunk into Aria's skin, jolting her with a shiver, but it also soothed the wounds all over her body. Strom looked between the four of them limping through the doorway of the Library of Knowledge and out into the sun. He pressed a hand against where his heart may have been in shock. His eyes widened, trailing over each of them like they were his favorite piece of porcelain now broken. Celestia, however, was calmly sleeping on the griffin statue still, ignoring them completely.

Aria tucked her hands into the pockets of her jacket. "We need to get out of the city and then we can assess our wounds."

"B-but, Aria—" Avi tried to argue.

"If we stay in the city, we are putting ourselves in danger." Aria's eyes traveled over the empty rounded street. "The Dark Forces could be anywhere, and we already know there are spies for them within the city. We won't stand a chance against them. Especially like this."

"She's right," Willow agreed. "Strom, do you think you could carry Luke?"

"Yes, Strom carry L-Luke." Strom reached for him gently. "What happen to Diviner and friends?"

"We will tell you later, I promise." Aria glanced back at the golden doors. "But right now, we need to leave."

Avi lifted Celestia in his arms and slid his bag over his shoulder, the bird startling awake at the movement. Strom took Luke carefully, settling him against his chest while blood oozed from his leg, soaking his pants. Luke clenched his eyes shut against the agony and groaned. Willow and Aria slid on their backpacks and grabbed Luke's before limping back towards the busy city streets.

The hustle and bustle of people was suddenly all around them as they went back the way they had originally come. Children ran by them, businessmen shouted about their wares, and families walked to shops to purchase food. The smell of honey drifted out from a bakery as a man stood in the doorway holding a tray of honey-soaked pastries.

"Come get your Halfulas!" he shouted cheerily, before his eyes widened at the scene passing his shop. All the color seemed to drain from his face.

Heads turned in Aria and her friends' direction with looks of concern and maybe even revulsion, but no one stopped to help them. People stepped away to clear their path, drawing too much attention to them. Aria's mind raced, wishing she could cloak the six of them in shadows. All these eyes on her, and any one of them could be in league with the Dark Forces. A flash of black cloth caught her eye and her stomach leapt into her throat. Head snapping to the left, she blew out a shaky breath. It was just a woman hanging clothes on a clothesline outside her window—not the Dark Forces.

"Man, I could really go for a Halfula right now." Avi stared back longingly at the horrified baker. "I can't remember the last time I had one of those. It's kind of like a baked bread roll, but it's soaked in honey and cinnamon!"

Upon hearing that, Aria's stomach grumbled traitorously, and she had to force herself to keep her head from turning as well. The arms of others brushed her as they made their way through the thickly crowded street. Her eyes darted around at every passing person, searching for black cloaks with an embroidered golden dagger.

Gold flashed a few feet away and she tensed again, but instead of a dagger it was a crescent moon and stars symbol—one star at the top of the moon and one at the bottom. The Forces of Light symbol. It was embroidered on the shoulder of a figure draped in a white cloak. Aria's eyes followed the figure as they wove through the crowd until it had swallowed them whole.

"Aria, did you see?" Avi swiveled in the direction the figure had gone. "That was—"

"I know."

"Maybe they can help us?" He stood on his tip-toes to see above the crowd.

"No, they can't," Aria said softly. "They'll just stop our mission. They can't know who we are or what we're doing."

Silence fell between them and they pressed forward, ready to leave Viden far behind them. As they neared the gate to leave the city, soldiers in gleaming golden armor marched down the road, a man in grimy plain clothing being held by the arms. The man had dirty blond hair, pale skin, and his eyes were bright blue like that of the sky—a shade of blue Aria recognized. Bruises covered his skin and his hair was disheveled, looking like the definition of a prisoner. The man's head hung low with every step he was forced to take. Chains rattled from the soldiers' waists as they pushed the man forward over the cobbled streets.

There was something about the man that felt familiar.

Aria's eyes leapt between Willow and the man, something beginning to click in her mind. A darker shade of blond hair and a sharper jawline, but those eyes and those rounded cheeks; she saw a reflection of Willow in this prisoner.

Willow's eyes went wide with recognition too, and she rushed forward, reaching out like she could pull him toward her. Before anyone could stop her, her voice rose above the din of the crowded streets. "DAD!"

The man in custody looked about the road before his eyes locked onto Willow and his mouth fell open. Struggling against the soldiers, he tried to turn toward her and his mouth moved to form distant words.

"Willow—why—find—home—love—" was all Aria made out through the city noise.

Willow's father pulled on the shackles encircling his wrists and ankles, eyes locked on his daughter with a plea in them. The soldiers surrounded him and suddenly he doubled over, clutching his stomach. Being dragged forward, he was led past a wooden sign pointing in the direction of the Enchanting Control Building. The distance grew between them and Willow's father before the crowd abruptly obscured their vision of him.

"Dad! Leave him alone!" Willow's every word was full of torment, and then her voice broke on the last one. "He's innocent." She started after him, tears rolling down her cheeks, but Aria's hand caught her wrist. Willow's head turned toward her, expression pleading. "They're hurting him! Please, we have to do something. We have to follow him."

Aria put her hand on Willow's arm to stop her, saying as politely as she could manage, "Willow, I'm sorry, but we can't follow him." Her eyes stung saying the words. She'd once had to walk away from her own parents. "It's out of our control, and if we don't get out of here soon, the Dark Forces could find our location. There are too many people here to see us. If we follow him, we'll all be caught. We're in no shape to fight our way out of this one."

She felt pity curl through her stomach, along with guilt. She didn't want to run away from this. Everything in her heart said she should try to help Willow's father, but it would only make everything worse. Going toward Enchanting Control would end in coming across at least one person from the Dark Forces.

For a moment, Willow was silent. She stared at the space where her father had been just moments before. Everything Willow had been scared of since her father had been put on trial seemed to be coming true. Aria felt as if she could see Willow's heart breaking before her eyes. Guilt branded her heart as her friend's head fell forward. Aria knew all too well what it was like to have to leave loved ones behind.

At last, Willow hastily wiped the tears from her face and said, "I understand."

Avi stepped up beside Willow and wrapped his arms around her, guiding her toward the glistening gates of Viden. She leaned her head on his shoulder, breath shuddering as she tried to suppress sobs. His hand stroked her back in a calming rhythm. They turned their backs on Viden, the eyes of the crowd drilling into Aria's back. Her cautious mind had anxiety coursing through every vein, and her hands shook despite being in tight fists. When they reached the gates, the man and woman guarding them put their hands against the cold stone and they slowly swung open to reveal the wide fields beyond. Stepping onto the grass, Aria's mind repeated the image of Willow's father, hurt, resigned, and locked in chains. Glancing back at the glittering city of Viden, the richest city in all the

"I'm hungry. My feet hurt. I'm thirsty. I'm tired," Avi complained, hunching over dramatically. "Celestia healed the cut on my arm but she can't heal my headache."

Willow's lips tugged upward, clearly fighting a smile, and she shook her head. "You sound like a child, Avi."

"I *am* a child, smarty-pants. I'm not eighteen yet, so technically I am." He smirked and brushed shoulders with her, distracting her from earlier.

Every time Aria noticed him doing that, a surge of gratefulness flooded her.

After walking for about an hour, Strom had led them into a shadowed forest where leaves crackled beneath their feet. The canopy above was mostly empty, allowing streaks of sunlight to pierce the forest's shadows. Celestia sat on Luke as Strom carried him. She cried tears into his wound, as she'd done many times already, but it didn't seem to be enough and there were only so many tears that she could cry.

Spotting a clear spot to set up camp, Aria pointed toward it. "Alright, we'll rest here. The tent can go over there."

Avi sighed a breath of relief and settled himself against a tree, propping his arms behind his head. "Finally, I can relax."

The rest of them sat down on the forest floor, assessing their injuries as Willow pulled out medical supplies. Celestia wobbled around them, eyes trailing along their stained and bruised skin.

Beside Luke, Strom grabbed the backpack that had the tent in it and poked at the zipper. "Strom c-confused."

"You *pull* the zipper," Avi instructed. "But maybe we should set up the tent? No offense, Strom, but you don't exactly know how to set up a tent."

Willow snorted. "Neither do you, Avi. Remember the last time you tried to help set up the tent?"

"Hey—"

The two of them bickered teasingly as Willow sat beside Luke to deal with his injury.

Luke's hands pinched his wound shut just in case it might burst open or begin to bleed heavier. But he was looking at Aria's injuries rather than his own. She felt his eyes on her, and it made heat rush into her face despite the cold air that encompassed them. She'd taken her jacket off to see where the blood on her hands had come from, and the wind made goosebumps rise on her arms. Little knicks from glass littered her arms, cuts ran across her hands, and her pants were sliced through on her left leg to reveal a bloody gash. Her whole body felt bruised and ached for rest.

Avi sighed and stopped his bickering, assessing some minor injuries littered across his body. Strom sat back and watched them with softened eyes. His gaze shifted to Celestia as she flew past them. She perched in one of the pine trees above them, singing a melody for the wind to carry. It was a song that somehow sounded like rainy days and falling tears.

"If I can find the ingredients for a Jenie Potion—a Healing Potion—then I'll make one. Strom said he knows the area, so I'm sure he can help me," Willow said as she tore out thick bandages and cleaning solutions for Luke and Aria's wounds. "It's a simple enough potion, but it won't heal all of the damage… Not for Luke. It's too deep. I'm sorry, Luke. But if Celestia can give you more tears, you'll get better soon." She sat down next to him, pulling his shredded pantleg up, and gnawed on her lip. "We sure did draw a lot of attention in Viden…and I shouldn't have yelled for my father…" She trailed off and sighed as she pushed the cap off the peroxide bottle. "Hold still. This is going to sting."

Luke squeezed his eyes shut and clamped his lips together, teeth sinking into his lower lip as Willow poured the peroxide over the thick, bloody, fleshy wound on his leg. His leg shifted even as he tried to pin it down.

"Hold still, I need to clean it." She took a cloth and carefully cleaned the wound.

Luke let out a low cry of agony, fingers digging into his leg to keep it in place. Aria reached for his hands and forced him to turn his attention away from his leg for a minute. His blue eyes met hers, tears gathering in them. She gave his hand a reassuring squeeze, thumb brushing over his knuckles. He released a shaky breath and fought to smile.

"All done!" Willow put away the bloody cloth and pulled out a thread and a needle. "Now I just have to stitch it up. It's a good thing my mom taught me sewing."

Aria's brows knitted together skeptically. "Umm, I don't think stitching up a wound and sewing fabric together are the same thing." She let go of Luke's hand, her attention being pulled toward a tiny piece of glass embedded in her hand. Gritting her teeth against the stabbing it caused, she pulled it from her skin. They were all going to need that Healing Potion if Willow was able to make it.

After stitching up his leg as best she could, Willow wrapped Luke's leg up with the thick bandage. He fought to hold in the groans by biting down on his lip. Then Willow turned to help bandage Aria's hands and leg, making sure to pull out the tiny slivers of glass with her magic, and then bandaged up her own arm that had been scratched in the fight.

"We won't be able to stay here. Not so close to the city." Willow said and she paused, looking back toward Viden. Something in her gaze told Aria exactly what she was thinking about. A father who she couldn't help free. "But we all need rest and time to heal, so I suggest we camp for now."

Luke's head fell back against the tree as his eyes fluttered closed, struggling to stay awake. His body relaxed and went limp. Aria's heart leapt into her throat before she caught sight of the slow rise and fall of his chest. She could only imagine the torment he was in. Giving him a delicate pat on the arm, she hoped the Healing Potion and Celestia's tears would help.

A breeze swept through the forest and prickled Aria's skin. A shiver ran through her. "We should set up the tent," she said, turning back to Willow and Avi. "We all need to get out of the cold."

"I'll help!" Avi hurried to his feet, dusting off his pants and throwing Willow a smirk. "Let me prove just how very good I am at setting up a tent."

She shook her head at him, amusement flitting over her face.

Together, Aria and Avi pulled out the tent and put it up as Willow pulled out a small bowl from their supplies. Avi stumbled over the poles and tripped over the fabric of the tent multiple times, complaining about how the instructions didn't make sense. He held them upside down, looking at the side where the directions were in another language, before flipping it around. A minute later, Aria began stomping the stakes into the ground to secure it. Avi then stabbed his hand with one.

"Ouch!" he shouted and threw the stake at the tent like it was *its* fault.

"How did you even do that?" Aria's brows furrowed. "You're supposed to put it in the ground, not your—"

"My hand got in the way," he grumbled. When the tent

was finally standing, he put his hand on his hips and proudly announced to Willow, "See, I *can* set up a tent!"

Aria decided not to say that *she'd* actually done most of the work.

Willow looked back at them from where she was foraging. "Okay, Avi. Okay." She threw Aria a wink after Avi had turned his back.

Wandering around with Strom, they dug through the foliage to find the ingredients for the potion. Strom knew where to look for things, pulling plants aside and reaching into the trees where strange-looking plants grew on the bark. As they worked, Aria and Avi set up the blankets and pillows in the tent. The dimming light began to cast deep shadows inside it. The clouds above were painted pink and orange like cotton candy by the setting sun. The breeze turned colder and the blankets inside began to call Aria longingly.

Willow's voice broke through Aria's reverie and she turned away from the blankets. "Avi, can you come get Celestia out of this tree?"

Avi shrugged toward Aria and left the tent, turning to throw his pillow over to where he'd be sleeping. Aria strode through the door after him and over to Luke, dropping to her knees beside him. She shook his shoulders gently, trying to get him to become conscious again. His eyes fluttered open slowly, settling on her face above him. A smile split his face before falling, his jaw tightening in discomfort.

"Here, I'll help you into the tent." Aria reached out her hand and he grasped it.

"Thanks," he said as his body weight settled over her and her knees nearly buckled. He wrapped an arm around her and heat flushed her cheeks even in the icy air. A fluttering feeling settled in her stomach.

With all her strength, she forced herself forward and tightened her arms around him. Being this close, she could feel his body heat radiating off him. He used his one leg to help propel himself forward so that it wasn't all on Aria. Her knees shook from exhaustion and the majority of Luke's body weight leaning on her. She nearly tripped on a twig, stumbling forward and pausing for a moment.

"Aria—"

"If you're about to argue over me carrying you, I'm not going to listen. I'm not leaving you out here. You need rest, and there's loads of blankets and pillows in the tent."

"You're so stubborn," he told her, smirking.

They made it into the tent, and she dragged him to his and Avi's side of it. He laid back against the pillows, eyes fluttering sleepily.

"Thank you," he said as she covered him with a blanket. "Not just for helping me…For saving me earlier."

Aria met his eyes, pulling back as she recalled seeing her magic dancing in the air around her. "Of course. I wouldn't just leave you, Luke."

He gave her a faint smile at that. "What you did…your skin was glowing. Your *eyes* were glowing. You looked so… powerful."

Aria opened her mouth but found she was speechless. *Powerful. Fearful. A legend.* She swallowed and forced herself to stand. "I should go see what Willow and Avi are doing."

He sighed and let his eyes close. "Okay. Sweet dreams, Aria."

"Sweet dreams, Luke," she said before heading back outside.

Now the sky was a deepening blue, the moon shedding its light down on the forest. Wind wrestled with the branches high above them, shaking whatever leaves were still left in the darkened boughs. With night descending, fairies began to dance around the forest, covered in golden dust that glowed like the stars. Several feet away, Strom, Avi, Willow, and Celestia's silhouettes could be seen. Celestia took to the air from a tree with fire glittering across her feathers and casting a glow around them. When she landed on Avi's shoulder, her flames ceased, but even without the glow, Aria could still make out each of their faces.

Avi gave Celestia a little pat on the head. "Okay, she's down. Why did you need her?"

"I need her tears." Willow held up the potion for them to stare at the lime-green liquid swishing around in it. "They are crucial to the potion. The rest of the stuff in this potion is just to help you feel more refreshed and recover quicker. Without the phoenix tears, it won't work, though."

Willow crept closer, gently lifting the bowl to Celestia's pink fuzzy baby face again as a tear formed in her eyes. The little phoenix leaned toward the bowl, willingly giving tear after tear.

Willow gave Celestia a rub on the head and she tweeted. "That will be enough. Thank you, little firebird."

With a spoon, Willow stirred the liquid in the bowl before lifting it above her face and dripping it into her mouth slowly. She held the bowl out to Aria, sighing as the discomfort evidently eased from her body. Aria did the same, swallowing a few gulps of the potion before handing it to Avi. The foul, leafy taste of the potion lingered on her tongue. Immediately, the pain in her body ceased. The small cuts and bruises all over her body disappeared as if they'd never been there. She unwrapped the bandages on her hands and leg. She watched in awe as the gashes across her palms and leg grew less irritated. They began to scab over and heal almost completely. Almost.

Willow must have seen the disappointment on her face

because she said, "It's a Healing Potion, but it won't heal a deep wound completely right away. Your wounds should be gone by tomorrow night, though."

"Mine are already gone," Avi said cheerily as he examined his arms. "I feel great!"

"Me too," Willow said, throwing him a look before looking apologetically in Aria's direction. "But ours were more minor injuries."

"Can I have the potion?" Aria gently took the bowl from Avi. "I'll give the rest to Luke."

As the three of them climbed inside the tent, Strom called out to them, "Good night, friends."

"Good night, Strom." Aria smiled. "Thank you for everything—for getting us to Viden and for watching after us. It means a lot." With a wave, she zipped the door closed and shut out the night.

Celestia looked worn out and in need of a nap like the rest of them, snuggling up beside Avi. The floor around them was thick with plushy blankets that Aria longed to crash into on her own side of the tent. Before she could do that, though, she crawled in beside Luke and lifted the bowl to his mouth. He peered at her through drowsy eyes and she coaxed him to drink it before he fell into slumber at last. Aria slipped out of his and Avi's side of the tent quietly and put the bowl away in a backpack. After getting situated on her own side of the large tent, she fell fast asleep and didn't wake all through the night.

CHAPTER TWENTY

ARIA TOSSED AND turned in the early morning, tangled in a mound of blankets. Birds were just beginning to sing their tunes outside. She sat up out of bed and quietly tipped-toed to the boys' room to check on Luke. The frigid air trapped inside the tent clawed its way down to her bones and she shivered. Settling on her knees beside Luke, a cough racked his body. She pulled his blanket up tighter around him and her fingers brushed his trembling arm. It was cold, yes, but not so cold that Luke should have been shaking while being wrapped up in a thick pile of blankets. Not to mention Celestia lay next to Avi, warming the tent with her fiery presence; the warmth was stronger in Luke and Avi's side of the tent. Panic immediately began to dig into Aria's mind. She leaned over to touch Luke's forehead with the back of her hand and heat burned into her skin.

Fever. The word pounded into her mind as she raced through it to find a solution. *The wound on his leg must have gotten infected.*

Willow and Avi were still asleep and she didn't want to wake them. So, she leaned over to look through the medical pack herself. She had never helped anyone who was sick like this before. Her parents had taken care of themselves whenever sickness was in the house, and they had taken care of her. She tried to recall what they had done when she'd had a fever. She scrambled back into the main room of the tent and looked around. If there was one thing she wished she could have of the Diviner's powers, it was the gift of Healing. Then she'd be able to heal Luke's wound and infection instantly—if that was how a Healer's power worked.

She grabbed Luke's canteen and an extra blanket to help keep him warm.

Good enough, she thought, then crawled back into Luke and Avi's side of the tent and laid it carefully across him.

He peeked at her through half-closed eyes and a soft smile touched his lips. "Thanks—" A raspy cough broke from his throat.

"Of course." Aria tried to return the grin. "I brought you water."

He slowly pushed himself up and the blanket fell into his lap. Aria handed him the water and he drank it slowly, his face grimacing at the effort it took to drink.

"How do you feel? You have a fever."

"Oh," he said, putting the cap back on his canteen. "My throat feels sore, and I feel so cold. My head aches. I suppose I got sick from being outside in the cold so much." He leaned away slightly. "You should probably back up so you don't catch it."

"Could it be from your wound? It could have gotten infected."

"Possibly." Even in the dim morning light leaking through the fabric of the tent, the torment on his face was evident. His fingers traveled down to where the wound was underneath all the blankets. "I can feel it's swollen."

"I don't understand, though," Aria said. "Willow cleansed your wound with peroxide, and I gave you the Healing Potion."

"Peroxide cleanses, yes, but the wound Aero gave me isn't just a scratch," he said. "Healing potions can't heal everything. It can heal what's on the surface, but the deeper it goes, the harder it is to heal."

"Does that apply to sickness too?"

"Yes. Illnesses live inside a body and must be flushed out, but that is deep and takes time. At least, that's what my mother always told me whenever I got sick when I was younger." A sorrowful look passed over his face and he shut his mouth. Aria's mind wandered to everything he'd told her so many weeks ago.

"I never thought about it like that. I just assumed those with healing powers and potions could heal everything right away." Aria held up her hands to show the bandages she'd wrapped around them before bed. She glanced down at her own leg that had been cut sometime in the library. "But I guess I was wrong."

"Don't worry," he said, patting her arm. "Soon, I'll heal, you'll heal, and we'll be ready to leave."

Aria's lips tugged up, putting her hands on his chest to push him back against his pillow. "Well, if you're going to heal, you need to lay down, tuck in, and close your eyes." She grabbed the blanket, laying it across his chest again, then set his canteen off to the side.

His eyes watched her, a grin pulling at his lips despite the exhaustion and pain he clearly felt. He lifted his hand toward her face, then hesitated, his smile dropping. A cough racked his body. "Sorry. I'm sick. I don't want to get you sick too."

Aria knew she was playing with fire and was likely being reckless, but she reached out and grasped Luke's hand anyway. She wanted him to know how she felt about him. She couldn't ignore it anymore. She lifted his hand to her cheek, the heat of his fever burning against her skin. In spite of the heat, it sent a chill through her body as he cupped her face, a crooked grin on his lips again.

"Get well soon, Luke." She set his hand down, tried to smile, and then crawled back into the girls' side of the tent.

Later that day, Aria watched Strom chase a squirrel happily across the forest floor. Willow sat down next to her just inside the tent, wrapped up in a blanket. A layer of frost covered the ground and each breath clouded in front of their faces. Dark clouds hung in the sky above, casting everything in solemn gray below.

Willow gnawed on her lower lip, her eyes unfocused. There was that look in her eyes—the same look she got whenever she was thinking, but now it was tinged with sadness. Aria only had to guess what she was thinking about and it made her heart ache for her friend. All her panic and heartbreak weeks ago when she'd found out her father had been put on trial was likely intensified. Aria couldn't help seeing the similarities between her own parents and Willow's father. Both had been ripped away from them. Both had been put through torment. And neither of them could save the ones they loved—not yet, anyway.

Willow suddenly stopped chewing her lip and her eyes slid to her, catching that Aria had been studying her. Curiosity dawned on her face, ridding it of the aching that had overtaken it moments before. "So, Aria…in the library…"

Aria sighed and braced herself for what was coming. Her hands crept to her sunflower necklace like that could stop her questions.

"In the library, you did…Well, I don't know what you did, really." She searched Aria's face as if there might be answers written there. "There was all this light and you glowed, and then Aero was unconscious and covered in books. How did you do that? Where did you learn it? Because I know you've been having a hard time controlling your powers."

"I don't know what I did. I just sort of blanked out. I saw you guys needed help, felt my magic calling, and boom." Aria sighed, everything that had happened in the library forcing itself back into her mind. "I read in the library about the past Diviners. Turns out, I'm the first Diviner in three hundred years—the only one worthy enough in all that time. I have so much power. So much power that one of the past Diviners was the one that ripped the universe into three realms…because he couldn't control it." She shook her head and stared straight ahead at Strom gently petting the squirrel he'd been chasing. "I don't want to be like that. I don't want to lose control. I don't want to destroy things. But I knew that magic like that could help you, I suppose. I don't ever want to have to use it again, though."

"Aria, I see nothing wrong with the magic you have. What you did saved us—"

"It scared Aero. Did you not see the fear in his eyes?" She paused, her eyes turning glassy. "To make a creature as dangerous as him scared of me—"

"So? It's not like you killed him. You just knocked him unconscious," Willow said, waving it off casually. "Whether you believe in yourself or not, you saved us. You got us out of that library. You saved Avi when Yalecia threw him off the stairs. What I saw when you glowed, and there were colors everywhere…that was magic in its purest form. It was as if you'd pulled magic from you and then reeled it back in."

"I can do that?"

"I don't know, but you're the Diviner. You are capable of so much, and you don't even *know* how much. You don't have to fear that, Aria. Being capable of great things doesn't mean you're a disaster waiting to happen. If you were the only Diviner worthy enough in three hundred years, there has to be a reason. If the first Diviner was the only person worthy enough of the power then, and yet still ripped the universe into three realms, then that can only mean one thing."

Avi's voice rose in shock from the other room. "The first Diviner did *what?*"

Willow smiled. "These realms were meant to happen. And you were meant to happen. Think about that, okay?" Then she got up, dropped her blanket in the tent, and walked away, leaving Aria to do exactly what she'd asked. "Hey, Strom! I see you made another friend!"

Strom looked up from the squirrel in his arms with a giddy grin. "Hello, Willow friend, meet squirrel friend!"

Aria stared after them, thinking just like Willow had told her to. Everything Willow had said played over in her head. Her heart couldn't help but pound at the thought of the power running in her veins, but this time, something felt different about it. It felt as if chains around her heart were weakening, nearly ready to break.

As Aria stepped out of the tent a few days later, the bright rising sun shining above, a snowflake drifted down to land on her thick jacket. She sighed and zipped the tent behind her, sealing what little warmth there was inside. Strom was out of sight, most likely looking for food again like he had ever since they'd found him in the forest. Celestia sang as she flew through the trees, looking like a bright ball of fire up in the air. She didn't look so much like a half-naked chicken to Aria anymore; her feathers were starting to grow back.

Aria wandered off into the woods to look for food as well, her stomach feeling as if it was clawing at itself. Worry dug its claws in and stirred up an uncomfortable feeling inside her.

The snow began to fall more in light beautiful snowflakes that stuck to the frozen ground like shimmering gemstones. Her breath became clouds in front of her face as she walked away from the tent. Her hands and nose were numb from the cold, so she blew her hot breath into her hands and rubbed them together. The wind began to pick up, rustling the trees and bushes on the forest floor. The cold made everything feel a little lifeless, and yet peaceful at the same time. No rabbits or squirrels ran by, no birds chirped, and frost covered every leaf and piece of grass.

"Strom!" Aria called, but no creaking of his limbs or his voice responded. She gave a sigh, a concern chilling her bones. "Strom!"

He's alright, I'm sure, she told herself. *He's a Timber Giant. He'll be fine.*

She walked back to the tent, shaking, as the snowfall began to pick up. The fluffy snowflakes came quickly now and the wind blew them about in the air. She quickened her pace as she neared the tent and hurried to duck inside of it. Even as she closed the door to shut out the wind, the cold still managed to sink through all the blankets and layers of clothing.

Willow was wide awake, staring at the Death Stone Riddle and scanning her thick book of languages she'd stolen from the library. Aria had barely looked at it since they'd escaped; she was much more worried about getting Luke healed and then leaving.

Avi was also awake, gazing at the roof of the tent in silence. Luke was asleep and every so often, he'd wake in a fit of coughing. Aria had seen his leg the night before when Willow had made another Healing Potion for him. The swelling had gone down, the skin had pulled itself together, and it had scabbed over, but his fever hadn't broken, and it caused him extreme discomfort. She looked down at her hands and leg where cuts had once been. By evening the day before, they had been healed. There wasn't a single scar left, and her hands had never felt so smooth.

A sudden loud creak outside made Aria peek her head through the tent door. Strom was outside with a massive buck hanging limp over his shoulder, its eyes glassy. Aria's mouth fell open and her eyes widened in horror.

"Did you kill that?" The way its head hung told Aria its neck had been broken.

"Strom no find berries today, so Strom get deer so friends eat." Strom's voice was solemn as he gently placed the buck on the ground. Bending down beside it, he laid a hand over the buck and began whispering apologies to it.

Willow and Avi poked their heads through the door too, and a mixture of emotions passed over their faces. When Strom was finished, he strode over to a tree to pull branches from it.

"You expect us to eat that?" Aria asked, revulsion bubbling up inside her. She'd never had deer meat and she'd never planned on it.

"It doesn't taste bad," Avi said. "I've had it before. It tastes kind of like beef."

Strom began to build a fire several feet away from the tent. He made a spike to put above the fire and used a vine covered in frost to hold it all together. Then he began the work of actually cooking it. Aria couldn't stand to watch it be skinned, so she turned away.

"Let's hope you know how to cook then, Strom." She zipped the tent closed and sat back in her and Willow's room to look at the Death Stone Riddle.

Outside, the smell of smoke and the sounds of a crackling fire made their way into the tent. An hour passed of looking at the Riddle's crinkling worn paper before Strom called them.

"Friends! Food done!"

Avi quickly unzipped the tent and dashed out of it. "Awesome because I'm starving."

Aria and Willow followed behind him, abandoning the Riddle and the book of languages on their pillows. Luke crawled out of his mound of blankets and into the main room, blinking sleep from his eyes. A faint grin found Aria's lips when she saw he was awake. She got herself and Luke some food before settling beside him in the main room of the tent. Strom watched them all curiously from the outside as they ate beside one another inside.

Willow's brows furrowed as she took her first bite. "This tastes nothing like beef."

"Who said it tastes like beef?" Luke looked perplexed, looking between each of them.

Avi slowly raised his hand and they laughed. "So? *Po-tae-toe po-tah-toe.*"

That night, the wind shook the tent and snow fell against it. The cold chilled Aria to the core and made her teeth chatter. Celestia had dropped more tears onto Luke's leg before they'd gone to sleep. Not a cough had escaped his mouth since Aria had laid down and covered herself with blankets. She hoped that that meant the healing was working. Tightening the blankets around her, she welcomed sleep.

When Aria, Willow, Avi, and Luke woke up the next morning, something seemed different. Aria opened the tent to look outside to see several inches of snow piled on the ground, and next to the tent were a pile of nuts and berries different from what they'd eaten before. Strom smiled at her from where he sat against a tree. The sun made the snow glisten, shining like a blanket of tiny diamonds. Aria reached for the food and then slipped back inside the tent. She handed the berries and nuts to the three of them, shocked when her eyes met Luke's. He was sitting up and smiling at her.

"How are you feeling?" she asked and handed him the food.

"Amazing, actually," he said before piling it into his mouth. He then threw the blanket off himself and pulled up his pant leg. Aria saw nothing but smooth skin where the griffin's bite had been.

She gasped, relief flooding her. "I'm so glad!" She leaned forward, wrapping her arm around him in a hug, and his arms twisted around her, pulling her close.

"And my fever broke too, but I still feel a little icky. Other than that, though, I feel fine." Luke said before he let out a soft cough, pulling away with an apologetic smile.

"We should get moving, then." Willow stood and pulled the inner walls of the tent down to start packing up.

Aria nodded. "I'll get the deer meat from outside."

She stepped through the door, her shoes crunching in the snow. Beside the tent, meat from the buck Strom had cooked was wrapped up in fabric, snuggled beneath the snow. Shaking the snow off it, she strode back into the tent to pass it out.

As soon as they were finished eating, they gathered their things up and started putting them away in their bags. After that, they stepped out into the frigid air where the wind blew past them. Avi and Willow took down the tent together and rolled it up while Aria stuffed the last of the food in her backpack for later.

Strom strode up to Aria from the tree he'd been sitting by. "Strom and friends leaving?"

"Yes, but I'm not sure where we should go. We need to get farther away from Viden and find water. Could you lead—" Aria broke off when she noticed something black shift in her peripheral vision, and she spun.

Her heart jolted and dread spread through her like prickly needles. Every muscle in her body tensed. Her blood ran colder than the ice clinging to the trees. Luke, Avi, and Willow paused what they were doing to stare in the direction of what had caught her attention. A hooded figure was making its way toward them, their cloak billowing in the wind.

CHAPTER TWENTY-ONE

LUKE HURRIED TO grab Aria's hand, intertwining his fingers with hers. He pulled her closer to him and shoved her backpack into her arms. Aria could barely concentrate on anything else but the Dark Forces member, so the bag fell from her hands to the ground.

"No," Aria whispered to the wind. "No, no, no…"

The hooded figure was stalking closer, though they were still at a distance. Her eyes were glued to them, blood rushing in her ears. A million thoughts ran through her head. Could they make it out of the forest? Could they escape?

"We need to go, now." There was urgency in Luke's voice and Avi nodded in agreement. Luke wrapped his arm around her and tried to get her to walk away, but she pulled away and remained where she was.

There would be no getting away, even if it was just one figure. There could be more coming. They'd just be hunted through the forest until they grew too weak to fight. There'd be no out-running them. There was nowhere they could go that would be safe, not with four people and a Timber Giant. They were trapped, and Aria was sure the Dark Forces knew that.

Aria turned to her friends and Strom, fear flickering in her eyes but also a fierce, burning determination. *I'm done running away.*

"You guys go, and I will distract them," Aria said, her voice cracking. She didn't want to have to do this. "Then I will meet back up with you somewhere in the forest."

If she could get away quick enough.

"Aria, no!" Luke objected, reaching out to grab her hand again.

She pulled away and took one step backward. "It's the only way to keep you guys safe. They want me, not you. We *can't* let them get the Life Stone or information on how to solve the Riddle."

Willow's face fell with understanding, but she still shook her head. "True, but you shouldn't have to be the distraction."

"And if one of you were the distraction, they likely wouldn't care. They'd just get rid of you and come after me anyway." Aria looked them in the eye, willing fierceness into her voice. "I'm *not* going to let them hurt you."

"But you're the Diviner—they shouldn't have you either… What if I lose you?" Luke's voice broke. Pure heartache washed over his face and he reached out to hold onto her arms, stopping her from running away.

At those words, Aria's heart melted like water in her chest and she searched his eyes. She thought of what Willow had said, about how she'd saved them. She knew she'd do that over and over again if she had to. "You won't lose me. I'll come back. Now go!"

Before either of them could object, she attempted to run in the direction of the Dark Forces member off in the distance, who was just standing there. But Luke caught her arm and spun her toward him. She collided with his chest and looked up at his face, now so close to her own. She remembered that moment in the hallway back at school, that urge that had risen up inside of her. A warm fluttering feeling lit within her stomach and a blush crept over her cheeks. He lowered his head and her lips parted in surprise.

Everything seemed so still as a question flickered in his eyes. "Is it okay if I kiss you before you go?"

In answer to that question, she let their lips collide. His lips were warm and sure, and all around them was silence. Tears ran down her cheeks as if she was saying goodbye to him forever. She reminded herself that it wasn't a goodbye, but she couldn't help but pull him closer, her hands holding the back of his head as if it really *was* a goodbye. Snow fell softly around them, and the breeze blew through her hair. He smelled of pine and sweet mint. She pulled back, grinning up to her eyes, and he looked stunned with a flush of red across his cheeks.

"I—I" Luke tried to say.

"I saw that coming," Avi commented with a smirk.

Aria glanced back at the hooded figure who strangely remained where they were. They wouldn't have the patience to wait much longer, though. They'd come and tear their group apart if Aria didn't get her friends out of there soon. The smile fell from her face as she turned to Strom.

She grabbed her backpack off the ground and shoved it into Luke's hands. "Strom, take them and get them out of here, please."

"As Diviner wishes," Strom replied solemnly, his face falling. "Diviner will come back."

"No, Aria, please don't do this…" Luke pleaded, scrambling to grab her. But Strom had already wrapped his arm around Luke and pulled him into his arms.

Strom's arm wrapped around Willow and Avi next,

swinging them up off the ground. With a bow of his head, he ran and shook the trees with every step. Their screams and shouts echoed into the forest, but within moments, the snow and trees blocked sight of them.

"I'm sorry," she whispered into the icy wind, knowing they couldn't hear her. *I'm not running away anymore.*

Aria bolted to the right, both in the opposite direction of the hooded figure and her friends, watching to make sure the hooded figure followed. She could still feel Luke's kiss on her lips, and making Strom take them away was like a stab to the heart.

I'll see them again. I'll make it out, she reminded herself.

The hooded figure followed her like a lurking shadow, but she didn't stop. She wove in between trees and over fallen branches sticking out of the snow. A growl in the distance made her heart pound faster. Her eyes searched the trees but she couldn't spot anything. She turned abruptly to the left as she noticed another hooded figure enter her peripheral vision. Trees and foliage passed her in a blur, her head clouded in panic. A twig snapped somewhere behind her and she glanced back to see nothing but forest. The growls and animal-like sounds resounded through the air, seeming to come from all sides even as she saw nothing for them to belong to.

Running in between trees, she moved to the edge of a large clearing. It was a serene place covered in an undisturbed blanket of snow. There was a small cabin in the center of the clearing with rotting gray wood and shattered windows. At first, Aria thought it was strange that there was a cabin in the middle of the woods, but maybe it wasn't since they were so close to Viden. Perhaps it was an old house for the farmers who worked in the fields or someone who wanted the opportunities Viden offered but didn't want to always live amongst the hustle and bustle. She ran through the clearing towards the abandoned cabin, snow seeping into her shoes. Her skin prickled and she had the distinct feeling of being watched.

A sudden strong force from behind hit her back and she was flung forward, landing face-first in the snow.

"You should really learn to not draw so much attention to yourself, little girl," Kora's voice came from her distant left.

Aria quickly raised herself to her hands and knees and turned to see that Kora and Viola were standing next to each other at the edge of the clearing.

"That is number one of going into hiding. Has no one taught you that?" Kora tutted. "Though, I suppose not, since your parents are rotting away in chains…"

The words dug into Aria like nails and she rose to her feet, raising her hands. Magic crackled over her fingertips in rays of colorful light. Viola took in a whiff of the air and Aria's gut tightened.

"And soon you will join them," Viola said before low growls tore through the air.

Aria's attention was pulled to just beyond the trees surrounding the clearing. Massive wolves with scrunched-up snouts to exposing their drool-covered razor-sharp teeth surrounded the clearing. The wolves ranged in many different colors, from black to reddish brown and white, but all had dark yellow eyes glaring at her with malicious intent. Werewolves. That was what she'd heard in the forest. There had to be ten, possibly more. And they were making sure there would be no way out.

She immediately began to regret her decision.

Her blood ran cold. The fear that dug its claws deep into her skin would not relent, but she couldn't submit to it. She couldn't give in no matter how badly she wished to fall to the snow-covered ground and give up. Letting her magic rise inside her, it crackled in the air around her like it had in the library. She hesitated, watching the werewolves creep closer and Kora and Viola watch her curiously from the edge. She didn't want to show them just how powerful she could be, because she didn't want that power…Her chest squeezed with fear and uncertainty. Her heart and mind battled over what to do. The werewolves were growing closer, pawing at the ground like they were getting ready to lunge. Magic sizzled in the air around her, calling her to use it. But everything she'd read, all the things she knew she could do, all the destruction she could cause reigned in her mind. And yet, with that same power, she'd saved her friends and countless other Diviners had created peace. She squeezed her eyes shut, blocking out every thought of doubt and forcing herself to believe in who she was.

"You are the Diviner," her mother had said to her in the Malamone Mansion.

Embrace who you are. Colorful light bloomed around her, a glow radiating from her skin as her magic took off across the clearing. Her eyes lit gold and embers danced around her like little stars.

The werewolves fell to the ground with resounding yelps and Kora and Viola collapsed into the snow. Several of the werewolves fell unconscious and a few branches from the trees broke off. The cabin shook with the force before Aria pulled all the power back into her. Her magic crashed back into her, filling her veins with intense power. Yet, her energy felt drained, and her head spun with a dizzying blur. She shook her head of lightheadedness and bolted across the clearing, kicking snow about. A growl behind her sent shivers up her back and she ran faster, glancing back to see three werewolves chasing her down. Their evil yellow eyes were narrowed in fury. One of them leaped and a set of teeth lodged in her leg, tripping her. She screamed, feeling the venomous bite start to take effect already as pain surged up her leg and her limbs grew tired. She fought the sensation, kicking at the wolf's head. Her heel collided with its eye and it backed away. Blood dripping into the snow, she forced herself to her feet and her vision blurred for a moment. Then she took off, only glancing back at Kora and Viola getting to their feet at the edge of the clearing.

The door of the cabin swung open and a thick vine sprouted from the ground beneath her, covered in frost. The vine wrapped around her ankle and held her firmly in place, making her fall into the snow again. The ice chilled her bones and she saw double of everything. She shook her head, pushing away the venom rushing through her veins. Her blood ran colder when she saw two Violas coming towards her with rage written all over her pale face. When her vision cleared, only one Viola was running toward her. Her hair was a mess with snow from her fall clinging to it. The collar of Aria's hoodie tightened on her neck as Viola pulled on the back of it and dragged her to her feet. She steadied herself on the ground again and the vine released her, slipping away beneath the snow.

"L-let go of me!" Aria screamed and attempted to pull away. Viola threw her back into the snow, and with a groan, Aria hit the forest floor. Pain shot through her back and head so fast that she gasped. Her head spun and she felt she might puke.

"This is what you get for setting me on fire, you brat," Viola spat out the words like poison and approached Aria again.

Aria got on her hands and knees before getting to her feet and running back toward the cabin. A werewolf blocked the way with its massive jaw hanging open to reveal its drool-covered teeth. A vine shot out from the wall of the cabin, sending splinters of wood into the snow. The vine wrapped around Aria's arm and pulled her toward the decaying wall.

Ebony came around the corner of the cabin, chuckling with her hands raised. A delighted smile appeared on her lips. The vine tightened and slammed Aria up against the cabin's wall. Pain to shot through the back of her head and her breathing quickened as panic took over her mind. Viola was in front of her in a flash. Another three vines burst through the cabin's wall, one pinning her other hand to the wall, and the other two locking her ankles in place. She struggled against her restraints, but when that was useless, she started pulling the water from the vines. Sharp pain pierced her arms, making her stop, and a scream tore through her throat. Viola had her hands encircling her arms, digging her dagger-like nails through Aria's jacket.

"Stop!" Aria screamed, tears escaping her eyes. Her vision danced in and out from the werewolf venom.

"This ought to teach you better!" Viola said, a wicked smile of satisfaction playing across her face. "If I were mortal and were able to have mortal wounds, I'd have scars from the burns your fire caused. But I still felt the pain, and that you'll pay for."

"Enough," Kora commanded as she walked towards them, werewolves on either side of her. "She is for Malus to punish."

Aria's head fell slightly, fighting the werewolf venom that was consuming her. Her muscles became limp, her skin growing numb with the cold. She gritted her teeth and glared, willing strength into her arms as she pulled at the vines.

Viola released her and stepped back, licking her sharp fangs like an animal. She raised her hand to her mouth and licked the blood from her nails. "Very well. Let's take her to him, then."

"No! You aren't taking me anywhere!" Aria screamed, her voice hoarse, and she tried to pull away from the vines. Ebony tightened them with a squeeze of her fist. Aria hissed as they cut off circulation.

"Sleep," Kora said and there was a hum to it that made Aria still.

Aria's eyes fluttered closed for a moment, but she opened them again, trying to resist the urge to fall asleep. The venom and enchantment pushed into the edges of her mind. She gritted her teeth against it, but it seeped in and flooded her mind.

No, no, no...I made a promise. I said I'd come back. Her breath grew shallow against her will and she balled her hands into tight fists.

"Give up, girl. You don't stand a chance against us." Kora smirked as Aria's limbs went limp, the vines the only thing holding her there.

Sleep washed over Aria like a suffocating wave and she was drowning in the force. It pushed her eyelids closed and pitch-blackness took over.

CHAPTER TWENTY-TWO

THE SECOND HE heard the high-pitched screams, Luke tore out of Strom's arms and sprinted in the direction they'd come from. He knew that voice. He knew that scream, and hearing it made his heart pound even faster. Strom bounded after him as Willow and Avi escaped his arms as well. Luke hated the thought of Aria getting hurt, hated that she would sacrifice herself for them. His hands were clammy as he bolted through the snow, replaying the kiss they'd shared. Then the look on her face as she turned and ran from him drifted into his thoughts. His heart sank as blood rushed in his ears. He ran as fast as he could, wanting to see her and hold her and know that she was safe. Her screams were silenced now, and it made his heart squeeze tighter.

He ran through the trees, jumping over snow-covered sticks before stopping in the middle of a large clearing where a log cabin sat in the center. The snow was punctured with footprints and clear signs of a struggle. A small puddle of blood had soaked into the snow several yards from the cabin. Luke's heart seemed to stop beating and his whole body shook. The cabin itself was splintered and dead vines hung from giant holes in the wall. He crept closer to it, eyeing the specks of blood that lingered on the vines.

His world felt like it was falling down around him. He couldn't breathe. He couldn't think. "No, no, no! NO!" He screamed, falling to his knees as tears ran down his cheeks. The snow soaked through his pants, but he didn't feel its cold sting.

They'd taken her, and he hadn't been there to help. Who knew what would happen to her or if he would ever see her again. If the Dark Forces had her, they'd use her for their own gain. Those monsters would hurt her. They'd try to break her.

Willow laid her hand on his shoulder, tears gathering in her own eyes. "They must have just left."

"Oh, look, its Captain Obvious!" Avi rolled his eyes and let out an exasperated sigh. His face fell and he said softly, "She risked herself...for us."

When Luke stopped screaming, he asked, "Where do you think they took her?"

"The Malamone Mansion?" Avi suggested, looking around at the scene the Dark Forces had left behind.

Willow shook her head. "No, I don't think so. Last time, Malus wanted us to leave the mansion. He told Kora to take us to...Ugh, I can't remember." She rubbed her temples and squeezed her eyes shut.

"Hora?" Luke got to his feet in a rush. "Didn't he say something about an underground mountain base?"

"Yes! But where is that?"

"Maybe Strom knows?" Avi said, gesturing to the Timber Giant.

They all turned to Strom, who stood in the center of the clearing. He looked down at a clump of fur in his hand, his eyes narrowed. "Werewolf fur. Werewolf prints."

Willow stepped closer to him, reaching for what he held. "Where did you find this?" She took it in her hands, examining it.

"In snow." Strom pointed to the paw prints littered across the snowy ground. They were massive and deep, much bigger than any wolf print Luke had seen.

Luke and Avi glanced at each other, then joined Willow and Strom's side.

"Why would werewolves be here?" Avi asked, grabbing the fur from Willow. "Don't werewolves hang out around villages, not the woods?"

"We are near enough to Viden and the farms that they might hang out around here…" Luke shook his head, his thoughts leading in a dark direction. Something didn't seem right. "But they're fresh. They were here when Aria was attacked. Why else would the paw prints be here?"

Something seemed to register in Willow's head and her eyes widened. "Werewolves are half-human half-wolf, but they can't change at will. They either change each night under the moon, or they can be cursed to be stuck as a wolf until the end of their life. It's broad daylight out. What if the Dark Forces cursed them and are using them as a weapon? One bite from a werewolf infects its victim into weakness and exhaustion, not allowing them to fight back."

"Are you saying Aria could've been bitten?" Luke's heart thumped louder against his ribcage.

"Then Aria would turn into a werewolf!" Avi shrieked. "Why would the Dark Forces do that? They need her as the Diviner!"

"No, that's not what I'm trying to say. It's possible, but—" Willow sighed, exasperation written all over her face. "Unlike vampires, werewolf venom can be cured. You have to have the venom in your body on the night of a full moon to change.

If Aria's healed, that won't happen. The Dark Forces must know that."

"There you are acting like Aria *was, in fact,* bitten again," Avi piped in sarcastically. "And if they were just here, how did they leave so fast? Unless they're *still* here…"

They glanced around uncomfortably, listening to the silence.

"Wouldn't they have come out already, though, if they were still here?" Willow asked skeptically. "They probably teleported, which explains how they got away so quickly. Where the wolves are, though, I don't know…They'd have to have used a Teleporter for that." Her voice grew soft and contemplating as if she were simply speaking to herself.

"Well, let's go." Luke pulled his backpack tighter against his back and started for the edge of the trees. "We're going to find Aria."

"But you don't even know where you're going," Avi said, making Luke stop in his tracks. "What are you going to do? Wander aimlessly in the woods until you find her? I'm sorry, but you're not going to find Hora that way."

"Well, I'm not just going to keep standing here, staring at her blood soaked into the snow," Luke said, his face red with panic and worry. His gut twisted at the pity in all of their eyes. Bile rose in his throat. They couldn't keep standing here. They had to find Aria.

"Strom know where Diviner be taken." Strom strode to Luke and placed a hand on his shoulder caringly. "Hora sunsights away. Strom take you."

"Let's go then." Luke nearly begged, dread and fear pricking at him like tiny daggers. A knot was in his chest, twisting slowly at the thought of Aria being locked away somewhere.

"Wait, why can't we just teleport?" Avi quirked a brow up. "I'm sure we can get there with little injuries if it's a mountain.

We know what being near a mountain feels like. And it would be quicker."

"I don't think that's a good idea," Willow said. "The base is likely well protected. If we teleported there and found ourselves surrounded, we'd stand no chance. Creeping up on it would give us an advantage rather than giving ourselves away the second we get there. We have to catch them by surprise. They'll never see us coming."

"But Aria—" Luke tried to argue.

"Luke, I want to rescue her as much as you do. But we have to use our brains. There's too much at stake here to rush through it and take risks." Willow nodded to Strom. "Take us to her, please."

Strom spun and started for the tree line, and they followed. Silence fell between them as they walked through the crunchy snow, but what they weren't saying was clear through that quiet. It didn't have to be said—they were all terrified of what was coming for Aria.

The ground was rough and hard beneath Aria, digging at her back. The cold air that filled the dark space around her seeped through her clothes and bit at her nose. Her head throbbed, feeling as if it had been bashed against something. The smell of stone and decay smothered her. Slowly, she sat up and sucked in a breath at the aching in her bones. A clanking sound met her ears. Through the dark, she could just make out the outline of bars to her side, but nothing else. A shiver racked her body as she felt around on the stone floor she was sitting on. Cold shackles dug into her wrists and ankles. Her jacket had been taken off, and when she felt her arms, she didn't find the punctures Viola had made. Smooth skin had been left behind, and goosebumps rose on her arms from the frigid air. At the realization, she reached for her leg to find her jeans had been raggedly cut short. Where she'd been bitten by the werewolf, there was nothing to indicate she ever was. Her heart thumped in her ears.

A deep man's voice rang through the dark. "I had Healers attend to your wounds."

Aria was startled by the noise and quickly rose to her feet, raising her hands. Torches across the walls of the room lit with a flick of a shadowed hand outside the cell. Now that dim yellow lighting filled the room, a hooded figure could be seen standing outside the door of her cell. A wide stone staircase led upward outside of the dungeons, and the walls were made of a dark brown, ancient stone that crumbled in places. The room was full of cells, all the exact same size. They were all empty… except for a few bones lying in one. Aria's stomach jolted at the sight and she stepped back against the wall.

The hooded figure outside her cell pulled down his hood to reveal an almost completely shaven head, thin scarred cheeks, and bright malicious green eyes. Malus Malamone. Aria's heart hammered against her rib cage and she tried to step further back, but she was already against the wall. Kora had said he hadn't really been imprisoned, but a part of her hadn't wanted to believe that. She wanted to believe he was out of her life for good. She'd wanted to believe she'd succeeded. She'd wanted to believe she hadn't been a *fool*.

He turned the key in the lock and stepped inside the cell. "Hello, Aria." A cruel half smile twisted at his lips as if they were old friends seeing each other after such a long time.

"Stay away from me!" Aria yelled and raised her hands.

She pulled on her magic, trying to pool it into her palms,

but nothing came. There was a tugging at her core like she was pulling on a taut string. She looked down at her hands to see a shimmer radiating over the surface of the shackles. Not a single hint of magic appeared in her palms.

"What did you do to me?" Aria's breath came in quick and she balled her hands up into fists.

"Those shackles are cursed, just like your parents' shackles," he replied, watching relief flood her face. Her parents were alive. "Yes, Aria, they live still. For now. Anyway, let's get straight to the point. It seems that you believed you had imprisoned me. Am I correct?"

Aria stepped to the right as he strode closer. There was a hostile gleam in his eyes. She glared back at him, her hands shaking, and gulped down the lump rising in her throat.

"Kora has told me everything." Malus smirked. "But you see, I am stronger than that. I cannot be easily defeated. I chose to let you go that day at my mansion, so you could lead me to the Death Stone. I knew your parents would have told you about it. You took something from me that day, though. And I want it back. The Life Stone does not belong to you, so where is it?"

Aria moved away from him again. "I don't know what you're talking about," she stalled as she inched towards the open door. Her chains rattled against the floor they were chained to. If she could just make it to the door, if she could slam it against the chains…Maybe, just maybe…

"Do not lie to me!" Malus yelled. "I know you took it. We searched you, but you don't have it, so *where is it?*"

"I—I lost it." She was almost to the door now, but her eyes were trained on Malus' scarred, heated face.

"I know very well you are not stupid, girl. You wouldn't just *lose it.*" A cruel smile bent at his lips like it all was just a game.

"Your parents know that too, which is how I know that. You see, that little curse of theirs is broken, and now I know *every-thing* they knew. I picked their brains *little—by—little*. I know they hid you for over fourteen years so that I wouldn't find you. I know how they translated the Death Stone Riddle, but I had already known that. I met them when they started that mission for the Forces of Light before you were even born." He paused, studying her. "But your parents never found the Death Stone, did they? They wanted to free your powers so badly when they realized who you are. But there were still pieces of the Riddle they didn't understand, and pieces of it they wished weren't true…So they stopped searching for it and hid the Riddle's copy in the Library of Knowledge." He shook his head. "But I don't give up that easily. Because of them, I know how to solve the Riddle now. And with their help and knowledge, I'll find the Death Stone soon enough." He grinned, watching her emotions war over her face. "It will be a perfect companion to my Life Stone once I get it back."

Aria's gut twisted, imagining Malus picking through all her parents' memories and forcing them to relive each one. It would drive them mad, possibly to insanity. "My parents would *never* help you."

Pulling a dagger from his cloak, he smiled and raised it so the light from the torches glinted off it. "I have my ways."

At that, fire rose up in Aria's core, kindling a fury that made her leap toward Malus with her hands clenched. She aimed her fist at his nose and a small crack met her ears. Malus raised his hands and a force pushed her up against the wall. Her legs buck-led beneath her and she tumbled to the ground. The impact of it knocked the wind out of her and she gasped. She grabbed her stomach, feeling the pain roll over her in waves. Blood ran from Malus' nose and he wiped it away with his sleeve, smirking.

"Hmm…" He squatted down to her level, rubbing his chin. "If you won't talk, we'll have to resort to other methods…" He flicked his hand and the cell door swung shut with a clang. "I'll give you one last chance. *Where is my Life Stone?*"

"Even if I knew, I would *never* tell you," Aria ground out through clenched teeth, her heart racing in her chest.

"Very well," he said as he stood. "*Pain.*"

The second he said the word, a high-pitched scream broke from Aria's mouth and she writhed on the rough ground. It felt as if knives were piercing every inch of her skin, shredding her to pieces. Tears streamed down her cheeks, but she didn't feel them. Instead, she felt fire scorching her flesh and burning her from the inside out. She clenched her eyes shut and twitched in extreme agony. It was worse than anything she had ever felt.

Please make it stop, she begged in her own mind. *Make it stop.*

It was as if hours were bottled up inside of a minute, and then it finally ended. Her whole body was shaking and covered in sweat, her fingers twitching from the aching, but she was physically unharmed. She lay on the cold concrete floor, sweat dripping from her hot skin. She stared up at Malus as he scowled down at her.

"That hurt, didn't it? Did it make you change your mind?"

Despite the pain, suffering, and misery he was putting her through, she kept her mouth clenched shut. She glared daggers at him. Fear of what she knew would come next bit through her and she felt bile rise in her throat. It took every bit of strength she had to remain defiant, unwilling to talk. Just his eyes on her made her flinch.

Malus tutted and the red-hot pain came over her again. She twisted and squirmed on the ground as if there was some way to escape it. It burned her and stabbed through her skin. She screamed at the excruciating agony that took over her body, making her wish it all would end right then and there. Finally, Malus made it stop. She was on her side now as Malus squatted down again to see her red, sweating face covered in her tangled mess of hair.

"*Where is my Life Stone?* This is your *last* chance." His jaw was set tightly as he cocked his head to the side, raising his thin eyebrows.

"I will never *ever* tell you anything, you *monster*," Aria stated and tensed her whole body up, expecting the pain to wash over her again. She couldn't tell him the truth, not after she handed Luke the Life Stone back at Camp Enchanted over the summer, not when it would put the friends she loved in immense danger.

"Fine." Malus stood up and strode towards the metal door of the cell. He walked through it and swung it shut behind him, saying, "If you won't answer me, I will have Ciaus pick through your brain like he did to your parents. And believe me, you're not going to like it."

"No!" Aria yelled as her heart jolted, panic twisting through her like a vile snake.

"*Pain.*" Malus walked away with a vicious smirk playing on his lips and the agony came over Aria tenfold, mentally burning and tearing her apart from the inside out.

CHAPTER TWENTY-THREE

ARIA WAS ON her side, hair splayed around her. Her puffy red eyes stared blankly ahead at the darkness, exhaustion taking over her mind from all the screaming and crying. Her face was stained with tears and her whole body ached as if screws had been driven into her bones. Each breath she took was sluggish. Time had passed in a blur, but she guessed it had been hours of lying on the rough ground of the dungeon, staring up through the pitch-blackness. The door swung open with a loud creak and Viola grabbed her roughly by the arms, forcing her to stand. As the realization of what was happening sunk in, Aria's eyes shot wide open and her limbs sprung into action. She tried to twist out of Viola's grip and was shoved from the cell. Her chains were pulled taunt, straining her arms.

Her eyes pinned to Ciaus outside the cell, a tall, skinny man with a bald head, lavender eyes, and a creepy smirk plastered to his face. Recognition chilled her bones. He was the judge from Malus' trial at Enchanting Court. Kora hadn't been lying at all.

Beside Ciaus, the man who'd promised she'd be safe and

get her parents back, stood Malus. He watched her struggle, his face void of any emotion.

Aria shook her arms, trying to pull away from Viola even as her nails dug into her arms. Malus flicked his hand, so the shackles fell from her wrists and ankles. Viola pinned her arms behind her back, causing her shoulder blades to hit each other, and Aria gritted her teeth. Her heart raced against her ribcage in a desperate panic that made her dizzy. Malus and Ciaus walked toward the steps that led out of the dungeons, followed by Viola pushing Aria.

"No! Stop!" Aria yelled and felt her magic swirl through her veins. She called on it and caught on to Viola's cloak as she was pushed up the first step. Heat began to bloom in her palms. Malus turned abruptly and wrapped his gloved hand around her bicep. His fingers pressed brutally into her skin. The move startled her and the magic in her palm went out.

"Don't try anything or you *and* your dear parents will pay the price," he said through clenched teeth. "Be careful with her, Viola." He released his grasp on her arm.

Viola quickly shoved her up the steps with Malus and Ciaus surrounding Aria. She made sure to tighten her grip on Aria's wrists. At the top of the steps, they rounded the corner. Viola pushed Aria as they crossed the polished, shiny black stone flooring. Yellow light from the torches lining the smooth stone walls cast a dancing shimmer on the floor. The corridor was long and branched off in every direction down long hallways and off to unknown rooms through black metal doors. The air felt thick and warm, and the walls felt unbearably close as if there was a mountain pressing down on them. Ciaus led the way past hooded figures, all in the same signature Dark Forces clothing. The other Dark Forces members were going up and down the hall with a purpose set into their steps, carrying papers, daggers, maps, and letters. Eyes locked on Aria and people paused to stare at her passing them. They gasped, awe in their eyes.

"They know what you are," Malus said, glancing back at her.

Aria's heart sunk into a large pit opening in her stomach. *"What you are..."* It made her sound as if she weren't human, like a monster.

Her magic swirled in her palms, waiting to be used. Viola had her hands angled in such a way that she'd likely end up hurting herself, though. Not to mention her parents and the threat hanging over them. So, she kept the magic at bay, waiting for the right moment to release it.

Viola pushed her around a corner and down another hallway before a black metal door swung open and they entered. The door thudded shut with a loud clang of metal behind Viola as Malus closed it. Aria's eyes scanned the room, and her heart drummed in her ears at what she saw. Trays of knives and daggers sat on a counter, and a wash basin was there too. On another counter were lined up bottles of potions and some medical supplies like syringes. The yellow light flickering in the torches made her feel like she was trapped inside of a nightmare.

Viola dragged her towards the metal table bolted to the floor in the middle of the room, which had a hook welded onto it at the top and bottom. A pile of chains sat in the middle. Ciaus walked over to his potions while Malus went to the other side of the table. He reached across to grab Aria's arm and pull her onto it, but she thrashed and kicked and yelled. She managed to land a punch to his shoulder, but he didn't even flinch.

"No!" She let out a yell as magic gathered in her palms. The magic shot from her fingertips toward him in one quick motion while one of her hands was released.

Malus hit the polished stone counter with a snarl. He hurried to grab the chains lying on the table right in front of him. Aria turned, blasting Viola with an Immobile Enchantment. She slumped to the ground, motionless, and shot a hostile glare at Aria. Free of hands, Aria bolted to the door and grabbed the handle. She shook it frantically, but it didn't budge. Grunting in frustration, she pressed her hand to the lock and closed her eyes, trying to enchant it open like she'd learned in school. It stayed locked.

Cursed, she figured, panic seizing the breath from her lungs.

"Where do you think you're going to go? You're outnumbered," Malus spoke from behind her, striding away from the counter she'd blasted him up against. "Even if you got out of this room, hundreds of others are out that door…Just think of what we could do to your parents."

Aria spun, raising her hands in defense. Her eyes stung because she did know what he could do, but she couldn't let him get ahold of the information she had. Magic crackled over the tips of her fingers like an electric current. "Stay away from me."

Malus strode closer to her anyway, lifting his own hands with a smirk. "Who do you think will win this fight? You or I?"

Without hesitation, Aria summoned an Immobile Enchantment and shot it at him. He stepped out of the way and a ball of red, angry sparks came barreling her way. She ducked to avoid it, but it found her anyway. She was forced up against the wall, her breath squished out of her. It felt as if a snake were constricting her. She gasped, trying to suck air into her lungs. Then she fell to her knees, oxygen filling her before it was stolen again. She coughed and sputtered as hands grabbed her arms and pulled her across the floor. Her heart raced too fast against her lungs, which felt bruised and useless. She couldn't get enough air. She was lifted from the ground and dragged onto the metal table as Ciaus bent down to help Viola. His palms lit with the counter-curse, and she rose to her feet, a furious look cast in Aria's direction. Aria coughed, trying to breathe. Black dots crowded her vision.

Ciaus went back to his counter to grab a syringe dripping with some kind of concoction. Then he turned to Aria as she was flattened against the table, her vision a dizzying blur.

"For this to work correctly, I will need you to not resist," Ciaus said, his eerie voice making Aria's skin prickle. "A special potion of truth serum and immobility should do the trick…"

Viola and Malus grabbed ahold of Aria's arms as tight as they could while she tried to escape. Ciaus lifted the syringe to her neck and she shrunk away, eyes clenched closed. The potion worked almost immediately. Her limbs went slack in Viola and Malus' grasp and they grabbed her wrists and ankles, tying them to the hooks on the table.

"No, no, no," she murmured. Her vision blurred and she tried to lift her head from the table, but it fell back with a thud. *They can't know the truth. They'll go after Luke, Willow, and Avi. I can't let that happen.*

"Now, this will only last about ten minutes, but it will open up her mind and guide me to the truth," Ciaus said as he set his syringe back down and turned to Aria again. He reached out his hand and laid it on Aria's forehead. She turned her head sideways to shake his hand off, using every bit of effort she had. He gripped her head harder, holding it in place as his hands began to warm and the world faded away.

Colors swirled around her like dust, forming a memory. It felt as if she had been thrown into the air, and then slammed back down to the ground. She gasped in shock. She was at Incanting Academy with Luke and Avi, meeting them for the first time. Luke and Avi were introducing themselves. The uncertainty and insecurity she felt as she stared at them bubbled inside her. And at the same time, her heart sank and leapt. Her friends sat in front of her with unheeded joy, but it was unsafe. They needed to run, yet she wanted to stay there with them. It was safe here in the past before her life had been unraveled. Her mind was clouded, and she couldn't think straight.

"Get out of here," Aria tried to say to them, but couldn't hear herself speak.

Then the world around her blurred and reformed, showing her the moment Luke and her had kissed. All her emotions came at her like a raging storm, and she felt Luke's lips on hers. Everything changed again and she was ripping the Life Stone from Malus' neck. She could feel its evil pulsing in her palms, making her head spin. Her friends were beside her and Malus in front of her, but then that faded away too. Panic surged through Aria at the memory she felt coming next. She fought against the Mind-reading, trying to push away the control Ciaus had over her. But the truth was there, coming to the surface without her permission.

Luke was now hugging her, holding the Life Stone that she had just handed him. Tears streamed down her cheeks. Whether in the memory or in reality, she didn't know. With all the might Aria could muster, she shoved Ciaus from her memories and he stumbled backwards, hitting the counter. She breathed heavily, her mind aching.

"A boy named Luke has the Life Stone, Master," Ciaus said, turning to Malus. He gasped, his chest heaving as if from exertion. "It's her boyfriend."

"No!" Aria cried, trying to move her limbs, but they remained stuck in place on the table. She didn't have time to ponder what Ciaus had just called Luke, all she could think of was that they'd just torn the truth from her. "Luke!" Tears ran down her cheeks, and her heart felt as if it might lunge out of her chest.

"Well done, Ciaus. Pick through her mind more. See if you can find anything else that her parents might have not known, especially if it has to do with finding the Death Stone." Malus said, his eyes narrowed at Aria. "Let's go then, Viola. We have things to take care of…"

CHAPTER TWENTY-FOUR

A WEEK OR MORE of walking made it feel like nails had been driven into Avi's legs and feet. They'd barely slept, wanting to get to Aria before it was too late. It felt like they were all walking on a tightrope. If they fell, they failed Aria. And staying on that tightrope, unwilling to give into the fear and uncertainty, drew the energy out of them.

Even now as they trekked through the frosted woods, everyone remained quiet. The trees creaked in the soft wind, blowing snow around in the air. From a distance, mountains rose above them with ice-topped peaks and dark, tall pines running up the inclines. Clouds surrounded the tops of the mountain range that was so wide, Avi couldn't see half of it. They had to be in Hora if those were the Hora Mountains. Seeing them made unease swirl in Avi's stomach. With every step, they were growing closer to the Dark Forces. But they were also getting closer to Aria, and that alone made him keep moving.

Celestia perched on his shoulder, nestled closely to his neck. He gave her a little rub on the head and she chirped affectionately. She'd grown a little and her scarlet and gold feathers had come back too.

Willow walked next to him, juggling her massive book in her hands and the Death Stone Riddle on top of it. Her eyes scanned the pages, trying to match up what language the Riddle was written in, even though Aria was the only one of them who could translate it because she was descended from its language. Still, Willow wanted to at least find what language it was.

"Do you think you'll be able to find the language in there?" Avi gestured to the book, trying to create some kind of conversation between them. Silence was an unbearable thing.

"Yeah, eventually." Willow's eyebrows were drawn together, her eyes unmoved from the book. "The pages go on and on. I bet there are thousands of languages written in here."

"Do you think you'll find it in time?" Avi asked, then immediately regretted the question upon seeing Willow's face.

Her jaw grew tight, and she looked up at him with hard eyes. Avi turned away, feeling the tension rolling off her in waves until she looked away and sighed. He didn't blame her for feeling the way she did, and he didn't need to be a Mind-reader to know how she felt. There was so much relying on all of them. He just wished he could do something to ease the worry. His hands ached to reach out and brush her tangled, bushy blond hair back. But he kept them still at his sides, already feeling the heat start to creep into his cheeks at the thought.

"I just meant that Malus is no doubt looking for the Death Stone too…" Avi sighed. "He may have even found it already. And he has Aria."

Willow pulled herself from the page again. "Don't let fear and doubt cloud your mind. We'll get Aria back and we'll stop Malus from getting his hands on the Death Stone. You forget he hasn't solved the Riddle yet."

We actually don't know that. He could have and we just don't know. Avi tried his best to kick the thought away. He locked eyes with Willow. Even with dirt and leaves in her hair, grime smears on her cheeks, and bags under her shiny blue eyes, she looked gorgeous. His face flushed and the corner of her mouth pulled into a small smile. He couldn't help loving how she saw the light in even the darkest of times. The doubt in his stomach faded to nothing.

"We're going to get her back," Willow said, and Avi wondered if she'd somehow read his mind. "And when we do, the Dark Forces will wish they'd never started this battle."

Avi kept his eyes on her, again wishing he could pull her into a hug. He couldn't remember how many times she'd read his mind, though, and how many times he'd given away the fact that he liked her. She probably even felt his emotions right now, and it made him take a step away. He didn't want to pressure her or overwhelm her. He pushed the feelings away, knowing there were more important things to focus on. Looking up at the mountains before them, he thought about how there would be another time. Another time when they weren't always on the run.

Hunger had never hurt so much before in Aria's life. It was like tiny knives stabbing her in the stomach and causing it to cave in on itself. She lay on her side on the rough stone floor, pitch-blackness all around her. Everything ached from her head to her toes, and the cold draft did nothing to help the fear digging its claws deep into her skin. Her throat was dry, and her tongue stuck to the roof of her mouth as a cough shook her body. The cursed chains made her feel small and lifeless as they cut into her skin, stopping the swirl of magic in her veins. Time seemed frozen like the air that filled the dungeons, slurring the hours together. Had it been days? Weeks? A single tear dripped down her cheek.

She had receded into her brain, not murmuring a word but thinking every thought in her mind. Voices came as soft footsteps touched the stairs, but she didn't look up. She knew who it would be—the people who brought her tiny amounts of food and water. It was enough to keep her alive, but she felt as if a punch to the stomach would be enough to kill her and her skin was stretched over her bones. Someone was saying something about the Forces of Light, as they always were. Aria wasn't sure if they were spies for the Dark Forces, or if that was just the only topic they wanted to talk about. All the torches in the dungeons suddenly lit and light reappeared for the first time in what had to be at least a day. It burned Aria's eyes and she had to blink a few times. The footsteps grew closer, and the creaking of the metal door's hinges signaled that the door had swung open.

"Get up," a woman said, her voice rough and full of hate as it usually was.

A man's voice that Aria didn't recognize spoke. "So, this is the legendary Diviner?" Aria could hear the disgust in his voice.

"I know, right?" The woman paused, probably glaring at Aria's back. "Get up and eat," she commanded, but Aria continued lying on the rough ground, facing the wall.

"I would say the universe chose wrong," the man said before setting the water cup down on the floor with a soft clang of metal.

The woman laughed and then their footsteps faded away as they went back up the stairs, slamming the door shut and sending a ringing into the silence. The dungeons descended into darkness again.

Aria sat up, whimpering from the pain of using her stiff

muscles, and crawled to get the food. She drained her cup of water as fast as she could, but it was not enough to erase the dry, sandpaper feeling of her tongue. Then she stuffed the foul food into her mouth, trying to force it down her throat. Her stomach lurched at the taste and she gagged. Tears began to drip down her face, burning her eyes, for what had to be the millionth time.

She used to scream their names into the dark, as if her friends could somehow hear the warning. It was only a matter of time before Malus found Luke…if he hadn't already. All of them were in danger and there was absolutely no way she could help them.

After swallowing the last bite of food, she let herself fall sideways back to the floor. Her shackles clanged on the stone, the very shackles that made her feel as if life itself was being drained from her. She was the Diviner, the most powerful enchanter or enchantress in the whole universe, and yet she was powerless at the same time.

Luke, Avi, Willow…He's coming, she thought as tears streamed down her face like a waterfall, and another cough racked her body. *Please run…Just like I should have.*

She looked down at her hands, wishing she could see some hint of power. It had been less than a year of knowing that magic ran through her veins, and yet her heart still sunk to her stomach each time she tried to call on it and it didn't appear. It was a part of her, but Malus had made sure it was taken away. He confined her and tried to break her. Still, there was something flickering inside her like a fire coming alive. It was a tiny sliver of hope that Aria held onto tightly just like she held onto the sunflower necklace her parents had given her.

"You are the Diviner." Ever since she'd heard those words come out of her mother's mouth, she'd refused to accept it. She'd

wanted to shove away the title, the power, and very idea of it. But now, she clung to it as if she could feel the very essence of who she was now missing. She didn't have the Divining Powers, and now she didn't have her magic at all. Tears dripped down her cheeks as she realized she was wrong. Malus had broken something, but it hadn't been her. It had been the chains of lies she'd placed around her own heart—her fear of being the Diviner.

She sighed, her breath trembling and forming clouds in the air. *I'll find you guys again. I promised I would, and I will keep that promise. Just find the Death Stone before Malus does and stay safe.*

It was all the things she wanted to say, but only the darkness would listen.

As Avi, Luke, and Willow crept up through the trees, the sun peaked over the mountains and began to spread across the forest. Celestia soared not far above them like a lookout. Up the incline ahead, a massive wall of stone loomed with a dark cave carved into it, surrounded by a small rocky clearing. In that cave, Strom had said there'd be a door that led into the base. Apparently, trees can communicate through some kind of bond and share information. That's how Strom had figured out where to go, and where the entrance to the base was. There had been a lengthy conversation about it in which Willow spewed some very big scientific words that Avi couldn't even hope to remember.

Now he tiptoed through the snow carefully as they began to slow their ascent. Luke, Willow, and Strom stopped behind a large tree, waiting in the shadows. Avi stepped out of the tree line slightly and warm sun brushed his skin.

"Wait, Avi," Luke said, grabbing him by the back of his jacket. "There's werewolves."

Avi immediately paused, walking backwards as he searched for where Luke might have spotted them. Across the clearing and hidden in the underbrush, lay three sleeping werewolves. Avi's heart stopped in his chest, fear crawling over his skin. They were massive, with sharp teeth poking out from beneath their drool-covered lips.

Avi kept his eyes trained on the beasts and tightened his backpack around his shoulders in case they needed to run. "Do you think there's a *back* door?"

Strom crept past the werewolves with Celestia silently flying overhead. She must have sensed the danger and evil lurking by, as they all had. Luke, Avi, and Willow followed behind in silence. Avi couldn't spare a second to take his eyes off the werewolves, panic etched into his face. He watched the rise and fall of their bodies, their snores carrying through the air. They were almost to the cave when one of their eyes opened. In a heartbeat, the werewolf was on its feet, barreling toward them. Strom stepped in front of it, swinging his arm against the wolf's face. It fell to the ground with a yelp. The other two werewolves rose, howling for backup, and bolted toward Strom. The snow stirred up as paws skidded through it and werewolves lunged their way.

"Friends, go!" Strom yelled and knocked his fist into another wolf's side. "Get Diviner!"

Luke grabbed Willow and Avi by the arms, pushing them out of the way and into the cave. Avi nearly stumbled over his own feet as shadows enveloped them. Celestia dove in with them and landed on the rocky ground. At the back of the cave was a wide, black circular door made of metal that looked to be at least a foot thick. Luke let go of Willow and Avi and ran forward. He grabbed its handle and tugged as hard as he could. The door didn't relent, and when Luke pulled away, the frigid metal had turned his skin red.

"It's locked," Luke said, evidently resisting the urge to scream in frustration. He balled his hands into tight fists instead, turning his knuckles white.

Willow stepped up to the door and pressed her hand to it, light glowing from her palms. She leaned her ear against the door and closed her eyes. After a moment, she turned back to them and shook her head, lips twisted like she was thinking.

"Well?" Avi asked, raising his eyebrows.

The growls and yelps of the werewolves outside the cave met his ears. He couldn't stop his foot from tapping anxiously. Hopefully, Strom could manage to keep holding them off.

Willow blew out a puff of air that clouded in front of her face. "I don't know how to open it. It's clearly locked. My guess is it's cursed to open with some kind of password…or there is someone on the other side waiting to open it and we are being watched right now," she said. "Either way, it won't open with magic."

Avi walked towards the door, squinting at it and waving his hand in the air as if there might be a camera there to see him—not that there were cameras in the Vezchia Realm. The thought of the Dark Forces watching them try to break into their secret base sent tingles down his spine.

"Hello, evil door! If you could please open up so we can free our friend, that would be very nice." He paused as if it might actually listen but knowing it wouldn't. He still huffed. "I *did* say please."

"If it is a password, what do you think it might be?" Luke scratched the back of his neck.

"I don't know," Avi said, unable to resist the smirk that

spread across his face. "Maybe something like 'I'm super evil,' or something."

"I'm being serious!" Luke nearly yelled at him in agitation. "Aria's in there!"

"I was only half joking…" Avi said. "But maybe it's—" He broke off as Strom ducked into the cave.

Strom made his way to the door and pulled on its handle, making the door creak. Claw marks from the werewolves were scratched into his bark, but Avi couldn't spot anything else different about his overall barky appearance. Avi glanced out the cave entrance, his eyes locking on three unconscious werewolves. He turned back around to watch Strom pull on the door. Crumbles of dirt and stone rained down from the ceiling, but it still didn't budge.

Willow's eyes brightened. "Luke, Avi, throw a strong Zilomi Enchant at the door."

"A Breaking Enchant? Why?" Avi asked but still raised his hands. "You just said the door might be cursed. Magic won't work against it."

"Just do it, but don't hit Strom. Aim the enchant at the hinges. Strom, you pull on the door. On the count of three. One…Two…Three."

Luke, Avi, and Willow copied each other, aiming the force gathering in their palms at the door. Strom stepped to the side, still pulling with all his might. The force released from their hands, shooting through the frigid air and hitting the metal door with a loud clang that dented it. Dust and pebbles fell from above and the hinges creaked.

"Again," Willow said and another three powerful blasts hit the door.

The doorway gave a loud shrill as Strom tugged. The hinges quaked in the wall before snapping. Strom ripped them off completely, letting the thick metal door clatter and fall to the ground.

Avi's mouth fell open, feeling magic recede from his palms. "How? How did our magic work against it?"

"I said the door might be cursed, but maybe it was the lock, which we just broke." Willow pointed at the door, where a thick lock was snapped in half by Strom's strength. Stuck in a hole in the door's frame was the other half of the bolt.

Shouts and yells resounded from inside, but Avi didn't spot anyone coming for them. Yet. The hall beyond was short and empty, curving off to the right. A single torch illuminated the small, dim space. Luke stepped over the door, onto the smooth polished black flooring, and gestured for the rest of them to follow. Celestia took to the air from the ground and settled on Avi's shoulder, raising her head as if she was ready for a fight. Together they stepped into the Dark Forces base.

CHAPTER TWENTY-FIVE

SHOUTS AND THUDS resounded from the floor above, but nothing could make Aria move from the icy stone floor. Her eyes were closed, half sleeping, but even if she opened them, darkness would still meet her eyes. She focused on keeping hope rather than what might be going on up the staircase that led out of the dungeons. Her brain barely functioned while she drifted in and out of sleep. Pain shot through her stomach and she groaned, clutching her sunflower necklace. Pounding footsteps made the ceiling shake, but it didn't register in her mind. The only thing that she could take notice of was the immense aches spreading throughout her body like scalpels poking at her skin.

"Timber Giant!" The words were screamed from a distance, echoing off the walls.

All the noise passed through one ear and out the other. She shifted to cover her ears and rolled over. The ground scratched at her back. All the sudden noise after days of endless silence and darkness instantly gave her a thumping headache.

"Aria!" a familiar voice called from close by, but she squeezed her eyes shut. Tears began to drip down her cheeks. She let out a cough that scratched her throat like sandpaper. Luke could not possibly be there.

A dream, she thought, and another cough escaped her throat. Everything felt so real, but she knew it wasn't. It hadn't been real the last time she'd hallucinated.

"Aria!" Luke's voice called again, and fresh tears spilled down her cheeks.

If only he was here…

A rattling of metal met her ears and then the loud creaking sound of the door filled the air.

"Aria!" There was a relief to this make-believe-Luke's voice now and footsteps padded across the rough stone floor. "Aria!"

"Luke…" was all she could manage before another cough shook her body. She knew it was just a dream and Luke wasn't really there, but why not indulge in it?

She was lifted off the ground and an arm wrapped around her back. Slowly, she opened her eyes and the sudden dim lighting of the torches burned them. Her eyes fluttered open and closed, her vision blurring with exhaustion. Her head spun as hunger and aching prodded at her, limbs numb and useless.

"Aria…" Luke let out a sigh of relief, his face just inches from hers.

"Luke," she said, her heart feeling as if it had just been punched and now the air was knocked out of her. "This isn't real…"

"What? Aria, I'm here." Luke tucked a brown strand of hair behind her ear, and Aria's eyes went wide. She felt that—his hand brush her pale, burning cheeks. "It's me, Luke. I'm here."

"Luke?" She reached her frail, small hand up to touch his warm, sweating face.

"Oh, Aria." His voice dropped with a worried tone and he pressed a hand against her forehead. "Your skin is burning up. What did they do to you?"

She ignored his question, too shocked to comprehend anything else other than the fact that Luke was really there, holding her. "You came back…"

"I will always come back."

"Willow, Avi. Where—"

"They're at the top of the stairs with Strom. Strom's holding off the Dark Forces," Luke answered. "I have to get you out of here." He reached to grab the shackles latched on her wrists.

"You can't," Aria said as he picked up the ring of keys he must have stolen. "Malus cursed them. He's the only one that can take them off. I'm trapped here."

Luke looked away for a moment and Aria couldn't see the emotion that flickered across his face. "No, no!" He banged his fist down on his leg in frustration before running his hands through his hair. "I'm going to get you out of here, Aria."

All the fear and desperation that had clawed at her in the midst of darkness now fought its way through her.

Sobs shook her body and tears streamed down her cheeks like a river. "He knows you have it, Luke. You have to get out of here. Leave me. He'll kill you if you don't. Leave before he comes back."

A sudden loud bang that made dust and small crumbs of stone fall from the ceiling came from the stairway. Luke turned from her abruptly but kept an arm wrapped around her. A cry echoed against the walls and Aria's heart froze, knowing the voice was Willow's. Loud thumps of boots hitting the concrete floor grew closer, and Luke straightened up. He stepped in front of Aria as she struggled with all her might to pull herself into a sitting position, but her muscles strained against it.

"Well, how sad is this that I have to break up this little reunion…" a crooning voice said as a black-cloaked figure came down the stairs and turned into her cell.

Malus lowered his hood just as Viola ran down the steps to stand at his side, savagely giggling.

"You have something of mine, boy," Malus snarled. "And no amount of magic you throw at me will stop me from getting it, so just hand it over."

"Never." Luke widened his stance before shooting a ball of radiant blue magic toward him.

Malus sidestepped out of the way, causing the enchantment to bounce off the wall and dissipate in the air. He raised his hands, white light glittering across his palms as a force blasted from it. Luke was blasted up against the metal bars and his head snapped back, banging against them. A gasp escaped his lips. His face turned red as he tried to suck air back into his lungs. Aria reached out her hands and tried to grasp the rough stone ground. It dug into her fingertips and each muscle in her body screamed in protest at her attempt to drag herself toward him. The chains rattled and her skin scraped against the floor with each move. Malus placed his boot on her side and kicked her backwards, knocking the wind from her.

"Then I'll take it myself," Malus ground out as he reached for something hidden in his cloak with his free hand.

Luke struggled against the force holding him in place. Aria saw a glint of silver peek out from Malus' cloak and her heart dropped to her stomach like a boulder. With all the might left in her frail body, she reached out to grab Malus' boot. Malus quickly turned, momentarily distracted, to kick Aria's hand away. The force in his hand went out, and Luke collapsed to the concrete floor.

Viola let out a feral growl. "Malus! The boy!"

Malus turned back to Luke, but he wasn't quick enough to stop a colorful glow shooting at him from Luke's raised hand. Malus stumbled backwards, slamming against the bars of the cell with a loud painful clang. He slumped to the ground, glaring as the enchantment Luke shot at him sunk in. Malus' head slid to the side and his eyes fluttered shut.

Viola lunged for Aria and Luke with a hostile glare, dagger-like nails outstretched and fangs bared. Luke dove forward to separate Aria from Viola's claws, and her nails scratched his arm. Blood dripped down his tanned skin and he stumbled back, tripping over Aria's leg and hitting the wall. Viola opened her mouth to reveal her fangs, hunger in her golden inhuman eyes. Even as magic soared through the air, Viola dodged it and her hands encircled Luke's neck, baring it. Fear gripped Aria's heart and she opened her mouth to scream, but no sound came out.

A sudden screech broke from Viola's throat as a bright orange glow filled the cell. Flames danced across Viola's cloak, and she fell into the bars of the cell, trying to pull it off. Avi and Willow stood over all of them, bright fire flickering in Avi's palm. Viola writhed and screamed on the floor, ripping through the fabric of her cloak even as the flames burned her skin.

Blood trickled down Willow's face, her hand pressed to her bushy blond hair, but when her eyes fell on Aria, she breathed a sigh of relief.

"Willow and Avi! What happened?" Luke asked with wide eyes as he wrapped his arms around Aria and tried to bring her to her feet.

She bit her lip at the pain caused by losing strength in all her muscles as Luke held most of her weight up. Holding onto him like a lifeline, she brought her arms around him, struggling to keep her eyes open. Stars danced in her vision and everything seemed to blur together. Her body shook with fever and sweat glistened on her forehead even in the frigid dungeon air.

Both Avi and Willow ignored the question, and instead, stared wide eyed at Viola. She was now still, her eyes closed as if she was in a deep sleep, and her cloak was burnt in spots, down to the dark purple and black leather outfit she wore beneath. The ribbon lacing up her leather corset and boots began to wither away. Willow blew a gust of wind through the cell with a swish of her hand, rustling their hair and putting out the flames.

Willow bent down and examined her with intensity. "She's alive."

"How do you know?" Avi raised his eyebrows. "Vampires don't have a heartbeat and they don't need to breathe."

"Yeah, but Viola *does* breathe. She's breathing, but only just." Willow indicated the slow, barely visible rise and fall of her chest. "Strange."

Malus stirred in his unconscious state and their eyes widened. Aria's knees nearly buckled beneath her, bile rising in her throat.

"He cursed her shackles," Luke said urgently, his voice breaking on the words. "We can't take them off."

Willow and Avi's mouths fell open and one of them said something, but Aria was slowly slipping back into the darkness that had consumed her mind since Ciaus had picked through it.

"Aria, wake up!" Luke shook her, and she felt herself being lowered to the ground.

Willow said something about waking Malus up from his stupor, but it was all a slur of words to Aria. She managed to peek her eyes open to see Willow grab hold of Malus' shaven head, but her eyes then slipped closed again. She struggled against the suffering in her mind, forcing her eyes open to watch things unfold.

Malus let out a shout before an eerie silence fell over him and his eyes slipped closed. Willow's eyes shut, and they moved behind her eyelids. A determined and focused expression crossed her face, then revulsion just as Malus got to his knees. His eyes jolted open, but they looked glassed over and lost. Willow forced him forward toward where Aria lay on the ground. Malus' limbs moved limply as he crawled, Willow's hands on his head. He looked smaller and helpless, but something changed in his eyes. Fury flickered on his face before it was replaced with blankness. Willow's breath shuddered, the muscles straining in her arms. Whatever she was doing, she was losing control.

Malus' hand wrapped around both of Aria's shackled wrists tightly. When his fingers brushed hers, she flinched against her will. A pulsing like a heartbeat traveled down her wrist to her fingertips before the shackles cracked open and fell to the floor with a loud clang, both the ones on her wrists and the ones on her ankles.

Magic poured through Aria's veins suddenly as if a dam had broken. It had been too long since her magic had been free. White light filled her palms and radiated from her skin for a moment. It was like pure energy, filling her up to the brim until it dissipated and she was nothing but an empty shell.

"L-Luke, g-get Aria out-t of he-here," Willow breathlessly ground out through her teeth. Her eyes were screwed shut and her whole face was strained in pain.

Luke wrapped an arm underneath Aria's legs and carried her from the cell, his breath shuddering as he carried her whole weight. Her body was limp, arms and legs dangling in the air. She cupped her wrists, rubbing the raw skin there and relishing the way she could feel her power flowing freely through her again.

Behind them, Willow let go of Malus' head and fell to her knees. She took a deep breath and her eyes fluttered open. Sweat glistened on her forehead, her hands trembling at her sides.

Malus' eyes widened and returned to normal as he fell sideways, crashing into the rough ground. His hands grabbed hold of the metal bars to hold up his body and he shook with the effort. Willow rushed back to her feet and bounded across the stone flooring toward them, pulling the cell door closed behind her.

"Malus is conscious!" she yelled as she came up behind them.

Aria's eyes slid closed again, but she pushed them back open with all the might she could muster. Out of the corner of her eye, she saw Malus struggle through the door of the cell to follow them up the stairs. He caught Willow on the ankle and she tripped, slamming into the stairs. She quickly spun around and shot what looked like ice toward him. The ice spread across Malus' body in a consuming wave, and he froze like a statue, a glare plastered to his face.

Luke and Avi hurried forward, bursting into the hallway above, as Willow scrambled back to her feet behind them. She was right at their heels in a moment, but Aria's eyes were falling shut again and she couldn't keep up with the chaos happening around them. Even the shouts and magic being thrown through the air couldn't register in her mind as darkness overtook her again.

Carrying Aria was like carrying a boulder, and after seeing her eyes slip closed, Luke knew there was no way she could help carry some of the weight. Since he had to use both arms to carry her, he could offer her no protection, and the feel of her bones so close to the surface made anger burn in his chest. Members of the Dark Forces surrounded them and tried to break through the protection Strom was offering. Strom was tall, but the ceiling was taller, like a domed cave. He swung his arms back and forth to knock out the cloaked men and women before they had a chance to harm him. Screams and shouts resounded off the walls that loomed on either side. Avi and Willow moved to stand on either side of Strom, helping push the Dark Forces backward. Cloaked figures fell to the ground and others stepped over them, forcing Avi, Willow, and Strom down the hall. Luke had the horrible feeling of being prey forced into a corner. Figures cloaked in black swarmed in from a hallway to the right, like smoke gathering around a fire. There were too many of them.

"We need to go, now!" Luke yelled over the loud shouts and Aria stirred in his arms. He looked down at her, heart seizing at how frail she was.

Celestia, who'd been picking her own fight with the Dark Forces, flew above the crowd and landed on Aria's stomach. The little firebird stepped forward toward Aria's face. Tears formed in the phoenix's eyes and they dripped down on Aria's cheeks. The tears soaked in, but Luke doubted they'd do any good. What they'd done to her was on the inside.

A hooded figure managed to run beneath Strom's tall legs with raised hands. A flickering ball of blue summoned in their hands, drawn back and aimed for Luke and Aria. Without thinking, Luke spun so that it would hit his back, shielding Aria. But the enchantment never made contact. He looked over his shoulder to see Strom kick the figure to the ground. The magic went out in their palms as they rolled down the stairs leading to the dungeon. A crash sounded and Luke looked back to see Malus had been pushed to the floor. The ice that had encased him now lay shattered on the ground like glass. He wiped the ice shards from his cloak as he came to his senses.

Strom held off the Dark Forces as Luke started down the corridor as fast as he could, Avi and Willow guarding his back.

Celestia clung to Aria's grime-covered shirt as they ran. Luke didn't look back, forcing his feet to move faster and faster, away from the man who'd broken the girl in his arms.

"They're getting away with the Diviner!" a voice called from behind.

"Friends, run!" Strom yelled and pushed Willow and Avi behind him. "Get saved."

Strom stepped backwards to follow while still kicking at the hooded figures barreling toward him. Willow and Avi turned and ran, glancing back as the Timber Giant threw Dark Forces members into the walls. They continued down the hallway, leaving the exact way they'd come, before turning down the darker hall that led to the exit. Luke wanted to wrap his arms around Aria and teleport, but he kept running. There was no doubt an Anti-teleportation Charm on the place. She weighed him down and pressed his feet into the ground, slowing his pace despite her being frailer than before. A sudden yell of rage from the distance startled Luke and he jumped out the broken door. He caught himself nearly tripping onto the rocky ground outside, icy air wrapping around him. Avi, Willow, and Strom stumbled out of the door last, glancing back behind them. Malus' unintelligible voice rose above the shouting and crashing making its way through the door.

Without looking back again, they bolted down the mountain, past the unconscious werewolves, and back down into the forest. They didn't need to speak to know where to go or what to do next. They just needed to run.

CHAPTER TWENTY-SIX

UNRELENTING DARKNESS TOOK over Aria's mind. She drifted in and out of consciousness but couldn't keep her mind focused long enough to figure out where she was or what was happening. It seemed she was in some sort of house, and the cold was now only lingering near the foggy windows. The blankets wrapped around her kept her warm and she was sinking into a soft mattress. After so long laying on rough concrete that dug into her back, she felt like she had been taken away to a haven. But her mind didn't feel the same peace. It showed her pain and darkness that made her wake up screaming for the agony to end.

Another sudden scream broke from Aria's throat and she rolled over in her sleep. Her skin was drenched in sweat as her limbs shook. Cruel voices and wicked grins appeared in her memories as if to remind her again and again of everything that she'd been through.

"Make it stop," she whispered.

Something cold and wet was placed on top of her head and she pushed it off, cringing away from the nearby hands. Something pressed against her lips. Her skin crawled and images of being in that room with Ciaus picking through her memories flashed behind her eyelids. She whined, trying to pull herself from her state of sleep. She needed to get out. She couldn't let the Dark Forces know more than they already did.

"Aria, please. You need to drink this," Willow's voice floated to her ears.

No, another hallucination, Aria concluded. *It's not real. It never is.*

"It's a Healing Potion. It will help."

She pushed Willow's hands away, wrenching her eyes open. Her vision was a dizzying blur crowded with stars. Aria sat bolt right up, heaving to get air into her lungs. Her eyes widened and light flared up from her palms.

"Leave me alone," she ground out, though she couldn't keep the desperation out of her voice. All she could focus on was getting out as fury burned through her. One word echoed through her mind: *Fight.*

Willow hurried to grab her hands, setting the vial of Healing Potion down on the table next to the bed. "Aria, relax. It's okay. You're okay." She pushed Aria back against the pillows. "It's me, Willow. Luke, Avi, Strom, and Celestia are here too."

Aria's vision righted itself, and their faces became visible. Relief flooded her and the magic in her palms sputtered out. Her head pounded, and after the rush of adrenaline, nausea gripped her. She touched her wrists where the chains had been to find the irritated skin was gone.

Looking around, she took in everything from the dusty brown carpet to the open window that had flurries of snow creeping in. Strom stood outside, bent down to watch her from the window. An old brown bedcover was laid on top of her and oil lamps glowed on the two bedside tables. Luke and Avi sat in worn out armchairs across the small room, watching her intently. In Avi's lap, Celestia sat watching her as well. There was an odd smell in the air—the kind that reminded her of something that hadn't been touched in a while. And she supposed the room hadn't because there was a soft layer of dust on everything, and cobwebs hung in the corners of the room. She clutched the blanket tighter and pulled it closer. The slight chill in the room reminded her too much of the cold dungeons and the icy chains that had cut into her skin.

For many moments she was quiet, just staring and counting the beats of her heart. Her eyes looked distant, as if the brilliant blue of them had faded and left behind a shell.

"W-where are we?" Her voice was quiet and broken on the words.

Willow turned to grab a glass cup of water off the bedside table next to her and handed it to Aria, clearly noticing her cracked, bleeding lips. "We're in a town called Ludia. In an inn. The innkeeper, Mr. Hushtleborn, is letting us stay here for free until you get better. We made up an excuse as to why we're here and why you were…unconscious," Willow said, pausing to search Aria's anxious face. "He offered us food and this room out of the kindness of his heart. It's only been a day since we rescued you…The Dark Forces haven't found us yet, but as soon as you're recovered, we'll have to leave." There was a tinge of sadness in her voice, as if she hated the thought of leaving the town.

"I thought—I thought—you had been a dream," Aria whispered. The darkness of the dungeons clung to Aria like a blanket, covering everything and sinking into her mind. The pain and wickedness lurking within the place had taken over, letting no light in. And yet, she had been saved. It felt like a dream breaking through a nightmare.

No one replied as she leaned back against the pillows, the

plushiness of them comforting her aching back. She let out a cough. Her eyes slipped closed for a moment, but she pushed them back open and they landed on Luke. He was watching her with concern flickering in his eyes. Shame and guilt prodded her mind and she looked away from him. Malus knew where the Life Stone was because of her. She sipped the cold water in her hand, the liquid washing over her dried, cracking lips.

Willow lifted the vial of Healing Potion from the bedside table and handed it to Aria. "Here, take this. We had the Healers here make it for you to get better quicker."

Aria took it and swallowed it before handing it back. She didn't know what the Healing Potion was for if she was simply weak and frail. Maybe it could help her gain weight and strength again, but she doubted it would heal her mind. She continued to drink the water. Her stomach clenched painfully, needing more than just liquids.

"I'm hungry." Her voice sounded hoarse.

Willow patted her arm and stood from beside the bed. "We'll go get something."

⸺✶⟨✶⸺

The hours had passed in silence, no one saying much. Willow and Avi had walked to get food for all of them hours before, and now a pile of plates sat on the scratched-up table by the door to their room. Luke's stomach growled with hunger as the sun began to sink in the sky. He looked across the room at Aria, and she avoided his gaze. His heart sank and he tried to push the feeling away. It felt so wrong to be hurt by someone who'd endured so much.

"What happened?"

The question repeated in his head for the thousandth

time. He'd asked her that a few hours before, and though she'd opened her mouth, no sound had come out.

It had been about a week of Aria being trapped within the walls of the Dark Forces base, and it seemed to have broken her. Red-hot anger scorched inside of him at the thought of what they might have done to her. Would she even be the same after enduring Malus' brutal cruelty?

Luke eventually got up to join Willow and Avi to get something to eat or drink. The three of them gave her a slight wave as they stepped into the hallway of the inn. She just stared at them with glassy blue eyes and Luke didn't miss the fear she tried to mask. Thinking of the Dark Forces hunting her, his heart squeezed. He didn't want to leave her, but he reassured himself that Strom was right outside, looking in through the window; he'd never let harm come to her. Closing the door with a soft click, Luke followed Willow and Avi down the hall of the old inn and out into the lobby.

Outside, Luke, Willow, and Avi started down the cobblestone street. Shadows were beginning to form around the wooden and gray-bricked buildings as the clouds in the sky grew pink. Avi kicked up the snow as they walked, huffing to make air cloud in front of his face. Strom was nowhere in sight, likely hiding from view of all the people walking around the town. Everyone around them was busy carrying baskets of wrapped parcels, each one adorned with a flimsy brown bow and lots of branches and pinecones. Red berries hung from the oil lamp posts, and red banners streamed from the buildings.

"Looks like they're celebrating," Avi commented as they walked past a bakery, the smell of honey-soaked pastries wafting out onto the street.

"Of course, they are. It's almost Yule'ta'yula, their version of Christmas." A faint smile appeared on Willow's face as she surveyed the festive crowd bustling through the streets. "Nearly all of the Vezchia Realm celebrates it. You should know that."

"I—I did, just forgot," Avi muttered and blushed.

"Sure," Willow replied, sarcasm lacing her tone. She rolled her eyes, but there was a grin tugging at her lips.

"We should be celebrating with them or something," Luke muttered. "But it would break Aria's heart."

"Aria just needs time," Willow reassured. "Time and a warm cup of hot cocoa." She reached out to grab Luke's frigid hand and he didn't bother pulling away, an understanding dawning in her blue eyes as she read his mind. "I know you're worried that Malus broke something inside of her—we all are, but she's strong. She'll open up to us when she's ready. How about we go get that hot cocoa?"

"I like the sound of that! It feels like a bucket of ice out here," Avi said before hurrying down the street to the stand someone had set up to sell candied fruits, chocolate, and warm beverages.

Luke and Willow followed after him, a worried expression still etched into Luke's face. *Aria just needs time*, he reminded himself. But the memory of Aria's lips pressed against his and the daring look in her eyes as she ran away from him flashed in his mind. The pressure in his heart didn't cease.

"Celebrating might not be a bad idea after all, and it just might lift our spirits before we leave," Willow said cheerily.

The silence in the room broke as the door creaked open. Luke, Avi, and Willow stepped back inside with steaming cups in their hands. Strom was just outside the window again, his trunk molded into the ground to look like a normal tree as he drew energy from the ground. Aria had just been talking with him moments before about how they'd escaped the mountain base, about the old innkeeper who was allowing them to stay at his inn for free, and about what the town of Ludia was like.

Aria still sat on the bed with the cover wrapped around her, Celestia asleep beside her. The firebird had given her a few tears before falling asleep, but Aria didn't know if they were doing anything to help her feel better. Aria's eyes lingered on the fluffy snowflakes falling onto the windowsill and coating Strom's branches. Outside, people could be seen putting up red banners and hanging red berries from the lamp posts. A memory floated into the edge of Aria's mind.

In the memory, the lights on the Christmas tree glowed brightly among the branches as she and her parents hung the ornaments. The whole house had been decorated with greens and reds and blues, covering everything with the reminder of happiness. Her parents turned to her, beaming, and handed her an ornament to hang on the tree. Now her parents were out of reach and so was a joyful Christmas.

"Aria, we brought you some hot cocoa if you want it," Willow's voice broke through into her mind.

Aria turned her head to look at the three of them walking over to her bedside. She parted her lips to speak but just nodded instead. Her eyes caught Luke's and quickly glanced away, guilt burning a brand on her heart.

Willow walked over to her side and handed her a steaming cup of the creamy, chocolatey goodness, before feeling Aria's forehead. "Good, your fever broke. We should be able to leave soon, then. The Dark Forces are no doubt out looking for you, so we will need to leave after Yule'ta'yula."

Aria took a sip of the hot chocolate and a shiver ran through her body at the sudden heat. She looked up at Willow with a questioning face.

"Yule'ta'yula is like Christmas but celebrated on the fourteenth of December and celebrates hope, food, and family. It's so much fun." A grin appeared on her face.

"Oh," was all Aria could manage.

Willow walked back towards the armchairs as she said, "I just want you to know that we're here to help you and if you need anything, don't hesitate to ask."

Aria nodded before taking another little sip of the hot chocolate. Though she knew they would do anything for her—Willow didn't have to tell her that—she wished they wouldn't. She was what had gotten them there in the first place—the reason none of them could be safe anymore. And now, she was a heavy weight on all their shoulders. Every one of them was carrying a massive burden—and it was her.

She quickly set the hot chocolate down on the bedside table when it burned her tongue, and the thoughts came to an abrupt stop. As she threw the covers off her, the sudden drafty air kissed her skin and caused a shiver to go up her spine. Celestia woke from her sleep, the shift startling her, and chirped. Everyone's eyes were on Aria as she pushed to her feet and her knees gave out. She tumbled onto the carpet before anyone could catch her fall. She tried to catch herself on her hands, but those gave out too. Luke quickly set his cup of hot chocolate down and rushed to her aid, wrapping his arms around her and pulling her back to her feet.

"Thank you," she nodded, her voice cracking on the words and tears welled up in her eyes. People shouldn't have to help her. After all, she was the Diviner—she was supposed to be the one helping others. "I'm fine. Why is this happening? What about the Healing Potion?"

"Aria, it's your muscles," Willow spoke from across the room. "They're weak. It's not a wound, so the potion can't exactly heal it. All you can do is use them until they get stronger again."

Aria caught onto the bedpost and tried to hold herself up, but her muscles trembled. Luke slowly let go of her, allowing her to try to use her legs on her own. She used all the strength she could muster up to take one step towards the door.

"I—I just need some air," she said as she took another slow step, letting go of the bedpost. Her breaths started coming in heavy, quick gasps as she put one foot in front of the other, slowly inching towards the door with shaky legs. Luke was right behind her, ready to catch her should she fall over like a baby just learning to walk.

"Aria, are you sure? You just got better. Maybe it's best to stay in here?" Willow asked, her eyes soft and kind, but there was something else there. Pity—that was it.

Aria knew exactly what was going through her head as Willow eyed her, the same thing that was going through Luke and Avi's heads as well. It was evident that they pitied her—Mrs. Mckinney had as well. It strained on her heart and she felt as if a huge weight were being set upon her shoulders.

"I'm fine," her voice cracked and she hurried forward as tears began to swell in her eyes. *Can't let them see me cry.*

Her foot caught on the edge of the carpet and she tripped, falling back to the floor with little grace. She gave a frustrated, angry shout, banging her fist on the carpet. The pound of her frail bones hitting the floor sent aches up her arm and she bit her lip. Luke offered her a hand and helped pull her back to her feet.

Willow sighed. "Fine, you—you get some air, and Avi and I will go ask the innkeeper if he can send some food in."

Aria nodded, the tears dripping from her eyes now as Luke

helped her to the door and they walked out into the inn's hall together.

Aria started to feel less of a tremble in her muscles when she and Luke stepped out into the frigid cold. The air stung at her lungs, but it felt fresh and cleared her mind. Luke was right at her side, his warm hand holding on tight to hers. Luckily, the cold gave her flushed cheeks an excuse to be red.

They hadn't said a word about that kiss they'd had. Luke's arm wrapped around her back, though Aria knew it was just because he was worried she might fall into the snow. She dared a glance at him to see that he was staring at her, a deep concern evident in his eyes. In a rush, she looked away, taking in a shaky breath of the rich air.

They stood outside the inn on the cobbled road outside a window. All around, people were bustling to get from place to place, carrying goods in their hands. From the outside, the inn looked small, like every other little home and shop from what Aria could see. All of the buildings were made of logs and bricks, and everyone was bundled in warm deer fur coats. Everything was covered in snow and festive decorations, which tugged on Aria's heart like the memories that were starting to flow into her head. It was like a waterfall, causing a stream of tears to run down her face.

"Aria?"

Her eyes looked distant, as were her thoughts. Lips trembling, her breath shuddered at the festive memories she had of her parents, but also at the darkness that ran in the shadows.

"Aria—" Luke's voice cut through into her mind and she turned to face him, realizing there was no other option. She would have to talk to him. She would have to explain herself— explain how Malus had gotten the truth. "Aria, I'm worried about you..."

She stared blankly at him, trying to find the right words—ones that would not crack as she spoke.

"You have barely said a word since we rescued you and I know you've been asleep, but—but Aria, I just—I'm just worried that—that—" Luke looked flustered and he ran his free hand through his hair.

"I'm not broken if that's what you mean." The words escaped her mouth before she could stop them, but they were confident and didn't crack. "Malus…he may have his ways, but—but—"

"Aria, what did he do to you?" Luke tucked her hair behind her ear, desperation etched on his face.

"He—" She turned her head away, tears running down her face. "He knows you have the Life Stone…I tried to stop him. I tried not to tell him, but—" Her voice cracked on almost every single word and the tears streamed down her face in a waterfall, her breath shuddering. "I'm so, so sorry, Luke. I tried."

"Aria, what—did—he—do—to—*you*?"

She looked back at him with her shining, glass-like eyes and tried to find the words for a moment. Her voice was soft when she said, "He had a Mind-reader infiltrate my mind. I'm sorry. I tried. Now you're in danger, more danger than before. Malus wants you dead."

"I'm sure he wanted me dead before he found out." He wrapped both his arms around her, pulling her against him. She pressed her face into his shirt as tears ran down her cheeks. "I'm just glad you're safe," Luke said, brushing his hand through her hair. "Malus will pay for what he's done to you. But I doubt that's all he did, Aria. And you don't have to tell me." He paused and sighed, his breath tickling her hair. "I was just worried about you. I was worried that—that he might have stolen a piece of you…or somehow hurt you in a way I cannot see…"

"Luke, I'm not broken," Aria said as she pulled away from him, looking him straight in the eye. Her expression was determined and she stood up straight even as her muscles trembled. She took a deep breath, thinking of that little kindling piece of hope she'd held onto in the dungeons. Of her power being locked away, just out of reach. "Malus wanted to break me, but he didn't. He may have tortured me, starved me, and threatened to take away all that I love, but I will not break that easily. After all, I'm the Diviner. The Diviner doesn't break as easily as glass."

Luke's eyes widened at her words, sounding breathless when he spoke. "Diviner?"

She smiled and tears pricked her eyes, but they weren't sad tears this time. A weight felt lifted off her chest suddenly and something in her heart felt stitched back together. "Always have been. I just needed to accept that, I guess."

A grin started to curl his lips as he gazed at her. The way he looked at her made heat creep into her cheeks, like there was something about her that was so fearlessly and beautifully different.

"Should we head inside? I'm sure that food is almost done and I'm *starving*," Aria said, taking hold of Luke's hand.

He nodded and his mouth parted as if he was speechless. She got on her tippy toes to press her lips to his cheek, but her legs gave out and they landed on his soft lips. His eyes went wide. She blushed harder despite the snowflakes falling around them. With a sheepish smile, they parted. Aria grabbed Luke's hand and he helped her back into the inn, blinking at her in astonishment.

CHAPTER TWENTY-SEVEN

IT HAD BEEN days since Aria first woke up and discovered they were in an inn, and the days had passed sluggishly. Most of the hours had been spent resting, gaining more strength, eating, and enjoying the hot baths that the inn offered.

Luke had helped her walk back and forth across the room, his hand often linked with hers and every time they had caught eyes, they had both smiled like they were children with a silly secret. But maybe that was what it was—she liked him and he liked her, and they had kissed *twice*. It felt like a big deal to Aria, but it wasn't something they'd had the chance to talk about. Both Willow and Avi clearly knew something was happening between them, but they just smirked and kept their mouths shut. It felt like a strange secret that no words could explain the complexity of, and maybe that was why neither of them had brought it up in conversation. That and they had very little alone time.

The rest of the time spent over the days had been spent looking at the Death Stone Riddle. Aria had barely looked at it let alone touched it. It reminded her too much of Malus, evil, and the pressure that was on her to find that Stone. Willow had been flipping through the book of languages and trying to find one that matched the scrawled-out words, but she still hadn't found it. Avi had tried to help her, but after a while, he stuck to entertaining Celestia.

Every one of them was on edge now because the innkeeper would be wanting the room he had given them back any day now. He was well-aware that Aria had gotten better and was now simply regaining her strength. Aria had even seen Willow talking to him in the hall about when they would be leaving. If they didn't figure out where the Death Stone was hidden soon, Aria was not sure where they would be forced to go. Nowhere was safe.

Now, Willow lay next to Aria on the bed, Luke at the foot of it, and Avi sitting in an armchair with Celestia. Willow was going through the book of languages again to find the language the Riddle was written in. She was at the back of the book, yet the pages never seemed to end. More would always appear, as if there was a never-ending number of languages in the universe. Luke plucked at the blanket in boredom while Aria rested her head against the headboard, her eyes closed. She had a headache from the song Celestia had been singing all day and the wind that kept making the window rattle loudly. Aria's head thumped like a heartbeat, exhaustion pulling at the edges of her mind. She was just starting to fall into a light sleep when Willow sat bolt right up, her hands clapping together. Aria jolted wide awake and she turned toward Willow, whose face was lit up like a lightbulb had gone off in her mind.

"Have any of you ever heard of Tungsinn? There's this language in here called Tungsinnian," Willow said as she stared around the room with her finger pinned to the page.

Aria thought she'd heard it somewhere but shook her head.

"It says here that Tungsinn was a countryside area here

in the Vezchia Realm. It often received rain and storms and therefore was often foggy…It even has a picture!" Willow lifted the book and turned it to show Luke, Aria, and Avi the little sketch of rolling hills, buildings, and streets lined with people.

Something in the picture caught Aria's eye and she grabbed hold of the book from Willow, pulling it closer to examine. There it was sketched in ink—a tall and wide house with shaded windows, and a tall metal gate, which Aria had seen as it is now: broken. And there was the brick driveway leading up to it. Aria pointed to it and they all inched closer to see. Even Avi shot up from his seat, startling Celestia, and ran to see what all the fuss was about.

"The Malamone Mansion," Aria gasped.

Avi's brows furrowed. "But there aren't any other buildings around the mansion. No one but Malus lives there."

Something dawned in Willow's eyes. "No wonder we've never heard of the language before…What happened to everyone? The language is a perfect match to the one the Riddle is written in."

Everyone looked up at her then, their eyes wide. Aria's heart thumped in her ears as Aero's words repeated in her head.

"Miranda Chesler is descended from the people of the Riddle's hidden language."

"My mom—she's Tungsinnian…like Malus…That's what Aero said…" Aria's voice was soft, but they were all close enough together that they heard it. "My ancestors are Tungsinnian."

"Wow," Avi said, his eyes wide as that new piece of information sunk in.

Confusion swirled through Aria's mind, making her nauseous. How could everything make sense and yet not at the same time? How was it that her mother's family had come from Tungsinn just like Malus? Aria had never even been told—yet another secret her parents had been careful to keep. Her breath caught in her throat as she looked down at the sketch of brick buildings, rows of homes, and streets lined with shops. What had caused them all to disappear and leave nothing but the Malamone Mansion behind?

It didn't matter, at least not for now. Aria needed to get the Riddle translated before Malus had the chance to figure out exactly where the Death Stone was.

"Umm…May I?" Aria reached for the Riddle, taking it from Willow and laying it next to the language book. Her eyes wandered across the pages covered in letters and translations. "Is there a spare piece of paper and a pen anywhere?"

Avi reached over to the bedside table, pulled open the drawer, and grabbed a rolled-up piece of parchment—which he'd doodled at the bottom of—and a quill to write with. He passed both to Aria and she began scrawling down translations.

After hours of sitting on the bed, writing and translating, Aria's hands, arms, and back were aching. Her eyes begged for rest now that the sun had set, but she forced herself to keep going. Avi had fallen asleep at the end of the bed, rolled up with Celestia in his arms, and Luke was starting to doze off on the floor next to the bed. Willow was wide awake, reading what Aria had already translated over her shoulder.

I, Alaric Malamone, hath made two Stones that, together, will grant the owner eternal power. Not only that, but they hath stripped the Divining Powers from the Diviner. I hath titled them the Life and Death Stones. The Life Stone lies on the chains of a person's neck while the other lies in the dark depths of flame. Hither is the guide I hath written, so that I may findeth it again at which hour I am eft to yield it:

I did hide in one of the universe's many rips,
There lies a stone as black as the obsidian round it.
Findeth it in the biggest flame named Darkness.
But beware of the many fiery beasts.
They are loyal beyond the end.
The Diviner's blood—

"It sounds strange," Willow said. "Nothing like any riddle I've ever read."

"Yep, sounds like gibberish to me." Aria nodded in agreement, yawning.

At least they didn't have a sphinx telling them a riddle this time.

Aria continued jotting down the rest of the Riddle in the next few minutes while Willow stared at the copy written in Tungsinnian. Just as the quill came to a stop, having finished the Riddle, it dropped and rolled off the bed. Aria's wide eyes drifted over the last words of the riddle. She sat straight up, her hands growing clammy and shaking uncontrollably. Her head spun and she couldn't get enough air. She tried to breathe, but it wasn't enough. It was as if a fist was wrapped around her lungs, squeezing everything out as her heart thumped too loudly in her ears. Everything in her brain told her to throw the Riddle off her and run out of the room. To cry and smash something. To get to the fresh cold air outside, away from where the walls felt like they were pressing in on her. The last lines of the Riddle read:

The Diviner's blood must spill upon the stone.
Every last drop should do the trick,
To put a dent or a crack in the power I hath created.
Only true power can destroy power.

Aria let out a strained breath and just stared. A beat passed, maybe two, before she threw the Riddle off her and sprinted from the room. Willow called after her, reaching for the Riddle written in English that had fallen onto the bed. Celestia chirped at her worriedly from Avi's lap. The window was thrown open and Strom peered in, confusion on his face. Aria hadn't even noticed he'd been watching them. Avi and Luke were both startled from their sleep, rushing to stand up as the door swung shut.

Aria was already bolting down the hallway, her steps heavy with the same weight that had seemed to grow within the last couple minutes. She had to get fresh air into her lungs, but it already felt as if she'd pass out from lack of it. Dots began to edge into her vision like sparkles dancing in the air. She needed to get out before people saw the panic on her face and the tears in her eyes.

She burst through the inn's wooden doors out into the night, frigid winter air engulfing her with an icy wind. The air stung her nostrils, but she sucked in as much as her lungs would allow. Then she fell to her knees in the snow, the cold seeping through her pants and chilling her bones. Her heart squeezed and she found herself staring down at her hands in horror.

The words from the Riddle engraved themselves into her mind like a haunting melody. A deadly riddle with deadly words.

She didn't want to die.

CHAPTER TWENTY-EIGHT

WILLOW'S EYES WENT wide, feeling like a hand was squeezing her heart. She looked up from the readable version of the Riddle before passing it to Luke in a rush. He scanned it and looked up with terrified eyes, then set it down on the bed. His head shook back and forth, eyes unfocused, as if he could simply pretend the truth wasn't sitting in the room. In a single moment, Willow could feel the emotions filling up the space, making the air heavy.

"Well, I want to read it too," Avi grumbled and grabbed the Riddle for himself.

Luke turned to look at the door as if Aria might walk back through the door at that moment. "We shouldn't find the Death Stone."

Avi set the Riddle back down, brows knitted together. "But how *much* blood?"

"All of it. All of it, Avi," Willow said softly. "That's what the Riddle says."

Avi's face fell, unable to meet their eyes. "Oh…But there's no way we'll be able to stop her. She's the Diviner. She'll do whatever she feels she needs to do. Especially when her parents told her she *needs* to do this."

"What is wrong, friends?" Strom's voice came from the window. He stared at them in confusion, looking between the Riddle on the bed, them, and the door Aria had run out of. "Diviner sad?"

Luke opened his mouth to speak, anger flaring from him. Whispering an apology, Willow rushed toward the window and shut it in Strom's face. His mouth formed a circle in shock, looking hurt, but such an innocent soul shouldn't have to hear this.

"Did you not read the Riddle?" Luke asked, an edge making its way into his voice. He picked up the Riddle again to read off of it. "*The Diviner's blood must spill upon the Stone. Every drop should do the trick… To put a dent or a crack in the power I hath created. Only true power can destroy power.* Destroying the Death Stone requires Aria to die! And I know she will go through with it if it means stopping Malus from getting his hands on it!"

"There must be another way—" Willow tried to say, but she could feel that Luke wasn't going to stop. Her hands shook at her sides and she felt the urge to cry. Why did things always have to be so hard and painful?

"No, Alaric Malamone did this on purpose. It's genius, honestly." Luke got up and started pacing the room, one of his hands anxiously raking through his hair. "If the Diviner has to die to get the Divining Powers back, then it defeats the whole purpose. No one would die for nothing, so the Death Stone would be safe. Malus got his twisted mind from somewhere." He sighed. "Aria, however, has a reason. If she destroys the Death Stone, Malus can't use it on her or any future Diviner's. Even if she dies, they'll always be another Diviner in the future."

"But what about what her parents said?" Avi asked. "They

said she had to destroy the Death Stone and then the Life Stone. She can't do that if she's—"

"Don't finish that sentence!" Luke shouted, his face flushed red, and his breath heavy.

Willow's gaze fell, feeling the weight of all their hearts breaking.

Avi put his hands up as if in surrender. His voice was barely more than whisper when he spoke. "Why would Aria's parents ask her to do this if they knew what the outcome would be?"

"It's a riddle, Avi. It can be interpreted in many ways," Willow said softly, her voice cracking. "Aria's parents must have misinterpreted it."

"So, we need to stop Aria from searching for it," Luke said, plopping back down on the bed with a thud.

"That's nearly impossible. She's the Diviner," Willow said. "She has a right to search for it if she wants to. And we promised we would help her." She found herself looking out the window at the innocent town turning off its lights to go to sleep. "If we don't help her at least find it, Malus will get his hands on it and we will *all* be in danger. All the realms will be."

Luke gave a frustrated grunt, looking down at his hands.

"I mean, she has a point, Luke," Avi said. "Even if you hate it."

"Fine," Luke ground out through clenched teeth. Willow could feel him trying to push his anger down to keep it from seeping out. He wasn't angry at either of them, she knew that. Like herself, he was angry at Alaric and Malus for all they'd done, and upset over everything Aria would do to stop the evil they'd put into the world.

Aria was leaning against the side of the inn, crying and sniffling into her hands. Her heart hurt as if it knew one day it would be forced to stop beating. Her hands clutched her sunflower necklace, wishing more than ever that she could see her parents and be held by them. She wanted to tell them what the Riddle meant, what being a hero would mean, and ask them if they'd known their baby girl would have to sacrifice herself in the end. She found herself talking to them in her mind like she had in the dark dungeons beneath the mountain.

Mom, why does it have to be like this? Tears poured down her face. *I'm only fifteen. I want to live. I don't want to die.*

I know, sweetie. I know. Her mother's voice floated into her mind. Suddenly, Aria wasn't seeing the little alley she was tucked away in. She saw her mother sitting across from her on the couch in their old home. *How about you come home to us? You don't have to do this.*

But I don't have *a home anymore, Mom.* That fact being spoken aloud in her mind made her choke on another round of sobs. Something about walking away from the journey she'd started didn't sit right with her, either. When her make-believe-mother didn't reply, she continued, *And the future Diviners… Malus will still be able to use them. He'll never stop hunting me. All the people in the realms will be in danger because he won't be stopped.*

Aria waited for her mother to reply, but then she was sitting in the alleyway again. It hadn't been real. Her mother hadn't been talking to her. Just like in the dungeons, it was all in her mind. Still, she came to a conclusion. The headache pounding in her head was like a voice telling her to stand up, wipe her tears off, and find the Death Stone. Her heart told her that it was the right thing to do—to follow what her parents had told her to do and prevent Malus from getting his hands on it. Her brain on the other hand feared death. She wrapped her arms around herself, feeling weak because of that. It's strange how death might be something a person never really thinks about, and the next moment it is thrown upon them and they can't escape it.

She stood up, deciding it was time to piece herself together and go inside. Her skin was numb from the cold and the warm air in the inn's hallways made her shiver as she stepped through the door. She wasn't wearing a coat or a sweatshirt, so the icy wind had bit into her skin like glass. As she turned towards the door of the room she and her friends shared, her hand reaching out to open it, a squeeze in her chest made her pull back. She didn't want to go inside the room. Luke, Avi, and Willow were sure to have read the Riddle and would know why she'd run out. They would want to comfort her and tell her not to go after the Death Stone. She had to, though. And she didn't want them to see the weak frightened side of her that she was trying very hard to cover up.

She turned around and walked back into the dim little lobby. Grabbing a thick blanket from the mismatched patched-up chairs arranged around the crackling fireplace, she walked outside with tears in her eyes. A flame appeared in her palm and she held it in front of her, soaking in its warmth. The wind wiggled through the blanket she had pulled around her, but otherwise, the frigid air was kept at bay. The oil lamps that lit up the street cast golden glows on her as she walked, but she didn't stop. The town of Ludia was lovely at night. It reminded her of what an old town in England might look like. Shops were closed up and all around was silence. She wandered around under the stars, torches casting firelight on the wet, snow-paved roads. It must have been twenty minutes before she finally turned back around, nearly sprinting to get back indoors. Her nose was running, and not just from the cold. Every limb was shaking to the core and covered in prickly goosebumps. She quickly slipped inside the inn and sighed at the sudden warmth that washed over her. In the lobby, there were a few people whispering, all of which were crowded around the fireplace. She dropped the blanket back down on one of the chairs and headed down the hall towards the room, exhaustion begging her to sleep.

When she opened the door to the room, everyone leapt from their places. Avi had been anxiously tapping his foot on the ground from where he was sitting in an armchair. Luke sat on the bed with Willow, staring down at the Riddle. And Celestia lay sleeping in the corner like a cat, the only one unmoved. The Riddle fell back onto the bed as they stood.

"Aria, where have you been?" Willow asked, concern flickering in her eyes. She strode across the room and pressed her hand to Aria's forehead, tsking. "You're lucky if you don't end up with hypothermia. Your face is red from the cold."

"I—I just needed air," she said, not able to meet their eyes.

"We were just…um…taking a look at the Riddle," Luke said. Something flickered in his eyes and he ran a hand through his hair. "We were able to work a few things out."

Aria looked up then, striding quickly towards the bed despite the pull of her heart.

Willow picked up the translated Riddle, scanning it. "You wrote down *Soaipkia* off to the side with an arrow pointing to *Findeth it in the biggest flame named Darkness*. The book here says Soaipkia translates to *darkness* and that it's a place, but that's it. It doesn't say anything about it or where it is." She pointed to the translated copy of the Riddle and then the language book.

"Yeah, that's why I wrote it down." Aria nodded. "I figured it meant something."

"Exactly. Now in another, more recent language—" Willow started flipping to another page that was dog-eared. "Soaipkia translates to *Temnota*. I've never heard of either of these places—if they even are a real place. So, I was thinking we could go to the library here in town. They should have maps of the Vezchia Realm and information on a place called Temnota."

"No, no, no. Not another library!" Avi complained, and Willow rolled her eyes. "We almost died in the last one we went to."

"Aria." Luke caught her wrist and sparks of heat went up her arm. "We don't have to look for the Death Stone if you don't want to."

"I have to find it, Luke. I've come this far. I can't stop now." She looked down, unable to meet his pleading gaze. "Malus can't get his hands on the Stone. I can't let him control me or a future Diviner. And I'll do whatever it takes. My parents and the realms—they're counting on me." Her eyes stung thinking about her parents in chains. "Sacrifice is what we do for the people we love. It's what I do." She turned to Willow. "You and I can go to the library in the morning."

As the rising sun turned the sky pink, Aria and Willow set out to the town's library. Ludia's library was far less dusty than the Library of Knowledge…and far less dangerous. Everything was organized in neat little aisles with the occasional potted plant sitting on a shelf or larger ones were on the floor. It smelled faintly of lemons and fresh paper. There was the distinct feeling of the building being old, yet nicely kept. The quiet librarians were just getting to work, hanging ribbons and red berries from the shelves and doors. Storybooks for children were being drawn from the shelves with talk of a Yule'ta'yula event in the library. As Aria and Willow split up to explore the shelves, the view of the sunrise outside the vintage windows was welcoming.

It didn't take long before Willow found a book on ancient natural structures. Aria raised an eyebrow at why she'd grabbed a book on such a thing, but otherwise didn't say anything. She herself had a pile of maps in her hand as the two of them sat down at the wooden table.

Aria began scanning the crinkly yellowed maps one by one, her eyes gliding over all the cities, regions, and smaller towns. If she could just find the word *Temnota* or *Soaipkia* somewhere in the midst of the pages…

Willow looked up from where her finger rested on the page, something seeming to occur to her as she turned to Aria. "Hey, Aria. Um…" She gnawed on her bottom lip, hesitant. "I—I was wondering if after we get the Stone, you'd like some lessons on—on…"

Aria's gaze lifted from the maps and her brows furrowed in confusion. "Lessons? On what?"

"Mind-reading. Well, blocking Mind-reading." Willow looked away nervously. "The mind is a great weapon and must be well protected from evil."

Aria's heart thumped loudly in her ears and suddenly, she felt anger and shame welling up inside her. "Luke told you."

"What? Luke didn't tell me anything." Willow bit her lip before lowering her voice even more, "I…I read your mind. I'm truly sorry, but you'd been screaming and crying in your sleep."

"When?"

"When you were still unconscious. You were having a nightmare." Willow held her hands up as if in surrender, shaking her head guiltily. "I promise I didn't go through your memories.

I only read your mind. I shouldn't have. I know it was wrong, but when you were screaming, I just thought…" She sighed.

Aria felt so many emotions all at once that she couldn't decide just how she felt about it. Willow shouldn't have read her mind. Aria looked down, wishing she didn't know just how horrible it had been. But Willow was offering to help so Aria could grow stronger, and Aria trusted her…

"Okay…that would be a useful thing to learn then." Aria paused as she remembered Willow in the dungeons, holding onto Malus, forcing him toward Aria, and the shackles coming away. "In the dungeons—you did something to Malus. Did you…did you control him?"

Willow gnawed on her lip for a moment before speaking softly. "Yes, I did." Her hands fidgeted on the table. "I controlled his mind and actions. It's illegal, but I had to save you. It's not something that everyone can do. I barely even managed it. He was *really* strong and there were so many walls up in his mind. I honestly only think I managed it because he was unconscious, but once he realized what I was doing, he fought me."

Aria let that soak in, remembering how hard Willow had to fight to hold onto the control she'd had over him and the pain on her face.

"There's no denying it now," Willow said. "The Dark Forces know I'm a Mind-reader. I used to always keep it a secret from everyone…But now our enemies know."

Aria didn't know what to say to that. She frowned, knowing the fear Willow had felt at revealing that to just her, Avi, and Luke over the summer.

Willow hastily ran a hand over her face. "Well, we should get back to figuring out the Riddle. We'll talk more about the blocking Mind-reading thing later."

The chair next to her scraped against the wooden floor as

Willow stood and wandered down the aisles again. The map in front of Aria was covered in sketches of mountains, rivers, lakes, and vast forests. A massive circle filled the bottom left corner where *Viden* was written in large letters. On the right side of Viden was a long strip of water that ran off the map, likely an ocean. Aria looked closely at it and tried to understand just how big Viden had to be if she'd never even seen the ocean that touched it.

But nowhere did it say the words she was looking for. Aria glanced behind her where Willow scanned a table of contents in the middle of an aisle. She shoved the book back on the shelf, sighing, and moved to look at a different collection.

Aria's skin prickled with anxiety and she pushed the maps away as Willow came to sit back down beside her. Now she had a book about a volcano. Aria remembered when she'd first met her friends, Luke and Avi had said something about Willow being obsessed with two things: cats and volcanoes. Aria had wondered how exaggerated that was—apparently, they hadn't been exaggerating at all.

"Willow, we're supposed to be looking for leads on where the Death Stone is," Aria whispered to her as a reminder. "Not volcanoes…"

"I am. Look." Willow pointed to the page where a massive volcano towered over ashy, dry, dead lands.

The volcano has been around for thousands of years, and since then has become a home for the Moltens. These are massive creatures of rock and lava. Living without a heartbeat or breath, they can live forever if not destroyed.

"Okay…" Aria looked at Willow. "I don't understand. What do these *Moltens* have anything to do with the Death Stone?"

Willow pointed to the page again, her finger hovering over one word. "Not the Moltens. The volcano. It's Mount

Temnota…also known as Mount *Soaipkia* in the Tungsin-nian language."

Aria turned back to the page, her eyes wide with realization. There it was on the page a few paragraphs down—*Mount Temnota.*

In the Firelands, hundreds of volcanoes spew ash and lava across the land. It is entirely uninhabitable except for creatures of fire.

"Firelands…" Aria repeated, letting the information sink in and start to make sense. "It did mention fire a lot in the Riddle."

There lies a stone as black as the obsidian round it.

Findeth it in the biggest flame named Darkness.

Aria shifted the maps she was holding to look at one that had the Firelands drawn on it, as well as the mountains, forests, and plains surrounding it. She stared at it, her eyes landing on a little triangle shape that above it could have read *Temnota* if not for the ink being smudged. Her stomach swirled at the skull and warning drawn at the top right corner of the Firelands. The whole of the Firelands looked desolate and filled with vol-canoes. The map was marked up with red and black coloring, indicating fire and ash. It looked like a place of ruin.

"Do you think you could find a book on the Firelands?" Aria asked. If they had to journey to such a place, knowing more about it wouldn't hurt.

Willow nodded and started down the aisles again. In a matter of minutes, she was back with a thin hardcover book on the Firelands. She flipped it open and began reading aloud from page one.

"The Firelands are the least mapped territory in all of the Vezchia Realm, as they are the most dangerous. Moltens, Feiary Tigris—Lava Tigers—Dragons, a deadly heat, and an ever-falling ash reside in the Firelands, which make them nearly impossible to

survive in. Over a hundred active volcanos are in the Firelands, one of them being Mount Temnota, the largest in the Vezchia Realm. Mount Temnota is an estimated 35,000 feet tall, but due to the harsh climate and dangerous creatures within the Firelands, not much is known about it. It is known, however, to be home to rare gems, stones, and diamonds, which attract the Moltens."

Stones, Aria thought. *What a perfect place to hide the rarest stone of them all.*

Together, the two of them went through book after book on the Firelands. They couldn't get through the whole of each book, but they skimmed the pages they felt contained the more important information. When they'd finished, the sun was high in the sky and Aria's stomach growled with hunger. She gathered up the maps, folding up a few to sneak out of the library as Willow shot her a disapproving look.

"You know, that's not very kind." Willow closed the book she'd been reading. "But I hope we know enough about the Firelands now...Even still, I know it won't matter when we're looking danger in the face."

Aria understood—that same thought was circling in her own mind. She took a deep breath to steady the jittery feeling coursing through her limbs. "Let's just get this information back to Luke and Avi. I suggest we leave tomorrow...But there's one problem."

"What's that?" Willow asked, standing from her chair and grabbing the books she'd found.

"We're going to have to tell Strom he can't come with us."

As soon as they got back to the room, Willow and Aria confirmed that they would leave in the morning and they left Aria with the maps to find a route to the Firelands. Willow talked to the innkeeper about it and ordered dinner for them so they could have their fill before their leave. For over an hour, Aria sat hunched over maps. Luke slid onto the bed beside her, draping his arm behind her to look over the maps too. From outside, laughs and joyful voices resounded. Willow and Avi were out there partying with the rest of the town, their faces likely pink from the cold. It was Yule'ta'yula, so Aria should have been happy and excited. She should have been able to join in the cheers, hot chocolate, and festivities happening right outside the inn, but she couldn't bring herself to. There was an itch inside her, needing her to find the Death Stone. Luke decided to stay indoors with her, keeping her company and giving her a hand to hold onto. Even still, they hadn't talked about whatever it was that was happening between them. Now they had the alone time, but Aria was too jittery to bring the subject up, so she continued to look down at the maps.

The Firelands were so far away—on the opposite side of the realm. A nauseating headache throbbed in her head just looking at the map. There was no way they would be able to get there before Malus could. In fact, he could have gotten there already.

Willow and Avi abruptly burst through the door, laughing and nearly falling to the floor with joy. They both had coats on and were covered in hats, gloves, and scarves—which the innkeeper had been glad to supply for them. Despite being bundled up, their cheeks and noses were red from the icy bite. Their smiles faded at the sight of Aria's flushed, concerned face.

"You two should come outside and join in the fun," Willow told them, a pleading glimmering in her eyes. "Right now, they have a choir singing! Their Yule'ta'yula songs are a lot like Christmas songs, and they might lift your spirits."

"I can't," Aria said quickly. "I have to figure out how we're going to get to the Firelands before Malus." She sighed and shifted the maps.

Luke grabbed the map from Aria's hand and moved them all out of the way, making her pause what she was doing. Her gaze snapped to his sulkily.

"If only we had a Teleporter," Willow said as she slipped off her gloves and rubbed her hands together, plopping down in an armchair. "That would make things so much easier."

Aria gave her a questioning look. "What is a Tele-port—"

"Teleporter. It's an old device used to teleport long distances to places you've never been before…but they're no longer made," Willow replied. "Any that are still around would be at least a century old. They stopped making them in the early 1900s, but before that, they had been around since the 1500s."

"Oh, yeah. I heard about them from somewhere…But I thought they were made over a thousand years ago." Avi looked a little confused as he went to sit down next to her, slipping off his own gloves and putting his hands to his rosy cheeks. "Aren't they supposed to be dangerous?"

Willow stared at him blankly for a moment before replying, "Honestly, you really ought to pick up a book."

"I've learned reading can be dangerous after the whole library incident. So, no thank you," he said, a smirk spreading across his face.

"Anyway," Willow sighed, turning back to Luke and Aria. "Teleporters *are* dangerous. They could get anywhere. They could transport groups. Even creatures who had had their magic stolen from them like vampires could teleport with it. And they were meant to be safer…until they weren't anymore. Something happened where so many began to have malfunctions. It became just like teleporting to a place you've never been before yourself—there are risks. That's why they stopped making them. They didn't see a point to them anymore…and there were…uh…casualties."

"Casualties?" Luke asked, raising his eyebrows.

"Yeah…people had been found dead or fatally injured all over the Realms, some people even torn apart. Others had been accidentally lost in the never-ending void of the Space Realm." Willow cringed, her lips thinning as if it was a pain to tell them such things, but they weren't little kids anymore. This was reality.

"What kind of books do you read?" Avi looked disgusted, his eyes just about popping out of his head. "Because that is horrible."

"It was just a book about teleporting. Mrs. Helma gave it to us to read last year…Didn't you read it?"

Avi looked down at his hands for a moment before softly saying, "No, but I still passed the teleporting exam, so…"

"But we don't have this Teleporter thingy, so how do we get there?" Aria asked. It was the obvious question, and she had an obvious answer. One that was ringing through her head and creating a knot in her chest.

No one answered.

"What if we just teleported there ourselves? Maybe right outside the Firelands?" Aria suggested, then bit down on her lip as she took in their reactions.

"Aria, do you even hear yourself?" Avi's eyes went wide at her words and he shot his hands up.

"That is very dangerous." Willow shook her head. "Every one of us could die."

"Then don't come with me. It's dangerous enough as it is that we have to go to the *Firelands*. If you go back home, you'll be safe. I have to stop Malus from getting the Death Stone."

"Aria, no. I'm coming with you," Luke said with determination and something else that Aria could not pinpoint lacing his voice. "I will go to the Firelands with you. I'm never going to walk away from you."

She wanted to convince him not to continue this dangerous journey with her like she had over the summer, but she didn't. She knew in her heart that he would do exactly what he said. And that would mean she wouldn't be alone. Being alone was one of the scariest things because then she would have no one to turn to.

So, instead of following what half her heart was telling her to do, she said, "Thank you."

She turned to Willow and Avi then. Avi looked like he was contemplating something with his eyes squinted and Willow was biting her lip, turning it a bright red like her flushed cheeks.

"I'm going to the Firelands too," Willow said. "If we have to take the most dangerous route, then so be it. I'd do anything to help. You're my friend."

Avi stood up then, pretending to dust off his coat before saying, "Yeah, what she said. I'm coming too, of course. So, what time were you thinking we should hop aboard the train ride to our dooms?"

Aria tried to restrain her snort, but it escaped and Luke smirked beside her. "As soon as we're ready to. But definitely not dawn—I need my sleep. And first...we have to tell Strom he's not coming."

She'd been holding off telling him all day, but now was the time. Outside the window, he was still rooted to the ground with snow collecting on his head and arms. Luckily, the window was shut so he couldn't hear the news yet. She would have to tell him, though. Plans were set in motion and there was no turning back now. While one half of her heart was knotted up with guilt, urging her to not bring her friends along, the other half wanted them to be with her. She hated that she felt that way when she knew very well that there was danger ahead. But that half that wanted her friends to be close by felt it would break without them. She needed them—her friends, who had grown to be like family to her. Without them, she didn't think she'd be able to handle anything she'd be forced to face.

CHAPTER TWENTY-NINE

S NOW DRIFTED DOWN from the sky while laughter and cheers came from all around the town. Willow and Avi had been right—Yule'ta'yula did look like a blast. Hearing the joyful sounds made Aria's heart squeeze. The news she was about to drop would not be cheerful at all. Strom had been with them through a lot. He'd taken care of them, led them through the wilderness, told them stories and all about life as a Timber Giant. He'd helped save her from the dark dungeons. He'd risked his life for them. And every time he talked about them, he called them *friends*. He loved them with such innocent unconditional love. Aria's eyes stung as she laid sight on him, as his eyes lit up when he saw the four of them coming toward him. Celestia soared above them and landed on his shoulder, tears in her own eyes as if she too knew what must happen. But Strom couldn't come. His skin was *bark* and there was *fire* in the *Fire*lands. He'd easily become a walking bonfire.

They stopped in front of him and Aria tried to find the words.

"Friends and Strom be leaving?" Strom's voice filled with excitement as his eyes flicked between each of them.

A lump caught in Aria's throat. "Yes, we are leaving, Strom, but—"

Strom smiled and lifted his legs from the ground, detangling his roots from the dirt. "Where friends and Strom going?"

"But you can't come with us." Aria rushed the words out, watching Strom's heart break into a million tiny irreparable pieces before her eyes.

The excitement fell from his face. "Strom…Strom no come?"

Aria looked to Luke, Avi, and Willow for help. She hated how heartbroken Strom sounded and wanted to fix it, to make it up to him.

"We're going to the Firelands," Avi said solemnly. "You'd catch fire, dude."

"We wish we didn't have to go." Luke's hands fidgeted. "We wish we didn't have to leave you. You've done so much for us. You helped us save Aria. You helped us in so many ways even though you didn't have to. Even though humans have hurt your kind for centuries, you still chose to be our friend."

"And Strom would do all again if Strom has to," Strom said, pressing his hand to where his heart may have been.

"Thank you, Strom." Willow's voice broke, tears running down her face. "Thank you for everything."

"Now we must part ways." Aria gulped down the lump in her throat, trying not to break down. "You can't come. We must teleport to the Firelands and end what we've started. You can't teleport and it's dangerous there. We want you to be safe."

"Safe," Strom repeated. "Will friends be safe?"

Aria paused, feeling they'd never truly be safe and knowing what the Riddle said she'd have to do. Still, it looked as if his heart depended on her saying yes, so she did.

"Will Strom see Diviner and friends again?" Strom asked,

abruptly pulling them all into a group hug with his long branches.

Aria's face was pushed into his bark-covered torso, a Timber Giant arm around her back. Her side grew uncomfortable as she was squished.

"I don't know," was all they could manage to tell him.

"But I hope we will," Aria said as she pulled away, massaging her aching side.

A tear ran down her face as they waved goodbye and choked down sobs. Strom turned toward the forest that stretched out behind the fence several feet away, head hanging low.

He looked back at them and said, "Strom wait for friends' return. Strom be here." Turning away, he disappeared into the snow-dusted forest and trees of icicles, and Aria wondered if she'd ever see him again.

It's better this way, though, she thought. Strom needed to find more Timber Giants and socialize with his own kind. Now he would be free to live his life as he wanted it. He would not have to be a slave, an endangered friend, or a hunted being. He could be Strom—a happy, caring, sweet Timber Giant. But Aria would miss him with every part of her being.

The sun was just starting to rise into the sky when Aria started tossing and turning the next day, not able to keep memories of pain, misery, and suffering from merging with her dreams. Malus' vicious scarred face and Viola's thirst for bloodshed haunted her. Then Strom's saddened face floated into her conscience, breaking her heart. Her eyes snapped open.

Beside her lay Willow, quiet in her sleep and probably much more comfortable than Aria—Willow had taken all the blanket. Luke and Avi were asleep on the floor with all the other pillows and blankets from their bags, wanting to be honorable and manly enough to let the ladies have the bed. Luke was right below on the floor from where Aria slept. She watched as his chest rose and fell, looking at such peace meanwhile she felt like a tangled knot.

Looking out the window and not seeing Strom gave her a fresh wave of sorrow. The sun was softening the indigo sky to a pale blue. She shook Willow awake and the two of them jolted the boys to consciousness. As soon as they were wide awake, the room came alive with preparations to leave. Everyone got changed in a freshly washed outfit—Willow had done laundry—and bundled up in as many layers as they could find. They brushed their hair and packed up the maps. They'd stuffed their backpacks into one bag, the other bag and everything inside of them shrinking to fit in Willow's, so they could pack light. Soon enough, they checked out of the inn and stepped into the morning cold.

The harsh and brutal wind shifted in a way that reminded Aria of a storm coming. It made every hair on her arms stand on end. The four of them walked down the nearly emptied streets in silence as the icy wind wiggled through their many layers. Celestia sat on Avi's shoulder, her head raised and alert as if she knew they were on their way to a dangerous place. They'd agreed they would take her to the Firelands. With her being a phoenix, they figured a place with heat and fire wouldn't be too troublesome for her. And she and Avi were too attached to part ways.

They turned into a little alley powdered in snow with brick buildings on either side. Checking to make sure no one was around, they joined hands. Celestia nestled down into Avi's jacket and held on tight with her claws sunk into the fabric.

"Remember, keep your mind clear and focused," Luke said. "Aria, would you like to guide us to the Firelands?"

Aria nodded before closing her eyes and picturing what she had seen from the maps and pictures Willow and her had collected at the library: a forest that grew dead and desolate, not a thing daring to step too close to the fiery, smoke-filled, dark ruin of a land. Dragons soaring above. Volcanoes fuming and spilling lava. Huge rocky magma creatures with fire for eyes. She heard the wind blow around her ears and then she was engulfed in the teleporting sensation that made her stomach flip. It was as if she had been thrown up into the air and then she was falling rapidly to the ground and her eyes flew open in shock.

Colors swirled around her in a dizzying blur and spun out of control. Places rushed past, the speed of teleporting threatening to pull her hands from her friends'. She held on tighter as her head spun at the nauseating feeling. Her hands grew sweaty and they started to slip away. At least a minute ticked by of falling through a blur of places. An electric energy grazed her skin. Panic rose in her chest; teleporting didn't usually take this long. The pressure increased in one of her hands as Avi tried to hold on. Her hand slipped from his and his scream filled the void around them.

It felt like Aria fell miles from the sky, and when she hit the solid ground with a painful thud, it sent horrible aches through her body. She quickly pulled herself to her feet, stumbling over into a tree. As soon as her skin made contact with it, she recoiled. The tree was gray, like a picture of death, and it flaked to the ground like ash. It bore no leaves, and Aria doubted it would stay in the ground much longer. Already, it looked as if it could fall over. She hurried away from the tree and swerved around to look for her friends. The sky above was inky black with the moon high above and surrounded by twinkling stars.

Willow was a few feet away, looking shaken as she got to her feet from the dusty, grassless ground. And Luke was close to her, searching for his coat. One sleeve remained on his arm, but the rest of it had been torn right off of him, leaving behind dangling strings of fabric.

"Good thing we all wore coats," Willow remarked. "Or you would have been torn apart."

"Where's Avi? His hand slipped from mine while we were teleporting." Aria's heart rate spiked as she walked towards them and picked at the buttons of her coat. She tore at the coat and quickly slid it off, the heat getting to her. After that, she unzipped her hoodie and slid that off as well.

Willow opened her mouth to speak before a scream permeated the air.

The three of them turned in the direction of the scream. They were standing in a field of dead trees, each one looking just like the one Aria had stumbled into. The ground beneath their feet was dry like dust and covered with a thin layer of ash, which ironically looked like snow under the silver moonlight. Other than that, the field of dead trees was empty and silent as Avi's scream faded away.

He suddenly came running from the distance, growing larger and larger as he approached them. He was holding up his arm to show that his whole coat, jacket, and shirt sleeves were ripped clean off and the teleporting had left a nasty bruise on his arm. Celestia's talons had left scratches on his neck, likely from her trying to hold on. She peeked her head out of his shirt and let some tears flow onto the scratches.

"It's winter, and I'm missing sleeves!" Avi shrieked.

They stared at him blankly.

"Avi, we are about to be entering the Firelands, where it's hot," Willow told him, shaking her head.

"Yeah, but if we get out of there—"

"*When*—when we get out, you can get a new shirt," Willow said confidently before turning to Aria. "Are you ready?"

Aria nodded reluctantly, biting on her lip to keep herself from saying *no*. She turned and stared down the Firelands ahead. Pulling a map from her bag, she took the lead. They stepped forward, every nerve on edge and every hair on their arms standing up, and walked towards the volcanoes rising into the sky. Even at a distance, Aria could see the smoke that rose up into the sky, filling it with darkness. The smell, even from where they were, burned her nose.

"We should each have an air bubble," Willow said as they walked. "If we walk into that smoke and breathe it in, we'll die."

A force pushed against the back of Aria's head, and suddenly, her lungs were engulfed in fresh air. The smell of smoke and death disappeared and instead, it smelled sweet like air on a rainy day. She looked over her shoulder at Willow, to see that the rest of them had clear orbs around their heads, making them resemble astronauts.

Avi aimed to poke the side of the orb surrounding his head. "Where did you learn how to do this?"

"Don't touch it!" Willow shouted, grabbing his finger and pushing it away from the orb. "Something hard touching it will make it pop. I read it in a book at the library in Ludia."

"But it's just so shiny, I want to touch it," Avi pouted.

"Well, thank you for these, Willow," Aria said before turning her gaze back to the volcanoes in the distance.

One of those was Mount Soaipkia. One of those was where the Death Stone was hidden.

The further they went, the more ash fell from the sky until they were walking through a blizzard of it in the dark. The smoke, heat, and ash were nothing like snow though—it burned and stung, clung to them like a new skin, and coated the ground. Powdery ash kicked up around Aria's shoes as she walked, and the ground beneath it all was rocky earth. She squinted her eyes against the oncoming ash that swirled around her air orb. She kept glancing down at the map in her hands, but trying to follow it when she didn't know where she was turned out to be a lot harder than she'd thought. She put her arm up to block the ash from the map.

A few trees popped up, but they were dead to the core. In the dark distance, plumes of golden fire blew through the air and the faint outline of bony wings could be seen. Aria's eyes trained on the dragons and watched as they disappeared from view. Nothing had spotted them yet, but she had a feeling they saw much better in the dark than she did.

Luke, Avi, and Willow were behind her, trudging through the barren landscape. Celestia, who didn't seem affected by the atmosphere at all, flew above them. Barely aware of it, Aria was ahead of everyone in an attempt to get to the Death Stone. The faster she found it, the faster they could get out of this deadly land of ruin.

There was no water anywhere to cool off, only heat that was quickly draining the energy out of her. Sweat slicked her skin. They had already been traveling through hours of silence, and they still hadn't caught sight of the volcano that was said to tower above all the rest.

"It's so hot," Willow huffed through the smoke, her voice sounding hoarse as she hurried to catch up to Aria.

Smoke and dark clouds hid the moon, making the night a shade darker. The ground started to incline, and Aria had to gather all the strength she could to push herself up the rocky hill. She put one aching foot in front of the other until the ground began to slope down into a shallow valley. A river of lava ran through the center, toxic heat rising into the air. Towering above the river was a volcano so tall that most of it couldn't be seen through the smoke. It rose from the little valley at the far right on the other side of the river with lava running down to join it. A long cracking stone bridge was built over the river of lava with chunks of the stone missing. Signs covered the entrance to the bridge, all of them made of cracked stone.

"What do you think that is?" Avi said from behind Aria.

"Umm…a bridge?" Willow said as if it was the most conspicuous thing in the world.

"No, not that. The sign-looking things." Avi pointed down at the valley where the bridge was and Celestia started to slowly fly that way.

"Well, there's only one way to find out," Aria said and started forward down the slope. In one step, her foot sunk into a pileup of ash and she slipped on the smooth surface. Her feet fell out from under her and her back crashed into the ground. A desperate high-pitched scream breaking from her throat, she slid down the decline towards the lava. The map fell from her hand and drifted through the air toward the boiling river.

"ARIA!" Luke's voice echoed through the air like Aria's scream.

Ash covered her like a blanket as she slipped down it. Her hands grappled for something to grab hold of, but there was nothing but hot powder. More ash rained down on her from the sky and from Willow, Luke, and Avi shuffling down the slope after her. The dark substance stuck to her skin and stung her eyes. Hitting the ground must have popped the bubble around her head because the thick, smokey air was filling her lungs. Her mouth and lungs burned as she gasped for breath.

The wind was knocked from her as she hit the bottom of the slope. Several feet away, two small pixie wyverns—dragon-like creatures that walked around upright with two legs and two wings—sat by the river of lava. They startled and took to the sky with a shriek. Aria rolled to a stop and quickly got to her feet as Luke, Willow, and Avi ran down to meet her. Their map drifted through the air and landed in the lava, turning black with heat. Before Aria could start toward it, it was gone. The heat in the valley was sweltering, causing her to gasp for air, but only getting a breath full of burning smoke that lit her lungs on fire. She wiped sweat off her forehead with her hand, ash coming away on her fingers. Luke grabbed Aria by the shoulders, steadying her, as Willow began to conjure up another air bubble.

"Aria, are you okay?" he asked, his eyes wide as he took in her expression. Her eyes were drooping and sweat was dripping from her skin.

"Y-yeah," she replied, and took a big gulp of the air the moment the air bubble was around her head again. "I'm fine. But there goes our map." She pointed at the river of lava that had eaten their only guide.

A headache pounded in her brain. Celestia landed on her shoulder and rubbed her face on Aria's arm, dripping tears onto her skin. Aria gave the bird a pat on the head before Celestia took off back toward Avi, but Aria wasn't sure what good the tears would do for her burning lungs. She forced herself to turn towards the signs built into the bridge that stood before them like an ancient monument. The stone was cracked, and pieces of the bridge were missing entirely, probably washed away by the flowing river of lava. A gold reddish glow filled the alley and reflected on their faces.

"We're not going to cross that, are we?" Avi gulped. His voice shook with the same type of fear that was coursing through Aria at that moment.

Before answering, Aria read the only sign in English.

Turn back now. Walk the bridge and die.

Avi peered over Aria's shoulder. "Well, that sounds cheery."

All the other signs on the right side of the bridge were painted in a different language, so Aria didn't look at them too closely. One word on another sign caught her attention, though. *Soaipkia.* Her head snapped to the right, to the volcano towering above the valley and out of sight into the smoke above. There it was—what they came to find. Her breath grew heavier, and her stomach tightened into a knot, but she took one step forward onto the bridge anyway.

Avi hesitated. "Maybe there's a way to go *around* the lava?"

Aria looked to her left, where the lava flowed all the way down the alley and out into the distance. The right was blocked by the towering volcano with lava running down the side. "There is no other way. Besides, there's a bridge."

"Yeah, a crumbling one," Avi grumbled under his breath.

Luke was the first to carefully follow Aria onto the bridge, then Willow. Avi finally joined with a huff, mumbling inaudible complaints to himself. Celestia seemed to agree with him as she shrieked at the popping lava. They stepped around the cracks that allowed the lava to be seen below. Crumbs of stone fell and sizzled in the river of magma every few steps. The heat from the stone was seeping through Aria's shoes, so she hurried quickly around the missing chunks of the bridge and to the other side. Reaching safe ground, they started up the opposite incline and away from the red-hot magma.

Aria tried to say *"water,"* but it came out hoarse and soft from her dry, burning throat. "Water."

"Huh?" Willow came closer to her, leaning in to hear her repeat what she'd said.

"Water. I need water."

The ash fell more heavily now, and the sky grew even darker with it. Willow dug through her backpack to pull out a water bottle and handed it to her. Without pressing it to her lips, Aria dumped the water into her open mouth. The bubble around her head popped, but Willow was already preparing a new one. The water was warm and did nothing to help the scorching feeling in her throat and chest. After handing the bottle back, they continued towards the towering volcano. The closer they grew to it, the thicker the air grew with smoke and humidity. Random pools and streams of lava offered light as they passed, heading toward the towering volcano that rose from the valley.

A sudden faint orange-yellow light appeared in the distance, and Aria could only hope it was not another river of lava to block their path. They crept closer to it, every one of Aria's nerves firing off. Something didn't feel right. The hairs on her arms and back of her neck stood up, and she felt as if eyes were bearing into her back. Celestia let out a little shriek of alarm. The light grew closer, then it moved to the left. A low growl filled the air. Aria took one step backwards and knocked into her friends. She pushed against them, urging them to head back.

"Run." The word left her mouth like a breath.

In the blink of an eye, the light rushed at them. Aria was pulled off her feet and razor-sharp fangs sunk into her leg. Head hitting the ground, the air bubble around it popped.

Pain shot up her shin as her skin was shredded, tears falling down her cheeks. Aria screamed in agony, writhing to get away from it as her back scraped against the hard ground. Luke, Willow, and Avi screamed her name from a distance. Black dots edged into her line of sight, and everything blurred through her tears. The pressure on her leg increased as she kicked out. Ash and dust clouded her vision as she struggled and screamed. She couldn't see anything but the golden light in front of her, pulling her away. It felt like knives were shredding apart her leg, and then everything shattered against the pressure of teeth digging deep into her skin. She screamed and writhed, but it was no use. She was pulled up a rocky slope, the stone digging into her back like blades. The agony was overwhelming. She could only focus on one thing: *I'm going to die.* Grappling for her leg to pull it from whatever had her, she was dragged to the side abruptly and swung out, her head smacking against stone jutting out from the ground. Her eyes fell closed and everything went black.

CHAPTER THIRTY

WILLOW'S LUNGS HEAVED as she ran, ash shuffling around her feet. Aria's high-pitched screams had been silenced, and it made Willow's heart pound in frantic panic. She stopped, Luke and Avi halting next to her as they glanced around. Eyes squinted, she tried to see through the darkness of the smoking atmosphere.

"I think it took her up the volcano!" Luke shouted, his fists tight at his sides. He pointed ahead, where it looked as if something had been dragged through the fallen ash.

"What exactly is *it*?" Avi's voice trembled.

"I don't know, and it doesn't matter." Luke started up the slope of the volcano, eyes locked on the trail left behind. "What matters is that it has *Aria* and it's dragging her up a *volcano*!"

Willow and Avi heaved their feet through the fallen ash to go after him. The darkness loomed all around like walls pressing too close. Willow's eyes darted back and forth, searching for predators in the shadows. Luke moved quicker up the slope with determination and worry set into his steps. He swerved around a large boulder jutting out from the ground with a furious huff.

Willow's whole body shook and she felt like her knees might give out; Luke and Avi's emotions were piling on top of her. The air was laced with fear. Celestia screeched and sang a call from up in the air, her eyes darting around in panic too.

Willow and Avi had to struggle to keep up, moving carefully as the ground grew rougher. A heavy silence weighed on all of them. Through the clouded air, hot magma gave off a reddish haze in the distance.

For a while, they pushed themselves further up the volcano. The layers upon layers of ash caused Willow to slip and fall backwards against Avi. He managed to catch her and steady her back on her feet. His hands lingered a second too long in hers and she noticed. His emotions quickly changed to embarrassment, the feeling radiating off him. Willow thanked him and started forward again with a fluttering in her stomach. Her already hot cheeks grew warmer.

They were still so near the bottom of the volcano, even after nearly an hour of walking up it. Luke was in the lead, looking left and right for any sign of Aria. But there was nothing. Everything was silent, ruined, and burning.

Avi gasped for breath beside Willow as Celestia came back down to land on his shoulder. Willow's sweaty face softened and she reached out to pull him closer to her, allowing him to lean on her. The air bubbles may have stopped the ash and smoke from entering their lungs, but it didn't stop the heat and exhaustion.

"I'm so hungry. And thirsty," Avi said, his voice dry and hoarse. "And hot."

"Okay." Willow stopped, guiding Avi toward a massive boulder a few feet away. "Luke, we need to rest for a moment. We haven't rested all day. If we don't take a break, the heat here will kill us."

From several feet ahead of them, Luke turned around. He came back, running a hand through his sweat-slicked hair. "I understand that. But Aria—"

"—Will be lost to the Firelands if we end up dead. You two just sit here on these boulders and I'll get out some food and water." Willow grabbed Luke by his hand and forced him to sit down. When Luke didn't argue any further, she blew out a sigh of relief.

She slipped off her bag and took out the water, handing a bottle to each of them. They immediately gulped them down, and handed them back to her, empty. She downed her own and put them away in the bag, pulling out food they'd packed from the inn. Avi let Celestia pick at a handful of his food and she rubbed her head on his shoulder affectionately. It reminded her of her cat, Twilight—no Malus—and she looked away. She desperately wanted to forget everything about him.

Willow sat down on a boulder next to Avi and took deep breaths. A deep gravelly roar resounded from the distance and her head snapped to the right. The Firelands were darker than before and shrouded in smoke. Only small slivers of fire and magma could be spotted. Whatever was out there, she couldn't see. Heat flared up in her palm as she summoned magic, creating a small dancing flame. She cringed at the heat, but light appeared around them, and she couldn't help but sigh in relief at being able to see better again.

"I don't think there's ever been a hotter winter," Avi said, his lips quirking up at the edges. His hair and face were covered in grime.

Willow shook her head in amusement. Leave it to Avi to make a joke while everything was falling apart.

"We should get moving again." Luke dusted off his hands and gestured for them to follow.

They started up the volcano again with the fire as their guide. The ground beneath was a rough, rocky incline that caused them to stumble. Willow's eyes darted around as she tried to find something to indicate Aria had been taken this way. Celestia flew low to the ground, inspecting everything they passed. She pecked at pebbles and ruffled her feathers whenever a noise came from the depths of the Firelands. With a sudden shriek, the little firebird's eyes went wide and she darted to the left. She bent closer to the ground and examined a rough wall of volcanic rock. Her feathers ruffled in a way that indicated she was agitated or terrified.

Willow stopped in her tracks as the firelight glinted against a crimson substance splattered near the stone wall. "Is that... blood?"

The rough stone ground was covered in it, leading right up to the stone wall, as if it went through it. Luke and Avi stepped up next to her and she could feel the moment they saw the blood; horror soaked their emotions.

"That's Aria's, isn't it?" Avi's voice was barely a whisper.

Willow touched the stone wall and her hand went through it, as if it were merely air. She gasped and drew back. "A veil?"

"What's a veil doing here on a volcano?" Avi reached through it too before stepping back.

"The blood leads into it," Luke said, pointing. "That means we follow it."

He pushed his way through the veil without a second thought, leaving Avi and Willow in the darkness of the Firelands. Her stomach twisted with unease. Another low growl filled the air and the flapping of wings grew nearer. Willow's eyes shot up to see a shadowed, bony pair of scaled wings fly overhead. Celestia blinked at the two of them and quickly hobbled after Luke.

"Yeah, I think I'll choose the mysterious veil and trail of blood over dragons," Avi whispered and followed.

Willow didn't hesitate; she sped through the veil, the airy feel of it brisking her skin. But as she came through to the other side, the scorching heat hit her. It was humid and the smell of smoke and gas managed to leak into her air bubble. There were rock walls all around them, which were carved to make the hallway they were standing in now. The ground beneath them was rough, matching the ceiling. The hall of stone stretched out ahead of them before becoming a fork at the end. The sound of something hacking away at rock was off in the distance. Willow forced herself to take a deep breath against the anxiety squeezing her chest. The stone walls surrounding them seemed to press in from all sides and the heat was sweltering like they were inside of a—

"Are we *in* the volcano?" Willow's brows furrowed as she took in the surroundings. No hallway of stone would be there without purpose, and that veil probably wasn't an accident either. But who made them?

"Well, this is odd," Avi said, turning in a slow circle. Celestia repeated what he did as she watched him. "It's kind of like Alaric Malamone made himself a fortress here."

Willow's mouth fell open as he answered the very question she'd been thinking.

"Yeah." Luke nodded. "This definitely has to be where the Death Stone is."

⸺⭒☾⭒⸺

The ground was hard and rough, pressing into Aria's side, which felt like it had been beaten with a bat. The second her eyes fluttered open, the agony of her leg came to her in a rush, tearing a

356

scream from her throat. It felt like white-hot knives had shredded her skin and shattered the bones running through her shin. There was no getting away from it—she was fully submerged in the pain.

She tried to tear her mind away from the feeling, forcing herself not to stare at her leg, and instead, looked around where she was at. She was in what appeared to be a cave, lying down against one of its walls. Everything was made of stone, except for the wooden crates stacked up against the opposite wall. The crates had *Minerals* messily painted in black on each of them. She didn't pay them much attention, guessing they might be minerals that had been mined. By what, she didn't want to stick around to find out. To the right of the crates was an arched doorway and past it looked to be a stone hall.

Aria reached out her hand to push against the stone floor and prop herself up. Her leg moved ever so slightly and she screamed in agony. She slumped back to the floor, squeezing her eyes shut. Nausea hit her and bile rose in her throat. She wanted to pass out again, so she didn't have to feel the pain anymore.

A roar came from her left, shooting her heart up into her throat. Her breath hitched, burning in her lungs, and she slowly turned.

Right behind her was a massive black tiger with stripes of what looked like raw, golden and crimson lava. The stripes pulsed and flowed along its body; they wove in the same pattern as a regular tiger's, going all the way to its face where it had golden eyes. One look at it told her what it was: a Lava Tiger. She remembered it from the book Willow had found in Ludia's library but couldn't for the life of her remember its scientific name.

The Lava Tiger strutted towards her, shoving its face inches in front of hers, and bared its fangs. The same fangs that had torn through Aria's leg. Aria tried to back away, but her shin felt as if knives were stabbing through it. She sunk her teeth into her bottom lip to keep from screaming, and then looked down at her leg. Her pants had been torn where the teeth of this monster before her had bitten into her leg. Blood oozed from the punctures, and her whole leg was swollen with a blue tint. She gulped and gagged at the sight. Her head ached and her heartbeat drummed in her ears. She leaned her head back against the wall, her vision darkening and blurring. Lips trembling, she tried to breathe, but her lungs felt tight. Her body shook uncontrollably as she began to hyperventilate.

She needed to get out of there, but there was no way she would be able to walk. Hopelessness seized her. The tiger walked to the stacks of crates, leapt onto the tallest one, and laid down. Still, its eyes never left her. That was when Aria noticed the golden, glimmering dagger-shaped bracelet tightly secured around the Lava Tiger's ankle. Something about that bracelet told her the beast belonged to someone.

"Why did you bring me here? Why not just kill me and get it over with?" Aria asked to distract herself. She winced at the hoarseness of her throat and the burning in her chest. Her air bubble was gone, and now every breath was a pain to take. There was a faint smell of rotten eggs in the air.

The tiger simply cocked its head to the side, unable to answer her even if it wanted to.

Aria sucked in a deep breath, grinding her teeth against the overwhelming agony. "Well, if you're not going to kill me, then I'm leaving."

She braced her hands against the wall behind her, biting her lip to keep herself from crying out. Pushing her back against the wall, she dragged herself to her uninjured leg while the other one hung limp and useless, shooting waves of white-hot agony up her whole leg. She leaned her head against the wall, breaths coming in shallow and pained. The Lava Tiger leapt down from the crates and let out a low growl that sounded like a warning. It paced back and forth in front of the arched doorway to block it.

Aria's eyelids hung low as her body threatened to pass out. She forced herself to stay awake and took one step around the tiger. Her leg gave out and she fell onto the tiger's back. As soon as she touched it, it lost its lava glow. Her hands gripped soft black fur and she longed to fall asleep on the surface. A gruff accented voice that sounded like rocks being ground together came near the exit, jolting her back to her senses.

"We must go. Master Malus is on his way to get the girl. She shall lead him to the Death Stone as he has commanded."

Aria's stomach lurched and she looked up quickly to see a bulky being made of rocks. The being looked like magma and volcanic rock molded together with a face carved into its head. Hot magma filled in the creases between rock and stone, and its eyes were a burning red like fire. Aria only had to guess what it was based on the books from the library. A Molten.

Her body shook as she tried to push herself off the tiger's back. Panic surged through her, her mind spinning. "No! You're not taking me to Malus!"

She needed to get out. She needed to find her friends. She had to get the Death Stone before Malus.

"That is *Master* Malus to you now. You will belong to him just as Cinder does," the Molten gestured toward the Lava Tiger. "We Moltens were first loyal to Master Alaric Malamone, and now are loyal to Master Malus. He will change the realms for us."

The Molten waved the Lava Tiger forward, seeming to grin wickedly. Cinder strode through the arched doorway to follow the Molten, Aria clinging to her back. The hallway outside of the room was empty and completely carved from stone. Aria tried to push off the tigress, but there was hardly any strength left in her. The thick air stung her lungs, making her dizzy. She drew a deep breath, then another, afraid that any breath could be her last. Her eyes dropped low and her breath became shallow as they came to the end of the hall.

They entered a massive cavern that extended all the way to the other side of the volcano. A spiral slope wound around the circular cavern, to the top where the shrouded night sky could be seen, and to the bottom where the lava bubbled and boiled hundreds of feet below. Small caves and crevices in the stone walls allowed thousands of Lava Tigers to lay down. Their eyes followed Aria as they soaked in the poisonous heat and gases from the lava below. Many Moltens were going up and down the slope, carrying pickaxes or crates. Everything seemed to blur together as they started walking down the slope toward the lava. Black dots speckled her vision and she went limp against the tiger. Her lungs strained, unable to handle it anymore. As they rounded the bend of the slope, Aria lost her grip on Cinder's fur and tumbled through the air. The last thing she saw before her eyes slipped closed was the pool of lava rushing up to meet her.

"C'mon, Luke," Willow begged again.

Aria's trail of blood had faded out and now they were lost. The panic filling up the stone hallway pressed down on Willow like a mountain.

She stopped walking, forcing Luke and Avi to pause, and wiped sweat from her forehead. "We are never going to get anywhere by simply wandering this maze of halls. Everything looks the same and I'm sure we've already been this way. We're just going in circles. We need to stop and think."

Luke leaned against the wall and grunted. "Fine. What do we do then?"

Avi relaxed against the wall next to him while Willow tried desperately to think of a strategy to find Aria. Celestia wandered in circles on the ground, inspecting tiny pebbles and bits of rock.

"If only we had chalk," Willow said. "Then we could mark off what hallways we've already been down."

"What's that?" Avi squinted his eyes and stopped resting against the wall.

"What's chalk?" Willow pinched the bridge of her nose. "I didn't think I'd have to explain it, but—"

"No, not chalk. That!" Avi pointed down the hall where purple light was dancing across a wall like a suncatcher reflection.

"Well, that's definitely something different." Willow started toward it and as she approached the light reflections, they danced across her skin.

To the right, there was a jagged opening in the wall, and through it, thousands of pointed blue and purple crystals. The crystals stabbed out of the walls in every direction, making the small cave crammed. The opening of the cave was very slim and the crystals blocked the view of the other side. A few pickaxes lay abandoned along the wall outside of the cave, but it didn't look as if they'd ever been used inside it.

Luke and Avi stopped beside Willow and she heard their breaths catch.

"I think we should go in there," she said and started toward the opening.

"But why?" Luke asked. "Why would Aria be in a crystal cave? It's small and cramped in there."

"So?" Willow carefully stepped around a crystal cluster. "It's a place we haven't checked yet. Perhaps it leads to somewhere else on the other side."

She looked up at the shadowed ceiling, where stalactites hung and slowly dripped water. As Luke and Avi joined her, there was a soft splash. The edges of Willow's pants were soaked in the collection of warm water at the bottom of the cave. A reddish-golden glow flickered high above them, reflecting through the crystals and making their colors sparkle across the walls. Weaving through the cave, Willow stepped out of the shallow water and onto a raised flat stone surface. A few pick-axes were littered across the ground, but otherwise, there was nothing. Willow stared at the dead end in front of her, at the stone wall with an indent in it. The indent looked as if a crystal or stone had been hacked from it. Willow turned back around and shrugged. The crystal cave didn't lead anywhere after all.

Avi and Luke joined her on the raised ground, looking at her with annoyance.

"Luke tried to warn you, Willow," Avi said. "This cave has nothing in it. It's pretty but it doesn't go anywhere."

"I just thought—" Willow sighed and moved away from the wall that indicated a dead end. "Whatever, let's just go."

She and Avi turned to go as Luke's eyes suddenly went wide. He stepped toward the wall and his fingers grazed the indent there. He studied it for a moment, then the wall rippled as if it were made of water.

"The backpack!" Luke beckoned for Willow to come back, urgency in his voice. "I need the backpack."

Willow's brows knitted together and she took the bag off, handing it to him. The crystals' sparkly reflections danced across her and Avi's confused faces. Luke unzipped the bag and pulled out a white faintly glowing stone with a golden necklace chain. The stone looked so pure, and yet vile intentions seemed to radiate from it. The Life Stone. Luke held up the stone and placed it in the indent. The wall rippled again like a liquid and Luke reached out to touch it.

Willow stepped forward. "Luke, what are you—"

His hand went through the wall and it changed to look solidified again.

"What did you just do?" Willow stood stunned, trying to comprehend.

"I think…it's another veil," Luke said slowly, as if he too were trying to understand. He pulled his hand back. "I saw the indent. I saw it look like water. It looked like a stone had once been there…And then I thought of the Stone we came for and what if it was once there in that spot. So, I put the one it's related to in its place."

"But why? If you think the Death Stone was once there and it's gone, then Malus has it already." Panic at the thought surged through her…and then another thought entered her mind. *Lost in the universes many rips…'* "A veil is a rip in the universe!" The words tumbled out of her mouth. "The Death Stone Riddle—it says the Death Stone would be found in a veil. Why else would there be a veil here?"

"Willow, you're a genius!" Avi exclaimed. "If you're right, the crystal cave was worth entering after all."

Luke put his hand through the stone wall. "Let's go then."

He stepped through the veil and Willow, Avi, and Celestia followed, leaving the crystal cave behind them. A coldness washed over all of them in an instant, relieving them from the heat that was burning them up in the volcano. Celestia chirped and ruffled her baby feathers in surprise at the change. Everything around them was dark save for the sparkling, faintly glowing crystals situated around a shining, golden platform in the center of a very small room, which was no doubt in the Space Realm. On the golden platform was a red cushion that looked to have been made hundreds of years ago. Which they all knew to be true—this place had not been touched in hundreds of years because there was what they had been looking for. A black stone with little glimmers of golden flecks and a golden ring attached to it, shiny and unused. The Death Stone.

CHAPTER THIRTY-ONE

LUKE QUICKLY GRABBED the Death Stone up, a cold lethal feeling pulsing in it just like when he had held the Life Stone. It felt like the corrupt power of a million raging seas was locked inside. The feeling of holding it tugged at his veins with a call to use it. It felt ancient and wrong and like it would ruin everything and everyone it bent to its will. After a minute of looking at it, he shoved it deep into his pocket, wanting the feeling to disappear. As soon as it was hidden from view, the feeling faded. He glanced over the room, eyes lingering on the darkness around them as if in a trance.

"You good, dude?" Avi asked, snapping him back to reality.

Luke shook his head, trying to clear it. "Yeah. I'm just ready to get out of this place."

They turned back and stepped through the veil. The cool air from the room disappeared and the heat of the volcano hit Luke in the face again. The three of them wove back through the crystal cave, water droplets hitting their faces from the stalactites above. They checked to make sure the coast was clear before emerging from the cave.

"Now to find Aria." Willow pointed at the hallway stretching out before them. "We haven't gone this way yet."

With her leading the way, they crept down the silent, smokey hallways. The sound of something popping met their ears after a few minutes and they turned the corner. Willow stretched out her arm, stopping Luke and Avi in their tracks. She gestured for them to step closer to the wall where the shadows hid them. In front of them, a large cavern stretched out. Filling nearly the whole expanse of the volcano was boiling lava. Moltens and Lava Tigers stood all along a winding slope and in carved out spaces, but none of them had spotted them yet. Celestia ruffled her feathers and hid behind Avi's leg, shaking.

Luke looked up towards the top of the volcano, where smoke was slowly rising from the lava, and then his eye caught sight of something else. Aria falling—rapidly.

"ARIA!" He couldn't stop himself from screaming her name as she plummeted towards the lava, and every eye turned on them.

"YOU!" a familiar vengeful voice shouted and Luke's stomach jolted.

Luke, Avi, and Willow's eyes jerked to across the lava, where Malus, Viola, Kora, Ebony, and Chad were standing as if waiting for something. Malus' eyes pinned on Luke, a craving for violence glimmering in them.

"You have something of mine, boy! Give it to me *now*!" Malus shouted across the volcano. "Give me the Life Stone!"

Luke ignored him and turned back to Aria as she neared the lava. Her eyes were closed and he couldn't tell whether she was breathing. He reached out his hands as if he could catch her as she grew mere feet from the lava…and then stopped, hovering above it limply. He went to dive for her, but Willow caught him by the arms and pulled him back.

"Luke, of all the stupid things you could do right now, jumping into lava has to be number one," she said.

"Oh, the little Mind-reader," Viola teased from across the pool. "I should have known what you were from the start, but I suppose the scent of the Diviner always masked it…But I know now. Oh, I know now." She giggled wickedly, flashing her fangs.

Beside her, Malus had his hand reached out toward Aria with a shimmering white glow emanating from his palm. He was holding Aria up, but he could also let Aria fall. He allowed Aria to grow a little closer to the boiling lava.

"STOP!" Luke shouted, his voice scratchy from being so loud. "You need her alive!"

"Oh, yes, I do," Malus said as a brutal smirk spread across his face. "But I have Healers, and you have something I want."

Luke's stomach clenched at his words. He would harm Aria if it meant getting the Life Stone back. He dug through his brain, trying to find a quick solution. Landing on one, Luke dug into his pocket and pulled out the Death Stone. He raised it high into the air so Malus could see. Striding closer to the lava, he hung it over the edge. The heat stung his skin and he gritted his teeth.

"Luke, what in the name of Viden are you doing?" Willow whispered frantically.

"Giving Malus a taste of his own medicine. He takes things from us. How about we take another thing from him?"

"But Luke, the lava won't destroy that," she whispered back. "Only Aria can. That's what the Riddle said."

"Yeah, but I'm sure *he* doesn't know that," Luke whispered, then raised his voice so Malus could hear his every word. "If you take Aria or let her fall, I will drop the Death Stone into the lava."

"Hmm…" Malus said, narrowing his eyes. "So, you found

it. You think you're a genius threatening me like this. But I picked through the minds of the Cheslers. I know what they know now, even if most of it was jumbled up and unable to be understood. I know that the Death Stone can only be destroyed by a Diviner's blood being spilt on the Stone as they die."

"True. I know that too. But good luck finding the Stone in all this lava." Luke waved the Stone in the air threateningly. "I wonder just how deep it goes…"

Malus' face twisted into a snarl. He leaned over and whispered something to Viola. A grin appeared on the vampire's face as she eyed Luke with vile intent.

"Luke…" Willow warned.

"Fine, have her," Malus said and pushed Aria through the air, away from the lava.

Aria's body knocked into Luke, Avi, and Willow, causing them to tumble to the ground. Celestia shrieked and dove out of the way. Pain ricocheted through Luke's body as he hit the floor. The Death Stone fell out of Luke's hand and rolled across the rocky ground toward the lava. It stopped just inches from it. He carefully pushed Aria out of the way and grabbed the Stone again, shoving it back into his pocket and kneeling at Aria's side. He wrapped his arms under her own, trying to pull her up, but only managing to pull her torso into his lap.

"No, no, no, no." Willow gently moved Aria's shredded pants out of the way so she could look at her bleeding leg. "Her leg is broken. Shattered even. She needs immediate care."

Celestia hobbled over to Aria's leg, dripping tears onto the blueish swollen skin. The tears slowly soaked in but the state of her leg didn't change; the wound was too bad to be fixed so easily. Bile rose in Luke's throat looking at it. He searched for her wrist and felt the slow beat of her heart beneath his fingers. Hands shaking violently, he looked back across the pool of lava. Malus was smirking now with his arms crossed as he watched them struggle. Beside him was an empty spot. Viola was missing.

A flash of black passed Luke, and then Viola was at his side with a twisted grin on her face. In one quick move, she grabbed him, tore him away, and his back slammed up against the wall. He groaned at the impact and toxic fumes flooded his lungs as his air bubble popped. Viola pushed his head back, baring his neck. Blood rushed in his ears and his heart thudded against his ribs. Her nails scraped against his skin.

"I'm going to get the Death Stone from you one way or another," she said lightly, a cruel smile bent at her lips.

Luke gritted his teeth and tried to push her off him, but she was like a cold marble statue. With a sudden screech, her grip on his neck was torn away. She hit the ground hissing like a feline. Luke rubbed his jaw where Viola's hand had been and blood smeared across his palm.

Avi stood a few feet away, lowering his hands from saving Luke. "Are you okay?"

"I'll be fine," Luke said and rushed toward Aria, falling to his knees beside her. "It's her we need to worry about."

Celestia gave up trying to help Aria and flew to Avi's shoulder. The volcanic cavern suddenly was filled with noise. Lava Tigers stared down at them from their slopes, growling and scraping their claws across the stone. Kora and Ebony were running around the pool of lava with air-bubbles around their heads. An enchantment soared over Luke's head and he ducked. Magic crackled over Kora's fingers. From every side, something rushed toward them. Viola got to her feet, snarling and baring her fangs. With her dagger-like nails outstretched, she leapt toward them.

"Teleport!" was all Luke could manage to shout before he

was gripping Willow, Avi, and Aria with all his might, and teleporting them far, far from the Firelands.

She's taken in too many toxic fumes. If she wakes up…She might not be able to function, the Healer had told them the day before. *It may affect her brain.*

When *she wakes up, you mean*, Luke had said with an edge he hadn't managed to hold back. *And when she wakes up, you can heal her even more. I don't care what you have to do. Just heal her.*

He stared down at Aria as she lay on a cot in the hospital of Viden, the one place he'd thought could heal her, the place that wanted to tell him there was a chance she wouldn't be the same Aria he remembered if she woke. It had been days already, and those words wouldn't stop pounding through his mind. Everything that had happened wouldn't stop replaying in his head—the volcano, Aria falling, the Death Stone, teleporting to Viden's gates, being loaded into a wagon and brought to the hospital, and calling for Aria as she was taken away from them to a different room.

The rest of them had been healed of burns and cuts and bruises, but Aria still lay with her shattered leg in a cast, unable to move, her chest rising slowly with each shallow breath. Her eyes were closed, lashes splayed across her cheeks, like a corpse. His heart hurt as he thought back to the Riddle and what it said would need to happen. This was too reminiscent of that. He couldn't take it anymore.

Luke stood up and paced the room, hands sliding through his hair.

"He's pacing again, isn't he?" Avi said from a chair across the room, his eyes closed. "He walks so loud, like he's stomping."

"I bet you'd be angry too if you talked to the best Healers in the Vezchia Realm and they said there wasn't much else they could do!" Luke leaned against the wall, turning to look at Willow and Avi.

They were in fresh clothes like him, wearing the kind of wool shirts and baggy brown pants that other people in Viden wore in the winter. The air inside the massive marble and white-stoned building was cold, and yet plants still grew in pots in every corner. Golden flecks were embedded in the floor and walls, like the hospital was a palace for the sick. And on every wall, there was the shade of blue that represented Viden, along with its golden pegasus insignia. Seeing so much blue and white everywhere was getting exhausting.

"It's been days and she still hasn't woken," Luke said, his voice breaking. "If she doesn't wake up and the Dark Forces find out we're here—I don't know what we'll do."

He longed to see her forget-me-not blue eyes, to see her smile split across her face, to make her laugh and forget everything that had happened to her.

"Luke, I understand," Willow said. "I know the Dark Forces won't stop. I know that next time we face them, they won't hold back anything. I mean, you know what Viola was going to do to you. She was going to *kill* you. And now that they all know I'm a Mind-reader..." She trailed off, fear warring over her face. "I don't know what they'll do. But for now, they don't know we're here. We just have to wait. Aria has been through a lot, but she's the Diviner. She's stronger than anyone could have thought. Just sit down and wait for Healer Zelia to come back in. She should be coming soon."

Luke forced himself to sit back down in the chair beside Aria's bed. The Healer Zelia was the Healer who actually offered kind words and reassurance, always asking how she could help and making sure they got fed. He took a breath and tried to think positively, laying his hands on the light blue blankets that were pulled over Aria. Her freckled face was now clear of the ash that had been stuck to her days before. He tucked a strand of hair away from her face.

"Stay strong, Aria. Stay strong," he whispered and pressed a kiss to her forehead.

Her eyes suddenly fluttered open and a pained look crossed her face. Her lip trembled and she bit down on it to keep from crying out at the agony of her leg. Her eyes darted around, panic flitting across her face before finding Luke's gaze. He didn't miss the glassy tears gathering in the corners of her eyes, even as she tried to blink them away.

"Aria, it's okay to cry," Luke said, grasping her hand and brushing his thumb over her knuckles.

One tear slid down her cheek and Luke stood up as he wiped it away. Willow and Avi were suddenly out of their seats, rushing over. Their eyes widened and they crowded around the bed, gazing at her with crinkles around their eyes.

"Oh, Aria, I am so glad you're up!" Willow exclaimed, clutching the spot where her heart was. "We haven't left your side since the moment they released us."

"You really are one tough cookie." A smile swept Avi's face.

Celestia began to sing a celebratory song from where she perched on Avi's shoulder. She swayed to the rhythm with a twinkle in her eyes. It was a song that sounded like friendship and affection.

Aria's eyes wandered across the white walls, blue bed sheets, white clothing she now wore, and blue banner hanging on the wall near the door. When Aria's eyes landed on the smooth wooden door, anxiety flitted across her face, as if someone were about to burst through it. Her gaze snapped back to Luke. "Where are we?"

"In Viden. In a hospital. We're safe. Malus is far from here," Luke said, grabbing hold of her hands gently. "*You're* safe."

A sarcastic smirk spread across Avi's face. "I already asked him why he brought us *here* of all places, so I wouldn't bother asking if I were you. This place gives me the creeps. You know, with dangerous libraries and whatnot, but he said it was the only thing he could think of so…"

"Do you feel different at all?" Luke said urgently, searching her face. *Please be the Aria I remember. Please let the Healers be wrong.* "Do you remember what happened?"

"My leg hurts…" She looked away, thinking. "A Lava Tiger bit it dragging me up the volcano. The Lava Tiger belongs to Malus, and he was coming to the volcano to get me and the Death Stone. He knew we were close to finding it…" Her eyes snapped to Luke's. "Did you find it? Did you find the Death Stone?"

At that, Luke's heart sank. He glanced at Willow and Avi and they shot him a look, urging him to listen to what they'd said numerous times already.

But he knew what he had to do. He had to tell her. He gave her hand a reassuring squeeze with one hand and with the other, he felt in his pocket to make sure it was still there. It was, cold and pulsing its evil rhythm. It seemed to call him, tugging at his core and telling him there was something immensely powerful nearby that he could use it on.

He immediately let go of it at that and looked Aria straight in the eyes. Then he said, "I'm sorry Aria…We couldn't find it."

A Letter to the Reader

Thank you so much for reading this book! If you enjoyed it, please spread the word. You can leave a review on Amazon, Goodreads, Barnes and Noble, or another online retailer where the book is sold. Reviews are a powerful way to get this book in the hands of other readers who will cherish it.

The story will continue...

-Aaralynn K.

ACKNOWLEDGEMENTS

Wow, was this book a roller coaster of a ride! (Yeah…sorry I had to end this one the way I did lol!) This world and these characters have become a part of me. Aria, Luke, Avi and Willow's journey feels like more than just words on paper to me, and I hope their story impacts readers in a meaningful way—that they will walk away from it knowing there is always light at the end of the storm. I'd be kidding if I said writing Deadly Riddles *and getting it out into the world was easy (in fact I wrote it and then rewrote it in 2022). I'm thankful that I am able to share* The Great Diviner Series *with others, but none of it would be possible without the people who have stood by my side through it all.*

Firstly and always, thanks be to the Lord—who has moved mountains for me, who put writing in my heart, who gave me this story and the purpose of writing it. I pray that this story sparks hope in the hearts of others like it has sparked hope in me. Throughout this entire journey of being an author, the Lord has stood by my side and I am beyond grateful for the work He's done and continues to do in my life.

To my wonderful parents: Heather and Jason—thank you for being by my side. You've supported me through each of my ideas no matter how crazy and impossible they seemed. My books would not be out in the world today if it weren't for you. From the moment I said, "I want to publish Meeting Twilight," *you have continued to uplift me and help me to succeed. You two were the first people to actually read* Deadly Riddles, *and I am so thankful for your input, the silly inside jokes we now have about its early drafts, and the laughs we shared.*

To my siblings—I am so grateful to have each of you in my life. You guys mean so much to me. Thank you for letting me rant about my books and all my crazy, wild ideas. Thank you for being excited about the stories I have, and for always wanting to listen to them. I started writing for you, and I'll never stop striving to write books full of hope and light in darkness because of that. Y'all are the best hype team!

To Meme—thank you for always encouraging me to reach for the stars and believing that I could make my dreams a reality. I've always loved sharing my stories with you. I love you, xoxo. And to Pap, who may be in heaven, but I know he continues to watch over me.

To Grandma, Papa, and Grandpa—for cheering me on. Thank you for your thoughtful words, your love, and your encouragement. It really helped me to keep going when things were tough.

To my beta readers: Katelynn, Ameleah, and Hamza—for reading this book and providing me with feedback to make it even better. Thank you for gushing with me over it, reviewing it, and making this journey so exciting! I loved reading every comment, reaction, and kind word.

To Cheyenne Nielsen—thank you for editing this book to bring it to where it is now, and for all the encouragement! My heart truly warmed reading all of your comments on things. You make editing less scary and a lot more fun. I absolutely love getting to work with you!

And to my readers—thank you for picking up my books and giving them a chance! I hope you love this story as much as I do. It is truly a dream come true to be able to share my stories with the world and for people to cherish them. Your support means the world!

ABOUT THE AUTHOR

 Aaralynn Karman has always had a strong passion for music, but at nine years old, writing entered her life, and a new dream was born. Ever since then, she has been writing stories, and obsessing about the ones she reads too. Inspired by the imaginative world she created as a small child, Aaralynn often writes of magic, adventure, friendship, and finding the light in a world of darkness. When not typing away on her laptop, you can find her juggling a bajillion art projects (like painting, drawing, and illustrating children's books), or hanging out with her large family in Michigan.

Aaralynn wrote her debut novel, *Meeting Twilight,* at fourteen years old and published it at fifteen.

aaralynnkarman.com

IG: aaralynnkarman.writes